Foresyth Conservatory

FORESYTH
CONSERVATORY
A. L. STERLING

First edition, October 2025

Hardcover ISBN: 9798998805608
E-Book ISBN: 9798998805615

For more information, visit:
www.alsterlingauthor.com

Interior design by Yana Murashova
Cover design by Luisa Galstyan
Edited by Caitlin Lengerich LLC

Dedication

To my favorite fortune teller: my grandmother, Valentina Murashova

"Do not imagine that art or anything else is other than high magic!—is a system of holy hieroglyph. The artist, the initiate, thus frames his mysteries. The rest of the world scoff, or seek to understand, or pretend to understand; some few obtain the truth."

Aleister Crowley, *The Equinox Vol. 1. No. 6.*

Table of Contents

Author's Note

My legs were tethered over the chair, toes barely kissing the ground, when I received my first Tarot reading. The woman seated across from me was a stout figure of Russian-Ukrainian blood with a prominent nose and shining hazel-green eyes. Her long, thin fingers shuffled my future.

"You're meant to be a seeker of knowledge," my grandmother cooed as she turned over the High Priestess. I sat up straight, peering at the image of a woman with her back to a grand library, a scroll tucked under her arm.

"You'll do very well in school, of course. But the most important source of your knowledge will come from here"—she tapped at her chest—"your own discernment."

I stared at the esteemed woman, a swell of excitement rushing in my chest. How could she be so certain of my future, all from a simple image on a card? I wanted to see what she saw, to know the things that she knew. I wanted to claim the superpower she suggested was my *discernment.* But then I sighed, the picture muddled in my head again. I thought maybe it was something only old people could do. When I asked her to teach me the cards, she smiled and said, "One day, when you're ready."

But my lessons never materialized. A week later, my parents and I moved to the United States. I thought about my grandmother's reading on the plane as I stared out at the cotton candy clouds. I daydreamed about the cards, inventing their names and meanings. *A seeker of knowledge*, her words echoed. But by the time I arrived at school that week, I had already forgotten about the Tarot reading, my focus shifting to learning English and adjusting to my new life.

Tarot only resurfaced years later, in college. I was browsing a thrift shop when I found a Rider-Waite-Smith deck, its brown case all but crumbling in my hands. I pulled out the cards, their symbols strangely familiar. By then, I was in my third year as an engineering student, taking pride in my sensible path. Buying the deck felt like a betrayal of that identity. I consoled myself by saying it was nothing more than an eccentric paperweight.

And so it was, until one night, my roommate barged into my room looking for something I'd borrowed. She knocked the deck off my shelf and placed it back at the center of my desk, right on top of my chemistry textbook and a scattered pile of differential equations.

There was something magnetic about that moment. Maybe it was fate, maybe curiosity, but I reached for the deck. At the time, I was drowning in a failing relationship and starving for clarity, something that couldn't be known but *felt*. I pulled three cards at random and laid them on my homework.

I didn't know what they meant, but the images stirred something in me. When I turned over the Three of Swords—a bleeding heart pierced by three blades—my stomach dropped. Those cards brought to the surface my feelings of futility, desperation, and heartache. The coincidence was uncanny, but with it I found the courage to stop avoiding my own truth. I left the broken relationship and stepped into a new kind of union with myself.

Since that night, Tarot has remained a quiet companion. What began as a crisis ritual became a daily practice. It bridged my overwrought mind and my quiet knowing. The cards taught me to sit with ambiguity, to unearth the unspeakable, to name the beliefs I had inherited but never questioned. Each pull became a conversation not just with myself, but with the women who came before me—a lineage of seekers whose wisdom was stored, not in books, but in their bodies. In this way, Tarot became a sacred act of reclamation.

Of intuition over intellect.

Of feeling over proof.

Of feminine knowing over patriarchal logic.

This practice of self-listening is the beating heart of *Foresyth Conservatory*. The novel was born from that same tension—between the sanctioned knowledge of institutions and the liberating truths that lie within us.

It's a story about the cost of knowledge, the way the past bleeds into the present, and how trauma echoes through generations until someone is bold enough to name it. *Foresyth Conservatory* subverts the polished veneer of Western occultism and instead asks: What is the true cost of magick? How do our fathers' choices compound across time? And what might we discover when we stop seeking permission—and start listening inward?

This book is the novel I needed when I was younger—when I was taught to chase certainty, to worship logic, and to earn love through achievement. When I believed that there was only one true way of knowing. When I believed the mind knew better than the soul.

Now this book is my offering to you.

With it, I offer a reminder that the deepest truths do not shout, they often whisper.

A.L. Sterling

Chapter 1: Blackburne Bookstore & Gifts

Greenwich, North Carolina, December 1919

Most children inherit jewelry or surnames. I inherited death, debt, and a door I should have never opened. A brooding sky pressed down on Wicker Street, its clouds limned in spectral light, mourning the path that led to my decaying little bookstore. I was wiping down the windowsill and balancing a stack of unsold books against my hip when I saw him.

A flicker of movement beyond the window—sharp eyes, green as cut glass, watching me. For a moment, I thought I had only caught my own reflection, blurred by the damp cloth in my hand.

Then came the knock.

I turned so quickly I nearly dropped the books.

It was well past closing, the street outside empty save for the lengthening shadows. I cursed under my breath, realizing I had forgotten to flip the sign on the door.

"We're closed," I called, blinking away the afterimage. I turned back toward the shelves—Another knock.

I sighed, setting the books down with a quiet *thump*.

New patrons always unnerved me. There was nothing more cumbersome than reading for a *tabula rasa*, as my grandmother called them.

It took more mental effort to sift through the rummage of their lives, finding the true crux of their nature. And on this dark December day, with the sun already setting behind the hills, I wanted to spare my faculties for my latest treasured tome waiting by my bedside.

I had just acquired a third edition *Lesser Key of Solomon* from a rather adamant seller, who claimed the book's seventy-two demons haunted him. I had chuckled at his assertion, but my curiosity got the best of me, and I left with the book tucked under my arm. Gabriel would be furious with me for making such a ghastly purchase. But given that I'd read every book in my store thrice over, I desperately needed something novel.

Being haunted seemed better than being bored, anyway.

Ignoring the stranger at the door, I returned to the counter and began counting the day's total. I wetted my forefinger as I thumbed to the most recent page in my ledger. I recorded just shy of three dollars, a dreadfully low sum.

"I'll pay double your rate," a deep voice called through the door.

He waved through the window and tipped his hat back. When I caught his gaze his eyes glowed, shifting to a bruised green. The window was most certainly filthy.

My arm jerked toward the door instinctively. I knew I needed every penny after my mother's procedure, but this stranger unnerved me to the core. If there was such a thing as intuition, I should have listened to it. It was only a whisper, but it pleaded with me to close the curtains and run upstairs.

Maybe I could summon those seventy-two demons to deal with him.

"Triple," the voice called through the door.

A vile mix of curiosity and greed made me stand up. Against my better judgment, I closed the space between myself and the door. I opened it to greet the stranger, itching to satisfy my curiosity about his color-changing eyes.

But when he raised his cap, I found two steady, sage irises staring back at me. There was nothing supernatural about them, but they glinted with an internal light, reminding me of my grandmother's emerald necklace—the one I had sold to keep the bookstore alive after my father died. It wasn't just the hue that drew me in, it was the depth of intellect. I wanted to read him—no, I *needed* to. And if he was so generous, I wouldn't mind getting my hands on his pocket money, either.

My hands shook as I opened the door further, but I forced a smile and said, "Welcome to Blackburne Bookstore and Gifts."

He tipped his hat, removing it. And as the stranger entered my shop, I suddenly felt bare without my shawl. I grabbed the iridescent fabric from the coat hanger and wrapped it around my hair, tugging it tight. The thin veil tamed my mass of frizzy black curls and gave me the mystical air befitting my trade name.

"Madame Blackburne, is it? I've heard a great deal about you. I'll honor my price—triple a regular patron. That'll double your earnings today," the stranger said, the corner of his mouth twitching upward.

"How did you—" I began, tightening the shawl to mirror the knot in my stomach.

"Well, you aren't the only one who does their research. I've read much about you in the *Observer*. Please, lest I keep you longer than necessary. My name is Christopher Renate, though most call me the Meister. I must say, your moniker ages you—you can't be more than twenty."

"I'm five-and-twenty, sir," I huffed, lifting my chin. "And one does not need to be old to be wise." I narrowed my eyes. "Meister, is it? And what do you 'meister' over?"

"Well, that's for you to tell me, Madame Blackburne. If your talents live up to their reputation, of course," he said with an uptick in his voice. Not quite mocking, but testing. What an infuriating stranger. Was he here to ask about an extramarital affair? Or an investment property in the Glades? It didn't matter what he came here to ask, the truth was I'd seen it all before.

Earlier that day, I'd counseled Lady Florance out of jaw-wiring her twenty-year-old orange tabby and recommended a timed feeder instead (I even equipped her with the invention myself, for an additional price).

The Lady's senility caused her to set out supper multiple times a day, and was also evidenced by her frequent visits to my shop—each time forgetting the last. I was only slightly ashamed of accepting her reoccurring payments. But given how lavishly the fat cat lived, I figured she could part with it.

And now, I would welcome my next new source of income.

"Very well," I said, leading the patron past the main display table of books to the nook nestled between two grand bookshelves, next to the only other window in the shop.

Outside, blanched clouds cast gloom over the stained glass, their colors becoming opaque, closing the room into a tighter space. I kept my gaze on the Meister as I moved, taking in the details of his form. What he didn't realize was that he had lost his advantage the moment he stepped into my bookstore.

My eyes darted to the cane in his hand. An old injury—I could tell by the smooth cadence of his walk. As if he'd lived with a limp his entire life. An injury from birth, or perhaps childhood? The grass outside had wetted the wood of his cane, but a resin coating kept the water from soaking through. It beaded instead at the tip, leaving a mark on the rug—pentagonal in shape. An odd, custom design. He must be wealthy to afford such a custom build. Then there were the markings on the cane—jagged, angular, and not from this century. Nordic runes, perhaps?

An admirer of old magick? Now *that* was interesting.

As the Meister sat down, a rumble of thunder resounded outside, filling the shop with a burst of light. I noticed a scar on his face, running from the top of his eyebrow down to his cheek, interrupted only by the edge of his bespectacled eye.

Meister . . . of music, or of art? My eyes scanned upward, noting the fabric and fitting of his attire. When he placed his hand in his pocket, I caught a glimpse of the fine silk lining of his coat—a geometric design in red and blue. A stark contrast to his otherwise dark, plain outerwear. His fingers bore no calluses from playing instruments; on the contrary, they looked soft, refined. So, I bet on the latter.

"A wealthy Meister of art, with a proclivity for old magick, I take it?" His eyes widened for a fraction of a second. I suppressed a smile as I circled the table and gestured for him to sit. He was indeed one of the most interesting people I had come across in Greenwich.

"Very impressive. But not just a proclivity, I must admit—an obsession." His grin widened with eyes alight. "Let's see what else you can tell me from the cards."

I prepared the deck in my usual custom. First, a sage smoke cleanse to dispel any residual energy from previous patrons. Then, a twig of Palo Santo for a sacred cleanse against demonic or otherworldly forces. I wafted the cards through the rising smoke, carefully ensuring every edge was covered. From the drawer beneath me, I selected the stones for the final step in purification, narrating each movement as I worked.

"I'll select a collection of crystals that represent your aura, so that we may imbue the cards with your energy, now that all others have been cleared."

The Meister nodded slowly, his eyes following my every move. I feathered my fingers across the minerals and stones. This step was crucial. Gaining the patron's trust was what kept them coming back. I had to choose the exact right combination of stones, making him feel as though I'd peered into his very soul and plucked the crystals right from within him.

Patrons needed to feel *seen* by me. Hence, I became the seer.

"Obsidian—a protector stone—to ward against harmful forces." I placed the black, glossy stone atop the deck and studied his reaction. Unmoved.

I needed something more. I brushed my fingertips across the other stones, their colors twinkling under the lamplight. What was he after—knowledge, power, or sex? The three greatest motivators of the human spirit. As I thrummed my fingers across the stones, I recalled Carousel Michelle (as I'd dubbed her after uncovering her circular romantic proclivities). Today she had wanted to know if she should visit her cousins up north without her husband in attendance. I had pulled the Ace of Wands, the most lascivious card in the deck, and assured her that her time away would be full of passion and new awakenings. Her eyes widened just as her wallet did.

But now, as I admired the well-groomed man before me, I realized he already held power (anyone pretentious enough to call themselves *Meister* surely did), and his expensive dress hinted at a sincere self-obsession. It was hard to imagine he lusted after anything aside from his own reflection. So, what did he want?

I plucked a blue stone from the drawer and set it atop the cards. "Lapis Lazuli. A stone for the seeker of enlightenment. A spiritual intelligence."

His brow arched slightly. I was getting warmer.

Another thought pulsed through me. There were five sides on his cane. The pentagon.

I pulled the drawer out as far as it would go, reaching to the very back. This was where I kept my more obscure stones. Not lesser in value, but far more unusual. Most patrons were drawn to the shiny ones. The deep, rich colors with obvious beauty. But this gentleman was no stranger to magick—he wouldn't be swayed by amethyst or citrine. He was an astute believer, perhaps even a practitioner. He needed something real, something raw.

I grabbed a jagged stone from the depths of the drawer and placed it alongside the others. In between the beige limestone, bits of metal sparkled. I watched as the Meister's eyes narrowed, focusing on it.

"What is that rock?" he asked, leaning in closer.

"I find 'rock' too vulgar a term for this precious stone," I replied. "It's an alloy of aluminum, copper, and iron, scavenged from Russia's Koryak Mountains. It harbors an icosahedral crystal structure with five-fold symmetry."

The Meister's eyes widened. I was getting closer.

"It's a rare stone indeed. In fact, it was my father's prized possession. Even when he died, my mother couldn't part with it," I continued. Though it would have kept us fed for a year, my mother preferred to starve rather than sell off my father's private collection. At least I re-purposed it for my readings, finding a way to generate income.

"It doesn't have a traditional spiritual meaning, as its unique composition was only discovered in the modern century. But given the rarity—improbability, in fact—of five-fold crystal symmetry, this stone represents a great unification. Perhaps even of the five elements mirrored in the suits of Tarot—fire, water, air, earth, and spirit." I played with the arrangement of the stones on the deck. "You're seeking a great union, are you not, Meister?"

The Meister leaned back, releasing a breath. He smiled and said, "Go on."

I continued my ritual, indulging in a faro shuffle, breaking the deck in half and weaving the cards together. I studied the Meister as my fingers worked quickly and effortlessly. It was at this point—when I'd cracked through my inquirer's exterior—that I brought out the pickaxe to start unearthing the layers beneath. The gooey center was what I sought.

Magick might be the Meister's obsession, but this was mine: seeing people for who they truly were. Most of the time, there was nothing worth seeing—but still, I hunted, hoping to be proven wrong.

My eyes drifted to the empty coffee cup sitting at the edge of the table as I shuffled, a ghost of the last patron I saw before closing—Marcus. A ghastly twig of a man, I ventured to guess I was the only woman he'd spoken to in five years. Though I hardly counted, seeing as I wore men's trousers and didn't bother to brush my hair most days. Marcus always asked about business ventures and bets on the market—stocks to buy and exotic animals to trade. Once, he asked if purchasing an endangered African spurred tortoise for five hundred dollars was a smart choice. It took all my willpower to stifle a chortle. Five of Pentacles for you, sir. A bad investment, and quite illegal in Greenwich County.

The truth was, when people came into my shop, they already had half the answer in mind. Most were afraid of making decisions, of being the hero of their own story. They asked for the cards dealt by Fate, all the while knowing the answer before it slipped from my lips. A bit of confirmation bias is all they wanted, and I was happy to offer it, if it kept my mother and I fed, and this shack of a bookstore over our heads.

I delved into people's worlds of wants and desires all the time, but no one has ever stopped to ask me what I wanted. Not that I have time for desires (or that it's fathomable for a woman to even allow such things). After my father's death, survival was paramount.

Maybe one day I'll travel east, like in the books I've read. All the latest discoveries were being made there. Perhaps I could convince Gabriel to come with me. We could go searching for the secret tombs of King Martiah, or a first edition of Robert Fludd's alchemical treaties.

It doesn't matter, as long as it is far from dreary Greenwich and its drearier inhabitants. But deep down, I knew it was just a dream, a story I told myself. I've lived in stories my whole life: the ones I read to myself, and the ones I read to others. *This was just another story*, I thought, but something stirred in me in betrayal. Something that said opening the door for this green-eyed stranger was the moment my own story would begin to unfold.

I lifted my eyes to the Meister and made a final cut of the deck, stacking the bottom half on top. The last chance for Fate to speak.

"Now, we take hands." I reached for him, and he obliged. His hands were strangely warm in my clammy palms, and I let the sensation ground me. "A truth spell, so that the spirits don't play tricks on us with your reading." I glanced around the shop, exaggerating my movements. I read the incantation aloud, bowing my head and tugging the patron's hands to follow suit.

Lowering my voice, I asked, "What is it that you wish to know, Meister?"

He paused, deciding. "The union you spoke of. I want to know if it will be successful." He looked up to meet my gaze, expectant.

I nodded and began to draw ten cards for the spread. I placed each down with care, as if all the truths of the world lay on the other side. I wasn't typically this slow or methodical, but with new patrons—whose inner selves I had yet to unearth—I took my time.

"A Hermetic Kabbalah spread, is it?" the Meister asked.

"Yes, very old. And my favorite. Well-suited for your inquiry." My eyes squinted for a fraction of a second. He'd given me something else: Runic Norse, now arcane Tarot? He was not an amateur practitioner; perhaps he was even a reader himself. But that fact didn't deter me. No one could read the way I did. I finished laying out the cards and opened them one by one.

"In the first placement, you have the Tower. An upheaval of order has brought you here today." He didn't blink. *Too ordinary*, I chastised myself. I needed something to grip onto, something real from his world.

"The Chariot. You're determined to create this spiritual union by any means necessary. You're exploring unconventional routes." I looked up from the cards, and his eyes flashed with something akin to surprise.

I continued through a few more cards, carefully watching his face as I revealed each one, tailoring my analysis based on his micro-reactions. *Why* are you here? The question tumbled through my mind like a stone down a mountainside. Finally, it found its mark.

"Seven of Swords, represented by the air element. There is deception at play." I watched his throat bob and pressed on. "Someone is holding back the truth of the matter, manipulating the very air we speak."

The Meister swallowed hard, his hand covering his mouth. "There's no way . . ." he said, his voice breaking.

I had him now. "And now, the challenge you face . . ." I flipped the card in the eighth placement and revealed the Hanged Man. "It's a man. Someone who is no longer with us?" I wasn't quite sure what possessed me to say it, but his face was all I needed to confirm the budding knot in my stomach.

The Meister swallowed again and covered his mouth with three fingers. "You . . ." he whispered.

I leaned in, pressing deeper. This was what I did best: I made people fall apart. And then, carefully, oh-so-carefully, I put them back together again. It's what my father did to suspects, and now I did to my patrons. The search for the truth being core to it all.

"And now for the *how*." I turned over the next card. "Three of Wands . . . you've traveled a great distance to find this person. You believe they can help you overcome the tragedy you've faced. You believe they hold a truth that others have failed to see." I reached for the final card, regretting it even before I saw it. I already knew what it would say.

I turned over the card and beheld the image of the Magician, the first card in the Major Arcana. The archetype represented a person who used all the elements—earth, fire, water, and air—to create a reality of her choosing. She manipulated the very fabric of the material world to dictate her will.

All knowledge was material.

All knowledge was accessible.

Fact over fiction, reality over illusion. My father's words echoed in my mind as I stared down at the Magician.

"You're looking for me."

Chapter 2: An Offer to Not Refuse

The Meister sat across from me, dabbing his handkerchief at the corners of his eyes. I was familiar with handling emotional reactions from my patrons—occasional fits of rage, minor tantrums, and tears of revelation. I was no stranger to coddling others' emotional woes, because I know that the cards—well, by proxy, me—brought up old wounds. After all, tapping into someone's subconscious was a dangerous game.

But my own emotional reaction was not something I had become accustomed to. I was rarely, if ever, involved in my patrons' readings. I was the unbiased third party, bearing witness to the secrets of the universe as they unraveled before me. These were not *my* secrets.

Fear clogged my throat, but I began. "You come to my shop after it's closed to ensure no one else would be here. To avoid interruption, or to avoid being seen?" My finger twitched in the direction of my drawer, where I kept a ceremonial dagger. Well, perhaps not *ceremonial* for much longer. My father's work had exposed me to the darker facets of humanity; I knew better than to assume the best intentions from anyone.

"You claim to be a scholar—you have a depth of knowledge in arcane magick, as evidenced by the runic glyphs on your cane and your discernment of my type of reading. You seem to know how many clients I have, the rate I charge them, and exactly what my shop hours are, as if you've investigated me and my business before you entered."

I paused, my lip quivering as the Meister nodded in approval of my deduction.

"You're not interested in my Tarot readings; you're interested in *me*." My brows knitted into a scowl as I spat out the last words. "Who are you, Christopher Renate? And what do you want from me?"

I followed his motions carefully as the Meister opened the drape of his coat, revealing the dazzling swirls of the red-and-blue lining. But all he pulled out was a crisp white envelope with the initials D. B. clearly written in typeface. With his other hand, he brought out a velvet pouch of coins and dropped it on the table. It made a loud thud, indicating the weight of his payment.

"Here—for the reading—Ms. Blackburne. But I won't let you keep the money unless you open that envelope first."

My jaw clenched as I detected the undercurrent of threat.

He pushed the envelope and pouch in front of me. I peered inside—several solid silver coins reflected off the dim overhead light. Gabriel would've had heart palpitations if he saw the amount of silver sitting in front of me. Everything in my bones told me to run, to throw the envelope into the hearth, kick the Meister in the teeth, and bolt upstairs.

But I didn't.

It was as if Fate had sunk her talons into me, coaxing my hand across the table, toward the money, and then toward the envelope. It was *her* fingers that opened the letter, *her* eyes that read it.

It was Fate's voice that read it aloud.

Dear Ms. Dahlia Blackburne,

Congratulations! It is my utmost pleasure to inform you that you have been selected for admission to Foresyth Conservatory for Magickal Arts and Occult Sciences. Foresyth selects only a handful of students each academic year for structured intellectual liberation, and we are delighted to welcome you to our prestigious community of magickal scholars and elite artists.

You will dedicate yourself to the scholarly preservation of magick through both academic research and applied artistic creation. Additionally, you have been awarded a coveted research fellowship amounting to six-hundred dollars annually, reflecting our commitment to supporting and nurturing your potential. At Foresyth, you will have the opportunity to conduct research of unparalleled rigor alongside your fellow peers and renowned magickal scholars.

I broke my reading to look up at Meister who was now studying my reaction. Forgetting any semblance of decorum I spat out, "Is this some kind of jest? You want me to join your magick school? One I didn't even apply to?"

The Meister cleared his throat, pushing his pince-nez higher up his nose. "Ms. Blackburne—Foresyth Conservatory is not *just* a magick school. Firstly, it's a Conservatory. Students are artists and creators, first and foremost. They are not pupils learning by rote memorization. We don't hold classes *per se*. Secondly, it is a one-of-a-kind program—rigorous, taxing, and certainly not for the faint of heart . . ." He trailed off.

I stared at him blankly.

"You mistake me, Meister. I am not a follower of any kind of magick," I began.

"Please, I know your skepticism. I know the tools you use for your readings are mostly based on keen observation and Jungian psychology. You also happen to have a deep knowledge of esoteric religions and ceremonial magick, thanks to your father, which you lavishly display in your . . . performances."

I swallowed hard. No one had ever seen through my carefully crafted ruse—a charade I'd spent years perfecting. No one had ever called me for what I truly was: a charlatan.

"I'll ignore your ingratitude for the moment, because the academic position at Foresyth isn't the true reason for my visit. I have a more honest proposition for your skill set. One I couldn't commit to ink and paper, and one that certainly couldn't be overheard."

I squinted harder, searching for any sign of deception. His face remained steady—no common tells. A swell of intrigue rose in my chest, and I cursed my morbid fascination, a relic of my father's imprint on me.

"Go on," I said.

"D. B.—those were your father's initials too, weren't they? Daniel Blackburne? The famous detective who solved the Rothwell murders—the serial killer that terrorized Greenwich in the early turn of the century, ending in a grisly triple homicide. What a catch that was for him. Such a shame, his daughter wasting away her talents on commoner trinkets and show-and-tell." The Meister stacked his fingers into a steeple and clicked his tongue.

"It wasn't a show-and-tell a few moments ago when I had you dabbing your eyes. Did I strike a chord with you, Meister?" I replied, steady and sharp. I knew I ought to kick him out right now—he had overstayed his welcome. But the money sitting on the table held me fast to my seat. It could be enough to cover the repairs this month.

"Ah, no need to get defensive, dear Dahlia. If I may call you that? It's much more befitting, given your girlish appearance. Though your display is quite impressive and accurate, I must admit." The Meister's eyes narrowed his eyes. "Still, your talents of foresight do not go unnoticed. I'm not here to make you a student—no, I think your skills are far better suited to other endeavors. Not to say you wouldn't excel at the Conservatory, should you choose to stay."

"I won't repeat myself: what exactly do you want from me?" I said very slowly. The vestigial light from the grey afternoon had all but faded, a flash of lightning momentarily illuminating the room. The overhead lamp quivered with the distant rumble of thunder.

"Dahlia, I'm upgrading you to *detective*, and I'm here to hand you your first case."

A long pause stretched between us before I found my voice again.

"Detective?" I let out. I hadn't realized I'd been holding my breath. The word felt both familiar and bitter on my tongue. "I can't. As you can see, I run a prosperous and profitable business here," I countered.

"Be reasonable, girl. You haven't moved half of the original inventory since your father bought this place on mortgage for your mother ten years ago. Yes, of course I've seen the lien. I don't hire anyone without proper diligence. I know you peddle your readings just to make your payments on time," the Meister said, his tone almost bored. "And besides, your mind must be turning to mush, hearing the same sodden stories day after day. People really aren't that interesting, are they?"

My chest clenched and my eyes stung at the corners before I even realized it. I studied the ageless face of the stranger across from me—the sharpness of his jaw that met with a narrow chin, the dark eyebrows that looked coarsely drawn with charcoal, and the avian eyes that peered straight through me like I was nothing but the moth-eaten silk of my shawl. It was almost enough to make me tell the truth. Almost.

I raised my chin higher. "My patrons are loyal, and I love what I do." It was only a half-lie. I found contentment in taking care of my mother and the books—it was the last of what we had from my father. The last that bound us all together as a family.

"I suspect you crave much more than what the cards of Fate have dealt you. You crave *purpose.* Not to mention, you despise being a fraud, and that's what this place makes you feel like. How's that for a reading?"

Touché. It wasn't as fun being on the receiving end.

"Fine. I'm not enamored with being a reader, but it covers my expenses. Plenty of people dislike their professions."

"Did your father dislike his?" the Meister pressed.

I shot out of my seat, pointing my finger at the door. I wouldn't let this stranger speak of my father. "You, sir, are kindly asked to leave now. Keep your money—the reading's on the house. But make haste out of my property."

The Meister swallowed but didn't move. "I'm sorry, Dahlia. I only meant to imply that you'd find employment under me far more gratifying than being the sole proprietor of a business you lack respect for," he said, adjusting his spectacles.

I sank back into my chair as he continued. "I've come to you because I find myself in somewhat of a precarious situation. You see . . . a dark stain rests on the Conservatory. Last semester, we lost a student." He paused for a moment, his tone turning grave. His eyes darted to the Hanged Man still upturned on my reading table.

"Though the authorities ruled it a suicide, I personally suspect foul play. That's all I can say before we're under agreement, you understand. And, well, I have limited options for hiring a private detective as the Conservatory is not so hospitable to outsiders. We don't trust many people. Hiring you as a detective as well as a student solves my tricky situation. You are the daughter of the infamous Detective Blackburne, and you more or less have the right background to be admitted as a student."

"You want me to investigate the other students?"

"Yes, precisely. I need to know who did it and why. I can't bear this stain of darkness on my school—not after all I've done, all I've invested to get magickal sciences taken seriously in the academic world. I don't want anyone thinking we're just another faction like the rest . . . We are a prestigious institution of higher education.

"And you, my fine madame detective, not only will you hold the prestige of attending my Conservatory—as I noticed you do not have any secondary education—but I will be glad to pay you handsomely. If you find the killer, I'll reward you with a two-thousand-dollar bounty. Plus, the stipend you'll make as a research assistant, of course."

Two thousand dollars. Did I hear him correctly? That was enough to pay off the bookshop mortgage three times over, and then some. I could double my collection of antique tomes. Maybe even take a trip east or west—maybe circle around and do both.

"I can see you're thinking it over. That's all I ask. Keep the acceptance letter—show it to anyone who might miss your absence for the year. I'll be back in a fortnight to collect your answer at the start of our spring term."

The Meister picked up his cane from the back of the chair and sauntered to the door, just as he had come in. He left the sack of coins in the middle of the table, along with the letter.

"And one more thing, Dahlia. Look too long into the void, and it will begin to recognize you. You'd best follow me out of it."

As he exited, the Meister flipped the sign on the door to *Closed* and smiled once more over his shoulder before slipping off into the storm. And I was left alone in the deafening silence of my bookstore.

"There are two main reasons a person would choose the career of a detective. The first is that they are a man—or woman—of justice. They believe that no wrong deed should go unpunished, and that the closure justice provides can heal the soul of the victim and those beloved by him. The second reason is that the man—as is usually the case—sees great darkness within himself and pursues vanquishing darkness in the world in an attempt to rid himself of it. I have not yet decided which reason is mine. Though deep down, I have a guess."

—*The Journal of Daniel Blackburne*, 1906

Chapter 3. Burning a Hole in Blackburne

I closed the shop and spread the money out on my reading table. Ten whole dollars—over three times my usual daily earnings. The money went quickly.

Half went to the roof thatcher, as the tiles had been rotting for years, and he required a "hazard" charge due to the patch of black mold growing on the shingles. I paid another dollar to replace the waterlogged window panels and re-board the doors (luckily, no hazard fee was required). I also spent a bit on a new glass case for some of my rarer tomes, something I should've done years ago. Some of the pages had already crinkled from the summer's humidity.

I had enough left over to buy goods from the market and prepare a lavish meal for myself and my mother—a fatty leg of lamb to roast, two pounds of golden potatoes, a pound of lard, two loaves of sourdough bread, and a sack of cabbage and carrots to make a stew from the leftovers.

With my future research stipend, I could repair the bookstore and buy a meal like this every week. And that wasn't even counting the bounty the Meister offered for finding the Conservatory killer.

"He gave you how much?" Gabriel's chestnut eyes widened as I recounted the story over a pile of books at our usual picnic spot outside of Greenwich Library. I found him on his lunch break at our rendezvous point. He'd been working at the library ever since he could read.

While I was tagging along with my father during his investigations, Gabriel was here, reading and caretaking for books. At his core, he was a guardian of the written word—far better than I would ever be. I envied him in some ways. He lived contentedly among bookstacks, never desiring to reenact their adventures.

"Ten dollars in silver," I said between bites of my apple. My satchel was heavy from the trip to the market, and I sighed as I set it down on the grass. "And he offered me a job. Well, a stipend, technically." I passed him my acceptance letter. "But listen to this—the whole scholarship is a ruse. He really wants to hire me as a detective. There was a death there last year, and he suspects one of the students."

There was a dark part of me that delighted in the prospect of a murder—of a puzzle to solve. Maybe that was the reason I had become a Tarot reader—it was the closest I got to uncovering humanity's dark truths like my father had. But there was another part that remembered my father's scowl and the sallow pockets under his eyes caused by the sleepless nights he worked on a case. Before he died, he made me promise that I'd stay far away from his line of work.

Keep to the library. Books can't hurt you like people can, he had said. I swallowed the bite of apple, some of it sticking in my throat.

"You're not seriously considering it, are you, Dahl? That amount seems a bit high for a scholarship," Gabriel said, studying the letter as though it were a sacred manuscript with his fingers at the outermost edges.

"It's not just a scholarship. Like I said, it's a job offer," I said, chewing my next bite more slowly. This wasn't the time for my pride to get in the way. "I was hoping you could look into the Meister of the school. His name is Christopher Renate. He could be in his fifties, maybe sixties. His accent seems English. He came into my shop knowing too much about me, and I don't like that imbalance of knowledge."

"Sure, I'll have a look in the archives," Gabriel said, biting his bottom lip in thought.

"Thank you, Gabriel. There's nothing you can't find in a book," I said, smiling. But it quickly fell when he didn't return it.

"I don't have a good feeling about this. This is exactly the kind of work your father meddled in, and you swore off it a year ago." *A year ago, when my father died by his own hand*, was what he meant to say.

My eyes fell to my half-eaten apple. It suddenly tasted sour. He was right—I *had* sworn off detective work when my father died, anchoring my fate at the bookstore.

"I know, but I can't shake the nagging feeling that Renate knows something about my father. He's not like anyone I've met in Greenwich, Gabriel. He knows *things*. He's an actual scholar—besides you, of course," I quickly added when Gabriel grimaced.

"You know better than I do what it's like in Greenwich," I said, leaning in to whisper. "What are people reading these days?" He looked away, but not before his eyes flickered to my lips. I ignored it.

"Exactly. They're *not* reading. Maybe two or three people a day borrow a book, and I get even fewer patrons at the shop. Forget about anyone being interested in the old archives; it's being wasted on this agrarian town." The library's archives housed some of the oldest books in the collection—gorgeous tomes on alchemy and primordial chemistry, the origins of the scientific method. As far as Gabriel and I knew, we were the only ones in Greenwich who had read them in the last fifty years.

Gabriel's face softened, his boyish roundness becoming more pronounced. "I've known you a long time, Dahl. I know how your heart soars in mystery and legends, and I know how much you love a good ghost story. I just don't want you getting lost in all of this."

Like your father did, said the silence.

"What would be worse is me not getting lost at all. Staying put, always knowing where I am, never figuring out who I am."

I know who you are, his expression seemed to plead. There was a sadness in his eyes that I couldn't place. Was he grieving the potential loss of a friend, or was he, like me, longing for a life outside of Greenwich? At least his parents had afforded to send him to Sawyer Academy, even if they expected him to stay in Greenwich afterward.

My eyes darted to his hands—dry and ashy from handling so many books, yet delicate and refined. I knew he wasn't one for getting his hands dirty, not the way I was. He was satisfied living in books, but I was not.

A bell chimed in the distance, and he stood, dusting off his clothes. "I have to go, but I'll look into this Christopher Renate. Promise me you won't leave without saying goodbye?" A small smile crept onto his lips, and it made me want to throw my arms around him in a hug, despite how improper it would seem. Despite the fact he might get the wrong idea.

"I promise." I smiled back.

*

Accepting the Meister's offer would be dangerous—fatal, even. But he was right. I *did* feel like a fraud in Greenwich.

My patrons trusted me with their most intimate affairs, their fears, and their dreams. But I had no real counsel to offer. What could a twenty-five-year-old girl trapped in a bookstore possibly know? I'd never left Greenwich, save for a few trips with my father as a child. The shop was never my dream. It was my mother's. And the readings—well, those were just to pay the dues. I had become reliant on the readings to feed myself and my mother. A slave to a trade I scarcely believed in. I could memorize the meanings of the cards and study numerology, but what did I know of the future when I did so little to determine my own life?

In that regard, I was no better than my patrons.

The Meister's offer was a golden ticket to escape the shop. Maybe even to place my mother in a proper medical center, where she could receive proper treatment for her ailment.

I was the daughter of Detective Daniel Blackburne. I had stood by my father's side countless times while he unraveled case after case, and I had picked up a few tricks along the way. I could detect the slightest lie and see through the illusions people cast over themselves and others. It was time for me to take control of my own future—my own Fate.

I was going to accept the Meister's offer.

Now came the tricky part: convincing my mother.

*

I was fiddling with a broken music box when I decided to finally confront her. Repair work was a habit I'd picked up from my father. When my mind was too restless to focus on reading, working on a mechanical trinket seemed to help. But this particular music box was missing a gear, and I didn't have the right size, so it was a fruitless effort. I sighed and tossed it into my satchel for later.

I made my way up the stairwell slowly, savoring each creaking floorboard. Some part of me would miss it: the smell of old parchment, leather-cracked spines, and dust-pillowed antiques. Though the promise of financial relief brightened my outlook, the weight of the decision I had to make overshadowed any sense of ease. I found my mother in her room, sunk into her favorite armchair. She had mustered the strength to leave her bed today. Sunlight streamed through the lace curtains, casting a warm glow over the room.

"Estelle," I began, the words hanging in the air as I gauged her reaction. If my father was the moon, then my mother was the sun—nothing had ever dimmed her internal light. She was all starry eyes and fair complexion. Until my father died, that is. Now she lay as a husk of herself, greying, and a glimmer of who she once was.

She looked up from the book she was reading, a smile briefly crossing her face before it dissolved into a grimace of pain. "What is it, my darling?" she asked, adjusting the pillow in the arch of her spine. She started to rock back and forth rhythmically.

Taking a deep breath, I recounted the Meister's offer, embellishing a bit. "I can even learn bookbinding there and start a workshop downstairs." I found myself speaking quickly, out of nerves. I didn't know if the Conservatory even taught bookbinding, but it was a skill my mother had always wanted me to learn. Her arthritis had made it impossible for her to teach me herself.

Her rocking ceased, and she fixed me with a gaze that betrayed her emotions. I was a master of detecting her emotions after years of vigil at her side.

"*Foresyth*," she murmured, her voice carrying an undercurrent of dread. The last light from her eyes died.

"You've heard of it?"

I watched the memories stirring behind her expression. "Your father investigated that school before he died. It pains me to know that you've come across it. He did everything he could to keep you away from it."

My eyes widened. "Father investigated Foresyth? But why—what happened there?"

"Is this because we couldn't send you to Sawyer Academy? I wish we could have, darling, but you know how hard it's been to keep the shop running," she said, trying to change the subject.

"This isn't about Sawyer—it's about Foresyth. Why did father investigate the school?" I pressed.

She sighed, her gaze turning distant. "It's hard to talk about your father, Dahlia. I'd rather not."

"Mother, please. What happened there?" I pressed. The furrow of pain in her brows was almost enough for me to abandon my curiosity, but this was the most we had been able to speak in weeks.

Her shoulders fell. "I don't know what happened, but I do know this: your father became obsessed. His obsession with Foresyth led him down a path from which he could not return to me. It was his first love, and his last enemy. I lost him to it, and I don't want to lose you, too."

His first love? What could she mean by that? Was Foresyth one of my father's earliest cases?

I swallowed hard before answering. "I don't believe in all of father's notions about magick or the occult. They're stories, warped by men who wish to be Gods. Unlike them, I'm content with being mortal, and firmly planted in this world. But I can't make my own in this world if I don't take this chance."

"You were always my brightest star, Dahlia. Reaching further than I could ever dream of," she said turning her face away from me, her grief a mist stretching between us. I could feel her sadness intertwining with my own.

A voice in my head—my father's voice—seemed to whisper, *Listen to your mother, Dahlia.* Tears threatened to well in my eyes, but I swallowed them back, replacing them with a surge of determination.

You don't get to tell me what to do anymore, father. You left me.

I took my mother's pale hand, tracing the veins that crisscrossed beneath her paper-like skin. "I promise, I'll always take care of you, mother. I'll be back before you know it. And I'll hire Lady Florance's daughter to look after you while I'm gone. You won't be alone."

A heavy silence settled between us. She said nothing, turning away from me. I stood, trying to break the tension. "Let's eat the lamb roast I made. We can talk more over dinner, maybe read some Dickens afterward."

*

We didn't discuss it over dinner, nor over Dickens. My mother's pain had intensified so much that she couldn't manage the trip downstairs. Instead, we sat in her room—she in bed, and I in her armchair—eating the roast in silence. Despite my attempts to sway her, the conversation was over. Her concern for me was greater than any argument I could make. I understood her fear. Losing my father had been a severe loss, and the thought of losing her daughter must have felt unbearable. But the truth was, the Meister's offer had opened a door for me, and I couldn't ignore it.

And then, there was the discovery that my father's past intertwined with Foresyth.

After settling my mother into bed and administering her medicine, I decided to explore my father's old library. Tucked away behind a hidden door, it could only be accessed by arranging certain books in a specific order. It was a project I had helped him with before the shop opened, meant to safeguard his most valuable tomes and journals. I also enjoyed helping him design the mechanical locks as a diversion from my studies that summer. Now, I was searching for any mention of Foresyth in my father's journals.

I spent the entire night pouring over his notes, but I found nothing except for a passing reference to "*a mysterious greenhouse brimming with exotic plants from the four continents*" in 1891. Beyond that, there were no detailed notes on the Conservatory. Strangely, the years from 1891 to 1893 were missing entirely—the gap stretched the year before my birth in 1894. My father was meticulous in his record-keeping, so this absence stood out.

If it wasn't in my father's library, then there was only one place that held the answers: Foresyth itself. Whatever had tied my father to the Conservatory, I needed to uncover it. The Meister's offer wasn't just a way out of Greenwich, it was a path to the truth about my father's haunted past, and to myself.

An occult arts school, a potential killer, and a link to my father's past awaited me. I had better pack all my ceremonial daggers.

Chapter 4: A Final Goodbye

A week later, Gabriel found me at the shop just after closing. The sky had unleashed its torrent, and rain was coming down in fat droplets. He walked into my shop soaking wet. His hair was matted and stuck to the side of his face. He looked more like a bedraggled puppy than usual, and I couldn't help but smile at the sight of him.

"What are you doing out in this storm, Gabriel? Come in!" I pulled him into the store, the heat from his arm radiating through his soaked blazer.

"I needed to see you before you left," he said through his misty glasses. They were fogging up from the change in temperature, and I instantly reached over to swipe them off his face to clean. He caught my hand, and despite the warmth of his grip around my wrist, a chill ran down my spine.

"You can't go to Foresyth," he said. His face was set and grim, and his features were so stiff that I couldn't help but laugh.

"Let me guess, you've unearthed their terrible lies and secrets. A sex cult powered by virgins' blood? Or one of those voodoo sects that crucifies small animals?"

"Stop being so flippant and listen to me, Dahlia," he said, reaching into his soaked satchel and pulling out a folio. "I couldn't find anything on Christopher Renate. The archives are *blank*. Do you know how rare that is? I even called the Library of Congress but couldn't pin down a single fact about the man. He must have bribed someone high up to erase his name from existence, or it's a fake name."

"So, you didn't find anything?" My hand drifted down, confusion flooding me.

"Not exactly. I found records on Foresyth dating back to the 1870s," he said, unraveling the pages from his folio. "The school was founded in 1872 by a Brit named Edmund W. Foresyth—look at this announcement in *The Greenwich Observer*: 'Prestigious Academy opens in Enderly, enrollment welcome to women and all races,' the title reads."

"Supporting a diverse student body—what's wrong with that?"

"I think it's because they were struggling to *assemble* a student body. Look at this one from 1875: 'School set on top of a mass grave, raises questions from locals. Enderly locals complain about strange noises near school.'"

My arms tingled with the familiar excitement that only came when I worked on a case with my father. I grabbed the old parchment, scanning it eagerly.

"And this one from 1893," Gabriel continued. "'Mysterious disappearance of terminally ill child, Elizabeth Svenski, eleven, in Concord'—a neighboring town."

"1893 . . ." My heart skidded to a stop. "That's one of the missing years from my father's journals."

"What?" Gabriel said, breaking his gaze from the papers and meeting mine.

"My father's journals—his collection goes back decades. But there are three years missing: 1891, 1892, and 1893. My mother said he'd been investigating Foresyth sometime before his death. Could it have been that long ago? I don't remember him looking into it while I was alive."

"Maybe he was investigating Elizabeth Svenski's disappearance."

I pursed my lips but quickly broke into a smile. "This has been very helpful, Gabriel. I can't thank you enough."

His eyes darted to the counter of my bookstore, noticing my father's old leather briefcase and my packed satchel.

"You can't go, Dahlia. There's something wrong with that place—I can feel it," he said, gripping the folio so tightly that his fingers were turning white. I put my hands over his and lowered them.

"That's precisely why I need to go. If there's been a missing student, and now a dead one, there could be others who might get hurt."

"I don't care about anyone else getting hurt, I care about *you*. If it's money you need, I could talk to my father at the treasury. We could arrange something," he pleaded quickly.

Anger rose in my chest before I could snuff it out.

"Please, stop before you offend me. I don't need anything from Mr. Lexor or the treasury. It's not just about money," I said sternly. "My father lived his life putting himself at risk in the pursuit of truth. And what have I been doing? Wasting my life away in bookstacks, selling stories to anyone naïve enough to buy them." Gabriel flinched, and I realized how my words hurt him. How I was rejecting the life that he had set out, and accepted, for himself. Perhaps it was better this way. Perhaps this was the only way he could let me go.

"I refuse to live like this. I refuse to live in other people's stories." I motioned around the bookstore. "I appreciate you coming here, Gabriel," I said, standing, "but it's getting late, and I should bid you adieu. Thank you for the research file."

"If you're determined to go, then there's something else you should know." Gabriel fumbled in his satchel and pulled out another folio. "I didn't know what this meant, but maybe it could help you."

"What is it?"

"There are reservation files—there's an entity called the *Council* that's been reserving public grounds near Enderly since 1875. I wouldn't have traced them if they hadn't slipped up once in 1881, logging their name as 'The Council of Foresyth.' They meet regularly, seemingly according to the lunar calendar, every twenty-eight days. They've met everywhere from City Hall to Enderly Public Library."

My eyes widened at the information. "Gabriel, you sleuth! This is incredible," I said, scanning the files.

"Like I said, I don't know what it means, but maybe there's a higher governing body at Foresyth. If there's a string of unusual occurrences, maybe they'll know something." He stood stiffly then, picking up his satchel from the table.

"Well, I guess this is goodbye then," he said, walking toward the door. I could sense the hurt in his voice. He turned to me, his eyes searching mine, as if he was trying to memorize my face. I puffed my chest out, ignoring the swelling pang of sadness from saying goodbye to my oldest friend.

"Goodbye, Gabriel. You've been a big help. I'll write to you." I knew he'd be safe here in Greenwich; that would be solace enough. He turned back before exiting into the torrent of rain and said, "Try to stay alive, will you?"

I smiled and nodded, and he disappeared into the whitewash of rain.

"The venerable Lord Edmund W. Foresyth II, esteemed founding father of Foresyth Conservatory, dedicated nearly two decades in pursuit of the school's consecrated site before settling upon the grounds at Enderly in 1872. His quest commenced in 1854 during a scientific expedition intended to observe the rare transit of Venus. While en route to the island of Oahu, Lord Foresyth was beset by visionary glimpses of a grand academy crowned by an imposing clock tower. He surmised that the celestial phenomenon may have disrupted the temporal-spatial continuum, granting him a glimpse of the school's future grandeur."

"Over the ensuing years, Lord Foresyth traversed more than 50,000 miles in his search for these sanctified grounds. In a final twist of irony, he discovered that Enderly lay a mere 30 miles from his place of residence in the Tar Heel State. Reflecting on this journey, Lord Foresyth wrote in his memoirs that the spiritual and physical breadth of his expedition had been essential to attuning him to Enderly's unique energetic frequency, an insight that would ultimately lead him home."

—*Foresyth Conservatory: A Complete History, Unabridged*, 1891

Chapter 5: Welcome to Foresyth Conservatory

I packed only the most critical items for Foresyth: two Hermetic daggers (which I had taken care to sharpen), my bag of spare mechanical parts, a book of Nordic rune translations (I admit I had not committed them to memory), two changes of clothes, the only dress I owned, and a pair of Oxfords.

My intent was to return from Foresyth as soon as possible—investigate the scene of the crime, make my deductions, and give the name of the killer quickly. In between my official duties, I'd inquire about my father's past and his connection with Foresyth, but no more than that. It would take me a fortnight, perhaps two. I was committed, for better or for worse, to returning to Greenwich with the bounty in hand. If not for my own sake, then for my mother's.

I arranged for the care of my mother with Lady Florance's daughter, Angelise. She was a stout woman, twice my age, diligent, kind, and the only person I could trust to take care of my mother and the shop while I was away. I gave her a generous rate of ten dollars a week, and she was to send word if anything became amiss.

The Meister arrived just past five, two weeks after our first meeting, just as he had promised. He wore a black bowler hat and the same grey overcoat with the fine lining. We spared no time at the entryway as the driver took my suitcase and tied it to the back of the motorcar.

I tugged my coat tighter against the wind as the Meister helped me into the motorcar. As the door slammed shut, I stared back at the little bookshop I was leaving, with its crooked sign that read "Blackburne Bookstore and Gifts." Despite the new boards and windowpanes, the shop looked minuscule from this far down the main road, crowded in a sea of other little shops and passersby. I sent a silent goodbye to the flower shop and shoe cobbler sandwiching my store. I was grateful for the home it had been to me all these years, but deep in my bones, I was ready to leave.

I spared one last glance upward to the second floor and saw the curtains drawn. I couldn't see my mother, but from the angle of her bed, I knew she had drawn them to watch me. *I'll be back*. I sent the promise across space, hoping it would be true.

The motorcar rumbled to life and I tore my gaze from the bookstore. The Meister was seated next to me.

"Ms. Blackburne, I would like to congratulate you on taking this next step in your future." His green eyes twinkled as he handed me a beige folio. "I do wish the circumstances of our partnership were less unfortunate. But regardless, I hope your time at Foresyth will be illuminating. For both of us."

I took the folder from his gloved hands and pressed it into my lap to steady it against the bounce of the motorcar.

"There won't be time to meet the other students today, as we'll be arriving late. You'll pardon my tardiness, as I had a client of my own to attend to earlier in the day. Inside the folio, you'll find the police report with all the evidence collected during their inspection. The victim's name was Julian Earhardt, a six-and-twenty-year-old male. His concentration was in enigmatology. His dissertation focused on Eastern esoterism, specifically Gnosticism, an early form of mythological Christianity. He died last Spring Equinox, in March."

"I see. So, less than a year ago," I said without looking up as I scanned the police report. "Why didn't you advise the police to simply arrest the other students?"

"There was no evidence to indicate anything besides suicide," he said, lowering his spectacles. "And arresting all the students would effectively shut down my entire institution."

"And despite your suspicions of foul play, you didn't press the police to collect more evidence?"

The Meister narrowed his eyes. "Ms. Blackburne, you need to understand something very important. I wanted this case closed, publicly, as soon as possible. The reputation of my school is critical. We cannot let a scandal like this blacken our reputation, lest our donors cease their funding. The house is . . . demanding and takes funding to maintain. If I couldn't afford to keep it open, the school would not survive. That is precisely why I have hired you . . . Eliminating the threat under discretion is the only way forward."

A familiar tension coiled in my gut, tight and unyielding. My father had always placed his faith in process—trusted that truth, when scrutinized under the weight of enough evidence, would rise clean to the surface, like oil atop of water. But here, with no official sanction and cloaked under pretense, I was charting a path without precedent or protection.

Was I capable of this? Alone, and in defiance of the very system meant to safeguard it?

I exhaled slowly, pressing the doubt into the recesses of my mind like a footnote. The only course now was forward. Truth was not an elusive spectator—it was a pattern, hidden in plain sight, waiting for the right mind to reconstruct its symmetry. I only had to hold the fragments to the light and let them speak. How difficult could that be?

Look for the inconvenient truth. My father's words echoed through me.

"It says here that he died from a coagulation of blood in the brain. But the coroner's report also states that there was a lethal dose of valerian root mixed with nightshade in his system." I flipped to the next page. It was an image of the victim—a sturdy-built man, tawny-skinned, with neatly trimmed, curly, dark auburn hair, wearing an oxford suit and suspenders. His face was swollen, his eyes nearly bursting from his skull. The way his body was arranged was the worst of all.

He was hung inverted from a wooden tress, his legs forming the shape of a four. The Hanged Man. The realization nearly stole the air from my lungs.

"Yes, Ms. Blackburne. Your reading predicted the manner in which the victim died."

"It has to be a coincidence," I said, looking up. But that familiar knot of fear was tugging at my stomach again. I squeezed my eyes shut—I just had to think.

"It could be," he replied, but his tone seemed unconvinced.

My head raced for an explanation. "There are seventy-eight cards in the Rider-Waite-Smith deck. There's an almost thirteen percent chance that the Hanged Man would appear in one of the ten placements in my spread. Slim, but not improbable. And that's not even considering other cards with complementary associations . . . Death, the Devil, the Eight of Swords, and so on." The facts steadied me as I said them aloud.

"Very well. Coincidence. A hell of a coincidence, but let's accept it for the time being. Now, what can you deduce from the evidence presented thus far?"

I took a breath, flipping through the pages again before answering. "The victim died when his central nervous system shut down from the poison. The deadly effects of nightshade, if I recall correctly, take two to three hours to set in. That means he was hung, or hung himself, after taking the poison. But why? Wouldn't the poison alone be enough to kill him? Why go through the trouble of hanging the body in such a fashion?"

"Precisely the question, Detective Blackburne." The Meister nodded approvingly. "That's what I was hoping you could figure out."

*

I had combed through the case file until the words blurred and sleep overtook me. When the car finally lurched to a halt, the sky outside was ink black. A tap on my shoulder—light, but insistent—pulled me back to consciousness. The Meister's hand. I blinked awake, heart stuttering in my chest.

"Easy, I was just trying to wake you. We're getting close. There are a couple more details I need to share with you regarding your status and employment at the Conservatory."

I wiped the daze from my eyes and collected the papers strewn across my side of the motorcar.

"You, Dahlia Blackburne, were educated at Wesley College and obtained a degree in classics," the Meister handed me another folio, this one black. Inside, I found a Wesley College transcript and several other documents affirming my degree credentials.

"You have been accepted to Foresyth to develop your thesis on Hermetic Tarotology, with an arts concentration in theater. I hope you don't mind my presumption, given your predilection for the performative arts." The Meister winked. "You are here to obtain your graduate degree, and most importantly"—his eyes locked onto mine—"you know nothing of Julian Earhardt. Do you understand?"

I gulped, my throat suddenly tight as I nodded. I adjusted the locket around my neck that was tangled with my hair.

A feeling of dread crept into my chest. Was I really prepared for this? Not only would I be investigating Julian's murder, but I'd also have to maintain a fabricated identity in a house full of suspects. Every word I spoke, every glance exchanged, every interaction would be calculated.

The Meister continued to explain my cover, but his voice sounded distant as the weight of the situation sank in. I was no actress, no professional infiltrator. My readings were performative, yes, but that was different. Those were controlled, guided by my knowledge of psychology and human behavior. Here, I'd be playing a much more dangerous game. I was stepping into a world I barely understood, surrounded by students who might be complicit in a murder.

And I would have to deceive them all.

"If any of the other students discover your true intent at the school—well, you know I couldn't protect Julian."

The Meister's words pulled me back to the present, a shiver running down my arms. His warning was clear. If I failed, if anyone realized why I was truly at Foresyth, I would be left to fend for myself. My father relied on his allies, but I would have none.

"I understand," I replied, but my voice faltered. I didn't sound convincing, even to myself. The rational part of me screamed to back out now, to walk away from this mess before I found myself in over my head. But the other part—the part that craved purpose and erudition, the part that longed to prove I was more than a mere shopkeeper—kept me right where I was.

I'd committed to this. I couldn't turn back now.

"Good. You are to report to me every week on your progress with the case. You are my personal research assistant, hired to help with another clairvoyant topic I've been dabbling in: Nordic runes. If anyone asks about your whereabouts, you are on official research business. If there are any issues, you come directly to me." He tried at a smile. "Oh, come now, Ms. Blackburne. Who knows, by the end of this year you might not only have a murder solved, but also several papers published!"

*

The motorcar emerged from the endless blur of the black forest, ascending a steep hill along a dirt pathway. It led to an imposing black gate with spires jutting out, offering the least welcoming of entrances.

From what I could discern in the dim light, the house just beyond the gate was three stories high, its Mansard roof adorned with cupolas in each cardinal direction. In the middle, a stained-glass dome erupted from the structure, the only part illuminated was a clock tower seemingly lit with a light of its own. Ivy writhed along the outer facade, its serpentine tendrils clutching the stone in a grotesque embrace.

The coachman helped the Meister and me disembark, carrying my suitcase through the gate. We started down a cobblestone path that led to the main entrance. A lawn speckled with trees lined either side of the pathway. The wind rustled through the skeletal branches, their gnarled limbs casting eerie shadows. Once at the door, the driver handed me my suitcase and made a hasty retreat to the motorcar. I was alone with the Meister at the grand house entrance in mere minutes.

"Welcome, Ms. Blackburne, to Foresyth Conservatory." The door rattled open behind us as if it had been waiting for my arrival. Dim candlelight poured through the entryway, and as the door inched further open, two eyes became visible. "Mr. Richard will take you to your room. I'm afraid all the students have already retired for the night, so you'll have to wait until morning to meet them."

I handed my luggage to Mr. Richard with a nod of thanks. The warmth beyond the threshold beckoned. For a moment, I lingered—glancing toward the impenetrable dark from which we'd come, then back to the golden glow of the house. I stood suspended at the boundary between them, light and shadow pooling at my feet. A jolt crawled up my spine.

I swallowed my unease.

I had always believed intuition was a poor substitute for fact. So I dismissed the feeling and chose what could be known.

Julian. My father. My purpose. They were waiting for me here.

And so, I stepped past the darkness and into the light.

The Acolyte & The Alchemist: Part I

The boy with raven hair did not notice when the copper-haired girl sat beside him. He remained still, his focus steely on the manuscript before him. He preferred the library for its silence. Two dozen students could funnel in to study here and scarcely cross paths.

That was why he had come in the first place—to study and become an acolyte of lost knowledge. Such a pursuit demanded unwavering concentration.

And yet, the scent of cinnamon and clove curled toward him as the woman brushed her unbound hair over her shoulder. His head turned instinctively, betraying him before he even realized his focus had faltered.

"I hope you don't mind," she said, the threat of a smile dancing on her lips. "This side of the library has the best lighting."

Midday light bathed the grand room in gold. And yet, of all the empty seats, she had chosen one a mere breath away from his.

He furrowed his brows. "No, I don't—" He bristled, meaning to lie, but stopped when their eyes met. The words became truth. "—mind," he finished, the furrow in his brow disappearing. "You're the new student, aren't you?"

His gaze traced the sharp line of her jaw, the undulating curve of her lips, the proud arch of her brows. Her skin was the color of the coffee he preferred to drink in the morning—equal parts espresso and milk.

Why do novels always fixate on the color of someone's hair? He wondered, faltering when he realized her beauty could not be contained by words alone. The manuscript before him lay forgotten.

"New to Foresyth, yes. But I have been a scholar far longer than I have been a student."

The boy wasn't one for infatuation. He had always preferred books over people, but there was something different about this woman. It wasn't just beauty that held him captive. No, it was the depth of knowledge in her eyes, as if she harbored secrets vast enough that even this library could not hold them.

She slid a stack of books to the edge of the desk, and he traced the movement, trying to catch their titles. One stood out before she cracked the spine: *A Meditation on Khorvyn Occultism.*

"I'm Hamra." She extended her hand across the narrow space between them, as if closing a distance that had always been meant to shrink.

The boy took her hand, soft and supple in his. A faint prickle of static snapped at his fingertips.

The two spent the afternoon in companionable silence, reading book after book, each lost in their own respective world.

The boy did not yet realize it would be the first of many such afternoons.

"Lord Foresyth's considerable fortune was not amassed from his exploratory endeavors but rather inherited through his father's vast and distinguished art collection brought over from England, which the young Foresyth greatly enriched. As an ardent patron of the arts, he envisioned Foresyth to be rooted in these same values. His purpose was to culturally enrich the New World. While a subdued palette is not strictly prohibited, students are actively encouraged to attire themselves in vibrant and resplendent colors, a practice believed to invigorate the creative spirit. In his early writings, he proclaimed, "The human form is the vessel of the divine and should be adorned accordingly." A testament to his conviction that attire plays a vital role in honoring one's creative potential."

—*Foresyth Conservatory: A Complete History, Unabridged,* 1891

Chapter 6: Meet the Suspects

I rose early the next morning to explore my surroundings before the other students awoke. We were a week into the Spring term, the Meister had informed me, and the students were alerted of my arrival. It wasn't common for students to arrive in the middle of the academic year, but not unheard of. *Everyone is on their own divine timeline,* the Meister had said in the motorcar. Whatever that could have meant.

The sun was just beginning to crest over the hills that surrounded the Conservatory when I opened my chamber door and stepped into the hallway. The floorboards squeaked in protest at my intrusion, and I cursed under my breath. The House didn't trust me—not *yet.*

Doors lined both sides of the hallway, encircling the mezzanine and leading to a grand staircase at its center. This House must have once been a noble estate, built with fine oak beams, tiled floors, and iron grates securing the windows. Yet signs of decay were evident. Rot bloomed from the base of the stairs, mildew speckled behind the torn wallpaper, and the scent of damp wood and rust lingered as I walked down the halls. It struck me as odd that the Meister could afford my generous stipend yet neglected to repair the House.

Concluding that only the student rooms were on the second floor, I descended the stairs and began my exploration on the first. The foyer, which I had entered the night before, appeared much more opulent in the soft morning light. A rich burgundy carpet stretched from the two entry doors to the back of the hall, leading to a dining room with an open door. Near the grand entrance, a wooden sign hung with golden cursive letters reading *Our Founding Values* at the top.

INTEGRITY OF THE WORD
ACTIVATION OF THE MIND
TRANSCENDENCE OF THE SOUL
THE CARETAKERS OF ARCANA
UNDER THE VEIL OF THE ROSE

Moving further down the hall, I noticed a sitting room bathed in sunlight—and a *tree*? A giant oak tree stood improbably tall in the center of the room, its ancient limbs stretching toward the vaulted ceiling, as though reclaiming the sky it once knew. The massive trunk rooted itself in the floorboards, defying logic, as if the House itself had grown around it, accommodating the tree's silent dominion. The dark wood paneling of the room blended seamlessly with the rough bark, the patterns of age and grain in both almost indistinguishable, as if the tree had long ago fused into the very bones of the House.

How was that possible?

I pressed further down the hallway, passed the tree-harboring room and tried a black wooden door only to find it locked. I continued trying each door until I reached the end of the hall. Of course, a House with self-proclaimed *caretakers of secrets* would have so many locked doors.

At the very end, the sage double doors opened easily when I pushed them, revealing the most exquisite library I'd ever seen. Dark oak beams housed a vast array of leather-bound books from floor to ceiling. The familiar scent of ancient parchment and cedar-wood floors flooded my senses, and I inhaled greedily. Eyeing the shelves, I noticed large, oversized books on the bottom and minuscule, palm-sized volumes near the top. Awed by the enormity of the collection, something like giddiness welled up inside me. The sight of row upon row of books was almost dizzying, and it reminded me, just slightly, of home.

"What are you doing in here?" a voice called.

Startled, I turned to find a small, lithe woman standing nearby. Barely reaching my collarbone, she had sleek black hair framing her pointed chin. She wore a bright red sweater that contrasted starkly with her dark demeanor, and her narrowed eyes held mine in a quizzical expression.

"I was just exploring the library. I'm a new student here, Dahlia. Dahlia Blackburne." Remembering myself and my purpose here, I offered a small smile, signaling an attempt at acquaintanceship.

"I'm Nina Choi. You like books?" When I nodded, she added, "We all have that in common," though her tone held a hint of mockery. Were the students friendly with each other, or were there rivalries?

"You sign out books on this sheet—it's an honor system. I'm returning a few myself before breakfast. You're welcome to check anything out. No, really. I'm mostly in the cryptozoology section, aisle C, rows five to twenty-four. I'm writing on gremlins and their representation of techno-anxiety in the modern era. What's your concentration?"

"Hermetic Tarotology, with an arts concentration in theater. You're researching gremlins?" I asked incredulously.

She rolled her eyes. "Yes, but as a metaphor. Mostly."

"What do you mean by that?"

She sighed as if the answer was obvious.

"Monster lore reflects society's fears, anxieties, and, most importantly, offers explanations for the inexplicable. Imagine you're a pilot in the Great War, flying over the trenches in a biplane, when your engine suddenly sputters and dies. Would you prefer to think that your mechanic overlooked a crucial repair, or that you missed something during pre-flight inspection? Likely not."

I was amused by her reasoning but disagreed. "When I work on a machine and can't figure out its malfunction, I ascribe the error to myself—not some fictional deity."

She gave me a steady look. "Yes, but you're not working on machines of war, unless you have something interesting to share? These engineers faced the unsettling truth of human fragility—they couldn't flawlessly command such complex machines. It's easier, more comforting, to believe the failure was beyond their control, surrendered to something supernatural. Psychologically, it feels far safer."

"That's giving too much power to random chance," I replied. "You must have a strong external locus of control."

"I wasn't talking about myself. I control *all* things, living and inanimate," she said with a shadow of a smirk.

A faint warmth rose to my cheeks. I'd spoken too freely. She was, after all, a suspect—however brilliant her mind or disarming her curiosity. And yet, I couldn't deny the flicker of intrigue her research stirred in me, nor the unexpected pleasure of genuine academic exchange. I would need to be more careful. This wasn't the place to divulge too much of my own interests.

Still, a question budded inside of me, quiet but persistent: *Could Foresyth be a true institution of learning after all?* Not merely the shadowed sanctuary of occult ambition my mother and others had condemned, but something more—something real?

"Psychological threats can loom larger than physical ones," I noted. "Do all the students share your sentiments on magick?"

Her smirk died and she returned her books to the shelves. "It wouldn't be an academic Conservatory if everyone thought the same, would it? We all have our own notions of right and wrong here," she said, a hint of irony lacing her words. "Tarotology—you read Tarot or just study it? Don't worry, I won't ask for a reading. It's a bit low-brow, like asking a medical student to check your deviated septum. We're not amateurs."

I glanced away, fingering the books on the shelf in front of me. "Yes, I read Tarot. I believe the cards hold sacred iconography that taps into our collective consciousness."

"Ah, Durkheim's theory?"

"His, and Jung's archetypes," I replied, a thrill rising in my sternum. It had been rare to meet anyone who could discuss the psychology of Tarot with me. Even Gabriel shied away from the darker, mystical topics I found myself enthralled with since I was a child. But before I revealed too much, I quickly shifted the topic. "So, gremlins—that's your thesis topic here at Foresyth?"

"Mythological zoology, or cryptozoology, with an arts concentration in mixed media. I use natural fibers and elements in my taxidermy," she added, noticing my raised eyebrow. "It's not as gross as it sounds, and we have a decent science lab here. I mostly use the microscopes, but there's a lot of equipment that's just collecting dust. If you're into machines, I can show you after breakfast."

"I'd like that a lot. My dad was a sort of scientist before he changed careers."

"Is that right?"

"Geology, mostly, but he made his own lenses to study minerals. Nothing that could walk, though. Not as interesting as taxidermy," I added, hoping I hadn't lost her. I needed an ally at Foresyth. Even if I couldn't trust her, maybe she could trust *me*. That had to be worth something.

Nina smiled, placing her last book on the shelf. "I hope they don't walk," she joked, waving a hand. "Come on, breakfast is in the other room. I'll show you the way."

As we started down the aisle, she grabbed my arm, tugging me back into the stacks. She bit her lip, deciding whether to share a thought.

"I have to warn you," she whispered. "Aspen—the tall one—he'll try to play a trick on you. He always does on the new ones. Just play along, all right? It's a stupid hazing ritual. His father hates him, so he must take it out on everyone else."

I tried to mask my surprise at her bluntness. "Thanks for the heads-up. I'll be careful." Was Nina genuinely looking out for me, or was she part of the game too?

We made our way to the breakfast room, a bright, airy space with high ceilings and white curtains filtering the January sun. My gaze drifted to the table where three students were seated.

Across the table sat a woman with blonde curls like a Botticelli angel, her face flushed, lips forming a cupid's bow as she laughed with the man beside her. She exuded charisma, an aura of effortless charm wrapping her and everyone near her. She wore a long dress of blues and purples draping her figure elegantly.

Beside her, the man lounged casually in his chair, his strong jaw and deep-set hazel eyes catching the light. His tailored sports jacket was made from a rich, heavy fabric which complemented his bohemian poise. His arm was draped over the back of the blonde's chair, suggesting a familiar intimacy. He was the first to notice me.

"Look what the Meister dragged in. Another playmate," he said with a smirk, locking eyes with me.

The blonde smiled warmly. "You must be the new student. We've been excited to meet you. Come sit."

A man sat further down, seated in a wheelchair with a book in his lap. When he looked up, I saw the half-dazed look of someone pulled from another world. Nina settled into a seat, and I noticed everyone wore bright, whimsical colors like the lining of the Meister's jacket—everyone except me.

I stood for a moment at the edge of the room before joining them at the table. Individually, they seemed unremarkable—eccentric scholars, perhaps not too different from myself. Examining any one of them too closely would render them as separate, isolated pieces—like a jigsaw puzzle in fragments. But together, they formed a powerful, enigmatic ensemble. And one, if not all, could be dangerous. I would never fully trust any of them, but I had to secure their trust in me, at all costs.

"I'm equally excited to meet all of you. Though I must admit, the Meister didn't share all your names," I said with what I hoped looked like a genuine smile.

Nina busied herself at the buffet table, then returned to sit with the others. "These are the Trees—Aspen Barlowe and Sequoia Nightingale. Leone Beaufort is the one always reading. And I'm Nina, in case you've already forgotten."

The Trees. So, they were together.

"And don't worry, Sequoia and Aspen are only distantly related, so it's only distantly disgusting," Nina teased.

"Oh, don't be jealous, Nin," Aspen replied, striding toward me. "Maybe the new girl is more your type, hmm?"

Nina scoffed and returned to her seat. Aspen reached me, grinning. "Let me introduce you to our spread. And perhaps, over breakfast, you'll tell us everything—where you come from, your darkest fears, your deepest desires."

He was devilishly handsome, I had to admit, with perfectly symmetrical features and a birthmark on his neck. His hair was a few shades darker than Sequoia's, and his face carried a sharpness she lacked. His hazel eyes reminded me of the color of upturned moss after a rainstorm, dewy and rich.

"Very well, if you promise to do the same," I replied.

He grabbed a fresh plate and began piling on food. "We have Miss Seaward's famous buttermilk biscuits, eggs, bacon—the staples. Fresh quiche—Koi, was it mushroom and feta today? The crust is flaky and divine. Then there's the crepes station. I recommend the gooseberry jam; let me get that for you. And finally." He paused, looking at me gravely. "Under no circumstances can you miss the breakfast cookies. Lemon sugar cookies this morning. Miss Seaward really went all out for your arrival."

"I don't think I could eat that much," I started, but my stomach betrayed me with a growl.

"Nonsense. You've had a long journey, and, if you don't mind me saying, adding a few stones to your figure wouldn't hurt."

I squinted at him. Well, he was certainly blunt.

"Stop eyeing her like a Christmas pig and get back over here. You were helping me with this translation, remember? *No one alive has ever escaped it, neither brave man nor coward—it's born with us the day we are born.* Why were the Romans so damn roundabout? I'd rather be studying Gaelic," Sequoia mused.

"Death?" Nina offered over her biscuit.

"Fate," I interjected. "No one alive escapes Fate."

"And she knows her Homer. You'll fit right in," Aspen said approvingly. "Now, try the tea—it's my favorite, especially on a cold winter day. Isn't this turmeric chai otherworldly, Koi?"

"Mhmm," she mumbled through mouthfuls of crepe.

"Oh, I don't drink—"

"Milk? Sugar?" he interrupted.

How could someone be so charming and overbearing at the same time? I glanced at Nina, who winked over her coffee as if to say *play along.* Whatever game Aspen was playing, I had to let him think he held the advantage. I took the plate from his hands.

"You're too kind; I'll have both." The tea's aroma—turmeric, ginger, and something else, earthy and moss-like—wafted up. Was I being paranoid, or was something else in the tea? Nina's warning echoed in my mind. I noted that everyone else had varying shades of coffee beside their plates despite Aspen's claimed love of the tea.

Aspen set my plate beside Nina's seat and took his place across from me. I smiled at him and eagerly bit into the biscuit, then the quiche. The food looked delicious, yet it dissolved into bland mush on my tongue. How could something that looked so appetizing taste so dull?

"By your expression, I can tell you're not used to this level of fine dining. Don't worry, you'll adjust," Aspen taunted.

"Though Foresyth lacks many . . . modern amenities, the food more than compensates," Sequoia added. "Now, tell us—what's your name again? The Meister mentioned it, Delilah?"

"Dahlia—like the flower—Dahlia Blackburne."

"Ah, Dahlia. Flowers aren't too far from trees, are they, my betrothed?" Sequoia chimed, nudging Aspen.

"No, but trees are taller, closer to the Gods. We'll help elevate you, Dahlia. Though we're serious academics, the best part of the Conservatory is the community. No one has to live in their own head anymore. Isn't that right, Leone?"

"I might prefer mine to suffering in yours," Leone muttered, barely looking up. Aspen's self-declared authority didn't intimidate everyone, it seemed.

"Never mind Leone," Aspen retorted. "A brick has more personality than him. Though I wouldn't get on his bad side, he *is* an Olympic fencer."

As they continued to bicker, I let one of the lemon cookies slip from my hand to the floor with a thud, sending up a cloud of powdered sugar. I bent down to retrieve it, using the moment to slip a small wad of cotton I'd plucked from the chair upholstery into my cheek, a buffer for whatever was in the tea.

"Clumsy me," I murmured as I resumed my seat. Aspen's eyes were still on me. I took a loud slurp of the tea, letting the liquid soak into the cotton rather than swallowing. I couldn't eliminate the tea's effects entirely, but at least I could dampen them.

"So, Dahlia," Aspen leaned in, his tone suddenly sharper. "Why are you here?"

To investigate you, I withheld with a bite of my lip. Instead, I replied evenly, "To study, of course. I'm a scholar of Hermetic Tarotology."

"Funny—almost sounds like tautology. Anyone else feeling déjà vu?"

"What do you mean?"

The students exchanged knowing glances, stifling laughs. "Let's just say that Tarot isn't a new topic here. Several others have studied it," Nina said, her gaze fixed on her coffee. How many students? Was Julian among them?

"Yes, more common than I'd care to admit. And what did you do before coming to Foresyth?" Aspen continued.

"I went to Wesley. Majored in classics. Hence the Homer." More thanks to my mother's library than anything else. Even if the books didn't sell well, I'd read them all. And when I was done with those, that's when I moved on to the rarer tomes of occultism and ceremonial magick. All for fun, light-hearted reading, of course.

"Wesley's prestigious. My cousin Annabelle went there for theater. See, Aspen, she's one of us. Let her be." Sequoia looked me over. "Although, Dahlia, dear, we should modernize your wardrobe. The dark plaids really wash you out."

"Heard there were three suicides there last year, mostly in chemistry," Nina remarked, eyes gleaming.

"Shut up, Nina. No one cares about your twisted metrics of prestige," Aspen shot back.

"Bite me, Barlowe."

"No thanks."

The cotton ball in my cheek was beginning to saturate with saliva. It was time to excuse myself. "I need to find a restroom."

"Here, I'll show you," Sequoia rose to guide me.

When we reached the restroom, Sequoia paused and placed a hand on my shoulder, her grip gentle yet firm. She smelled faintly of lavender. "I'm sorry about Aspen. He's going through . . .," she started, looking away. "There was a student here before you, but he left unexpectedly. Aspen hasn't handled it well."

"Why did he leave?" I tested, the cotton was soaking onto my tongue, the ginger prickling my cheek.

"It's complicated. But I was looking forward to meeting you. The Meister only brings in students he deems worthy. I can't wait to see what you'll bring to our group." Her tone was warm, yet the statement bristled with expectation.

"I'm looking forward to being a part of it," I replied.

Once she walked away, I skittered into the bathroom, closing the door firmly before spitting the yellow tea-soaked cotton into the sink. As I rinsed my mouth, another timely Latin phrase floated to my mind, one that my father taught me before he died.

De omnibus dubitandum.

Be suspicious of everything.

"One of the most splendid assets of Foresyth is, undoubtedly, its library. A repository of knowledge matched in grandeur only by its impressive art collection. Boasting over 20,000 volumes and an additional 5,000 preserved within its exclusive archives, it is esteemed as one of the largest libraries on the continent. The collection spans a vast range of subjects: art, mythology, and history are all represented, alongside practical treatises on medicine and herbal remedies. One member of the illustrious Founding Five reputedly achieved a level of medical expertise equivalent to a formal degree through dedicated study within these walls. A truly remarkable collection, indeed."

—*Foresyth Conservatory: A Complete History, Unabridged*, 1891

"The seasoned detective does not ignore coincidences during a case. If something feels like it was fated, then it was likely *staged*."

—*The Journal of Daniel Blackburne*, 1906

Chapter 7: The Hanged Man

I took a shaky breath, my hands anchoring to the sides of the sink. There was no time to waste. I needed to make progress on the case before the ruse of my studentship at Foresyth faltered, especially with the threat of the other students looming over me.

When the breakfast hour passed, I crept back into the dining room to stitch up the chair I'd mutilated with my dagger. The food had been cleared from the tables, but my chair remained tucked in just as I'd left it. I bent down to the upholstery and began my quick work with a needle and thread before one of the students decided to appear.

As I finished the final stitches, I looked up to admire my handiwork. Barely noticeable, I decided. But, just to be safe, I switched my chair with Nina's. As I lifted the chair to carry it forward, a strong breeze from the next room caught me by surprise.

Was there a window open? I peeked into the hallway.

It was coming from the sitting room, the one with the peculiar grand oak tree erupting from the dead center. I stepped inside, a ray of light reflected off a gilded mirror, illuminating the oak's branches. My eyes followed the sinewy lines bursting through the floorboards and towering over the furniture. The House seemed to have molded itself around the tree, securing its branches as if it had long accepted the tree as part of its own architecture.

It was mesmerizing, if not entirely perplexing.

I crept in, half-expecting to be caught, as Nina had found me in the library, but the room was empty. The air was fresher than in the other rooms, and a breeze filtered through the cracks where the tree broke through, dancing with motes of dust suspended in time. Faded wallpaper, patched and peeling, covered the walls. Opposite a large fireplace, the gilded mirror I'd noticed reflected an aged but comfortable room, showing a worn chaise longue and loveseat at its center. The room felt familiar, though I couldn't place it.

Had I seen this in a dream, or perhaps a photograph?

That was it—I'd seen this room in the photographs the Meister gave me in the folio. This was the scene of the crime.

I went back upstairs to retrieve the photos, carefully sliding them into the waistband of my trousers and covering them with my blazer. I knew well that if I was caught with these, it would spell the end for my time at Foresyth.

Returning to the room, I compared the photograph to reality, noting a splotch of torn wallpaper in the corner where Julian's inverted body had hung limp. I found the damaged wallpaper and scanned up the wooden trellis. But after a closer look at the picture, I realized it wasn't a trellis at all.

It was a *branch* from which Julian hung. I approached the tree, staring up at it. *Why*, I wondered, the question burning in my mind. Why invert the body? The coroner's report said he had been poisoned. Why go through the trouble of hanging him? It wasn't to ensure his death—the dose in his system was lethal enough. There must have been another reason.

I racked my brain for connections. The Hanged Man. Card twelve in the Rider-Waite-Smith deck. Its interpretation spoke of suspension—surrender, sacrifice, a change in perspective. It suggested waiting, letting go of the past, or seeing things from an unconventional angle.

And then, the thought burst to the surface of my consciousness.

I slipped the photo back into my waistband and got down on my hands and knees, aligning my head with where Julian's would have hung. The eerie parallel between us felt unsettling—our heads in the same space, separated only by time. Ten months ago, Julian had been here, alive.

I took a breath and stilled myself. I needed to see the room from his perspective.

I looked, my head still, scanning my eyes across the room, studying every detail. At first, nothing seemed out of place. But before giving up, I pulled out the image one last time, studying Julian, his limbs twisted, his left knee bent to form the shape of a four. *His knee.*

I looked back at the room, following the line his knee would have pointed to—a shelf above the fireplace, filled with an assortment of knick-knacks. I stood, careful to steady myself, and walked to the shelf. There, among a collection of books, sat an old picture frame and an obsidian statue of Ra.

My gaze fixed on the picture—a group of six students and a teacher, shoulder to shoulder. Their clothes, perhaps from thirty years ago, showed an assortment of colors and textures, even in black and white. I turned the frame over, and my breath caught. Carved into the wood was a symbol—a creature with the head of a lion and the tail of a serpent.

I knew, deep down, that Julian had left this symbol, intending it to be found.

*

The image held no meaning for me. In all my years studying my parents' collections and the Greenwich Library, I had never come across this lion-serpent iconograph. But if there was a place where it could be deciphered, it was the Foresyth Library. I sketched the symbol into my notebook, returned the frame to its exact position, and slipped out of the room.

The library was empty, save for Leone, who barely glanced up as I walked down the aisles.

A trace of sunlight filtered through the curtains, casting a sepia glow on the shelves. The scent of aged paper enveloped me, a reminder of the hidden mysteries within these walls. I would be lying if I said I didn't relish delving into its labyrinth of knowledge.

Certain no one else was around, I opened my notebook and examined the symbol again. The lion, regal and fierce, entwined with the serpent's coils, seemed to guard its secrets as fiercely as the library itself. I started in Nina's favorite section, cryptozoology, rows five through twenty-four, losing track of time as I scoured tome after tome. But nothing matched the symbol in my notebook. Disappointment settled where my earlier excitement had been. I closed the last book with a sigh. I had come so close, only to be nowhere again.

I turned to leave the P section where I'd looked up *Panthera leo,* and my gaze fell on the plants and herbs section. I trailed my fingertips along the collection and found a field guide on brewing herbs, slightly jutting out, waiting for me to pluck it from the shelf.

I skimmed through its pages, noting pictures of various plants. One particular variety of hops caught my eye. The image showed a bristly bulb with yellow flowers, and the description noted grassy, pungent, earthy aromas. It sounded a lot like what I had tasted in the tea, masked by the turmeric and ginger.

Humulus lupulus, I read. Bitter and earthy in teas. Smoked or steeped, the herb promotes drowsiness and relaxation. In certain doses, it has effects similar to a truth serum.

Truth serum.

Aspen had dosed my tea with truth serum.

"At Foresyth, the annual Spring Symposium stands as the pinnacle event for students—a revered occasion where scholars present the culmination of their year's work. This gathering not only marks a significant milestone in each Scholar's academic journey, but also serves as a critical appraisal by the Foresyth Council, whose evaluations determine whether one may continue their studies. Ultimately, only the most exceptional and promising will earn the esteemed role of Advisor."

—*Foresyth Student Handbook*, 1920 edition

Chapter 8: Research Circle

A white folio rested on my desk when I returned from breakfast. Inside, contained the daily schedule along with the prospectus, detailing the amenities of the House, including the library, science lab, gardens, recreational area, and information about the weekly laundry service. Breakfast was at eight each morning, lunch was à la carte downstairs, and dinner would be held at six in the evening, following the Research Circle, which occurred daily except on Sundays. Aside from the occasional practicum or demonstration, the Conservatory's curriculum was entirely research-based.

At the bottom of the stack was a student handbook.

Under "Basic Expectations," I read that students were expected to spend eight to ten hours a day conducting independent studies. Then, I flipped to my weekly schedule and noted that I had meetings with the Meister twice a week—one for mentorship and another to discuss the assistantship project outside my research, which I assumed was a front for discussing the progress of my investigation.

Curious, I skimmed the graduation requirements at the back of the pamphlet. I wasn't planning on staying that long, but it was worth knowing what I'd be expected to work toward.

Publishing was mandatory by the end of the year to earn credits. I wondered if the Meister actually expected me to publish in addition to solving the Conservatory's murder; that hadn't been part of our agreement, as far as I knew. Most students, the handbook explained, were expected to publish at least one paper annually, with many leaving the Conservatory having authored a dozen scholarly articles. It described this as "structured intellectual liberation."

Interestingly, there was no mention of practicing magick, save for one line on something called an "Initiation" which had the most cult-like connotation out of the whole handbook: "*Initiation begins when the student has shown both a commitment to academic excellence as well as magickal aptitude.*" The former would be easy enough, but the latter made me pause. Hopefully I'd long finish my investigation before being subjected to this milestone.

The yearly requirements concluded with a Foresyth-hosted Spring Symposium, where each student was to present an exhibit of their intellectual work from the year. I swallowed, considering I had joined in the middle of their academic year, I would only have three months to prepare for the Symposium. *If you get that far,* doubt retorted.

As I sifted through these materials, I realized that the students here had all the time and resources in the world to pursue excellence in their chosen subjects. Although some topics were strange or macabre, it was clear they were all incredibly gifted. Hadn't I always dreamed of attending an institution like this, surrounded by peers who shared my drive and fascination with . . . unique topics? Excitement welled in my chest, but I quickly tamped it down. This was not Sawyer Academy. And I was not a scholar.

This was Foresyth and it was dangerous, as my mother and Gabriel warned. I'd need to use every skill my father had passed down to me if I wanted to solve this murder and leave Foresyth alive. All four students had the opportunity to kill Julian within these close quarters, but the question remained: *why?* What would motivate them to commit such a heinous crime and kill a fellow student?

That night the students settled around the table just after six, taking the same places they had in the morning. Richard, the steward, brought in dinner, piping hot from the kitchen, and served it family-style on large ivory plates. Given this manner of dining, I let out a quiet sigh of relief, knowing that poison was unlikely to be on the menu tonight.

I stole a glance at Aspen. His hair was brushed back, and he was wearing an evening jacket in lieu of his morning sports coat. It was well-tailored to his form, accentuating his imposing height and stature. A bud of lilac peeked out from his breast pocket, twinning the color of Sequoia's dress.

"Will the Meister be joining us?" I inquired over the steaming plates set before us. My mouth was watering, but I feigned courtesy before filling my plate.

"No, afraid not. He rarely does. He's got clients to attend to," Sequoia answered.

"Clients?"

"Yes, the ones he advises," she said slowly.

"Of course," I replied. I vaguely remembered the term from my earlier reading of the handbook.

"She doesn't know," Aspen said matter-of-factly. "The most prestigious position after graduating Foresyth is to become an Advisor. Holding the most powerful people in the palm of your hand, setting them on a course that runs the world. Foresyth has a long history of advising the world's most influential people."

That had certainly not been in the handbook.

"You don't really think that bloated bloke, Taft, secured the election himself did you? It wasn't just Teddy's involvement that won him the bid," Aspen continued with a knowing arch of his brow. "Why be the person in power, when you can be the one who *controls* those in power."

I furrowed my brows at the implication that Foresyth's advisors influenced American elections.

"Not everyone is as power-hungry as you, Aspen. Some people are here for the erudition. Maybe that's what Dahlia is looking for," Nina offered with a smile.

I was glad to have her as an ally, but I wasn't keen on the division forming against Aspen. At least, not yet.

"I'm here for both," I said, taking a sip from my wine glass. Aspen's mouth twitched to the side, appeased. He didn't know that I hadn't taken the truth serum this morning. At least, not fully.

"You might find this hard to believe, Nina dear, but I'm actually here for the *art.* And what better way than to treat your whole life as a piece of art, crafting each day with a brushstroke?" Aspen's twinkling eyes caught mine.

Sequoia cleared her throat and interjected, "So, how was your first day at Foresyth?" She was wearing that same warm grin from the morning, a silvery shawl draped across her shoulders. I noted that she squeezed Aspen's hand as she looked at me.

"Delightful. I'm just getting acquainted with my surroundings," I said, digging into the mashed potatoes, wafting off steam. I hadn't had this much food in front of me in years—at least not since my father died. My mother barely ate anything during her illness, and I lost count of the hours spent tending the bookstore, and rarely made time for multiple meals a day. It was like all the pent-up hunger was finally being unleashed.

"Nina said you saw the library. Isn't the collection here marvelous? It's one of the largest archives in the States, I've been told. Can you imagine being in the epicenter of such knowledge?"

"It's very impressive. My father owned a bookstore, but it was nothing like the collection here."

"A bookstore? Aspen, Dahlia's father owned a bookstore, how quaint." She squeezed Aspen's hand again.

"Why would he think that's impressive? It's not an oil empire the likes of Titus Barlowe's," Nina chimed.

"I have interests outside of my father's," Aspen cut in with a sharp tone. Nina must have struck a chord with him. Father wound, *noted.*

"And I'm keenly fascinated by everything about the newest addition to our class," Aspen said with a smile, turning toward me. "Now tell us again—you're a Tarot reader? What got you into that line of work?"

"Just something I picked up from my grandmother on my mother's side. It entertained her friends, having a small child of five telling prophecies," I said, hoping my candor would be returned. Aspen shouldn't be the only one getting answers tonight; I needed a few of my own.

"I could give you a reading one of these days, if you'd like." The table fell still, and Sequoia's cheeks flushed red. Nina let out a giggle. Even Aspen adjusted in his seat, pulling his gaze down from mine.

"I'm sorry, did I offend?" I asked.

Nina turned toward me. "Well, new girl, magick is an intimate affair around here. Not something you offer at a dinner table." The blood pooled in my cheeks when I realized the faux pas I'd committed.

"I'm flattered, Ms. Blackburne. Maybe there will be a time," Aspen said, looking over at Sequoia. "Do you do couples readings?"

"Oh, stop it, Aspen. Don't scare the poor girl," Sequoia chided. She smiled softly, looking over at me. "You said your grandmother taught you the cards. There must be something special in your blood. Most of us here have a magickal lineage, too." She kindly changed the subject. "Aspen and I are descendants of the occultist Paschal Randolph. He was our great great-grandfather."

"Well, most of us have lineage. Nina is a mutt," Aspen said.

"And yet, we're all at the same table," Nina said, biting a piece of bloody steak off her knife and smiling at Aspen as she chewed.

The group fell into an argument about lineage for the rest of dinner, and I was glad to have the attention averted from me. I studied them while they bickered, observing their roles.

I gathered that Aspen was the instigator, always throwing the first flames; Nina, the retaliator, spat back dirt with even more force, while Sequoia pacified. And Leone completely abstained, unless to correct the record. I had them in their archetypes, but I needed more. I needed to see who they were aside from their superficial masks.

After we all finished dinner and Richard took our plates away, we moved to the sitting room next door. It almost looked like a different room than it had in the morning. With the sun down, the only light source in the room was a roaring fire in the central fireplace. The breeze had settled, and drowsiness took over as I sank into the velvet lounge chair, the cushion swallowing me up.

The *Trees* sat on a loveseat next to the hearth, while Leone rolled up next to them. Nina took a seat farthest from the fire on the chaise lounge, spreading her lanky limbs over it as if preparing for a nap.

"All right, whose turn is it today? I want to get this over with sooner rather than later. I have a corpse rotting in the lab. If I don't brine it tonight, it'll stink up the whole House by tomorrow morning," Nina said, picking dirt out of her fingernails.

"I'll go; I haven't presented in a while," Sequoia offered. "Please, Nina, tend to whatever you have in the lab. We don't need a repeat of what happened during summer solstice."

"Hm, something about the hot summer and taxidermy just doesn't go together, does it?" Nina mocked as Sequoia grimaced.

The entry door opened, and the room fell silent. The Meister walked in, his steps lagging behind the tapping of his cane. He lowered his briefcase to the floor next to the chair I was sitting in.

"I'm afraid you have my chair, Ms. Blackburne."

"My apologies, Meister," I said as I rose and moved to Nina's chaise. She slid her legs down so I could take the space next to her. I cursed myself internally. Why hadn't the students corrected me? Unless . . . they wanted to see me subverting the Meister's authority, testing me.

"Now, let's open the Circle," the Meister motioned for all to rise. "*Sub rosa*," he said.

"*Sub rosa*," everyone echoed, then took their seats again. Under the rose, or in secret, I translated.

"We have a newcomer to the Circle, as you all see. I trust that everyone has done their part to welcome Ms. Blackburne to Foresyth," the Meister spoke, his eyes drifting around the room.

"Ms. Blackburne, we are bound here to this Circle in scholarly trust. Your ideas, no matter how controversial or disruptive, will be kept to this Circle. We are here to discuss in earnest and without fear.

We are also here to exercise unbiased judgment in our evaluation of academic merit."

"Thank you for welcoming me, Meister. I'll observe for this first one, given that I've only begun my studies today."

The iconograph I found in this very room swirled behind my eyelids still. I blinked and thought better of asking the group about the hanged man's symbol. Regardless of what the Meister said about secrecy, this was not a safe space for me.

"I'll begin," Sequoia said. "In my study of bardic incantations and their role in first-century BCE polytheistic culture, I've become acquainted with the Celtic Druids. Not much is known about them given their oral traditions, but I've found a few bards that could be interpreted as magickal incantations. I wanted to see if the group agreed."

"Lovely, thank you, Ms. Nightingale, for the proposal," said the Meister. "Anyone else?" He looked around expectantly, waiting for other topics. "Very well, then. Proceed. The Circle is yours."

Sequoia continued reading from a rose-colored journal, "Holding lineage to the original Norse Druids, Eochaid Dála experienced an analepsis in which he heard a hymn. A hymn, I believe, was acquired or written during a shamanic experience of his ancestor."

"That can't be right. The term 'Shamanism' originated with the Tungus-speaking people in Siberia. Connecting them to the Celts would be anachronistic," Leone said.

It was the first time I'd heard him speak since breakfast.

Sequoia cleared her throat. "I mean *Shamanism* as a universal conceptual framework for practices that involve people—*shamans*—serving as intermediaries between the spirit world and the real world," she retorted at Leone.

This seemed to quell Leone's rebuttal, and she proceeded. "Through these experiences, Eochaid surmised that the Druids would go into dreamlike trances in order to gain wisdom from the Otherworlds. As you all know, the act of entering such an ecstatic state is called soul flight. But these dream-states, typically altered states due to hallucinogens, made it difficult to remember the findings from these flights.

So, they created songs to better remember them. Here's the passage I found in a documented account:

Anam ar siúl, i gcoillte is gleannta,
Sióg le héisteacht, draíocht le brath,
An t-anamchéad, solas faighte.

"I've been working on a translation of this song, and here's what I have so far:

Soul on a journey, in forests and glens,
Fairy whispers, magic to sense,
Free from the body, enlightenment gained."

Sequoia's voice softened as she recited her translation, her gaze drifting, as if she was transported to some distant forest or mist-covered glen right there in the sitting room. For a moment, the Circle seemed spellbound, as if we were all catching glimpses of the Otherworlds through her incantation.

"And you're trying to use this passage to prove that the Celtic Druids were shamans and engaged in practices of soul flight?" Nina asked, her tone sharper and more probing.

"Exactly," Sequoia replied, her excitement untampered. "In another passage, it explicitly uses the word *léim,* which translates literally to 'jump' or 'leap' but could be interpreted in context to mean *transcend.* It's not a word that inspires physical movement, but rather a spiritual one."

"Impressive translation, Ms. Nightingale. Though I do wish your Latin were as good as your Gaelic," the Meister interjected, a glimmer of amusement in his eyes.

Nina spoke next, tapping her chin thoughtfully. "I'm not an expert in astral projection or soul flight, but the passage, if your translation holds, seems like reasonable evidence for shamanistic Celts. I haven't seen any research on it, so it could make an interesting paper." She sounded genuine, not merely appeasing Sequoia.

Aspen leaned back with a finger to his chin, looking less than convinced. "I think it's conjecture. We don't have any physical evidence that the Celts used songs for ritual purposes—just the Eochaid account, which was published, what, three hundred years after the Romans overtook the Celts? And he got this knowledge through some ancestral recollection?"

Leone nodded. "Exactly. It makes research on the Druids especially challenging. Oral traditions are difficult to substantiate. Perhaps stick to a culture with more tangible records, like the Greeks or the Sumerians."

The Meister looked over at me, his gaze inviting a response. "And what do you think, Ms. Blackburne?"

The weight of everyone's eyes found and settled on me. I hesitated, aware of the academic alliances already forming. Siding with Sequoia and Nina would be easy, yet I didn't want to risk my academic integrity in favor of politics. If honesty was my only reliable card, I might as well play it.

"Shamanistic practices are ancient and predate the Tungus," I said slowly, watching Sequoia's hopeful expression. "It's entirely plausible that the Druids engaged in those practices. But without physical evidence, like an account from a Druid herself, there's little weight to the argument that the song was part of a shamanistic ritual. It's speculative at best."

Sequoia's expression faltered while Aspen's seemed to brighten. "Ms. Blackburne is right; you ought to focus on written history, like the Greeks or Sumerians. Cultures that were a bit more . . . literate," he said, a touch smugly.

Sequoia's eyes flashed. "Oral history doesn't make a culture any less worthy of study. In fact, Julian wrote several papers on the Celts and their extensive oral tradition," she said, her voice pointed.

At the mention of Julian's name, a chill fell about the room. Aspen's face went pale, and his eyes narrowed as they fixed on Sequoia.

"Of course Julian would have preferred the Celts—romanticizing their scattered clans and tribal squabbles over Roman order. You should have known better than to take his advice," Aspen said, his tone a shadow of a whisper.

Sequoia's gaze hardened. "You are assuredly a Greco-Roman *snob.* Julian would have voted in favor of the Druids," she said, glancing in my direction. "Unlike some of us here who seem to dismiss anything without a concrete record."

"Enough," the Meister cut in, his voice slicing through the air. "The group majority has recommended not to pursue further research on the topic, Ms. Nightingale. You are, of course, free to continue at your discretion, subject to peer review."

"Julian favored you and would've endorsed any idea you proposed here. If only you hadn't been so friendly with him, you could've seen *reason,*" Aspen sneered.

"And what exactly is that supposed to mean?" Sequoia's voice trembled with anger as she rose from the loveseat, her cheeks burning red.

"The Circle is dismissed," the Meister said sternly. "And let me remind you both that personal matters are forbidden in the Circle. Unbiased judgment is required for the integrity of our discussions," he added, his gaze cutting between Sequoia and Aspen.

Nina stretched with a yawn and rose. "Well, that was entertaining. Good luck on your paper, Koi. If you'll excuse me, I've got a brine bath to fill."

Sequoia moved toward the door, sparing a quick glance back at me. Her expression was a mixture of hurt and, perhaps, betrayal before she disappeared into the hallway. Only Aspen and Leone remained.

Leone looked up from his book. "Welcome to Circle," he said flatly.

*

With the Circle dismissed, I watched everyone leave, each slipping back into their carefully-constructed roles. Leone retreated with his usual silence, nose already buried in his book as he disappeared into the hallway. The Meister offered me a careful glance before following the other students out.

Alone in the sitting room, the fire cast flickering shadows on the walls, its glow amplifying the rich, haunting atmosphere of the House. I leaned back on the chaise, letting my head rest against the cool upholstery. The entire evening had been a master class in psychology—a delicate balance of trust, manipulation, and academic posturing. And Julian's presence loomed over it all, a ghost conjured by Sequoia's simple mention of his name.

I stood, crossing to the hearth where embers crackled softly. I craned my neck to the ceiling and studied the trellis-like branches of the oak stretching upward, its ancient wood casting elongated shadows. It was a symbol, one that seemed to bear its own secrets, somehow entwined with this House. And now I was here, linked to that same branch as Julian.

The Acolyte and the Alchemist: Part II

Despite how swiftly the boy with raven hair had fallen for the girl, he did not act on his feelings for a very long time. It would have been improper, and besides, he had no interest in facing the inevitable sting of rejection. He held neither title nor status to secure a match, and that was not why he had come to study at the most prestigious Conservatory on the continent.

And so, he engaged with her the only way he knew how: as a rival.

They sparred relentlessly in academic debate, each determined to outwit the other. Their manuscripts competed for the Council's praise, and at mealtimes, he pointedly ignored the weight of her knowing gaze, throwing himself instead into discussion with his peers. He spoke at length of mythological Christianity, the transition from polytheism to monotheism—anything to keep his mind occupied, anything to keep from looking at her for too long.

One evening, as he scribbled furiously in his dormitory, a knock sounded at the door. His quill snapped in half. He cursed under his breath and rose, irritation simmering beneath his skin.

When he opened the door, Hamra stood on the threshold, a fresh pen in her hand.

"I had a feeling you'd need one of these," she said, amusement flickering in her dark eyes. "You're in the habit of breaking them. I ought to call you the Quill Killer."

His brows knit together. "How did you—"

She smirked, pushing past him into the room as if she belonged there.

"Fine, Quill for short," she declared. "I'd like to broker a deal. You take this fountain pen, and in return, you'll assist me with a research project. We can call it a collaboration if you like, though I'll be first author. I don't believe in any of that co-first nonsense."

She twirled the pen between her fingers. "While, at first glance, this may not seem a fair trade, you'll find the pen to be of the highest, furious-scribbling-proof quality. And, of course, you'll have the added delight of my company."

Quill sank back into his chair, not knowing what else to do with himself. His mind scrambled for something clever to say, but he could only watch as she spoke, commanding the space with effortless ease.

She leaned against the desk, tilting her head. "Well?" Her smirk erupted into a full, brilliant smile.

"Though Lord Edmund W. Foresyth II was indeed the initiator of Foresyth Conservatory, he was not its sole founding figure. The esteemed Founding Five consisted of figures such as Stuart Renate, Louis G. Rockwell, Patty Mearsheimer, and Aleric Khorvyn who each brought their distinct expertise to bear on the institution's creation."

"Stuart, for instance, was revered for a command of herbology and scientific illustration; Louis brought to life the kiln and sculpting studios; Patty, a virtuoso, laid the foundations for the music program; and Aleric, a talented painter and curator, helped to elevate the standing of Foresyth's gallery. Naturally, Foresyth served as the group's unifying force, having meticulously handpicked each member from a broad selection of distinguished scholars."

"It is said that the blood, sweat, and passion of the Founding Five consecrated the very grounds upon which Foresyth stands, creating a legacy through which all subsequent members would be forever bound to the school's destiny."

—*Foresyth Conservatory: A Complete History, Unabridged*, 1891

Chapter 9: The Lab and the Rock

There was one thing I had become assured of in the last twenty-four hours at Foresyth Conservatory: simply blending into Foresyth would not be possible. I had to take an active role in building alliances or enemies, or risk being outcast by the entire group. Perhaps even risk facing the same fate as Julian.

Sequoia was not at breakfast the next morning. I turned to Nina, who said, "She does this sometimes. The Trees fight, and it ruins the whole mood if you let it." She took a giant bite of her biscuit. "I can show you the lab this afternoon if you have time," she said with full cheeks.

"Yes, I'd like that. I'm free after my mentorship meeting with the Meister." I sighed, relieved I hadn't alienated her last night by siding with the anti-Druids. There was still a chance at forging an alliance—perhaps even the most advantageous, given her access to the lab. Even if I could pick a lock or two, it was always easier to have a key.

"I'll meet you in the sitting room."

The Meister's presence at Foresyth was elusive at best, which made seeing him as unsettling as seeing an apparition. There was a sense that he should be elsewhere, or else*when*. It was the first time I saw him in daylight. The white flesh of his scar glinted in the morning light as he lowered his spectacles. I wished I knew how he had gotten that scar.

I wished I knew anything about him. I grimaced, remembering how Gabriel had turned up with nothing from the archives.

"Ms. Blackburne, I can't tell you how delighted I am to see you at Foresyth. It suits you. Though, I'm afraid I must apologize for the behavior of the other students last night. Julian's death hasn't been easy for anyone around here."

"No, especially not Julian himself," I quipped before I could catch myself.

"I can't argue with that. He wasn't my favorite, but he was jovial and brought a lightness to Foresyth. In his absence, a dark cloud hangs over this place. One I hope you may dispel soon enough." He smiled, motioning me to sit.

"That's what I've come to discuss with you. I've made some developments on the case." I ignored his gesture and instead walked across the room to where he sat. I took out the case file and laid it down on his desk.

"Here, this is a picture of Julian's hanged body. We know from the toxicology report that he must have been poisoned. I don't think he hung himself to die, but to leave a message." I pulled out another sheet of paper, one on which I had drawn the lion-serpent symbol. "He left this for someone to find. He must've realized what had happened—that someone had poisoned him—and he wanted to make sure someone would find it. Do you know what it means?"

I studied his reaction. His eyes scrunched together in thought, and I traced his features for any sign of deception. I didn't fully trust the Meister, even though he was the one who had hired me. I couldn't shake the feeling that he was somehow more involved in Julian's death than he let on.

"I can't say what this means," he said without looking up from the drawing. He adjusted his spectacles further up the bridge of his nose. "But it doesn't surprise me that Julian would leave a clue—he studied iconography and thought in puzzles. The boy was sometimes an enigma himself."

I noted his word choice: *can't say*, not *don't know*. Why was the Meister holding back from me?

"That's lovely for him, but it gets me nowhere. Why couldn't he just write down the killer's name?"

A corner of the Meister's mouth lifted, and my stomach churned. "Ms. Blackburne, if there is one thing you should know about the students of Foresyth, it's this: when you're an artist—and all magickians are—everything becomes an art. Even dying." He read the disgust on my face and added, "They don't have your direct sensibilities."

"Can I ask you something?" I paused.

"Certainly."

"Why mix the two? Art and science, I mean. Are they not diametrically opposed?"

The Meister's eyes flickered with amusement, as if I'd just told him a joke. "Magick is simply science we've yet to understand. And what remains after the experiment—that's art. That's why we unite the two at Foresyth. Because art, like magick, grants the soul a means to transcend—to glimpse the universal human experience."

I furrowed my brow, uncertain of his meaning. In the quiet of my bookshop, the Meister had seemed legible—his intentions sharp beneath the surface. But here, steeped in the shadowed corridors of Foresyth and the weight of its obscure histories, I found his words increasingly opaque. Perhaps it was foolish to chase meaning through the thickets of philosophy. Better, for now, to return to what I knew: the facts.

"How did you come to be the Meister of Foresyth?" I asked, testing him with my directness. He chortled, reclining back in his chair.

I didn't see what was so funny.

"I was born here, metaphorically speaking. My father was Head Meister, and his father before him. Though we were fairly elected, Foresyth has always been in my blood."

Legacy. The students had used that word during dinner last night. It meant something special here, to be born into this school through parentage.

"And you like it?" I asked. Perhaps it was childish of me to think that people ought to enjoy their professions. My father hadn't become a detective because he enjoyed it necessarily, but because it served him a higher moral purpose. It *benefited* society.

"Yes, I do," he answered. "But not just because it was what my father did." His tone dropped, as if drawing a parallel between us. "But because it was my own path that I chose, independent of my predecessors."

I broke my gaze from his, frustrated by how much he knew of me when I knew so little of him. That was enough of him reading me. That's not why I had come.

"I'd like to see Julian's things," I said, changing the subject again. "His research papers and the like. If he studied iconography, maybe I can find the symbol in one of his papers, something that points to who poisoned him."

"That's a good idea. I'll see if I can have his personal effects sent to your room with discretion." He smiled.

"Thank you," I said and started to turn out of the room.

"Ms. Blackburne, you are not dismissed yet. We have your academics to discuss."

I narrowed my eyes at him. "You know I'm not here for that. I came to read suspects, not more books."

"Yes, but it would do you well to try to . . . blend in at the school. You've been excused from the first-year prognostication seminar given your background, but I still expect you to produce scholarly research. You wouldn't want to generate suspicion." He arched a brow. I thought of the past day—Aspen's truth serum, Sequoia's Research Circle, and all of them staring at me expectantly. As if I had an obligation to contribute. As much as I wanted to disagree with the Meister, I couldn't.

"If I may grant you some advice, Ms. Blackburne: the easiest way to act a scholar is to become one. *Esse quam videri.* To be, rather than to seem," the Meister added.

He had a point. Crafting a ruse, even just to feign interest, was taxing. Perhaps it was better to be rather than to seem. If I wanted to track down Julian's killer, I'd have to make a better attempt at fitting in. I'd have to fully embrace the type of person, the type of scholar, I had always dreamed of being. I had always been fascinated by mysticism, not because I believed in it, but because there was a part of me that was morbidly curious about the darkest parts of humanity, the *id* to their *ego*. If I just embraced into my natural curiosity, I could become a natural at Foresyth.

But I needed to toy the edge just right, such that I didn't get swallowed whole by the very same obsession that had claimed my father, and maybe even Julian.

How difficult could that be?

I smiled, resolution coating my lips, and looked up. "Very well. Let's talk about Tarot."

*

The Meister and I agreed that I would begin my research with a historical perspective on Tarot, which I was already familiar with, and then write a paper on how Tarot became affiliated with the occult. He asked me to present at Research Circle the following week. I agreed, if only because I could use the opportunity to garner more credibility with the other students.

Shortly after my conversation with the Meister ended, I made my way to the sitting room to meet Nina. She was there on the chaise thumbing through a book on mythical reptilian species.

"You were in there for an hour," she said, closing her book.

"Yes, the required mentorship meeting."

"The Meister never spends more than thirty minutes with me; he must really like you," she said with a genuine undertone of envy in her voice.

"I doubt that. It's just that, with me being new, I need a little more guidance."

"Fair enough, though I don't think you need much guidance. You spoke your mind pretty plainly last night. That takes a lot of courage to do—dispute, I mean. Not a skill a lot of first years know."

"And what year are you?"

"I'm a second, so are Aspen and Sequoia. Leone's a third, but he'll probably do his postdoc here. He has none of the softer skills necessary to become an Advisor."

"Right. Aspen alluded to as much. The Advisors?" I toyed with the line of my ignorance carefully. Maybe seeing my incompetence in some way would alleviate some of her envy.

"Yes, hired magickal Advisors, sourced primarily from Foresyth and other reputable institutions. They advise on all business and personal matters. They work for statesmen, executives, proprietors."

"Presidents?" I interjected.

Nina arched a brow. "I cannot neither confirm nor deny. Besides, we aren't supposed to know the identities of Advisors' clients. But it's possible . . . people come to us to ask which markets to invest in, whether or not to start an affair, if sending weapons overseas would create more unrest or forge a strategic alliance."

"It sounds a lot like what I did as a Tarot reader. Minus the war," I said without thinking too much of it. I immediately regretted it.

"You were a professional reader? That's . . . uncommon. None of us have made any money with our peculiar sets of interests. I've tried to sell a bit of my taxidermy, but it's not a huge market, as you can imagine." She shrugged. "You'll certainly be up for Advisor when you graduate."

"What are you working on right now?" I asked, changing the subject. I didn't want to reveal that I wasn't planning on sticking around long enough to graduate, let alone to be hired as the magick industry-equivalent of a Tarot reader.

"Let me show you. The lab is this way." I followed Nina out of the sitting room and down the main hallway. She unfastened a key from her necklace and twisted it into the keyhole of an unassuming door. It opened to a staircase leading down to what looked like the basement level.

"Lab access is only for second years and above. But since you asked about my work . . . I'll give you a tour." She winked before she started down the dark staircase, her form completely disappearing halfway down. "Well, what are you waiting for?" Her voice echoed from below.

"Coming." I took a deep breath and walked down into the darkness.

Seconds later, the room became illuminated by fluorescent lights, revealing a pristine laboratory with black marble countertops. It reminded me of my father's forensic lab but was several times larger. Mason jars of all sizes filled the shelves, along with browning textbooks and empty glassware.

"Welcome to Foresyth lab," Nina cooed. The bounce in her step told me she was fond of this place, perhaps even more than the library. I was equally torn over which I found more impressive.

"Everything at Foresyth is so . . . grand," I remarked, noting the rows of benchtops. There were nearly a dozen; each student could have two of their own.

"Foresyth used to have more students. Before it was a Conservatory, it was a college. There were dozens of students here, apparently."

"What happened? I mean, to make it smaller?"

Nina fell silent for a moment, and I read the pause for what it was—a quiet withholding. Whatever she said next would be a version of the truth, not its entirety.

"The school was grander once, if we're borrowing your word," she said at last, her voice measured. "But those days have faded. Keeping Foresyth alive now is . . . a political endeavor, as much as an academic one—or so I'm told."

"Interesting." The word slipped out before I could temper it. Did that mean the Meister had adversaries—perhaps even among the Council—quietly tugging at the threads of his authority? He had mentioned he'd been *elected*, after all. That implied politics. And politics implied opposition.

I rounded the corner to the next benchtop, and a bulbous bird with two black eyes startled me backward. The creature was a mosaic of orange and red feathers but was missing feet.

"You've found Ashes. Just a Resurrection pheasant I've been working on. Took ages to ship from China, and the customs paperwork was a nightmare. I think he's coming along nicely; just need to mount him onto something sturdy." She scratched underneath his chin affectionately.

"What is that smell?" I covered my nose.

"That's the brine bath I was working on," Nina cut across the lab space, and I followed her down the aisle. It became apparent that she was the only one using the lab, as I looked around, seeing stuffed birds, foxes, rabbits, and squirrels.

"That's Beatrice." I approached the aluminum bath slowly, pinching my nose as the stench of formaldehyde grew stronger. "Right, sorry. I've become desensitized to the smell; I don't know how bad it is anymore."

A giant brown hog was basking in the bath, rocks stacked on top to keep him from floating.

"It's all the fat. Makes him buoyant," Nina said.

"What are you going to do with him?"

"I don't know yet, but I couldn't give up a find like that. I found him in the woods next to the school. Maybe I'll make a shrunken head; I've been dying to try this Shuar recipe from a banned paper from the Academies."

"You've got quite an impressive collection here," I said, my eyes scanning the lab.

Nina shrugged. "Thanks. I've been trying to sell some of it after the Symposium, but it's slow, and the shipping costs are astounding. Julian had a cousin who worked for the post and was helping, but since he's been gone, it's slowed down. Even the most aggressive collectors don't want to pay for postage that's worth almost the price of the artwork."

"Julian was helping you sell these?"

"Yeah, now and then. That's just how Julian was; he always helped people around here. He wasn't selfish like the lot upstairs." Nina stepped away from the brine bath. "That's why when you showed up . . . I thought I ought to pay the favor forward. It's what he would have wanted."

"He died," I said factually, staring at the brown hog covered in rocks.

"Yes, he did."

"What happened?" I asked, turning to face Nina. The stench of formaldehyde had somehow become more tolerable the longer I stood in the lab.

"He killed himself, quite *dramatically*," she said, the word landing with a bitter edge. "Hung himself in the sitting room—a grand gesture to the school and the Meister, just like Julian wanted. He talked about wanting to bring down the school, do something so dramatic that it'd get the press involved. But I never expected Julian would *really* do it. He underestimated the Meister, how well connected he is. Even with the school being underfunded, he's from a long line of political magickians. They know how to bury things."

"He and Julian weren't on good terms, then?"

"No, not at all. Julian was from quite a powerful legacy, or so he said. But the Meister thought that was the only reason he got in. People underestimated Julian, especially his courage."

"Why are you still here, then? After all that happened?"

Nina shifted her stance, the movement subtle but telling. "Students who come to Foresyth . . ." she began, her voice quieter now. "We don't exactly have a wealth of alternatives. Especially not someone like me. We're all repaying some kind of debt, one way or another." She paused, eyes flicking to the floor before continuing. "I wasn't born into a legacy. I wasn't groomed for this. I stumbled into magick—and art—as a child, and it consumed me. Foresyth was the only place that ever offered me a way to make it more than a passing fascination."

We made our way back to the lab benches, our footsteps echoing softly. "This place . . . it has everything I need to build a real life. Not just theory, not just talent—*work*. It's the only shot I've got."

"You really believe in it, don't you? Magick, I mean," I said, grazing my forefinger across a lab logbook at the acid station.

Nina shrugged. "Magick is what's left over after reason explains. There's a lot that's still unexplained in the world, don't you think, Miss Tarot reader?"

"That's what the Meister said. That art was what is left over," I said, raising my eyes to meet hers. "But I disagree, I think there's a scientific explanation for everything. We just haven't found it yet."

Nina took the bench chair next to me, resting her chin on her elbows. "Really? You mean to say that nothing inexplicable has ever happened to you?"

I thought over her question, searching the archives of my memory.

"Once," I admitted.

Nina's eyes widened, and she leaned in.

"I was a kid." I turned to her. "My dad was just playing some kind of magic trick on me. He used to do those a lot, but he always made me guess how he did it. A sleight of hand, a double-sided coin, invisible ink. I'd agonize over it for a few days until I'd figure it out," I paused. "But there was one I never figured out."

"Oh?" Nina prodded.

"It was something so silly. He was a geologist of sorts, so he liked to play with rocks, minerals, anything he could get his hands on. There was a black stone—obsidian I think—that I found in a park once. He made me put it in this jar of dirt he had sitting in his lab. The container was clear, so I could see the dirt—there wasn't a false bottom or anything like it. I put the stone in it. He closed it and shook it up, and—a moment later, he poured all the dirt out onto his bench. The stone was gone."

"Gone?"

"Yes, it wasn't in the jar anymore. I searched everywhere in his lab after that. Nothing. He was so amused by it, how I struggled to figure out the trick. It's been years and I still haven't figured it out."

"You could always ask him."

"I can't anymore."

"Oh. I'm sorry," Nina said, looking away. "Both my parents are dead, too. Have been since I was a kid. Died in a motorcar accident—so much for technology improving people's lives. For the longest time, the only thing I wanted to do was bring them back." She moved over to the tub of brine, her fingers searching for something to fiddle with.

My heart sank, images of my own father flashing in my head. I had wanted to bring him back, too.

Something clicked in my mind as I thought back to my first conversation with Nina.

"The Gremlins, the techno-anxiety—it's yours, too."

Nina looked away, rolling her eyes. "I'm not afraid of motorcars, but I did want to understand *why*. Why did they have to die like that?"

"You want their death to mean something," I said, blinking away the sting in my eyes. When she didn't reply, I asked, "And you don't want to anymore? Bring them back?"

Nina turned to me, smiling. "Necromancy is a dangerous magick. They wouldn't come back the same anyway. Besides, I've found a better way of dealing with my loss."

"Oh?"

"Honoring them," she said solemnly, looking back at the tub.

"Perhaps you could use a friend in that pursuit." I forced my tone to be casual.

"And I guess you could use one too, new girl." A wry smile crested her lips.

I watched her for a moment as she toiled over the brine bath, carefully stacking stones atop her specimen with practiced precision. Her focus, her tireless resolve—it was animated by grief, not unlike my own. Loss had shaped us both, though in different molds. Was this blossom of friendship seeming or *becoming*, as the Meister had urged? I swallowed the lightness in my chest.

We spent the rest of the morning in the lab, Nina detailing every piece of equipment on the benches and me soaking it all up. I was especially pleased to find a light analyzer capable of chemical analysis of liquids and solids.

"I don't have the slightest idea how to use that, so it's all yours if you want it. There are also drawers of spare mechanical parts that I promised. I'll clear my stuff from that bench," she said.

I smiled and thanked her. Excitement welled up in my chest as I pried the drawers open and looked through them. A rusty gear stood out to me as nearly the perfect size for a music box I had been working on. I pocketed it, turning my attention back to Nina.

"And here's my spare key to the lab," she said, untangling a key from her necklace. "The Meister isn't here enough to enforce his silly rules."

I took the key from her, slipping it into my pocket. It didn't matter if our friendship was true or not, I decided. The most important thing was that it was proving to be useful.

"It is indeed true that Foresyth Conservatory holds lineage in high regard, though not for the reasons commonly assumed. The Council harbors no intention of preserving exclusivity based on notions of aristocratic breeding or the presumption that ancestry signifies inherent magickal ability."

"The reasoning is, rather, far more elemental. The House favors familiar blood, akin to the body's selective acceptance of compatible blood types. Just as a foreign element may be rejected by the body, so too does Foresyth resist unfamiliar presences, for its vital essence has already been established. Foresyth exists to sustain its legacy, not to alter its nature."

—*Foresyth Conservatory: A Complete History, Unabridged*, 1891

"Tis there's the stone that whoever kisses
He never misses to grow eloquent;
'Tis he may clamber to a lady's chamber,
Or become a member of Parliament.
Don't try to hinder him, or to bewilder him,
For he is a pilgrim from the Blarney Stone."

–*The Blarney Stone* by Francis Sylvester Mahony, 1837

Chapter 10: The Singing Tree

I hadn't dreamt much since my father died. But by the end of my first week at Foresyth, and after countless hours in the library, my restless mind began to conjure them again. It was as if some remnant of my father lingered in the House, coaxing me back into visions each night.

I heard his voice before I saw him. Deep and smooth, like velvet. Even though my resting body tingled with the sensation of falling, his voice anchored me to my bed.

"What did I tell you about following in my footsteps? You ought to be with your mother," he said.

My eyes were open now, but I couldn't move. Not my arms, not my legs. Father stood over me, brushing a hand through my hair. I relaxed, despite my paralysis.

"I'm lying down, not following anyone's footsteps," I teased, though my lips didn't move. He sighed, offering a small, sad smile, as if he understood.

"Death changes all of us. Sometimes for the better," he said.

I tried to shake my head—*your death didn't change me*—but my body refused to respond. His deep blue eyes—mirroring the shade of mine—traced my face, pausing like he noticed something for the first time. He froze, then looked up, startled by an unseen presence in the room. I tried to follow his gaze but only found the darkened corner of my room.

"The House. It knows I'm here," he whispered, his voice losing any hint of calm. I struggled to move, but to no avail. My throat tightened when my father's features began to shift. His mouth and nose split and pushed out into a feline snout, his eyes stretching, pupils turning to narrow slits. Scales erupted across his skin as his body twisted and elongated into a serpent.

The creature with a lion's face slithered under my bed, disappearing into the shadows. And then I began to fall.

*

I awoke on the ground next to my bed, the smell of rotting wood entering my nostrils. I pressed my palms to the damp ground, adjusting my weight, when one of the floorboards gave way, and my hand fell a few inches through. I rushed up to a seated position, putting distance between myself and the underside of my bed. After I collected my bearings, I crouched down and flipped the dust slip, sending a plume of grey into the air. I coughed as some of the dust entered my lungs, then. I peered underneath my bed but saw nothing, aside from my father's leather briefcase and dead dust moths.

A dream, of course.

Despite being stiff from sleeping on the ground, I gingerly donned my usual uniform of black slacks and a grey sweater, looking forward to getting back into the lab and putting distance between me and my bed.

I stuffed a letter to my mother and Gabriel into my breast pocket, intending to leave them with Richard to post, as I made my way out of my dormitory. After a quick meeting with the Meister, where I ran through the outline of my proposal, I then spent the whole day with Nina in the lab, deconstructing and reconstructing the light analyzer. It would prove useful in evaluating physical evidence, and it also helped to keep my mind off my unsettling dreams.

It took several hours, but I finally got the machine to work. Nina called it magick. I called it mechanics.

"Don't tell me you're becoming a lab rat like Nina," Aspen said, sitting as far across from me as possible at the dinner table. "You reek."

I sniffed myself and winced. I had to remember to take a shower after the lab. "I lost track of time."

Nina followed in soon after. "Dahlia fixed a light machine downstairs."

"Light analyzer. It uses polychromatic light to analyze chemical signatures," I corrected.

"Could it be used for artifact dating?" Leone asked, piqued.

"I think mass spectrometry would be better suited for that, but we could try if we get a suspension. It would be destructive, though," I said.

Leone considered. "I don't want to destroy the cartographs."

"We'd only need a very small sample. Just a scratch of the surface."

"Maybe that could work. You'd have to show me how." Leone nodded.

Aspen said nothing, but I could sense his discontent as he plated greens onto his dish.

"Is there anything you'd like dated, Aspen?" I offered.

"The only kind of dating I do is the kind where copulation is involved." He smiled. "Otherwise, I prefer to do the chronology of my work using scholarly means."

"Very well," I scoffed.

Nina and I continued chatting about the light analyzer and its potential uses in assessing the legitimacy of a species she'd received from Spain, while Aspen made conversation with Leone about a new sculpture he was working on.

"I'd like to see some of your work, Aspen," I said, interjecting into the conversation when mine was at a lull. Really, it was more of a monologue about the brilliance of his counter-Renaissance work. But I needed to find a way to investigate him without calling too much attention.

"A true artist never reveals their work until it's finished." Aspen smiled squarely, his eyes darting to Nina's for a split second. "You'll see it at the Symposium."

The Symposium—a once-a-semester public display of each of our works. The next one was on the Spring Equinox, less than three months away. I had to begin working on mine, even if I managed to get out of here before then. It would be suspicious if I didn't dedicate time to my project, like the others.

There was so much to be done.

I was on my way to my room when I heard the music. It was light and ethereal, as if it didn't belong to this world. It was strange hearing music in this old House, which at times felt like a deteriorating museum, or rather yet a mausoleum. But the music's bouncy echo down the hall gave the House a breath of life, and I was compelled to follow it like a siren's call. The music got louder and lovelier as I crept down the hallway toward it.

It led to a dormitory room like my own, cracked just an inch. Through the gap, I recognized the mass of golden curls as Sequoia's. I took a step backward, as if the curse had momentarily subsided, but the boards creaked loudly under my feet, and the singing stopped. A pair of brown eyes found mine.

"Dahlia," her voice floated.

"I'm sorry—I just heard—" I stammered. My cheeks flushed.

"No, it's okay. Please, come in," Sequoia said, widening her door. "I've been meaning to talk to you."

I weighed my options carefully. Entering her room would grant me access to her space—an opportunity to search for evidence—but I couldn't ignore the gnawing question of trust. What if this was another manipulation, another trap, like Aspen's?

I studied her face with forensic focus, searching for any trace of malice. But her lips were slightly parted, her eyes bright—not with calculation, but with something gentler. Curiosity, perhaps. *Kindness*, even. And that, in its own way, unsettled me more.

"It's okay, I promise." She smiled, and a blanket of golden warmth seemed to envelop me. I walked into her room.

"What were you singing?"

"Oh, just a composition I've been working on. It's in Old Gaelic."

I considered her, noting the undertones of red in her hair and the slight peppering of freckles on her nose.

"You're Irish."

"Kiss me," she said, her smile widening.

A deep blush crept up my neck. What would Gabriel think of this charming stranger? I think he'd hardly be able to put a sentence together in front of her.

At my silence, she elaborated. "Relax, it's just a saying. It comes from the Blarney Castle Stone—it's a poem."

"The interest in Druids," I said, making the connection. "It's your lineage."

"My mother was Irish, perhaps a modern Druid even. I want to bring some light into their practices. Irish history is rich and layered, but we've been persecuted so long."

"I see. That's noble of you, bringing light to your family history like that."

"I don't see it as noble." Her features shifted. "All scholarship comes from some form of self-obsession, don't you think? We look onto the world to see ourselves. Maybe it's the only thing we can do to make ourselves feel less lonely." Sequoia smiled softly, brushing a rosy curl out of her face. I couldn't help but think of my father and wonder why his form of scholarship seemed to be murder and mayhem.

"I wanted to apologize for the other night at Circle. You had every right to voice your opinion. I didn't mean to bring you into whatever is going on with me and Aspen."

"No, I'm sorry. I didn't realize the personal significance of your work. You should continue studying the Druids, even if the evidence is sparse," I said, hoping the last part wasn't too harsh. "You could become a leading scholar in the field," I added, and I meant it. There was merit in studying an underdeveloped field, of becoming the voice through the darkness.

"I wish Aspen believed in me as much as you do," she tore her eyes away from mine, and I immediately felt their absence. Everything about her drew me closer, like there was an invisible rope tethering me to her.

"What do you mean?"

"Aspen thinks little of my scholarship. He says I got here through lineage—as if it weren't the same case for him. His father paying off the Council is practically the same thing." She puffed hot air from her cheeks and collapsed onto her bed. I tried not to notice her legs stretching across the mattress.

"He relishes feeling superior to everyone. That's why he didn't like Julian. Julian couldn't have cared less about the prestige."

Sequoia took out a little mirror from her drawer and started patting her nose with powder. "I feel for him, I do. If my father were an oil baron the likes of Rockefeller, I'd feel the need to extend my shadow. Aspen's father never cared much for art, but he did care about being better than everyone else. Why must men constantly live in the shadows of their fathers?" she asked, closing the mirror and turning to me.

Sometimes daughters do too, I thought. But I didn't say anything.

"Oh, never mind that. I just hate it when he's so cruel to me."

"Then why are you with him?" I finally let out. *Why betroth a potential murderer?* was what I really wanted to ask. But the evidence I had against him held as much weight as Sequoia's Druid paper, even if he did try to poison me the first night at Foresyth.

Sequoia gestured to the space next to her. I took the seat, if only to make my face less visible to hers. It was easier to lie in profile.

"Dahlia, you're like a breath of fresh air in this stuffy House. I want us to be friends," she said, taking my hand. Her skin was silky smooth over my dry hands. She held them for a while before breaking apart and standing up from the bed. She ran her fingers through her hair, turning to me again. "Why don't we get you out of these clothes," she said.

My neck turned red, and I lifted up the collar of my sweater to conceal it. I pretended to sniff it. "I smell that bad?"

She laughed a melodious tune. "No, it's not that . . . it's just, these colors are too drab. They wash you out." She stood and crossed the room to her armoire. "You know, it's in the handbook—the dress code, I mean."

"I know," I said nonchalantly. "But I like my clothes as they are. Besides, I don't have anything bright or patterned."

"Well, that's why you have me." Sequoia turned, holding up a turquoise sweater. "This'll bring out the beautiful blues of your eyes." She handed the sweater to me. I took it, admiring the soft dyed wool between my fingers. It was certainly warmer than the one I had on and was made of a heavier thread. A siren bearing gifts?

I considered my options. If I didn't take it from her, she'd likely take offense. But if I did . . . it might help me in winning her over. Counterintuitively, human psychology tends toward favoring those for whom we do good. If I let her do me a favor, she'd be much closer to believing we were genuine friends.

"I'll have to repay you somehow," I said, biting my lip to feign hesitancy.

"Nonsense, that's what friends are for," she sang.

Friends, the familiar word echoed in my chest. Had I really been that effective at coaxing trust out of all these suspects that they extended their friendship so easily? Nina, and now Sequoia. At this rate, I'd find myself in bed with Aspen next. I blushed at the thought, cursing my foul expression, and refocused my attention to the sweater in my hands.

I looked up and sat frozen, searching her for deception.

After a moment, she burst into a fit of laughter, saying, "Well, aren't you going to try it on?"

"Right." I gulped, wiggling off my grey sweater. Sequoia turned to give me privacy, and I was grateful she wouldn't see my threadbare undergarments, lest she'd make me get rid of those too. I slipped the blue sweater over my head, pulling my braid through the top. The fabric was soft and plush against my cooled skin.

"You look fantastic!" Sequoia squealed, spinning around again. "Now, let's look for a skirt for you . . ."

"Wait, that's not really my style," I started to protest. I hadn't meant for this to get so out of hand.

"But you're a woman, Dahlia, unless I'm mistaken. It would do you some good to show off your feminine shape." I looked down at myself, at the slight undulation of my breasts and hips. I'd never paid them much attention.

"I—" I stammered.

"Look," Sequoia said, turning away from the armoire and coming back to the bed. "Don't let the boys fool you—there's nothing wrong with being a woman."

"I've never considered it much," I said. "I've always found myself relating more to my father than my mother in everything," I admitted. If friends were what she wanted to be, I had to make a show of vulnerability. The easiest lies were always the ones closest to the truth.

Sequoia sighed softly. "I wish I had known my father," she said. "Maybe that's the reason I am the way I am. I was raised by my mother and my aunt, though truthfully more by my aunt, since my mother was always traveling with her theatre company," she said.

"Your mother was an actress?" I echoed, letting my eyes widen just enough. I could tell it was what she wanted—recognition, a flicker of admiration. And, just as I had so often done for my patrons, I gave it to her. A performance, tailored to my needs.

Sequoia smiled. "She was. She was a musical actress, but mostly starred in smaller, foreign productions. She taught me everything I know about music."

"That's why you sing so beautifully," I mused. The way her chest inflated made me feel as though I had hit my mark.

I stood, placing an arm on my hip. "Okay then, show me your set of skirts. I can't be friends with the daughter of an actress without dressing like it." I hated how patronizing I sounded, but Sequoia didn't seem to mind. Her eyes lit up, and she danced across the room.

"Oh, Dahlia, I'm so proud of you for embracing change," she said, rifling through her drawers. "It starts with clothing, but you'll see how much it'll affect your whole outlook on life."

*

For the next hour, I slipped in and out of the countless garments Sequoia tossed my way, until we finally agreed on a light grey skirt with pinstripes that matched the soft weave of the sweater she had picked out. We collapsed onto the heap of discarded clothing strewn across her bed, and I couldn't help but laugh—light and breathless—at the sheer absurdity of it all.

"I've never seen so many clothes in my life," I said, still smiling.

She laughed through her nose. "Neither have I! I didn't realize I brought so many with me."

"I tried on seventeen different skirts," I mused.

We looked around at the puddle of clothing we lay on top of and both of us broke out into laughter. I couldn't remember the last time I had laughed this hard.

"Does Aspen's closet also look like this?" I teased through a grin. But at the mention of his name, I saw her spirit falter. Her eyes dipped down to look at her hands, though a trace of a smile was still on her lips.

"I don't want to think about him right now," she said, throwing herself back onto the pile of clothing. I followed her motion and lay back myself, acutely aware of the warmth of her hand inches away from mine.

I pushed my discomfort away and instead decided to press. "Why are you with him if you hate him so?" I asked, staring up at the cobweb-ridden ceiling. Pockmarks splattered along the vaulting, and I traced patterns on it with my eye, waiting for her to respond. It was such a long moment before Sequoia said anything that I was sure I had only thought the question instead of speaking it aloud.

"Have you heard of a mycorrhizal network?" she finally said.

I thought for a second, searching the internal archives of my mind. An image of a plant system appeared behind my mind's eye. "That's when plants share nutrients through their roots," I said.

"Exactly—but it's not just nutrients. Sure, carbon, nitrogen, and other minerals, but they also share a lifeforce. Their network can stretch on for miles; they communicate with each other when droughts and storms are nearby, warning to gather resources. Their lives are intertwined in a way that's inseparable without killing them both." She stared at me, waiting for my response.

"People are not trees," I said.

"We are. And I wish we weren't. I've been looking for a way to separate our connection, but it's impossible. That's why—" She turned toward me, taking my hands. "That's why I need your help. We're friends, right?"

Is that what all of this with the clothes had been about? I was foolish to think that Sequoia was being nice to me from the kindness of her heart—of course she wanted something. People always do.

"My help?" I wasn't looking forward to what was coming next. There was only one thing she could be asking of me, that anyone ever asked of me when they were in trouble.

"I want you to read my Tarot. Tell me how to break away from Aspen."

"Though construction of the esteemed Foresyth House commenced in 1867, its completion was not realized until 1872, owing to a series of unforeseen delays. The architecture, inspired by Lord Foresyth's alma mater, Old Souls College, required specialized building materials and construction equipment that was not readily available in the mountainous region of Enderly."

"Additionally, labor shortages, outbreaks of disease, and land disputes plagued the project, rendering the site inhospitable and exacting a toll on the workforce. Several laborers suffered grievous injuries, with some requiring hospitalization, a testament to the arduous conditions they faced in the House's formative days. Yet, despite these trials, Lord Foresyth and the remaining Founding Five remained unwavering in their commitment to the endeavor, ultimately opening Foresyth's doors to its inaugural class in 1872."

—*Foresyth Conservatory: A Complete History, Unabridged*, 1891

Chapter 11: The Wyrd

I had been sleeping dreadfully ever since my nightmares started, but last night was especially difficult with Sequoia's haunting melody stuck in my head. I hoped that the time I spent cultivating our friendship would prove fruitful in unearthing more about her and Aspen's involvement with Julian. Reading for her was just the window into her subconscious I needed to propel my case forward.

But first, I had to survive tonight's Circle—and deliver a proposal of my own. It was my chance to prove that I belonged here, to play the role of scholar convincingly enough to earn not just their attention, but their respect. Perhaps even their trust.

Failure, though? I couldn't afford to dwell on that. In a place like this, failure wasn't just embarrassing. It was dangerous.

I hurried downstairs for a quick breakfast before heading to the library. I was the first in the dining room and grateful for it. I stuffed my satchel with several tasteless biscuits and poured myself a cup of black coffee (no more tea full of mystery herbs). I left the dining room just as Aspen came in, a yawning Sequoia on his arm.

Had they spent the night together after I left Sequoia's room? I took a long gulp of the bitter coffee.

"Good morning, Dahlia. You look . . . different." The taller tree hummed, raising an eyebrow. He looked handsome as always, his hair neatly brushed to one side of his face, and his eyes twinkling with a morning alertness I envied.

I glanced down at the clothes Sequoia had dressed me in. The skirt cinched too tightly at the waist, the fabric clinging in ways I wasn't accustomed to. I didn't appreciate the way it traced the curve of my hips—I also didn't appreciate Aspen's gaze on me, lingering far too long as I slipped past them both.

"Thanks," I called from behind, not letting him see my face flush with embarrassment.

"You won't stay for breakfast?" Sequoia said over her shoulder. Her eyes glinted slightly, as if she had been crying. Why was she so attached to him if he caused her such distress?

"No, too much work." I waved my hand and left without another word.

*

I spent the next few hours in the library, stacking tomes onto the little section of desk I had claimed for myself. I had never seen so many books on a single esoteric topic. I was lucky to find one or two in my mother's collection, or even in the Greenwich archives, but here in the Foresyth library, I found three books on cartomancy, two on the Qabalah, and five books on Hermetic Tarot. Gabriel would have a picnic here.

My mind drifted to thoughts of him and how we'd spend hours reading outside and acting out the stories. We hadn't yet discovered the archives and spent those languid summers in his father's orchard, reading about sailors and pirates traversing rocky waters. We mounted apple trees, our ship's posts, and set to sail the waves of apple blossoms as our rolling seas. As children, the candor of our desires had come far more readily, unburdened by the complexities of adulthood.

I sighed, missing Gabriel suddenly. Sure, he wasn't as charming or enigmatic as the students here with morbid fascinations and curious practices, but he was still my oldest friend. I touched my chest, remembering the unposted letters I still had in the breast pocket of my blazer. I resolved to hand them to Richard on my way out of the library.

As I stacked my books on my worktable, I sighed, knowing I couldn't possibly finish reading all of these by tonight. By the time it was noon and time to report to my mentorship meeting with the Meister, I had scarcely gone through two books.

I carefully wrote down the title on the check-out board and slipped out of the library before heading to the Meister's office across the hall. I found Richard in the hall and handed him my letters, one for Gabriel and one for my mother and Angelise, including most of my stipend to cover the costs of caretaking for the bookstore.

"I'll have these posted right away, Ms. Blackburne." Richard nodded, taking the stack from my hands.

I thanked him and made my way to the Meister's office. The strap of my satchel dug into my shoulders from the weight of the books, and I adjusted them.

"Ms. Blackburne, good to see you again. I see you've been taking advantage of Foresyth's collections," The Meister said, looking up from a stack of papers on his desk.

"Indeed, an impressive inventory. One to rival my bookstore," I said, taking a seat across from him. As I sat down, the pen I had tucked into my breast pocket slipped out. I dove for it, but before it could land, the pen disappeared.

I looked up to see the Meister holding it with the barrel outstretched towards me. He extended his hand, and I took it from him, my eyes searching him. *How did he do that?* He must be incredibly fast. What other talents must he be holding back from me?

"Take as much advantage of it as you'd like. Foresyth is here for the students as much as the students are here for Foresyth." The Meister thrummed his fingers along the desk as he found his own seat again.

"It's curious—this place is unlike any in the world. It has a life of its own. You can feel it if you spend enough time alone here—the slight pulse of the House." The Meister laid his hand flat down on the table. "The intensity of the students' output is directly linked to the life force of the House."

"That's beautifully poetic," I said, tucking the pen back into my pocket.

The Meister gave me a soft smile, pushing his glasses up the bridge of his nose. "Shall we discuss your next assignment?"

"Oh, well, I've just begun—"

"Nonsense. Each student here has multiple research projects at a time. You should be no different."

I crossed my legs and leaned back. This wasn't going to be a quick meeting. "Very well, what research do you have in mind?"

"I want to continue where Julian left off. He and I were collaborating on a topic that intersected my specialty in prognostication and his in iconography. I'm hoping you can pick up the pieces. It might even help you with the case," the Meister said, pulling a black sachet out of his drawer and shaking it. The runes inside made a rattling noise.

"You recognized the runes on my cane, yes? Do you know where they come from?"

"They're based in Norse mythology. Northern Germanic tribes would use them to advise on the future," I said. Could Julian's research on runes be connected to the lion-serpent symbol?

"Ah, not just any future. Into the *Wyrd*. The tapestry of the world and how the threads connect us on a cosmic level. Where pulling one thread over here unravels another over there." He made a motion of pulling on a thread with his fingers. "That's what the runes tell us."

He emptied the contents of the sachet onto the table in front of us. Bone pellets with carvings came tumbling out. "And who writes the runes, you may ask? The maidens in Urd's Well, underneath the sacred Yggdrasil tree. The first maidens spun the Fates of every being and carved the runes into the tree."

"The Norns—I've read about them. They are the ones who not only see the future but determine it."

"Precisely, my child. They weave the fabric of cosmic destiny together through their unimaginable powers. Several scholars believe that the runes were first found carved into the Yggdrasil tree. Look here," the Meister said, leaning over the bones. "Uruz, the wild ox, is here in the center. It represents untamed potential."

"This is very fascinating and similar to Tarot in some ways, but what exactly is the research question here?" I stifled my instinct to roll my eyes. Not only was he adding to my workload, but now he was wasting my time with this lecture on basic runes.

The Meister pursed his lips, raking the runes back into their sachet. "I want you to figure out why they were carved into Yggdrasil. Many scholars have argued over this topic, but there is no consensus. Using the vast resources of our library, I would like you to do a meta-analysis of the scholarly work and come up with the answer. Why did the Norns leave behind a way to peer into their tapestry? And more importantly, is there a way to tap into the powers of the Norns themselves? Through the runes or otherwise."

"You mean influence the future yourself, not just see it?" I sat up taller.

"Don't look so surprised. We influence the future all the time. You walking into this very room set off a chain of future events. For better or for worse. If we could find a way to tap into the Norns, we could see exactly what it takes to get to where we are going, just more efficiently."

"This kind of meta-analysis could take months. And many of the books are written in old Norse . . ."

"Well, then you better get started, Ms. Blackburne. Feel free to collaborate with the other students on this topic, but I want you as lead author on the publication. I'm expecting an outline of the paper by this Friday."

"But Meister, don't you think—"

"That'll be all, Ms. Blackburne. Unless you want me to end your research assistantship? And the checks that come with it?"

"No, sir," I said, fully knowing that catching up on any sleep this week would be impossible given the increasing load of expectations. And there was still the case of Julian left to investigate.

"Very well. Then you're dismissed to go and continue your studies. And here, keep this." He tossed the sachet of runes to me. "This might help." I pocketed the sachet and stood.

"Oh, I'm sorry. There is one more thing. I did have Richard bring down Julian's personal effects. If you would like to take a look . . . for your other research project." He motioned to the grand piano in the corner of the room where a carton box sat atop the bench. My heart skipped a beat.

Finally, evidence to look through. Having so many distractions would make it difficult to make progress on the case, but at least I had evidence.

"Yes, indeed. Thank you." I cut across the room and peered into the box. There were journals stacked to the brim, along with several checked-out books on esoteric symbology and iconography. I'd have my work cut out for me, indeed. I picked up the box and started for the door.

My heart sank when the door cracked open, and in stepped Aspen. I should have arranged another time to come for Julian's things.

"You've run over fifteen minutes," Aspen said, his hands casually in his pockets. A devilish smirk ticked the corner of his lips.

"New research project," I said, slipping past him as quickly as I could.

"What do you have there?" Aspen asked, turning back away from the Meister's office and into the hallway where I stood.

"Research materials. I'm doing a meta-analysis." Both statements were factual, though they were disconnected truths.

"That's what the library is for." He furrowed his brows together, then took a step forward, letting the door go.

"From the Meister's private collection," I said and turned away. If he got a step closer, he might recognize Julian's journals. "You don't want to be late to your meeting," I shot back at him, disappearing around the corner and to the staircase.

The last thing I heard was the office door closing. I breathed a sigh of relief and scurried to my room as quickly as the weight of books on me would allow.

"'Sub rosa' is a common refrain among Foresyth scholars, used before engaging in magickal discourse. In alignment with Foresyth's core value of "INTEGRITY OF THE WORD," we encourage students to express and explore their ideas to their fullest extent."

"This pursuit is made possible only through "THE VEIL OF THE ROSE," a bond of discretion that we affirm to protect one another. It is our shared secrecy that binds us, shielding our discussions. Here, no words or thoughts of magick will be persecuted, as was so common in the not-too-distant past."

–*Foresyth Student Handbook*, 1920 edition

Chapter 12: The Tarot Circle

I was panting by the time I made it to my room with Julian's box, having narrowly escaped Aspen's interception. I couldn't risk Aspen—or any of the other students, for that matter—learning about my investigation. My throat tightened at the thought of Aspen seeing the journals I carried, clearly marked with Julian's initials. But had he already seen them? I slipped by him so quickly, it seemed unlikely. Unlikely, but not impossible.

I pushed the thought aside as I picked through Julian's things. I scarcely had time to search the box, given that my proposal was due in six hours, but my curiosity had gotten the best of me. My cursory glance found four journals—presumably one for each of the semesters he'd spent at Foresyth—two books on Gnostic symbology, and three on Norse mythology, plus a Norse dictionary.

But what connection had Julian seen between ancient Christian mythos and Norse runes? The two practices were separated by at least two centuries. Flipping through Julian's journals, I noticed something else peculiar: they weren't written in English. At least, not all of them.

They were written in strange markings that resembled a mix of Latin and Nordic symbols.

I stacked the books and journals back together in the box. I imagined Julian thumbing through these books in the library alcoves late at night, scribbling his findings excitedly into his journal, running his hands through his curly hair with each thought pulsing through him. He was only a year older than me.

Perhaps too young to leave a mark on this world, certainly too young to die, especially in the manner that he did. Whatever Julian was studying had to be connected to his death. But I couldn't afford to spend more time thinking of it, not when I had to speak at Circle tonight in front of all the other students. Tonight's performance might silence their doubts—or unravel the illusion entirely.

I trudged back downstairs and into the library, avoiding the route that would take me past the Meister's office, just in case Aspen was coming out of his meeting.

It was exceptionally quiet.

Richard had drawn the curtains to cast out the afternoon light. I retreated back to my workstation and started stacking the books out of my bag onto the table. Luckily, given my extensive knowledge on the topic, there were only a few gaps to fill before I could construct a coherent proposal.

The scent of aged, leather-bound books clung to the air, and despite everything, a small smile found its way to my lips. Whatever the circumstances that had brought me to Foresyth, there was a part of me—quiet and unshakable—that felt at home here, buried in the alcoves, surrounded by words.

I drew in another breath, letting the stillness settle around me, and then turned to my study. The fog in my head lingered, but I kept it at bay with steady cups of black coffee retrieved from the breakfast room. Each bitter sip cut through the haze, sharpening my focus as my eyes moved over the page, line by line, chasing clarity in the flickering lamplight.

An idea was taking shape in my mind, and I traced its contours. Could someone use the physical decks of cards to chemically date their age instead of relying on scholarly reports?

Granted, it was a first-principles question and would require a significant budget to loan and date the decks of cards from different libraries, but if I succeeded, I could put to rest the conflicting timelines found in the literature. A smile broke on my lips at the thought of imbuing this mystical field with scientific investigation. I only hoped the others could be convinced.

*

"Where were you all day? I didn't see you in the lab," Nina said, taking her seat next to mine.

"Preparing for this," I said, nodding to the center of the room. The old tree swayed, as if nodding in recognition.

"This is nothing. You could write a proposal in your sleep. Wait till you submit for review. There's nothing scarier than the Advisors evaluating your work."

"The Advisors are involved in publishing?"

"Of course. But it's not just quality inspection, even though that's what it feels like, it's also because they want to know the latest and greatest research. They're still scholars. It's just that *their* research happens in the real world."

My stomach churned at the thought of magick—*or worse, the presumption of it*—seeping into the outside world. It belonged in books, buried in the long-forgotten histories of vanished ages, where it could be studied, disproved, and ultimately contained. It wasn't magick itself that unsettled me. One cannot fear what one does not believe exists.

What frightened me was belief. The kind of belief that turns into certainty. Because with enough conviction, even fiction could be dangerous.

"Good evening, everyone," the Meister said, striking his cane down several times, opening the circle. "Sub rosa."

"Sub rosa," I murmured under my breath as I stole a glance at Sequoia and Aspen seated on the loveseat. He had a hand on her knee, strumming the fabric of her skirt. I closed my eyes, and the image of her warm hand in mine from last night flashed before me.

People are not trees.

But we are, she had replied. Her eyes met mine for a second before looking away. Or was it the glint of the fireplace playing tricks on me?

"Ms. Blackburne, I believe tonight it is your turn to start," the Meister beckoned.

I tucked a loose strand of hair back and sat up, straightening on the chaise. "Indeed, I'd like to begin with a brief history of Tarot, including the elemental suits and Major Arcana." I cleared my throat, ready to dive into the research I had gathered.

"That won't be necessary," the Meister said. "You can just dive into your hypothesis."

My stomach dropped. This was what I had been preparing for all day, all week. Hadn't we agreed to this?

"All first years take Prognostication seminar. We're familiar with the history of most methods—scrying, palmistry, and cartomancy, of course," Aspen said, wrapping his arm around Sequoia's waist.

I had prepared for a rigorous re-telling of Tarot, tracing all the threads of lineage, which would perfectly set the stage for my proposed research. Without an interest in history, what else did I have?

"I was trying to explain how there were conflicting timelines in its history—"

Leone chuckled. Sequoia crossed her legs away from me. Even Nina's gaze dropped.

Failure built thick and hot in the pit of my stomach.

"If we studied every conflicting timeline in history, we would never graduate," Aspen said factually. There was no menace in his tone, just academic objectivity. A part of me even appreciated it.

"Research isn't just about *doing* the research, reading books, and recounting what academics say—any first year could do that. What distinguishes you as a scholar—as an Advisor—is asking the right questions," the Meister said. "What is it that you really want to know? Absent any sense of how you would actually go about investigating it?"

I sat back in my seat, heat flushing my cheeks. What was there to know about card tricks? Aside from their methodology, there wasn't anything substantive in them. I read people, not Tarot. They were just the medium of my manipulation. I didn't believe in their intrinsic power; it wasn't something to find out, it was already a fact.

"I see you thinking, Ms. Blackburne. Challenge the status quo. Question everything, even what you think is an unshakable truth."

My pulse quickened, saliva gathering on my tongue. My mind raced with memories of my readings. Yes, I read people's micro-reactions and profiled them accordingly, but somewhere deep inside, I knew there was another force at play. Invisible, but ever-guiding.

The question sat at the back of my throat, rising with the bile in my stomach from all the coffee I'd had earlier in the day. I tasted the swelling truth.

"What I truly want to know," I began, feeling the weight of every eye on me, "is this: If the cards are indeed magick, if they can prophesy the future . . . where does that power come from?" I couldn't very well ask, *is the magick of Tarot even real?*

But if there was a source, then there was power.

"Ah, now that's a much more interesting question." The Meister leaned back, satisfied.

Sequoia's eyes flashed with horror, but the look was gone as quickly as it had appeared. Had I said the wrong thing? Or had I tapped into something I wasn't ready to know?

"Haven't you heard of *The Book of Skorn*?" Leone said.

I turned to him, feeling the weight of his judgement. "Of course I have, but it's a hypothesis, just like anything else. The truth cannot be derived solely from books, only through experiment," I said pointedly to Aspen.

Aspen rolled his eyes. "What a purist," he muttered under his breath.

"No, let's follow that thought," the Meister probed. "True magick, after all, comes from experimentation, not from reading books. It is the practice of doing, of becoming, that creates magick. What experiments should Ms. Blackburne perform to derive the origin of the cards' powers?"

An uneasy silence fell across the room. I had the feeling that everyone, except me, already knew the answer.

"She could call to different deities and then pull cards, see which ones are more accurate," Sequoia suggested. "I could help you draft a list of patrons," she added.

"That assumes that the power of Tarot comes from deities," Nina said. "What about sacrifice? I could lend you a frog or a pheasant. I would expect it back, though. After you kill it."

"You're disgusting, you know that?" Aspen frowned. "What she really needs is a hypothesis, like she said. Where do you think the powers come from? From there, test it."

I found myself agreeing with Aspen. But I couldn't very well say that I didn't believe the cards had power; otherwise, what kind of Tarot reader would that make me? Leone had mentioned *The Book of Skorn.* If I referenced the work, perhaps that would help me gain their favor.

"Aleric Khorvyn wrote *The Book of Skorn.* In his view, Tarot was a means to access the archetypal energies and universal principles that underlie the fabric of reality," I started, recalling a copy of the book I had read in my father's library. "He believed that by engaging with the symbolism and imagery of the cards, individuals could gain profound insights into their spiritual journey, the nature of existence, and the forces shaping their lives."

"I know you come from a sub-tier school," Aspen bated with a teasing smile, "but a hypothesis usually begins with an if-then statement."

I shot him a dagger with my eyes, but my mind was too preoccupied to reply. "As I was saying . . . if Tarot's powers come from engaging with these archetypal energies, then by engaging with them in a specific way—maybe even embodying them in the real world—one could strengthen their powers of foresight. If one's power of foresight does strengthen, then Tarot's power is derived from these collective energies."

Sequoia's excitement bubbled up and she started clapping her hands in a quick, hummingbird motion. "She's so good," she whispered to Aspen.

"Sounds like someone developed an experimental framework," the Meister said. "Does anyone have suggestions for which cards Ms. Blackburne could use to test her hypothesis?"

"The Moon—that's my favorite," Sequoia said, smiling.

"She needs something straightforward to study. The Moon is too ambiguous. What about Eight of Coins? That one's very literal," Nina said.

"Coins are so material. She needs cards with spiritual meaning. The Two of Swords is an excellent choice," Leone added.

"The Devil," Aspen said. Everyone turned to him, eyes scrunched—even Leone.

"What? She needs a card that has a strong, unambiguous meaning. The Major Arcana card representing rebellion should be easy for Ms. Blackburne to embody." Aspen crossed his arms with that same sly grin on his lips. I hated how my cheeks were blooming from his attention, and I let my hair fall to the sides of my face to conceal them.

"Then I think you have a path forward, Ms. Blackburne. Is there anything else you want to discuss with the group?" the Meister asked.

"No, that's all. Thank you," I said, sitting back, defeated.

What the hell had I just gotten myself into?

I wanted to propose studying the lineage of Tarot using empirical methods, not tapping into its magick. How was I even supposed to do that, when I'd never done magick before?

"What deck are you going to use?" Leone asked.

"I have my own," I said, severely wanting the attention to shift away from me.

"Your hypothesis is based on a Skorn deck. While nearly identical to the archetypal images in Tarot, the Skorn deck was penned by Khorvyn himself and imbued with his magicks," Leone said. "You should use one of those."

"He's right; otherwise, it's not a controlled experiment," Aspen said. "And we know how much you care about that."

"Well, I don't have a Skorn deck," I said.

"The Foresyth archives have it," Nina said.

"First years aren't allowed into the archives, and second years need explicit permission. You'll have to make an appeal to the Advisors Council to lend you a deck for your proposal," the Meister said. "Don't look so worried; they meet monthly. I'm sure they'll have time to hear your proposal next week."

Meeting the Advisors? That sounded mortifying. I bet they would have all of Aspen's pompous zeal and none of the Meister's even tolerance.

"I've done it before; I can help you prepare. That is, if you help me with dating some materials," Leone offered.

"Of course, I'd be happy to," I replied, swallowing the lump in my throat. Who were these elusive Advisors, and how was I going to survive being picked apart by them? If I refused, I wouldn't have a research topic, and the others would quickly realize that I was a fraud who didn't belong here. There was no way out of this for me.

"Very well . . . Leone will help you make the appeal. Your proposal has been conditionally approved, granted that the Council will approve your access to the archives to borrow the Skorn deck."

I sighed, sinking deeper into my chair. I had survived Circle, hadn't upset any of the students or the Meister, but it came at the cost of paving my future with even more impediments. I hoped Leone would be good for his word and help me prepare for the Council, lest they eat me alive.

After we closed Circle, I strode back down to the library. It was never too late to get a head start on the next day's materials. I had another research project to prepare for, thanks to the Meister's interest in Norse mythology. Besides, I needed the others to see me going to the library to prevent suspicion about my meeting with Sequoia later tonight. I began taking the books out of my bag, stacking them on top of one another on my desk.

I stopped when I got to the first edition *Book of Skorn*.

"Why did you have to go and make me promise to do magick?" I muttered to it, skimming the pages I had earmarked. I flipped back to the front to check the date of publication.

My heart dropped when I came to the title page. Not only was the book signed by Aleric Khorvyn himself, but there was a distinct marking drawn at the bottom of his signature, hand-drawn. I traced the tail of the serpent, all the way up to the head of a lion. It was the same symbol I had found on the back of the picture frame.

This lion serpent was what Julian had pointed to with his dead body. *The Book of Skorn* was undoubtedly linked to Julian's death.

The Acolyte and the Alchemist: Part III

The pen was a symbol, Quill thought. Or perhaps, an omen. Whatever it was, he knew one thing for certain—Hamra would rewrite his Fate, one way or another.

Now, when they spent time in the library, they were no longer confined to their separate worlds. Instead, they began to share one. They read the same books, collaborated on the same papers, alternating who would take first authorship. Their work was so prolific that, one day, the Council summoned them to a meeting to discuss their potential as future Advisors.

"You have collectively submitted twelve manuscripts in the last six months," a Councilman with a wispy mustache said, peering down at them from the dais. "That is the most in the College's history."

Quill swallowed his nerves, stealing a glance at Hamra. He had no experience with men in robes or wispy mustaches. Hamra smiled up at them.

"We are honored by your praise, Lord Councilman," she said, casting a brief look at Quill. "We hope to bring pride to Foresyth."

"You two are well on your way to becoming excellent Advisors," said a younger Councilman, his beard full where the other's was sparse. "We wished to extend our praise, and to ask if there is anything the Council might do to further support your studies."

"We feel quite supported—" Quill began.

"What my colleague means to say," Hamra interjected smoothly, "is that we extend our deepest gratitude. And, so that we may continue our research into the ceremonial practices of early Gnostic sects, it would be of great benefit to gain access to the archives."

Silence fell across the chamber.

Quill turned sharply to Hamra, mortified. The archives were strictly for Advisors—the practitioners of magick. They housed private collections of journals, accounts of ceremonial rites, and, more than that, artifacts—summoning boards, pendulums, priceless relics. No student had ever been granted entry.

The eldest Councilman folded his hands. "We will consider your request."

And so, history was rewritten.

Addendum to the *Handbook,* December 24th, 1893:

"In light of recent events, students are strictly prohibited from engaging in the practice of magick without the explicit authorization of the Council. As a reminder, Foresyth stands as an academic institution devoted to the stewardship of magickal history, art, and knowledge. Practical applications of magick are approved solely in instances that contribute to the scholarly advancement of the school and are not to be pursued for personal purposes."

–*Foresyth Student Handbook*, 1920 edition

Chapter 13: Sequoia's Reading

I clutched *The Book of Skorn* to my chest, the latest revelation crashing over me like a storm. Julian's death was tied to Tarot. Had the Meister known all along? Had he brought me here not just as the daughter of a famous detective, but as a Tarot reader?

I can't say what it means, his voice echoed in my head.

Anger burned in my ribs, sharp and unrelenting. I hated being manipulated. I had to uncover what had happened to Julian—and I had to do it quickly. It had only been a week since my arrival, but the moment I had the truth, I would leave. I didn't need the research stipend. The bounty was enough to support me and my mother. I didn't need the Meister, or the hollow weight of prestige.

The thought of leaving tonight was tempting.

Sequoia's words echoed in my mind—her quiet observation that Aspen might be living in someone else's shadow. Was I any different? Julian hadn't simply died; he'd been murdered. Of that, I was certain. And if I abandoned this now—if I turned back—the one who killed him might never be brought to light. Julian's story would end in silence. And so would mine.

My father's highest principle had always been the pursuit of truth. Now, I wrapped myself in it like a cloak—unyielding, unbreakable.

I carried this resolve with me all the way to Sequoia's room. Someone in this House had to know what happened the night Julian died, and Sequoia was as good a place to start as any. Even if I found myself drawn to her, I couldn't rule her out as a suspect until she offered an ironclad alibi.

"Dahlia!" she cooed, opening the door and swinging an arm around me. "You did brilliantly at Circle today."

I ignored the warmth of her arm around me, though it did feel pleasant to hear that I had performed well in Circle. "Well, I have my work cut out for me. I don't even know where to begin," I admitted.

"At the beginning, of course—with the Fool."

I squinted at her. "You all seem to know as much about Tarot as I do. All of you," I said, not hiding the suspicion in my tone.

Sequoia gave me a blank stare. "Nonsense, I've heard you're an illustrious reader. But we all know our fair share of the principles of fortune-telling." She winked. "Still, if I had any real knack for it, I wouldn't have asked you here." Her big brown eyes threatened to swallow me whole.

"I know students aren't supposed to practice magick together, but I really appreciate you doing this for me."

"We're not allowed to practice magick?" I asked, frowning. Not that I considered Tarot reading to be magick, but it seemed strange that an occult arts Conservatory would forbid the application of knowledge.

"Well, not alone, technically. The Council forbade it indefinitely, leaving it to the Advisors. But the Meister makes exceptions now and then. But we don't need one if we aren't asking him, right?" She fluttered her lashes.

I gently shrugged her arm off and fumbled in my bag for the deck. "Shall we, then?" I gave her a small smile. Sequoia was right; this was my strength. Reading was my best chance to access Sequoia's psyche and edge closer to the truth. And I wasn't breaking any rules if I didn't believe in magick.

She smiled and led me deeper into her room until we reached her bed.

"Do you . . . need anything in particular?" she asked.

"Sage would be great, and any stone or mineral you connect with," I said, setting out my ceremonial cloth on her bed. The whole room smelled like her—lavender and lilac. I inhaled, letting her scent fill my chest.

What is the essence of you? I wondered, studying her as she opened a drawer and pulled out a bundle of herbs and two crystals.

Her arms were lithe, almost feline, as she set the items on the bed. Could those hands have poisoned Julian? Poison was a woman's weapon of choice, after all.

"Thank you for doing this." She reached over, her touch sending a jolt up my arm. "I know everyone here is so strange about magick—I just want you to know it means a lot to me." Her brown eyes seemed to envelop me entirely.

"This is what I do. This is how I help people." *Even those who can't truly be helped.* I thought of my past clients. Did I really help them, or had I just told them comforting tales that satisfied them for a moment, only to lead them straight into the trouble they were bound to encounter anyway? I supposed if they'd wanted good advice, they'd have gone to a psychologist.

I brushed the thought aside and lit the bundle of sage over the spread I'd laid on her bed. I let the smoke billow under the cards, flipping them over to cleanse the other side. Relaxation was essential to the reading. Humans are social creatures, and if the inquirer sensed unease in me, they'd never let their guard down. And that was the entire point.

"You have to sit on them now," I said, handing her the deck.

She smiled. "How delightfully unconventional." I pushed away the thought of how close she would be to my cards.

"The purpose is to imbue them with your energy. This is the most effective method. I read for a lot of people, and you don't want the energies getting all muddled." I didn't believe a word of what I was saying, but the logic held for someone with a magickally-inclined mind. I had learned this over years of reading. Ceremony was all part of priming the inquirer.

"And have many sat on this deck before?"

"More than you'd like to know." I smiled. "That should be good."

"No, I haven't finished imbuing yet—you distracted me." She sat up straighter and shifted on the cards, closing her eyes and taking a deep breath, with a slight upward curve on her lips.

Ordinarily, I'd have to guide my patrons—ease them into a meditative, receptive state—but she slipped into it with unsettling ease. Her breath deepened, and I watched the tension drain from her shoulders like water from a clenched fist. After a few moments, she handed the cards back to me. They were warm. I swallowed hard, taking them from her.

"Do we invoke the powers of Sophia, our Shattered Mother, now?" Sequoia asked.

"Who?" I started to ask. But then I decided to play along, lest Sequoia question my magickal erudition. "*Sophia*," I repeated before Sequoia had a chance to catch my hesitation. "Yes, of course, we invoke the Goddess."

She giggled, covering her mouth with her fingers.

"What is it?" I asked.

"I've just never heard her referred to as a Goddess, but I quite like it." She smiled.

I nodded, trying to keep the confusion off my face. I would have to research this deity further—it might be important to Julian's case.

"Now that we have your energy on the cards, let's seal it. I usually do this with a few crystals I select based on the inquirer's energy fields. But since you're magickally inclined and in tune with your own fields, I've let you select them yourself." I looked down, picking up the two crystals Sequoia had provided. "Pink quartz—symbolizing the feminine divine, purity, and love. And this other one . . . black agate? A shielding stone, a protector." I glanced at her curiously. She nodded slowly, her features softening.

I clasped her hands. "Now, let's say a small truth spell. To let the creative forces move us toward the light of truth." I said the words with rehearsed sincerity. She nodded, gripping my hands firmly.

I spoke the incantation, and Sequoia echoed after me. As I said the words aloud, an electric current thrummed through our connected hands, followed by an almost imperceptible buzzing in the back of my head, rising in pitch.

"Do you hear that?" I asked.

"Hear what?"

"Never mind." I broke our hands apart, and the buzzing stopped. I took a deep breath, steeling my focus. *I'm here for Julian*, I reminded myself. Sequoia knows something about that night that I don't, and I have to figure out what it is. *Who killed him?*

"Aspen," Sequoia said.

"Excuse me?" I blinked.

"I want this reading to be about me and Aspen. I want to know how I can separate myself from him. Our relationship is . . . unharmonious, but I keep finding myself going back to him, again and again."

"We'll get to the bottom of it." But how was I supposed to connect the night Julian died to this reading? I wracked my brain, and a memory floated to the surface. *If only you weren't so friendly toward him.* Aspen's words echoed in my head. Why had he said that to Sequoia during Circle?

"I'm actually quite experienced in love readings—they're a specialty of mine, given their demand," I said as an idea started to form.

"I'll use a spread I call Love's Dagger. The sheath represents the past and present of the relationship; the hilt represents the core issues and opposing forces; and the pommel, the resolution." Sequoia's eyes widened as I laid the cards down one by one.

"This is a perfect spread for my situation," she said, her eyes fixed on the cards in awe.

My lips curved slightly. She was unaware that I had thought of it on the spot.

"We'll start at the hilt—the core of the issue." I revealed the cards on two opposing sides. On the left lay the Lovers, and on the right, the Five of Cups. A shiver ran down my arms. Sometimes, the cards' coincidences struck me, but I hardened myself. I could explain her situation with any cards that appeared.

"The Lovers—the core of your relationship is a twin flame, a soul connection. You are bound to this connection by a force greater than human nature. When you are together, you are one." I searched Sequoia's eyes, and she nodded slowly.

I hadn't said anything she didn't already know, but seeing reality mirrored in the cards was an almost certain way of gaining her trust. I needed to be careful with my reading. Unlike most inquirers, Sequoia had at least a cursory familiarity with the cards and their meanings.

"The opposing force—" I pointed to the card across from it. "The Five of Cups. A shrouded figure stands over three spilled cups, bemoaning his disappointment. Two cups stand upright behind him. The cups represent the element of water—everything that has to do with our emotions, their fluidity, their ever-changing nature. You've been emotionally wounded by Aspen, and despite any good in your relationship, there are always more spilled cups than upright ones." Sequoia's eyes glinted with tears, and I knew I was getting closer, but I wasn't quite there yet. I pulled another card from the deck and placed it on top of the Five of Cups.

"Strength, in reverse," I noted. "The core of your disappointment comes from Aspen's narcissism, his self-obsession with his work and himself. He holds himself to an impossible standard, and that expectation bleeds to those around him." Sequoia's eyes widened.

"Gods, these are eerily accurate. But I suppose you do have a lot of context—being our peer and all." Her voice flattened.

I needed something beyond the obvious. I needed a deduction, a hypothesis—something I couldn't know but could surmise from the facts. Something that would make her believe in the cards, and in me.

I swallowed and laid cards at the center of the dagger. I flipped them over. "The Three of Wands. Your discontent began when your affection fell away from Aspen and landed elsewhere." I placed another bet. Sequoia didn't move but stared intently at the cards laid before her. I continued.

"Your cup was empty, and Aspen wasn't filling you in the ways you needed. You were seeking validation in another. You looked away from Aspen to new lands." I pointed to the image of a figure perched on a cliffside, watching a distant horizon. If there was a perfect card for infidelity in the deck, this was it. I worked my way up to the tip of the dagger spread. I flipped another card, and the familiar Hanged Man appeared. A shiver curled down my spine, but I ignored the coincidence and went on. I was getting closer and couldn't falter.

"It was Julian—you developed affection for him. For his gentle nature, his passion for his work, which wasn't an obsession but a calling. He was obsessed, instead, with you." I read between the cards, tracing the lines on Sequoia's face, searching for what rang true and what didn't. Her features softened slightly, and I rephrased. "Or was it you who was obsessed with him? Was it unrequited?"

"It's true, we were close. All three of us were, at some point. Julian . . . he was kind and compassionate. He said nice things about my work. And he loved me, but it wasn't like that."

I held her gaze as I traced the edge of the next card, feeling a spark at my fingertips. "Your discontent with Aspen began long ago, but it only solidified recently. Something happened that made you doubt your connection to him, and it's represented by" —I flipped the card— "death." My heart nearly skipped a beat.

Could this really be? I stared at the skeletal figure riding a white horse, holding the flower of death in his left arm. A black dahlia.

Sequoia gasped and her lip began to quiver. "No, no . . . it couldn't be," she whispered. I steadied my concentration. This was the moment I had been waiting for—the crack, the break. Every reading had one. A moment when the person's facade began to fracture. The perfect moment to strike, to uncover the truth.

"Aspen was involved in Julian's death," I said. "He was jealous of the attention you gave Julian, suspecting that you favored him romantically. And he couldn't handle his favorite toy being handled by another." I winced at the harshness of my tone. But it was necessary to get to the heart of the matter.

Sequoia whimpered, tears streaming down her cheeks. "No, no . . . he couldn't have . . ." She covered her face with her hands. This was my chance to find out what happened that night. But as I watched her, sobbing into her hands, my heart softened. I was breaking this poor girl.

"What happened that night, Sequoia?" I whispered. My resolve weakened with her cries, but not enough to stop pressing. It was now or never.

"Nothing—I mean, I don't know." She looked up at me and started speaking between gulps of air. "Julian and I were working on a paper together; he was relying on me for Gaelic. There were a lot of long nights, you know how it goes. But nothing ever happened . . . *really* happened, I mean." She paused, taking a deep breath. "One night, while we were working on the paper, it was late, and we were sleep deprived. I think we were just trying to stay awake. I kissed him. Or he kissed me. I don't remember. But we both agreed afterward that it was a bad idea, and nothing came of it."

"But Aspen knew."

She nodded. "Somehow, he found out. I don't know how, but he has a way of seeing things. He told me I should stop spending time with Julian, that he was holding me back. Maybe he was jealous, I don't know. I honestly couldn't wait until we turned in the paper, so Aspen could let it go. So, we could all let it go. But then that night at Circle almost a year ago . . ." She hesitated.

"What happened then, Sequoia?"

"I . . . I shouldn't tell you this. You haven't been Initiated."

"Initiated?"

When she didn't answer, I pressed on. "Is that what you were doing that night? Practicing magick?"

"Oh, Dahlia," she said weakly.

I reached over, folding my hand over hers. I hardened myself. "I can only help you if I know the truth."

She was silent for a long moment, then finally began to speak again. "We were performing a ceremony. We drank an herbal concoction that made everything hazy; it made us more receptive to the magick. We were all fine the next morning, except Julian. I didn't know what happened that night—I suspected but didn't know. But when we woke up, Julian was tethered to the tree in that horrible position. And Aspen . . ." She broke into a sob. "Gods, he looked so pale. He looked as if he knew something none of us did. I always thought he was beautiful, but in that moment, he looked so broken."

Blood pumped behind my ears at an alarming rate, but I steadied my breath. I let the facts settle over me before speaking again. "You didn't see Aspen do anything to Julian?"

"No, no, I didn't. Like I said, everything about that night is so hazy. But we all drank the same tea, and none of us died. So, it couldn't have been the tea, could it? Gods, I feel so awful, like I was the one who hung him myself." Sequoia was red all over, tears and snot running down her face. Had Aspen given me the same tea on my first morning?

I had broken her, but I finally had more information about that night than I'd gathered since coming here. I had a motive, but I still didn't have any physical evidence. I had deduced earlier that Julian likely hung himself to leave a message pointing to his murderer and that he died from poison, not hanging.

"Did anyone else have access to the tea you made?"

"I guess everyone did. I assembled the herbs, but we were all there, close to the hearth." *Damn.* Any of these students could have been responsible. But how had everyone survived, except Julian?

"We all drank it—I poured it from the same kettle. That's why, when they ruled it as a suicide, I figured they were probably right. He hung himself that night, after all. But to think Aspen was somehow involved, that he said something to Julian about me—" She reached for my arm. "You have to help me—tell me how I can break free from him."

I looked down at the cards in front of us. There was only one left to turn over. The pommel, the resolution.

"Sequoia, I promise I'll help you. You just have to trust me and wait for the right time." If I could gather enough evidence against Aspen, I could make a case for his conviction.

I flipped the last card, hoping to seal my resolution. I grimaced when I saw the image of two figures leaping from a tower engulfed in flames, trading one horror for another.

"What . . . what is it?" Sequoia asked through her tears.

"It's going to be a lot harder than I thought."

"I have come to see the runes as more than just symbols—they are like the roots of the ancient Yggdrasil tree, digging deep into the soil of our understanding, connecting us to something primal and untouchable. Just as a tree's roots give life to its branches, so too do the runes give rise to all knowledge, from magick to philosophy to the fabric of reality itself. Each rune is a seed, and from it grows the branches of insight and power, stretching far beyond the surface of what we know. Yet, like the forest, the runes hold their secrets closely, whispering in a language almost understood, but just beyond reach. I cannot shake the feeling that the deeper I dig, the more I disturb something ancient and wild—something that, perhaps, was meant to stay buried."

–*Julian Earhardt's journal*, dated February 4th, 1919

Chapter 14: The Third Tree

I traced my fingers across the old tree, letting the coarse bark scrape against my palm. It was nearly five in the morning, yet I couldn't sleep, not after Sequoia's reading. I had been pouring over Julian's old journals and somehow found myself down here.

Aspen. The Trees.

There were really three of them in the House, if you included the monstrous oak in the reading room.

It's peculiar to have a tree within a House like this, I thought, letting my fingers dig into the bark. How did its roots grow without disturbing the foundation? I circled its trunk, as if tracing the tree would reveal something about its origins or the House itself. Julian had died on this tree, I was certain. But before he died, he had left a clue—the strange symbol on the back of the picture frame, a lion's head with a serpent's tail. The same icon I found in his journal and in *The Book of Skorn*. Was there anything else he had left behind that I'd overlooked?

The bark snagged on my sweater, tearing a small piece away to reveal the wood beneath—milky and smooth, reminding me of pale moonlight. But at the very edge of the exposed patch, I noticed a marking. It was faint but deliberate, clearly carved. It wasn't natural. Using my nails, I peeled away more bark, uncovering a symbol. Once enough bark had been cleared, I studied it closely: two triangles, stacked in a way that resembled a "B." Where had I seen this marking before?

The runes. The memory hit me suddenly, like a weed bursting through rubble. I was researching the origins of rune magick for the Meister's project. But why would this tree bear runes? And how had it regrown bark over the carvings?

"What are you doing up so early, Tarot reader?" I'd recognize that deep, thunderous voice anywhere. Acid rose in my throat as I turned slowly to face him.

"Couldn't sleep," I said, stating the truth as I turned to Aspen. No point in lying when it wasn't necessary.

He smirked, his teeth gleaming in the dim light. "Something on your mind?" He trailed two fingers along the edge of the red chaise, circling around to sit.

"I could ask you the same thing," I replied, crossing my arms. He might be a suspect, but I doubted he'd harm me here, with others due for breakfast in an hour. Still, I didn't like that smirk on his face.

"Relax. I think better in the morning than at night. Everyone here's a night owl, but not me. I'm an early bird, and today, I've found a worm." His smile widened.

He was infuriating, but I couldn't let him see that he was getting to me.

"I've never seen what you're working on. Why don't you show me some of your sculptures?" I changed the subject, hoping it might draw him in. Perhaps showing interest in his work was the way to get through to him. But he didn't take the bait; instead, his eyes narrowed.

"I don't show incomplete work like an amateur. You'll have to wait until the Symposium, like everyone else. Besides, don't you have your hands full with two research projects and investigating Julian's death?"

My heart dropped. Did he just say what I thought he did?

He laughed, the sound hollow. "Oh, don't look so surprised, little worm. Did you really think I hadn't noticed? I know the Meister hired you to look into Julian's death. I saw you carrying a box of Julian's things from his office the other day." He stood, moving toward me. My hand instinctively twitched toward the dagger sheathed at my ankle. Leaning against the tree, I adjusted my stance, my hand closer to the blade.

He inched toward me, a predator stalking toward his prey. Perhaps I should have left Foresyth last night when I'd had the chance.

"And what's most interesting is that you think you're getting closer to the truth." He was a foot away now, his eyes gleaming. It would take me only seconds to draw my dagger and another two to nick his throat. Not enough to kill, but to scare. I willed my heart to quiet. He leaned in so close I could trace the lines of his jaw, the curve of his mouth, and his almond eyes—like Sequoia's, but without her softness. He was her jagged reflection.

"And while I do love making a worm squirm, I've come to set the record straight." His breath was hot on my cheek. I inhaled sharply, taking in the scent of pine and wax. But in the next moment, he pushed himself off and turned away.

His back was to me. I could strike with a single swift motion if I wanted to.

"You can take this as an official statement: I didn't kill Julian. But I know who might have." My stomach lurched, though my pulse steadied now that he was at a safe distance.

Should I play ignorant, or admit my investigation? Aspen had seen the box of evidence. He already knew my true purpose.

"I must say, I underestimated you, Aspen. You might really be as clever as you believe yourself to be."

Aspen smiled, his expression unexpectedly genuine. If he had information, it might be worth letting him believe I was willing to listen. Then again, it would be safer to keep my distance.

"But you're wrong. Everyone knows that Julian's death was a suicide. The Meister gave me his things so I could continue his work on Norse runes. I'm his research assistant, nothing more."

Aspen's face fell as he considered. "Very well, reader. If that's the story you're sticking to." He paused, eyeing me. "You're hoping I'll still tell you what I know, aren't you?"

Damn. He was sharp.

"Well, you're in luck. I'm feeling generous today. Besides, I can't stand being falsely accused. Tell me, does Leone strike you as an honest man?"

I blinked, thrown by the question, but I gave it thought. "Yes, he does. He's meticulous with the truth—always the first to correct inaccuracies, even on small points. He has a purist's commitment to both thought and word."

"Clever observations, as expected of a detective."

I scowled, and he laughed—a surprisingly musical sound. "You know, in the right light, you're quite striking, even with that scowl plastered on your face."

"Is that your method? Insult, then compliment? Keep people yearning for your approval?"

"Oh, so you admit to yearning for my approval?" His smirk returned, smug and infuriating. My cheeks heated against my will.

"You think you're good at hiding your emotions, reader. But you're not the only one who reads people," he said, narrowing his eyes. "Now, back to Leone. Yes, he's rigorous with the truth, which makes him a good scholar. But don't you think the truth can be a bit dull? Sometimes a little embellishment adds color, makes things more interesting."

"Is there a point to this, or are you just waxing poetic?"

"Oh, there is a point," he replied smoothly. "Julian had a way of embellishing his work, weaving in stories and puzzles that made them fascinating. The Advisors loved it, even if it wasn't strictly necessary or even factual. But Leone . . . well, he didn't appreciate Julian's creativity. They were both third year rivals, in every sense."

"You're suggesting that Leone killed Julian?"

"I'm not suggesting anything like that." His eyes darkened. "I'm merely stating the facts: Leone and Julian were working on papers on the same topic—ancient Christian symbology. The Advisors, knowing about their rivalry, thought it would be fun to turn it into a competition. They're always thirsty for a bit of academic blood. Whoever wrote the best paper would be awarded a week-long residency at Trinity College in Dublin, with full access to their magickal collection."

God, that did sound like a dream for a scholar like Leone. But would he actually kill for it? He seemed the least likely suspect—as though he existed on a plane above the rest of them.

"Don't let the fact that he's crippled deter you from considering him—hypothetically, if you were investigating the case."

"And hypothetically, why would you help me?"

"Oh, come on, reader. That's obvious. I want to clear my name. I'm the best-suited candidate for the Advisor role, and I fully intend to secure it. The others will say whatever they need to make me look less than perfect."

So, this was about some petty promotion Aspen was angling for? I resisted the urge to roll my eyes.

"And speaking of Advisors, let's talk about Ms. Choi—your new friend. She's not what she seems, either."

"Let me guess, she's trying to steal your precious Advisor role too?" I crossed my arms.

"Actually, no, not that I know of. She has her own schemes. I don't know why she'd want Julian dead, but if he was poisoned, she's the only one with access to the lab where all dangerous substances are stored."

"That's not true. You're *stored* up here, and you're ridiculous if you think I'd suspect my friend." Nina was the first person who had shown me kindness here. She might have eccentric hobbies, but I owed her my gratitude. Still, her access to the lab might have been convenient for storing poisons . . .

Aspen grinned, pushing a strand of hair back from his face. "I'll take that as a compliment—that you think I'm dangerous," he said, moving closer.

"And exactly how do you know all these hidden motives and means?" I asked, barely masking my annoyance now.

A corner of his mouth inched upward. "The currency at Foresyth is secrets—it pays to know." He rounded the chaise, heading toward the door. "Now that I've set the record straight, I'll let you get back to whatever you were doing."

A part of me didn't want him to leave. As frustrating as he was, I still suspected him, and he was the only student who wouldn't stop talking about the case. I wanted to ask him about *The Book of Skorn* and what Julian was doing with it when he died, but I couldn't reveal my position as an investigator.

"Oh, one more thing, Dahlia." He paused, his voice softer. It was the first time he'd called me by my name, not some condescending nickname. "After you figure out who bloodied the poor lad, I do hope you'll stay at Foresyth. You might just save us all."

What could he possibly mean by that—save us all?

But before I could respond, he slipped out and closed the door.

Left alone with my thoughts, my mind spun, my heart racing. Aspen knew I was investigating Julian's death, and he was even more dangerous than I had realized. And now, I had more information—Leone as Julian's rival, Nina with access to potential poisons in the lab. They could be red herrings, or they might be leads worth pursuing. Perhaps Aspen wanted me on a wild goose chase to divert suspicion from himself, giving him enough time to strike again before the semester ended.

But I couldn't dismiss any possibility until the truth was clear. I'd need to dig deeper into both Leone and Nina and look beyond the surface. Not to mention, I needed to follow up with the Meister and figure out why he was holding back information.

Whatever chance there had been of me leaving Foresyth was now gone.

You're right. You're too far gone, I could almost hear my father's voice, resigned.

I was too deeply entangled in this case. Leaving before I solved Julian's death was no longer an option. It wasn't what my father would have done, and it wasn't what I would do either.

I glanced back at the tree I had been examining before Aspen interrupted me. Two triangles stacked to form a jagged "B." I sketched the symbol into my notebook, resolving to find it in my rune dictionary. I wanted to peel away more bark to see if there were other symbols hidden beneath, but I couldn't risk drawing attention by damaging the tree.

Besides, this wasn't the tree I was after.

*

With thoughts of Julian and tangled motives weighing on my mind, I decided to spend the following week catching up on my academics. This meant researching runes, preparing for my meeting with the Council, and, when I had time and was sure no one was around, translating Julian's journal. The Meister was away on business for the week, leaving Leone—the only third-year in residence—to lead Circle every night. That meant my mentorship meetings were postponed, and I wouldn't have the chance to confront the Meister about *The Book of Skorn* until his return.

Despite everything, I managed well in Circle and even found myself enjoying the intellectual sparring with the other students. Maybe the Meister hadn't been entirely wrong when he said I could have belonged here under different circumstances.

Midweek, I received a letter from Gabriel—another long-winded plea for me to come home—and a curt message from my mother. She informed me she was alive, listed the books she was re-reading, and complained that Angelise was overfeeding her. I wrote back to both in between my hours at the library and the lab. I was in my dormitory finishing the letters when Nina strode in as if it were *her* room and I was the intruder.

"Are you busy?" she asked, collapsing onto my bed and dropping her satchel beside it. "You weren't in the lab."

I rolled my eyes and turned away from my desk. "Not anymore, I guess. To what do I owe the pleasure of your company?" I asked, dripping mocking sweetness. Aspen's accusation still echoed raw in my mind as I considered her. If there *was* a poison master at this school, Nina would be my first suspect. But if I wanted to understand her motives, I had to tread carefully.

"I'm looking for something. I need it for my Spring Symposium project. I've been researching local folklore, and there's this one legend about a satyr . . ."

I furrowed my brows, readying a response, when the door creaked open again. Sequoia entered, a wide smile on her face.

"I didn't know Dahlia was throwing a party in here," she mused, coming to sit beside Nina. She made a shooing motion with her hand. Nina scrunched her features but, after an awkward pause, begrudgingly moved over.

"Why don't I call for Aspen and Leone while we're at it?" I said dryly.

"No!" they said in unison.

"Fine. No boys. I'll hang a sign on my door."

"I didn't mean to intrude. I can come back another time," Sequoia offered, though she was already leaning back on my bed, legs crossed. "I was working on my outline for my Druid paper and wanted a second opinion."

The light in her eyes made me pause. If the students were coming to me for help, then perhaps they were starting to see me as an equal. And despite their questionable personal boundaries, the ease between us warmed my chest.

"So, you decided to go through with it, huh?" Nina asked.

"It's a work in progress," Sequoia said, smoothing the wrinkles from her skirt.

I caught the tension between them and a thought took root. Was Nina's animosity toward Sequoia tied to her proximity to Aspen? If so, she needed to see Sequoia in a different light—separate from him. As I was starting to.

"Why don't we all help each other?" I suggested. "Sequoia and I can help you find whatever it is you're looking for, and then we can workshop your paper together."

Nina had granted me access to her lab—I owed her a favor. And I still felt guilty for devastating Sequoia with my previous reading. Maybe this would even the score. Maybe it would also bring me closer to understanding the students' potential motives regarding Julian's death.

"I'd be delighted. The girls should stick together," Sequoia chirped.

"Nina, what do you say?"

Nina sighed. "Fine. The more, the merrier." She pulled her bag onto my bed, unrolling several scrolls of parchment.

"Are those maps?" Sequoia asked.

"Yes—of Foresyth and the twenty or so miles surrounding it. Leone helped me dig them out from the library."

My eyes widened. Those could be useful to me, too. I approached the bed, careful to mask my eagerness. One was an interior blueprint of the House, the other a detailed sketch of the surrounding grounds. I hadn't realized how much land belonged to Foresyth.

"What exactly are you looking for?" I asked.

"Well, that's the problem. It's not *something*, it's *somewhere*." Nina tapped the map. "I'm looking for a region of Foresyth where the ground itself is said to have magickal properties of transmutation."

Disappointment flickered in my chest. *Magick?* After I had just started to appreciate Foresyth for its intellectual rigor.

"Oh, we could try scrying!" Sequoia said enthusiastically.

"I've done that," Nina said, rolling her eyes. "I was wondering if Miss Scientist could help me narrow it down with soil samples." She pulled several vials stuffed with dark earth from her pocket. "If they have different chemistries or whatever, it might help me pinpoint the right location."

Now *that* was interesting—using science to find magick.

"I could take a—" I started to say.

"You've tried scrying, but not with *us*," Sequoia interrupted. "And not with a professional Tarot reader." She turned to me. "Dahlia, if your cards can unearth truths about people and events, why not locations?"

Nina and Sequoia exchanged a look. I gulped.

"I've never tried that before," I said. The idea of using Tarot to locate a mystical site sounded decidedly unscientific. I much preferred analyzing the soil samples. But I couldn't let my cover slip—a student at Foresyth would be just as inclined, if not more, to believe in the magickal method as much as the scientific.

"We aren't supposed to be practicing magick according to the handbook, especially for personal gain, right?" I tested.

"This isn't for personal gain, it's for research," Nina said. "Besides, what do you think the Advisors do all day? Use their power for the personal gain of their clients. Isn't that right, Sequoia?" She cut a look toward her.

Sequoia's cheeks blushed red, and she turned her attention to the maps. "Why don't we grid the map, assign a card to each section, and have Nina pull the one she's drawn to?" Sequoia suggested.

That was certainly one way of doing it.

"If it doesn't work, we can try the *science* way later," Sequoia added with an exaggerated eye roll. "But this way is faster—and more fun."

"I'm okay with that." Nina shrugged.

The two of them looked at me expectantly. I thought it over and came to the simple conclusion that I had nothing to lose and only trust to gain from both of them.

"Oh, what the hell," I said and started to reach for the deck of cards.

*

Hours later, Nina and Sequoia finally shuffled out of my room. Nina had chosen the northeastern quadrant of the map, drawn to a card that turned out to be the *Five of Cups*, marking her next area of investigation. We'd also gone over Sequoia's outline, debating every point ad nauseam before I handed her a copy marked in red.

Satisfied I had settled my debts, I turned back to my unfinished letters. Then, sparing a few painful hours for Julian's journal, I set to work translating. Would anything at Foresyth ever be simple? Like Julian, I was only beginning to scratch the surface of this peculiar school—and its even more peculiar inhabitants.

Chapter 15: Uncomfortable Topics

The following morning, the breakfast room was steeped in an unusual hush, as if I wasn't the only one caught in the undertow of my own thoughts. I helped myself to lemon cakes and black coffee, then slid into the seat beside Nina. Leone was absent, but the ever-watchful Trees remained across the table, their visage like branches blocking the sun coming through the high windows.

My gaze drifted to Sequoia. I wondered if the reading we'd shared had shifted anything between her and Aspen—or if the Trees were simply experts at masking the fault lines.

"Nina, Leone and I are working in the lab later today. Will you be in?" I asked, trying to break the tension. I wanted Aspen to know that I was following up on this lead, just as he had suggested. Better to let him think everything was going according to his plans.

"Yeah, all right," Nina said distractedly. "I'm working in the field. I won't be in until much later." I nodded in acknowledgment.

"Still looking for that lost plot of dirt, Nina? I'd find a new treasure hunt if I were you," Aspen interjected. I turned to Nina and saw her cutting him a daggered stare. Whatever she was searching for must be important enough to rile Aspen.

"You'll be the first thing I put in that plot of dirt, if the legends are true," she shot back, standing from the table.

Then she hurried out before Aspen could say another word. I stuffed crumbs of dry cake into my mouth and washed them down with coffee. I'd gotten used to the dry taste of the food here—it at least filled my belly. Strange that no one else had mentioned the lack of flavor.

With just the Trees left in the room, I awkwardly stood and started to leave. I nodded goodbye to both of them before heading out.

Once in the hallway, I took a deep breath. It was Sunday, so luckily, no Circle tonight. I wasn't sure I could handle another mental sparring match with Aspen until I sorted through all his accusations. It was quarter to nine when I found Leone sitting by the door to the lab, a book in hand. He looked up nonchalantly, as if seeing me was the last thing he wanted to do today.

"So, there might be a problem," he said, pointing to the door.

It was locked, but beyond it, I could see a stairwell leading down to the lab. "From the looks of it, there's a stairwell."

"How have you gotten down before?" I asked. In my excitement to show him the light analyzer, I had completely overlooked how Leone would get down there.

"I haven't. I've never needed to with my line of study," he replied, returning to his book as if the real world didn't deserve more than five seconds of his attention.

I needed to figure out a way to get him down the stairs. Otherwise, I couldn't help him date his maps, which he had promised to exchange for advice on how to approach the Council for the Skorn deck.

I groaned in frustration. I was going to need help getting Leone down to the lab, unless I wanted to unintentionally contribute to another murder at the school by clumsily pushing him down the stairs.

"Stay here, I'll go get some help."

He muttered in faint agreement. I retraced my steps back to the breakfast room, looking for Richard. He was a stout man, but well-built enough that he could help me get Leone down safely.

"Looking for someone?" Aspen's voice came from across the hall, from the reading room. Was he following me now?

"How is it that we keep crossing paths today?" I asked with a forced smile.

"We are in the same House," he replied, over a book I now noticed in his lap. It was well-worn, earmarked, and heavily annotated, as if he had been poring over it for quite some time.

"I'm looking for Richard," I said.

He considered me for a moment, likely debating whether or not to lie. "Richard is probably upstairs, sorting the rooms, and no doubt planning the menu for tonight. Is there anything I can help you with?" His smile made my stomach twist.

"I wouldn't want to disturb you. I'll go find Richard," I said.

"Nonsense. I know this House like the back of my hand. And you shouldn't disturb Richard, or he might make a mistake on the menu, and we'll end up eating Nina's dead pheasants. What can I help you with?" He closed his book and set it aside. I sneaked a glance at the cover, which read *Playing with Fire.*

My eyes flicked upward, drawn to the breadth of his arms—muscles taut beneath the crisp lines of his dress shirt. He was certainly strong enough to carry Leone down the stairs.

Strong enough, too, to push us.

What kind of game was he playing? And how was I supposed to trust him when I couldn't even tell whether I was a pawn—or a threat—to him?

"You might not believe this, Dahlia, but I'm the most trustworthy person in this House. Let me help you," he said, rising from the chaise. I instinctively took a step backward.

"Fine, but only if you do exactly as I say." I faltered. Though I knew Leone would be content to read all day, I didn't have much time before this week's presentation to the Council. Forget the research report; I needed to get my hands on a Skorn deck, especially since it was tied to Julian's case.

"I need you to help me get Leone down to the lab," I said.

"I was wondering this morning how you were going to do that." He chuckled, a sly smile creeping up his lips. So, he had been eavesdropping, as I'd expected.

We started walking back down the hall to where Leone was seated. "This is the help?" Leone quipped.

"Oh, come on now, I'm much stronger than this tweed might suggest," Aspen said, tossing his sports coat on a hanger. The muscles in his forearm tensed as he gripped the handles behind Leone's wheelchair. I stepped up to intervene.

"We're going to move slowly, wheel by wheel, but I want you at the bottom," I said, quickly crafting a plan to get Leone and myself down in one piece. There was no way I was going to let Aspen topple Leone over me to our demise and then easily pin it as an accident.

"Dominant, are you?" Aspen said, wetting his lips. "Don't worry, I don't mind my women taking control." My stomach churned at the way he looked at me.

"Disgusting. Can you two not do that around me, please?" Leone said, half-irritated, looking up from his book. I winced and shot a scowl at Aspen, but his smile only seemed to widen at my embarrassment.

"Let's get this over with," I said, unlocking the door with the key around my neck. I flicked on the lights and counted the steps down. "Twenty-two." I turned and waved for Aspen to go first. He obliged without a word.

"Okay, Leone—let us know if anything feels off. And I don't mean Aspen's presence," I said, rolling him over the threshold to the landing. I angled him sideways and lifted one wheel at a time. My muscles, which hadn't been exercised in months, strained with the weight until Aspen took over the other side and lifted it with ease. His eyes followed me.

"Stop looking at me," I said.

"I can't. I mean, we have to coordinate our timing here," he said, his eyes drifting down to Leone.

"On my count . . . now." We both lifted at the same time, lowering the wheel another step. We repeated this twenty more times, until I was gasping for breath at the bottom of the landing. My legs were burning too. Aspen, however, didn't have a lick of sweat on him; he simply rolled his sleeves up.

"Haven't been down here in ages," he said, scanning the lab. He sniffed and winced. "Ah, yes, now I remember why. Since Nina took over, no one likes to come down here."

"You get used to it," I replied, making my way to the lab benches with Leone.

"Not even a thank you?" Aspen called.

"I'll thank you once you get him back up, too. It'll be a couple of hours," I called back, waving him off. He disappeared back up the stairs, and I exhaled in relief. I really didn't like relying on him for anything. Maybe Nina could help me get Leone back up when she finished with her fieldwork.

"He likes you," Leone said matter-of-factly.

"Well, that makes one of us," I muttered, guiding Leone to the benchtop where the analyzer sat.

"Hm," Leone hummed, finally looking up from his book and glancing at the machine. "That just looks like a brass box."

"It is a brass box," I replied, running my fingers over its sleek chassis. "But inside, it has a powerful light source. When we shine it through a sample, the sample absorbs different wavelengths of light. Using the photo signatures, we can determine the chemical composition and its age." My words tumbled out quickly as I got excited.

My father had taught me chemical aging methods back in his lab where he studied the chemistry of mud tracks left at a crime scene. He could determine the age of a footprint down to the day. I wasn't as skilled as he was, but I could tell samples apart by years, if not months.

"It's impressive, if it can do what you say," Leone said. "I brought these two samples as you instructed. I'm trying to determine when these two maps were drawn. Both are of the Polynesian islands, created by two scholars who claim to have discovered them first. One says he found the islands through a prophetic vision, the other through map dowsing."

"Map dowsing?" I echoed. It sounded similar to what the girls and I had done the other night.

"Yes, using a dowsing rod or pendulum over a map to locate water, precious metals, or anything of value," Leone explained, turning the two test tubes between his fingers. "Both scholars claim they were the first to discover the islands, but their claims predate James Cook by a hundred years. Verifying which one is true—and which method was used—could be invaluable to the field."

Which claim is true? The words echoed in my mind as I began setting up the machine, inserting the calibration liquid into the test chamber. Aspen had said that Leone valued truth over story, which was the source of his feud with Julian. If he valued truth as much as Aspen believed, could I trust him as an ally? Or was he compromised because of his potential involvement with Julian? There was no reason why poison couldn't have been stored anywhere in the House . . . even hidden in someone's book.

"Have you started the test?" Leone asked, interrupting my thoughts.

"No, not yet. I have to calibrate the machine first with a pure substance—gold." I pushed the buttons in the rhythmic pattern I'd discovered worked best for the machine. Whoever had stitched the machine together was a genius ahead of their time, but given the mismatched collection of knobs and pins, it required patience to operate.

"Can I ask you about someone? There was a student here previously," I began, testing the waters. Leone's expression remained neutral, fixated on the observation panel in front of us, dials turning to indicate the calibration was in progress.

"Julian," I said. His expression didn't change. "I heard he died under tragic circumstances."

"Yes, his whole case was quite tragic. A lineage acceptance who had no business being at Foresyth in the first place," he said. I studied his reaction, but his features were relaxed, eyes steady. There was nothing to indicate guilt or remorse over the situation.

"Oh, so you two weren't friends?" I asked, hoping my tone sounded innocuous enough not to raise suspicion. Maybe Aspen had been right—maybe there had been bad blood between them.

"We were academic counterparts. We disagreed on methodology, and our inclinations toward the truth. He favored story, and I favored facts. It was as simple as that. I told him he should stick to crafting puzzles instead of writing papers," Leone concluded, as if that ended the conversation.

"But his death . . . it didn't impact you?" I asked, hinting at the paper competition.

He paused, not taking his eyes off the chamber. "Come to think of it, it did eliminate him from consideration for the Advisor role," he said. "But he was clear that he didn't want anything to do with the Conservatory after graduation. He had some morale scruples he couldn't get past, so becoming an Advisor wasn't his aim."

The machine beeped, indicating that the calibration was complete.

"Were there any topics you two were collaborating on?" I pressed, removing the calibration sample from the machine.

"Hmpf. We were working on similar papers, but mine won out among the Advisors."

"Oh? I hadn't heard . . ." I said absently.

"Why would you have? We found out a week before Julian died. Then my research trip to Dublin got postponed with all the chaos surrounding his death. No one knew, but it shouldn't be a surprise to anyone that my paper won out. I don't waste my breath on bragging."

I turned around, rolling my eyes. Was there a man at this school who wasn't pompous? But if the competition had favored Leone, that would remove his motive. So much for Aspen's currency of secrets.

"You sure ask a lot of questions," Leone noted.

"Oh, I'm just curious. Students dying isn't something anyone should get used to," I said, switching out the calibration tube for one of Leone's test samples.

Leone nodded absently, but I could tell his mind was elsewhere, deep in thought.

"You said only you and Julian were next up for the Advisor role. What about Aspen?"

Leone scoffed. "Aspen is a second year—Advisor roles are reserved for graduates. And despite how impressive Aspen thinks his curriculum vitae is, he's not eligible for another year."

I furrowed my brow. That eliminated an academic rivalry as a motive for Aspen and Julian, but there was still the issue of Julian's relationship with Sequoia, and the jealousy it might have stirred. But Aspen's theory on Leone seemed to hold true. It seemed like Leone and Julian hadn't seen eye to eye, either. But why would Aspen be helping me?

"Is something wrong?" Leone asked.

"No, no. The test is running as expected. Here, this is the spectrum of the first one," I said, handing him the output with the spectrum lines. It would be foreign to anyone but me, but I could teach just about anyone how to read it. "I'll just cross-reference them with my book, and then I can tell you the approximate age of the compounds in the sample. I can show you how it's done."

"How long will that take?"

"About an hour or so."

"Very well," Leone said, cracking open his book again. That was indication enough that he wanted me to do the analysis on my own.

We spent the next hour in silence—me pouring over the spectra of the two research samples, and Leone engrossed in his esoteric tome. It was a comfortable silence for the most part. There was a part of me—perhaps just my intuition—that urged me to trust Leone, and that almost disqualified him as a suspect. But I couldn't tell if that was just my bias, ruling him out because he was simply unsuspecting. As it stood, I didn't see a clear motive for why Leone would want Julian dead, unless I bought into the idea that it was still the philosophical differences between the two. I couldn't imagine Leone being that spiteful, or Julian that competitive. But I couldn't rule out Leone, or anyone else—not yet.

"It's done," I said, looking up from my notebook. "It looks like Sample B is a good five years older than Sample A, based on these spectral lines."

"Map dowsing wins. Interesting," Leone said, looking over the spectra I had marked up with my reference text. "I can use these in my research paper?"

"Certainly. I'd be happy to write up the methodology section for you," I said, closing the lid of the analyzer.

"That would be very nice, thank you," Leone said, opening his own notebook and jotting down the findings.

"Not to make this transactional, I would've helped you either way, but I do need advice on how to approach the Council," I said, readying my own pen and notebook.

"Oh, that. Of course, I'll tell you what I know," Leone said, pushing up the bridge of his glasses and turning toward me. "I've submitted a handful of proposals to them during my time at Foresyth, and about a dozen or so papers. All but one has been accepted, with varying degrees of critique," he started.

Curiosity flared—I wanted to press him about the one paper that hadn't been accepted—but I held my tongue. Better to focus on what mattered: getting my proposal approved. Of all the things to worry about, publication ranked lowest. With any luck, I'd be gone from Foresyth long before that ever became necessary.

"There are two things you should know about the Council. Number one—they value academic rigor. If you have a hypothesis, you better be willing to defend it. They don't like to waste time or resources on half-formed ideas," he said.

"Fair enough, I wouldn't either," I agreed.

"Secondly, they value magickal devotion. They can see right through those who aren't true believers."

My heart sank. To me, magick had always been a parlor trick at best—a relic of forgotten histories, conjured by people who lacked the science to explain the world around them. Would the Council sense that? Would they see through my skepticism and tear my carefully constructed cover apart, like a forbidden book marked for burning?

"I don't know exactly how they do it—but it's necessary and part of their line of work. They advise clients using magick, but if the clients don't fully believe their methodology, it's hard to take an Advisor's advice. That's why observance to the sacredness of magick is so important to them."

"Is there anything I could do to strengthen my . . . observance?" I asked.

"There isn't really a prescription for believing. It's rather binary—you do or you don't. But my best advice is to experience it for yourself. It's sometimes difficult for me too. I gravitate too much to the facts of the matter," Leone admitted.

And for the first time, I felt like Leone and I were two sides of the same coin. I searched the clear blue of his eyes and saw an intensity there I hadn't noticed before. Perhaps he only reserved it for the things he was truly obsessed with. But now he was sharing it with me.

"It's why I've gravitated toward fencing." He shrugged. "Because when you are faced with no choice but to fight—to *believe* in your own power over your doubts—that's when something magickal can happen."

I furrowed my brow, considering him. "That's right, the others mentioned you're a swordsman. Books, magick, swords—they are all methods of claiming power, are they not?"

"I suppose, but they are also conduits to truth." His fingers feathered the edge of his book, index finger still jutting in the middle to keep his place. "You have to get out of your head, sometimes. Go and apply your learnings in the real world to find the truth."

"Now you sound like Aspen."

"Him and I don't agree on many things, but about the practice of magick we do. It's an application, an art. It's true power lies outside of books," his tone changed, becoming softer. "Magick is dangerous, but I believe it needs people like us, grounded in reality, in order to control it."

I nodded. On that, at least, we were aligned: magick was dangerous—whether real or not. Even the mere suggestion of it could drive people to reckless, even deadly, ends. I had no doubt it played a role in Julian's death. The Meister wanted me to test Tarot in the waking world—to embody the archetypes, to trace the source of its power, whatever that might be.

If Julian's unraveling was entangled with magick, then I needed to understand its pull—not just how it worked, but how others *believed* it worked. Belief, after all, could be just as potent as truth. And if I could decipher the shape of that belief, it might bring me one step closer to uncovering what truly happened to him that night.

"Thanks, Leone. That's very insightful," I said, stacking my books up in a neat pile. It was almost time for lunch. Nina was still out, so I'd have to call for Aspen to help get us out of here.

"And one last thing you should know. There's a woman on the Council," he said in the same hushed tone. "She goes by the name of Ash-Shaytan Al-Ahmar—the red devil, in Arabic. She doesn't appear at every Council meeting, but if she does at yours, you ought to be careful. She wields a kind of old magick that even the other Council members are afraid of. Superficially she's a kind of guardian for the Council, but I suspect she plays an even more prominent role than that. Just be careful of her."

"Ash-Shaytan Al-Ahmar. I'll remember her," I said, nodding.

"Just hope she doesn't remember you."

The Acolyte and the Alchemist: Part IV

To Quill, first love was like first snow—gradual, then all at once.

Quill was mystified by the force of it. For the first time, he thirsted for something other than knowledge. At least knowledge had an end—in theory.

He knew he was doomed when love and knowledge became one and the same. He and Hamra spent their afternoons nestled in the stacks of the library, unraveling ideas, twisting them like thread between their fingers. When the light faded, they moved to their dormitories, spilling ink and coffee as they poured their thoughts onto the page.

Their minds intertwined, distinct yet inseparable.

And when they disagreed, they set their pens down and took the argument to bed.

"Do you ever wonder where it comes from?" Hamra asked one night, her voice a murmur against the hush of their room.

Quill twirled one of her curls between his fingers. "Hmm?" he hummed, kissing the bare slope of her shoulder.

"Power."

Quill furrowed his brows. "That's why I came here—to determine how knowledge transmutes to power. It's a form of alchemy, in my mind. The Advisors have perfected it. They draw it from books and apply it."

"Not all power comes from books." Hamra traced a slow line from his chin down to his throat, resting her fingertip over his breastbone. "Some of it comes from here."

Her eyes met his. He was already smiling.

"If that's true, then call me power-hungry."

Quill flipped her onto the mattress, pressing her into the sheets. He kissed down the column of her neck, then lower, where her pulse thrummed against his lips. The sound of it stuttered through his own chest, a rhythm he wanted to memorize.

She laughed, and at once, he thought of a sound to rival the beating of her heart.

"I never want to lose this," he murmured, his mouth finding hers again.

But as soon as the words left him, he remembered how cruel Fate could be.

"To be a detective is not merely to sift through clues, but to confront the facts in their entirety, even those you'd rather turn away from. It is to weave a narrative from evidence alone, forsaking comfort and conjecture in the pursuit of truth. And when every piece has fallen into place, when what stands before you is the undeniable and irrevocable, it leaves you with no choice but to accept it—no matter how inconvenient it may be."

—*The Journal of Daniel Blackburne*, 1906

Chapter 16: Bloodless and Barren

The following afternoon, I stepped into the garden in search of Sequoia. The air met me like a surprise—unseasonably warm and heavy for late January, as if spring had arrived out of turn. I inhaled deeply, the humidity clinging to my skin, urging me to shed my coat. After weeks cloistered within the House's stone confines, the open air felt disorienting, almost indulgent.

And yet, beneath the soft breath of early warmth, there lingered a quiet tension—a reminder that winter had not yet relinquished her claim. She was only waiting—patient and unseen—to play her final hand.

Sequoia was sitting on a bench, nibbling on a blackberry jam sandwich, the edges dripping sweetness. She looked deep in thought, but her eyes brightened when she noticed me approaching.

"Dahlia, come join me," she said licking her fingers, scooting over to make space. Her coat and scarf lay in a pile on the ground next to her.

"It's strangely warm today, but I think it might still rain; the air is so heavy," I noted.

"I love being out here, no matter the weather. Look, you can see the inklings of spring, ready to burst forth." I followed her gaze, but all I saw were dried rose bushes. Perhaps she had a keener eye than I did.

"I just wanted to check on you. See how things have been with Aspen since our reading. It was . . . a lot."

A pang of guilt twisted in my chest as I remembered how hard I'd pressed her for answers. Normally, I didn't lose sleep over extracting information—especially from someone I suspected. But with Sequoia, it felt different. Not like strategy, but trespass. And for the first time in a long while, it felt less like investigation . . . and more like crossing a line.

"You can say that again," she replied, splitting her jam-laden sandwich and offering me half.

When I shook my head, she tucked the other half of the sandwich back onto the napkin in her lap and gestured for me to sit. I settled beside her, our knees brushing lightly. Suddenly, I felt self-conscious, her effortless grace a mirror to my own rough edges. I fidgeted with the clasp of my necklace, trying to free it from the tangle of my hair.

"Let me do that for you," she offered. Before I could protest, her fingers moved gently through my tangled curls, gathering them to one side. Her hands brushed across the nape of my neck as she freed the clasp from my hair, her fingers moving with the fluid grace of flowing water. Her calm confidence was almost electric, charging the space between us.

"How do you do it?" I asked.

"The clasp?"

"No, being you. You move through the world like a feather through silk."

She giggled, and I felt a pang in my chest. I wanted to hear her laugh like that many more times.

"There's nothing I have that you don't, Dahlia," she said, meeting my gaze. "Many things are difficult for me, but tapping into my femineity has always been the easiest."

"That has been anything but easy for me," I confessed. "I wish I could be comfortable in my own skin, but it's like I need a costume for the world to accept me." It was the same way I felt with my bookstore patrons; they only saw the image I projected, never the person underneath.

I turned my gaze toward the garden, to the withered rose bushes bowed beneath the weight of winter. I could feel her eyes on me, steady and searching, but I couldn't bring myself to meet them.

"I see you, Dahlia. Costume or not," she mused.

I turned to her, and her eyes were like two pools of caramel, warm and inviting, pulling me closer. I wanted to trust her; I wanted to believe that we could truly be friends. Until Foresyth, I'd rarely had peers of my own. It had always just been Gabriel and I, tucked away in the alcoves. But these students were different from Gabriel—they didn't just want to read stories and myths, they wanted to *live* in them, create new ones of their own, even. It was simultaneously exhilarating and unsettling.

"I actually came here to give you something."

"Me?"

I reached into my coat pocket and pulled out a small wooden box. "I just fixed it up recently; it was missing a gear. I thought you might like it."

Sequoia took it from my hands, examining it from every angle. Finally, she opened it, and an airy musical tune began to play. She squealed in delight.

"A music box, how lovely. Thank you, Dahlia."

"It's the least I could do . . ." I drifted off. The guilt of my reading was still hanging heavy in my chest, despite having helped her on her Druid paper. The music box didn't erase the ache in my chest, but I did feel a little bit lighter seeing her in such delight.

"Nonsense. You've already done so much for me. I'm glad to know I'm no longer alone in this House. It can be so lonely, being around people all day but not having them see who you really are. But now, neither of us are alone," Sequoia said, closing the music box and taking my hand. "I'm glad you're here."

And this time, I didn't instinctively pull back. Instead, I let my fingers interlace with hers. We stayed there, holding hands for a while. Despite the circumstances, a part of me was glad to be here, too.

*

After lunch, I made my way back down to the lab. Most students frequented the library after meals, but I preferred studying alone. Aside from the occasional visit from Nina, who sometimes worked on her taxidermy, I had the lab to myself. It felt like a sanctuary, a place where I could think and study in peace.

Today, I wanted to set Julian's case aside, if only to focus on the numerous research topics I'd been assigned. I had handed in my runic paper outline to the Meister, but now there was the looming Council meeting. Falling behind on my research tasks would only weaken my cover, and I couldn't give Aspen any more reason to suspect that I was a detective.

I stacked the books from my satchel in the order I planned to read them. Even though I could manage nearly a hundred pages an hour, it would take most of the afternoon to get through the stack I'd set for today. Preparing for the Council meant immersing myself in the history and lore of *The Book of Skorn*—the rare text Julian had been researching.

If academic rigor was what they valued, I was determined to deliver it. The magickal devotion, however, was where I was at a loss. How could I experience something I didn't believe in? Perhaps I'd ask Nina for advice when she returned.

A few hours passed as I combed through the books, jotting down notes. I found a steady rhythm and was content to stay there for the rest of the evening. But just as I was getting hungry for dinner, Nina came bolting down the stairs, several dead pheasants in hand.

"Dahlia, oh thank goodness you're down here!" she exclaimed, her excitement evident as she dropped the pheasants right onto my workstation.

"Hey, you're going to get that all over my notes," I said, pushing the feathered creatures aside. I looked up at Nina and noticed she was covered in dirt. Dark smears of mud ran down her cheeks; some was even caked in her hair.

"What on earth have you been up to?"

"Field research," she replied, plucking the pheasants off my desk and moving them to her brine baths. "That card scrying trick of yours worked. I finally found those grounds! Aspen is going to eat his words."

"Do you find them dead, or . . . do you kill them?" I asked, wrinkling my nose at the birds. "Actually, never mind. I'd rather not know."

"Once I put these away, you have to come with me. You have to see it for yourself," she said, her voice high with excitement.

"Out there? It's raining. And we aren't allowed out after dark. Plus, it's almost dinner time." I began stacking my books back into my bag. I hadn't spent much time outside since arriving at Foresyth save for this morning with Sequoia. The weather had been inhospitable, and Richard had mentioned that landscaping wouldn't start until March. "Maybe tomorrow, when it's light out."

Nina grabbed me by the shoulders and shook me. Despite her lanky build, there was a surprising strength in her grip. Her short hair was plastered to her head with mud, but her eyes were wild and determined.

"No, we have to go tonight. I need to make sure what I saw is real."

There was something in her tone that made me uneasy. What did she mean, *real*? What had she seen?

"Fine, but let's have dinner first. You missed lunch, so I know you must be starving. Besides, if we sneak out after dinner, it'll raise less suspicion than if we're both missing now."

Her grip loosened as she considered. "Fine, but you promise we'll go out afterward?"

"Yes, I promise," I replied, already wishing I'd held my tongue.

*

Dinner was uneventful. Richard was serving a vegetable dish, so luckily there was no risk of eating pheasants. Everyone was at the dinner table, including Leone and the Trees. I made easy conversation talking about the experiments Leone and I ran the other day.

"It worked like a charm. I didn't believe it at first, but that box works like magick. Plus, Dahlia's analysis itself was impressive," Leone said, raising his wine glass to me. He was in a jovial mood after I had resolved his timeline dispute. A swell of pride rose in my chest. This feeling of acceptance was new to me.

"How do you know it worked?" Aspen injected. "I mean, how do you know the sample that Dahlia said is the oldest, is actually the oldest? There's no way to verify it."

"That's why it shouldn't be the only method of dating. Leone has other conventional ways of dating the maps, such as the ink colors used or other markers," I defended. Why was he always so contrarian?

I stole a glance at Sequoia, who sat quietly twirling her fork through a nest of spaghetti, her expression unreadable. Despite the closeness we'd begun to share, something always shifted when Aspen entered the room—a subtle distance, as if I were intruding on a language only the two of them spoke.

I needed to make progress on the case—not just to find the truth, but to fulfill my promise. To get her away from him.

"Why don't you just run an experiment where you already know the answer? Date two pieces of paper that are separated by a known time period to confirm the method works," Aspen continued. "That way you can be sure that it works."

I hated to admit it, but it was actually a good idea. An additional control. But it was also adding to my pile of work, which was already overflowing. Was that his intent, to overwhelm me with more work so I would stop following him as a suspect? I eyed him carefully.

"I'd need two pieces of paper with dated ink."

"That should be easy. We all keep yearly journals don't we? I know you have a few to spare." He winked. He was referencing Julian's journals just to irk me.

"I have my own I could test on," I said, ending the conversation there. The rest of the dinner went on without further qualm, but I couldn't help but notice the rhythmic shaking of Nina's leg under the table. She had washed and changed for dinner, but there was a nervous energy about her. Whatever was out there, I wasn't looking forward to seeing it.

*

"Are you sure we need to do this tonight?" I asked, my last plea to get out of whatever Nina had in store for us.

I could easily say no to her, go up to my room, and close the door, but I'd be alienating her, after the friendship and trust she had shown me the past few weeks. Including access to her lab.

But hadn't Aspen said I ought to suspect her? Maybe this would be a way to let her guard down so I could ask her about the night Julian died.

Nina nodded, her spikey strands of dark hair swaying across her shoulders.

"Very well," I said, stepping out from the threshold of the House. It was starting to rain, and the air was cooling. It actually felt pleasant against my hot face.

I started after Nina, tracing her steps along the small dirt trail that went around the edge of the House.

"Here. It's to the left." Nina's mouth twitched upright, and a tiny pang of worry formed in the pit of my stomach. Maybe it hadn't been such a good idea to follow Nina. But a part of me was glad to be out of the House and didn't want to go back in—not just yet. My mind felt clearer somehow.

"Are you going to tell me at least where we're going?" I asked, but Nina was too far ahead of me.

"Northeast quadrant," she sang.

I ran after her as she slipped through a crack in the iron fencing that circumscribed the House, sucking in my breath to fit through the rails. We were definitely not supposed to be out here.

We traced the side of the forest facing campus for a while and then turned to enter deeper into the thicket. Having completely deviated from the path against the railing, we whacked our way through bushes of dried sweetgum and poplar as leaves squished beneath our feet.

"Are you sure this is okay, Nina?" I asked, swiping dead branches from my eyeline. "I don't see any trail."

"It's here don't worry; I know my way around these woods. Trust me," she replied, motioning me to follow her.

We walked through the wet foliage for another quarter mile until we approached a tall oak tree with a single, faded white marking painted onto its stucco truck. "This is it. This way." Nina disappeared behind the trees and I lost sight of her.

"Nina?" I called.

I rounded the tree, careful not to trip on the thick roots that broke from the soil underneath. The lights from the House had faded and the only source of illumination were the thin slivers of moonlight that fell through the dead branches overhead. An almost imperceptible buzzing was starting to bud from the base of my skull.

"Nina?" There was a slight shake in my voice.

Behind the tree there was a narrow path, just wide enough for one hiker to follow, tracing uphill. I followed the worn-down trail, feeling the blood rushing to my legs from the strain.

"This isn't funny, Nina. Where are you?" I called again, hunching over.

I heard a faint rustle of tree leaves behind me and turned around, but there was no one there. I continued the steep climb until I finally saw a clearing at the top and picked up my pace. The buzzing started getting louder as I followed the rustling shadows. My legs were burning and aching for me to stop, but then I saw the silhouette of a lone figure at the top of the hill.

I broke into a sprint.

"Nina!"

I was gasping in greedy breaths, expelling plumes of moist air once I got to the top of the hill. I braced my hands against the tops of my knees and lifted my head toward the figure. The rain had stopped but the ground was wet, and my heels sunk into the mud. I lifted my gaze. Nina was standing at the edge of what seemed to be a circle of barren dirt, inexplicably dry. I had the sudden realization of how strange that was—to find an empty plot of dry land like that in the middle of a wild and thick forest. It had stopped raining just a minute ago.

"This is it, Dahlia. This is what I wanted to show you!" Nina turned around to face me. In the clearing, unabashed from the trees, the moon shone brightly, and I could see a wild glint in Nina's dark eyes as a smile curled on her lips. The buzzing in my ears had turned into a fever pitch.

"This is the Devil's Tramping Ground," she said. "Nothing can grow here in this circle. Local legend says that Satan himself visits this circle and tramps it down bare with his hellish hooves, plotting and planning his sinister deeds against humanity. Everything that's laid to rest here in this circle is said to disappear." Nina's eyes sparkled as she recounted the story. A jolt of fear shot up through my ribcage.

"Nina, I think we should—"

"But it's a misnomer, you see. It's not the *Devil's* Tramping Ground." Nina shoved her hand into her pocket and fumbled for something.

I walked over to her slowly, wanting to grab her by the shoulder and lead her away from the circle before she got any closer. I wanted to run back down the hill and down to the safety and warmth of the House. We weren't supposed to be out here.

The bevel of a shiny pocketknife caught in the moonlight as Nina unfurled it from her pocket. She crouched down low onto her hinds like a dog and shifted the hair away from her face before she ungloved her other hand.

"I thought it was really strange that I kept finding dead animals around this area. But now I know why. This circle—it doesn't belong to the Devil." Nina toyed with the blade of the knife, twisting the point at the center of her palm.

This wasn't the dark pixie Nina I knew who got excited over brine baths and monster lore; no, this version was darker. *So* much darker.

I watched in shock as she plunged the point deeper into her hand, breaking skin. Rivulets of blood began pouring down her wrist and she guided her hand toward the inside of the barren circle.

"Nina!" I called, my voice catching in my throat.

The droplets of blood fell to the land and instantly sizzled on contact with the ground, as if they had been poured directly over a hot stove. All that remained of the blood rose into a trail of hot steam above Nina's head. I watched in horror and fascination as Nina squeezed her palm, sending thick beads to the ground that instantly evaporated back up as mist.

A few lone drops had fallen outside of the circle before she had directed her palm over it, and those were soaking into the ground, forming inky black spots.

"This isn't the Devil's grounds, because it is *Sophia's,* our Shattered Mother's," Nina said. "All material flesh in this circle ascends back to its spiritual realm." She said this as she traced the skyline with her eyes, resting her gaze at the bright moon.

Nina then pulled her arm away from over the barrier and redressed it with her glove. I stared up at her, completely frozen.

Sophia. The name was familiar.

I stared at the inky droplets of blood that were left outside of the circle. All those times when I had read for other people—when I had hammered into them steadily until I created a fracture—I never knew what it was like on the other side.

Until now.

Something fissured—not in the ritual, but in me. A hairline split in the façade I had always trusted as reality. Magick was no longer theoretical. It had become *physical* as soon as Nina's blood disappeared.

I shook my head, stunned, but the image refused to vanish—Nina's blood, disappearing the instant it touched the circle. I opened my mouth to speak, to demand an explanation, but no words came. Only silence, thick and unyielding, pressed at the edges of my thoughts.

"Come on Dahlia. Didn't I tell you it would be *amazing*?"

Nina's arm came around me and pulled me up to my feet. My legs were numb, my muscles weak. Without her, I'd have sat like that all night, staring at the dried droplets outside of the circle contrasted by the land within—barren and bloodless.

*

I didn't know exactly how I had made it back to the House, but I must have walked back because my Oxfords were caked in mud. I slipped them off at the door and walked to the fireplace in my wet socks, not caring for the imprints I left behind. I plopped myself next to the fire, and slowly, very slowly, began to thaw myself from the outside in.

Nina came into the room at some point, but I didn't acknowledge her. I was trying to make sense of what I had just witnessed.

It had to be a trick of the eye. It was dark, I was tired . . . the blood must have landed somewhere—soaked into the soil and was lost in the shadows. I clung to these explanations, turning them over in my mind like a rosary. But deep down, beneath the layers of logic and denial, I knew exactly what I had seen. And there was no undoing it.

I had seen *magick*. And it had shaken me.

Hours seemed to stretch on before I finally found my voice. Nina was curled up on the chaise, scribbling furiously in her notebook. A cup of tea appeared next to me, and I took it, letting the warmth ground me. I broke my rule of no tea tonight; I needed to warm my bones. And besides, I was the one asking questions tonight.

"What was that, Nina? You said the Circle was the Devil's Tramping Ground, and then you amended it to *Sophia's*. Who is Sophia?" I looked over my cup of steaming hot tea to her.

"I keep forgetting you haven't been Initiated."

I frowned. "Sequoia mentioned that. Would Sophia be there at my Initiation?" I sat up from the chair and bore my gaze into her.

Nina chuckled before saying, "No, no. Sophia isn't a person, she's an emanation, from the one true Source. The one we pray to for our magick—from where all other powers are derived." She looked away. "But I've already said too much—you should talk to the Meister. I can't really say more about her until . . ."

"I've been Initiated." I sighed, falling back deeper into the couch. More layers, more dead ends. I was getting annoyed by the lack of answers. Who was this Sophia figure, and why hadn't I heard of her? If she was connected to *The Book of Skorn*, surely, I'd have read about her before.

"So, you all do believe in the same thing," I said to no one in particular in the room. "I thought this was a rigorous academic institution, but it's just a cult." It stung to say the words, but I felt foolish for having believed anything otherwise. I had even teased Gabriel when he had made the assertion. And now I was falling for it too . . .

The students, their intellectual discourse, the fervor with which they studied—it had almost convinced me. Shame permeated through me in red hot streaks. I had been so desperate for a sense of belonging that I had let myself become convinced that Foresyth was an elite academic institution that had chosen me. So desperate that I allowed myself to let go of logic.

Neither of those things were remotely true—this wasn't an academic institution, nor had I been chosen. At least, not for the reasons I thought.

"I don't know why you're getting so upset. Did you just miss the part where my blood disappeared upon contact with the ground up there?"

"No, I didn't miss that part. I just . . ." I buried my hands in my face, "I just wish I could figure this out." It was foolish of me to break down like this in front of Nina—in front of anyone—but my exhaustion started to drown me. Nothing made sense to me anymore.

"I get it. I was overwhelmed when I first got here, too," Nina said with a reassuring smile. "But you're doing fine, really. You're meeting the Council this week—that's no small thing. It means they're taking you seriously."

It was comforting that she only suspected I was overwhelmed by the academics. "And nobody knows about Initiation until it happens, so don't feel too bad. It'll happen when the Meister thinks you're ready—and then you'll know everything."

Know everything. If the Meister really wanted me to solve Julian's murder, why wasn't I already made aware of everything? The secrecy and lies were enough to make my head spin. I looked down at the locket on my neck, the one my father had given me the year he died.

"Was there a particular reason you showed me the Tramping Ground?" I asked. I was too exhausted to be slyer about my questioning. But as it stood, I didn't know why Nina was letting me in on her secret. If secrets were currency around here, why was she sharing hers?

"I wanted proof that I wasn't going mad. But by your sorry state, it seems like it must have been real." She shrugged.

Real. I was the least certain of what was real anymore.

"It's going to entirely shake the Spring Symposium. I can't wait," she mused, back to scribbling in her notebook.

I forced myself to return Nina's smile with one of my own—thin, but passable. I couldn't afford to worry her, and I certainly couldn't risk revealing any more of what I was feeling.

Emotions were dangerous here. They made you visible. And visibility meant vulnerability.

"Thanks, Nina. For letting me in." My exhaustion was settling into me like paralysis. I stretched my legs out and set my cup of tea to the side. It was almost too heavy for my weak grasp, and I splashed a few drops setting it down.

"I should go to bed," I said, standing.

"Goodnight, Dahlia," she said, hesitating on the last word. "And just for the record, we don't all believe in the same thing."

"The history of the Council of Foresyth is veiled in obscurity, yet it is believed to have come into being three years after the consecration of Foresyth Conservatory, coinciding with the graduation of its first Advisor. As the Conservatory's academic contributions flourished, a governing body was deemed essential to discern which findings might be safely shared with the world and which must remain in secrecy. Today, the Council stands as the initial arbiter of what may be published, determining what knowledge is deemed fit for public consumption. Anecdotal accounts from former students suggest that only half of submitted papers ever reach publication; the rest are sequestered within Foresyth's private archives. Beyond guiding the flow of knowledge, the Council holds the esteemed power of appointing Advisors—a distinguished cadre of Foresyth graduates entrusted with applying their knowledge beyond the Conservatory's walls, guiding figures of influence through decisions that may shape the world's future. Additionally, they hold the authority to dismiss any student who does not meet Foresyth's high standards—a power they have not hesitated to wield."

—*Foresyth Conservatory: A Complete History, Unabridged*, 1891

Chapter 17: The Council

The following morning I woke up with a stiff neck. It had been the longest uninterrupted sleep I'd had since my arrival at Foresyth. My mouth felt like it was filled with cotton, prompting me to reach for the water on my nightstand. Blinking, my eyes scanned the walls of my bedchamber. Being outdoors the previous night had emphasized the oppressive nature of the House's walls. Were they collapsing, or was my mind deceiving me? They appeared to have an unsettling slant.

I blinked away my morning haze, looking through the window. An overcast sky obscured the forest, and a murmur of thunder threatened in the distance. Beyond the hidden tree line, I knew there was still that barren plot of land. I buried my head back into my pillow, squeezing out the memory of Nina and her hand dripping blood.

The memory of *magick*.

In the weeks that I'd been here, I felt like I'd only unearthed more questions about this place than answers. And I still was not anywhere closer to finding out who killed Julian.

You've felt like a fraud your whole life. This is your opportunity to discover the truth. About Julian and what you're capable of, a voice resounded in the back of my head.

The Meister had said something similar to me, the first night we met. Failure, I thought, is what I was capable of. My father would have been disappointed in me.

I untangled my locket from the back of my neck, coaxing myself out of bed. Slipping into a black sweater and trousers, forgoing the dress code, I readied myself for the day ahead.

The Council meeting was this evening. If answers were what I sought, then that's where I would find them.

*

Circle that night featured Aspen and his doctrine on political effigies. I stopped myself from rolling my eyes on more than one occasion. I had too many things on my mind to entertain Aspen's self-righteous research prompts. As Circle concluded Nina reached across her chair and tapped me on the back.

"Good luck tonight. I'm sure you'll be great." She smiled and I returned the gesture.

Out of the corner of my eye, I could see Aspen stealing a glance at us. I kept my eye on him as he and Sequoia left the room. Was he still warning me about Nina or Leone? Ignoring his gaze, I held back while the other students exited the room. The person I had to talk to wasn't any of the students. It was the Meister.

"We need to talk," I said to the Meister, as soon as the other students had left. "You're not telling me everything," I said.

The Meister looked up from his cane, green eyes sparkling in the firelight.

"I do regret that I've been traveling and have missed our mentorship meetings. Perhaps we can catch up on our way to the Council tonight. Have you made any progress?"

"You're not answering my question. You knew about the lion-serpent, about *The Book of Skorn.* Why didn't you tell me, when it could be connected to Julian's case?" I asked pointedly.

"As far as I understand, you're still a student Ms. Blackburne. I can't give you special privileges beyond that, or else I'd jeopardize the sanctity of the very institution I'm trying to protect."

When I was absolutely certain no one could hear us in the room, I closed the door and said, "You *hired* me. I'm a student here as a cover. Or are you forgetting that?" My tone was raspy, hushed but still coarse with indignation.

"I think you're doing very well as a student here, as well. Wouldn't you say? Your peers respect and admire you. I was very transparent about wanting to keep you here once all this mess with Julian was resolved." I had never heard those words, *respect and admire*, in that context. I ignored how they created a sickening lightness in my chest. As much as I respected him upholding the standards of his institution, murder should allow him an exception to giving me full disclosure.

"Who is Sophia?" I said through gritted teeth.

The Meister's eyes turned black as coal. He struck his cane down on the wooden floor and the sound reverberated through me. I shuddered, stepping backwards. "You are not to speak that name in this House unless you do so with *reverence*. Do you understand?"

I nodded, but the fire inside me was still raging on. "I need to know everything so I can help you. So I can help Julian," I said, softer.

"In due time. When you're ready, you will," the Meister said, striding over to the door. "Now, you best turn your attention to the Council. We mustn't keep them waiting."

"You're accompanying me?"

"Indeed. I'm presenting you. Follow me," the Meister replied, leading me down the hallway.

"Does the Council convene here?" I motioned to the House.

The Meister paused briefly before responding. "Occasionally, but not often. They choose different venues for their meetings. Tonight, it's in town."

He retrieved his coat from the rack, and I followed suit, adjusting my black coat. I dabbed at a mud stain on the sleeve.

"Wishing you both a pleasant evening," Richard bid us farewell, holding the door open as we exited.

It would be far from pleasant if I had anything to say about it, I thought.

Stepping outside, I drew in a deep breath of the night air, feeling the tension in my shoulders dissipate. We walked down the path to the awaiting motorcar at the gate. Climbing in, I took care not to soil my freshly-polished pair of Oxfords.

Though I felt a wave of relief as the House receded behind me, a new knot had begun to form in my stomach. I was confident in my grasp of *The Book of Skorn*—its symbology, its historical context—but how could I possibly demonstrate a genuine dedication to magick? Until yesterday, nothing had come close to convincing me it was real. And now that it had . . . I wasn't sure which was more unsettling—the doubt, or the belief.

"Are you all right, Ms. Blackburne?" the Meister inquired, closing the car door.

"Quite," I replied. "Is there anything I should be aware of before meeting the Council? Anything you're *willing* to share?" I couldn't hold back the sourness from my voice. If the Meister wouldn't give me answers, then I'd force the Council to.

The Meister offered a gentle smile. "You're well-prepared to meet the Council. I trust Leone assisted you in your preparations?"

"He did," I confirmed slowly. "He mentioned proving my devotion to the Council. You know I'm not . . ." I hesitated. Worry creaked into my throat. I needed to convince them of my magickal devotion. How was I going to get answers from the Council if they didn't deem me worthy of being a student at Foresyth?

"Don't concern yourself with that. They have methods of assessing your potential. It's beyond your control. This is a test, Dahlia, but not the one you think it is," he said.

I furrowed my brows. What kind of test was I walking into, exactly?

We traveled the remainder of the journey in silence, watching the scenery pass by outside the window—first the dense foliage rushing by, then the twinkling lights of the town. When we reached the town center, the driver stopped the car and opened the door. We stepped out and I braced myself from the wind with my coat.

"It's this way," the Meister said.

I followed him through the narrow alleyway, hemmed in by imposing stone structures on either side. It was clear we were using the rear entrance of the building we were about to enter. Keeping pace, I trailed after him, the rhythmic tapping of his cane guiding me along the uneven cobblestones. He halted abruptly, facing a weathered wooden door with an iron grate. With a practiced melody of taps, he unlocked it without touching the handle.

"How did you do that?" I whispered.

"Magick," he replied with a smirk. "Let's not dawdle; we're already behind schedule."

Descending the spiral staircase, I gripped the railing tightly as we bore deeper into the earth. The air grew heavy and musty, indicating our subterranean location. Finally reaching the bottom, we traversed a dimly-lit tunnel until we reached a grey tiled door. The Meister rapped out a different sequence of knocks, and the door swung open.

Entering the dimly illuminated chamber, a chill traced down my spine, a mix of anticipation and unease. The scent of damp stone and freshly disturbed earth filled the air, wrapping around me like a cloak of foreboding.

In the center of the room stood a circular stone table, adorned with Nordic symbols that seemed to pulse with an otherworldly energy. Eight shadowy figures encircled it, their features obscured by deep hoods, exuding an aura of ceremonial sacredness.

Seated among them was a woman of commanding presence. Her scarlet cape spilled around her like a river of blood, a stark contrast to her dark complexion. Her gaze was unrelenting—piercing through me, peeling back my defenses as if to unearth every secret I'd ever tried to bury.

I shuddered. She was certainly the woman that Leone had mentioned.

Approaching the table, my heart pounded with trepidation, yet I refused to yield to fear. I had come too far now. I stared back at her with an equally intense gaze. The chamber was cloaked in perpetual twilight, the darkness pressing in from all sides. A solitary raven perched on the table before the woman in red, its ebony feathers ruffling as it cocked its head. Its eyes traced my every movement.

The Meister followed behind, motioning for me to take a seat at the stone table. With a resolve born of necessity, I took my place, meeting the woman's stare with determination. I was going to get that deck from them, and I was going to get answers.

"Councilmen, Al-Ahmar. *Sub rosa,*" the Meister hummed. He said the woman's name with an air of discomfort.

The group spoke the Latin words back in unison. "Thank you for allowing this intrusion."

"It is no intrusion," the head Councilman spoke. "You are always welcome, Renate," he bowed, and the others followed the gesture.

The subtle deference to the Meister pricked the hairs on my arm. Perhaps he was more politically powerful than I had assumed. And I had just all but yelled at him an hour ago.

"Thank you, Gerald. I would like to present to you and the Council body Foresyth's newest addition, Dahlia Blackburne. She is lineage to Daniel Blackburne—his *daughter*, in fact," he said, turning to me.

My heart sank into my chest at the mention of my father's name.

My father wasn't just investigating this place—he had been a student here. My cheeks burned. I stole a glance at the Meister who nodded me on. I faced the Council, trying not to trip on my words.

"Thank you for allowing me at your meeting," I said, raising my chin higher. "I'm here to submit a research proposal and request access to an item from the archives."

One by one, the hoods of the Councilmen fell back, revealing a sea of faces. I swept my gaze across the room, meeting each of their eyes in turn. They were of varying ages—the youngest, seated at the far end of the table, could have been only a few years my senior. Only one figure remained cloaked: the woman in the scarlet cape. She alone kept her hood drawn.

"I know who you are, daughter of Blackburne," one of the older men said. "Yes, I recognized those eyes. Your father was quite the pupil."

My stomach lurched. Not only had my father also been a student here, but he'd left an impression on a Council member.

"Yes, it was quite disappointing when he didn't stay on to become an Advisor. But, given the circumstances, it was best for him to leave," he said, looking up to the red woman. Her features, still shrouded by the cape, remained unknown to me. Did she know my father, too?

"You've come to request the deck, have you?" the young man on the edge asked. He had a slight nasally tone that reminded me of Leone.

"Yes, I've come to request the Skorn deck. For my research project this term," I said. *And for investigating Julian's death.*

"It's the middle of the academic year—the Symposium is mere months away. I don't see the point in starting a new project now. It would be quite a waste of time," said another man near the middle. I swallowed hard.

"The body at Foresyth has discussed it in Circle, and we have concluded that the timeline would be adequate for Ms. Blackburne's project. She intends to do a first-principle's study on the origins of its power," the Meister interjected. I sent him an appreciative nod.

"I am a knowledgeable reader—I have much previous expertise to rely on for this study. I will have plenty of time to complete the study by the Spring Symposium," I said.

"I've heard of your reputation back at Greenwich," the voice under the red cloak said. It was smooth and low, like a purr. "You've been acting as an Advisor without training, have you?"

The woman in red lowered her hood slowly, so now I could see her face. She was ageless—she could be my age, or someone twenty years older. I had no way of telling. Her cheeks had the supple curvature of youth, but her eyes were deep-set and framed by shadows, as if they had seen many stories unfold. She stepped away from her seat and took the three steps down to the circular round table at which I sat.

Something about her tone told me that I wouldn't be getting answers from her or the Council members tonight. At least, not the answers I was interested in.

"I am not concerned whether or not you have the *knowledge* to use the artifact appropriately. I question whether or not you have magickal *connection* to tap into its powers," she said. I sensed the undercurrent of judgement in her words as they rippled through me.

I thought quickly. How was I going to prove my connection to magick? How could she even tell if there was one? I swallowed, an idea emerging. It was risky, but it might be the only way to prove to her that I believed in magick.

"I can do a reading for you," I said. "With the cards."

Some of the Councilmen gasped, others let out a chuckle, but most fell silent. I recalled something that Aspen had mentioned on my first night at Foresyth about magick being an intimate affair. Not something you offered across the dinner table.

Only the red woman did not make any noise. She smiled instead.

"You'll have to excuse Dahlia—she's not yet accustomed to our ways," the Meister started.

"It's fine, Renate." The red woman sent him a glare. "You are offering me a reading? You must be Blackburne's daughter for you are both foolish and brave." Her words coiled around me like an asp. "Given your determination, I will humor you. But you will not be reading for me as that goes against our rules at the Council, so, I will read for you. After all, Tarot and similar divination techniques are all decision-making tools. We'll let the cards decide whether or not they want to belong to you. Is this acceptable?" She looked straight at me, waiting for my answer.

"It sounds like a fair appraisal," the Meister said, but his tone didn't quite match his words.

"I was asking her," the red woman repeated. The deference he wielded from the Council clearly did not extend to her.

I nodded without taking my eyes off the woman, but my stomach dropped. I had never had my cards read for me. I hated being on this side of the table, the side with no control. I couldn't control the narrative of the cards. I just had to hope that the red woman had already made up her mind to give me the cards, and that decision would be reflected in the reading.

I shifted my gaze to the Meister, and he nodded in approval.

The red woman came closer to my table and took out the other chair tucked into it. She materialized the Skorn deck out of her cape, like she had known exactly what I had come for before I entered the room. I stared at the cards, their glossy golden backs casting a glare. Would the cards choose me, or would she?

She brought the cards up high, close to her chin and let them fall, rippling to her other hand, like they were all strung together by a string. I had to admit, the method was pleasing to the eye, but did a poor job of intermixing the cards. Was the woman planning on using this sleight of hand to keep the order of the deck as it was?

As if she read my mind, she switched her technique, letting her hands instead weave the cards into a farro shuffle. It was my preferred technique of choice as it statistically had the highest chance of randomization.

"Pleased?" she asked, her lips in a crescent shape.

"Of course," I said, biting my lip. I had to be aware of my micro-reactions. She was no doubt reading me, just as I read others. I couldn't give her anything she could use against me.

"I'm going to charge the cards with your energy for you, now. This should only feel like a pinch," she said, placing them flat down. What did she mean? I typically had my inquirers do this part to help coax them into a suggestive state.

But then I felt it. It was a pinch like she said, right in between my shoulder blades, that made me erect my spine taller in my seat. My hand instinctively reached for my back, but nothing was there.

"It shouldn't hurt that much," she said.

I blinked at her. How was her power of suggestion so strong over me? I closed my eyes and steadied my breath. I had to sit very still and relax. I couldn't give away anything. She's already made up her mind about me, likely, and I needed to just remain calm. I'm sure even if I didn't get the cards, I could do my research project on something else. And besides, I had plenty of other clues to investigate regarding Julian's death.

She plucked a card from the top of the deck and set it down. "You recently had a magickal awakening," she said, staring down at the card of Judgement. The card looked identical to the regular Rider-Waite-Smith deck that I used, save for the emblem of the lion-serpent at the top of the card. "You are skeptical about magick, just as your father was, but you've recently seen it before your very eyes."

I swallowed. How was it possible that the red woman could know that?

"You're here to discover a secret," she said, plucking another card from the deck. I stared down at the High Priestess. "Something you have a special skill or talent for unearthing. You're not here for magick."

I stared blankly at her, willing my expression into stone. My heart began to palpitate, but I would not let it show on my face.

She pulled another card, and I strained not to hold my breath. I forced myself to inhale through my nose. I didn't look down on it until she leaned back, as if deciding how to interpret it. "Hm. The cards are saying that despite your lack of truthfulness, you have a purpose here at Foresyth. A divine one." I finally broke my gaze from hers and looked down to see the Hanged Man.

I let out a breath.

We both knew that her interpretation of the Hanged Man was wrong. It didn't mean divine purpose. The last time I had pulled that card, I interpreted it as Julian's death. Did she also interpret it that way, but was refusing to say it in front of the Council? The way she was seated, with her back to the Council, and the cards stacked on top of one another, it would be impossible for them to see the cards. They must trust her.

But then, why was she lying?

The red woman picked up the upturned cards and shuffled them back into the deck. "The cards have spoken. They are willing to be loaned to Dahlia Blackburne," the woman said as she stood.

I let out a quiet sigh.

"But on one condition. You'll report your findings to me—personally," the red woman said. And based on the tremor in her tone, I knew at that moment that she knew what the Hanged Man represented. She didn't want to know the result of my research; she wanted to know my findings on who killed Julian.

I nodded in acceptance of her terms.

"If the Al-Ahmar votes in favor of loaning the deck to Dahlia Blackburne, then so do I," said the eldest Council man in the middle of the line. The others stood and an echo of "I's" followed.

"The deck is yours," the red woman said, handing me the cards in their sheath. As I took them in my hand, an undeniable jolt of energy shot down my arm, as if the cards possessed a heating source of their own. My eyes widened, and the red woman smirked.

"I wish you the best of luck on your research," she said before returning to the podium.

And with that, the Meister and I quickly left the Council chamber the same way we entered.

"The deeper I go, the more I realize that power at Foresyth is not simply earned—it is consumed. It draws from something deeper than knowledge or skill. It hungers. I feel it in my bones, and though I reach for it, there is a cost. I've seen it in their eyes—those who have tapped into this well before me. What have they lost, I wonder? And what will I lose, when the time comes?"

—*Julian Earhardt's journal,* dated February 20th, 1919, translation by Dahlia Blackburne

Chapter 18: Druid Like Me

I arrived back at Foresyth a few minutes past midnight. As I entered, the House greeted with its usual creaks and groans, and I carefully avoided the rotting board of the entrance steps. I had become accustomed to the sounds of the House. It was as if it had a life of its own, breathing and trembling, just as its inhabitants were prone to do. My knees ached from the drive, and I stretched them along the lanes of the hallway, readying myself for bed.

I had secured the Skorn deck and could count the day as a success. But still, thoughts of my father, the Council, and the red woman wrapped around me like a cloak of mist—ephemeral and difficult to grasp. My father hadn't been investigating Foresyth as I thought.

He had been *attending* it.

A migraine was budding at the base of my skull, and I rubbed the sensitive place with my thumb. As I rounded the corner up to the stairwell, I saw light pouring out from the reading room. Who would still be up at this hour?

The floor creaked again, and a backlit shadow appeared in the frame of the door.

"You made it back," the shadow said.

"You would have preferred I didn't?" I said to Aspen.

"Why do you antagonize me so?" he said, stepping into the hallway. I could hear the sly smile forming on his lips and saw a flicker of his thumb caressing the edge of his mouth. He was wearing casual slacks and a crisp white button-down shirt with sleeves rolled up to his elbow. Effortless, but calculated. Like everything about him.

"You know why," I said quietly and against my better judgement. I was tired and just wanted to retreat to bed. I'd had enough duplicity for one day.

He pretended not to hear me. "So, you got the deck, then?" he said, crossing his arms. He narrowed his eyes, studying me.

"Of course I got the deck," I said, crossing my arms back.

"I didn't doubt you. It's just that the Council is known for being a bit . . . skeptical."

"They didn't give me any trouble," I said, yawning. "I'm headed to bed; you can interrogate me tomorrow."

"I was just going up myself." He turned back to the reading room. "Let me just get these lights," he said.

When he flicked the switch off, the entire House turned dark. My body tensed and it took a few seconds for my eyes to adjust.

"You can hold my hand if you need help up the stairs," Aspen mused, no doubt noticing my hesitation.

"I'm fine," I said and started up without him. I blinked my eyes into focus and found the steps.

As we ascended the stairs, the sound of rushing water became audible. It sounded like someone was drawing a bath. At the top of the staircase, I flicked on the hallway lights as my Oxfords squished the carpet underneath.

Water was spreading in a slow, gleaming pool across the floor, seeping from beneath one of the doors. Sequoia's bedroom.

"What the hell?" he said.

Aspen and I exchanged a glance, then moved in tandem toward Sequoia's door. With each step, the sound of rushing water intensified, a low roar now pressing against the walls. I lifted my hand and knocked.

I tapped on the door, calling, "Sequoia?" No answer.

Aspen was right behind me. I kept him in my peripheral vision as I cracked the door even further. I called again. No answer.

"Sequoia, are you in there? You're overflowing the tub," I called again. There was a hitch of irritation in my voice. How could she be so careless?

"I'm coming in," I said, ignoring the splashes of water against my socks. I pushed the door open and strode into her room, calling her name again. Strangely the bathroom door was locked, even though the threshold under the door was spewing water through it. I wiggled the door handle again, but to no avail. I was going to have to pick the lock.

"Let me," Aspen said. "It'll take too long to pick," he said. He placed a firm hand on my shoulder, gently moving me out of the way.

"No way, I can do it," I said.

"It'll take too long," he echoed each word slowly, gritting through his teeth. He had lost any sense of his teasing self.

I stepped away from the door with my hands up in the air. He backed away as well, and the next thing I registered was him flying the length of the room and bolting straight through the bathroom door. He aimed with his shoulder, and the door burst open, sending a wave of water with it.

"I guess that was faster," I admitted.

I treaded in after him, my feet soaked up to my ankles. When I saw Sequoia in the bath my heart lurched to my throat. She was completely submerged, the faucet running open by her feet.

Aspen dove for her, raising her head to break the surface of the water. The way her body limped made my dinner curdle in my stomach. While Aspen raised her out of the bath, I prepared room for her on the bathroom floor and laid down a towel.

"Bring her out here," I said. My instincts kicked in and I immediately readied myself to resuscitate her.

"I can do it . . ." he trailed off as he groaned under the effort of picking her up from the tub. Her hair was completely drenched and matted to the side, her skin ghastly white. Aspen's hands were shaking as he set her down.

"And break her ribcage in the process? Move out of the way," I said.

"Fine," he said. His tone was so faint that my animosity for him momentarily subsided. Despite the trees' tumultuous relationship, something in his tone and the way he gently laid her down by my knees made me believe he really cared for her. His eyes knit together in a fear-stricken way that made my heart lurch.

I got to work immediately, brushing off Sequoia's hair from her face. I stacked my two hands on top of one another, aiming at the center of her chest. I pushed, over and over again, until sweat beaded on my temples and I was panting.

When that wasn't enough, I pinched her nose and pressed my lips to hers. They were cold—unnaturally so—and the chill sent a sharp twist through my gut.

I moved back to her chest and pushed down again, harder this time, willing her heart to remember how to beat.

I couldn't bring myself to look at Aspen. He was perched on the edge of the tub, his clothes drenched and clinging to him like a second skin. At some point, he must have turned off the faucet—the roar of water had stopped.

Now, there was only silence. And the relentless pounding of blood behind my ears.

After a few more desperate compressions, her body lurched—Sequoia coughed violently, water spilling from her lips. It was the most welcome sight I'd seen in months. A ragged breath tore through my chest, half relief, half disbelief. She was alive.

I guided her to her side, so she didn't choke on any more of the water. She coughed and spat out more liquid, finally catching her breath. I held her hair, but most of it had slicked down her back.

She shivered and I finally noticed that she was naked. Her breasts swelled into teardrops as she hunched over, coughing up the rest of the water. I hesitated only a moment before reaching for the towel hanging up by the sink and handed it to her.

"You're going to be okay," I said, wrapping the towel around her. She shivered and nodded.

I stole a glance at Aspen. His hands were covering his face, his hair sticking out between his fingertips. He didn't look up for a long time.

"What happened?" I asked once Sequoia caught her breath. Her eyes were big and wild, and she was staring off at a fixed point in space.

"It was beautiful, Dahlia. I saw *her*," she croaked.

"Saw who? You almost died," I said incredulously.

"I know. I was meant to," she said. She got up to her knees. Aspen finally unshielded his face and looked at her.

"You promised you wouldn't try it." His grief was replaced with anger as he seethed the words behind his clenched jaw.

"I know . . . but I couldn't help it. It was the only way I could tap into the Druidic power. Since you and the group didn't think ritual hymns had anything to do with soul flight, I had to try it myself—Dahlia gave me the idea," Sequoia said. My heart dropped at the assertion.

"I did what?"

"You said that the only good evidence for soul flight would have come from a Druid herself," Sequoia said, wrapping the towel tighter. It took me a moment to recall the words from my first Research Circle.

"Yes but . . . I meant it metaphorically . . ." I said, exasperation fully claiming me.

"The only way to initiate soul flight is, well, to die. I sang underwater until my lungs burned, and then I don't remember. But I had a plan to revive myself," she said, pointing to a string on the faucet. "Once the tub was full, it was supposed to bring me up to the surface. But the knot must have gotten untied while I was down."

"You idiot! You *died*," Aspen said.

"I know, I'm sorry. But you two were here for me. The Fates must've decided it wasn't my time yet." She blinked her giant eyes at both of us and my anger softened.

She risked her life for a research paper? I couldn't comprehend the absurdity of it.

Only the image of Julian behind my eyes coaxed me out of my stupor. Had *he* attempted soul flight as well?

"You could have asked one of us to help you," I said. I could have tried to talk some sense into the girl.

"I did, but Aspen said no. I don't think he would've liked me asking you . . ." she trailed off.

"If it meant keeping you alive, I don't care what you have to ask of Dahlia," he rumbled. "This was not what I meant when I said to be *rigorous* with your research."

"Well, I said I'm sorry. But the good news is that I got the proof I needed for my paper," Sequoia said, propping herself up to the edge of the tub next to Aspen. Her legs dangled long over the edge. She extended a hand to his knee, and his shoulders dropped just slightly, the tension easing.

I couldn't understand it—how Sequoia had so willingly risked her life, all in the name of research. It defied logic, defied self-preservation. No rational person would go to such lengths just to prove a theory. There was only one explanation.

"You really believe in all of this, don't you?"

She looked down to her feet, stretching her toes wide. "This is all I have that connects me to my past, that gives me purpose. Power. Of course I had to try it," she said so casually I thought she could have been talking about the weather.

This only further proved that the students here would go to any length over their research, and in their attempt to feel *powerful.* It terrified me to the core. I shook my head, standing up from the floor to grab another towel to dry off my knees. It was then that I noticed a flash of something golden at the bottom of the tub.

The gold shimmered under the water like a coin sunk in a wishing well. I reached for it.

"What is this?" It was rectangular and had a beautiful intricate geometric design, thicker than a piece of paper. One of the corners was soaked through and fraying, but the image of a woman was regal and her power undeniable: the Empress.

Realization dawned on me. I was holding an exact replica of one of the Skorn cards.

"Oh, that?" Sequoia said.

"*No* . . ." Aspen said. "You used the cards?"

"I used one. Just to help intensify the magick. I didn't think it was going to work. But then I saw Sophia, and she was chanting in Druidic. And I knew it had worked—I had channeled the Druidic power *through* the card."

"It's the Empress," I said blankly, staring at the matriarchal figure imprinted on the golden card before me. In my mind the Empress card toppled—first in a line arranged like dominos, each card falling in turn until they curved inward, closing into a seamless, inescapable circle.

Sequoia was using Skorn magick.

Of course.

"You are all Tarot readers. You're using the cards in the way the Meister prompted me to at Circle. He wanted me to use the cards to tap into their power, to prove their source of power. But I'm not the first to experiment with them," I said.

Aspen winced, turning to Sequoia. "How could you be so careless Sequoia?"

"I think it's stupid that we keep hiding things from her, Aspen, don't you? If she's here to help us, then shouldn't she know that?" Sequoia refuted.

"I suspected that the Meister was keeping something from me. But not this. I've been an idiot this whole time."

"You figured it out quicker than any of us have. We all went through the same process, detangling through the web of secrets before being Initiated," Sequoia said in between coughs.

"You're wrong about one thing," Aspen said. He didn't look up from the spot on the floor he was staring toward. "We're not all readers—not ones like you at least—we're practitioners."

"Save the semantics for Leone," I said, almost rolling my eyes.

Something changed in his expression. He became tacit, academic, the version of himself I knew well in Circle. "There is a meaningful difference. We don't read cards and make predictions. We use the power of the cards to *influence* the *present.* That's what Advisors do for their patrons," he said.

I frowned. "I've read an excerpt on that in *The Book of Skorn*, but I thought it was theory."

"That's because you've only read the published version. There's an unabridged version that Khorvyn never published. He didn't want to share the knowledge with anyone else; he wanted to keep it for his own gain. But one of Khorvyn's friends thought the knowledge was too important to remain hidden, so he shared it for a price, with Renate."

The Meister.

"Oh, I'm so happy we're telling her. It's going to be so much easier from now on," Sequoia sang, grabbing on to Aspen's arm, losing grasp of the towel around her.

"Well, it's not like you've left us much choice," he said, shrugging her off gently. "And if she's going to know, she better know the truth."

"The cards," I began. "You tap into their power, to influence things?" I echoed back. I strained to recall the passage I had read in Julian's copy of the book.

"Sort of. The magick isn't very well understood. But we have some hypotheses for how it works. So far, we think it feeds off emotion. We channel emotion through our artwork," Aspen continued, "the stronger the desire of an outcome, the more likely the card's power will work in favor of it."

"I have so many questions," I said. My thoughts were whirling years ahead of my words. "How have you used it? How effective is it? What are its limitations?" I rattled out. And then I paused, considering the most important question. "Have you used it on *me*?"

By the way Aspen's gaze darted to the ground, I knew the answer.

"So, you have," I said, biting down on my tongue to prevent myself from saying any more.

"It's not like that. We're always running tests; the Meister has us do these experiments. If you happen to be around, which you have been, then you can be in the crossfire," he said.

My thoughts snapped like a rubber band on itself. The way I felt so out of place in the House, the gravitation I felt toward some of the students. They were manipulating me.

That is, they had the intention to. Whether or not the cards' magick actually worked was a separate question.

Sequoia remained silent, looking down at her feet. "I might have used it on you, once or twice. Oh, Dahlia, I just wanted us to be friends!" She reached over to me, but I shrugged her off.

"I . . . I need time to think," I said. "Now that you're breathing, I trust that Aspen can take it from here." I started toward the bathroom door.

"Oh, come now Dahlia, stay with us," Sequoia pleaded.

"I just need to be alone right now," I said, stepping into her bedroom. "And I need sleep."

Sequoia nodded and draped her head against Aspen's shoulder. Aspen placed a hand around her naked body, and Sequoia's lips parted. I paused at the door, catching their still frame. They reminded me of Pygmalion and Galatea—an artist looking upon his muse. They looked beautiful and broken, just like the first day I saw them.

I tore my gaze away from them and walked out of her room.

Just a few doors down, I found my own. I climbed into bed and pried off my sticky Oxfords. The leather was going to crack at this rate of misuse. I shook off my wet slacks and sweater until I was bare. When I was finally alone, I let the guilt and horror wash over me.

The feelings swallowed me whole, twisting like twin serpents in my gut. I had spent weeks convincing myself I was the one unraveling the students' secrets—but all along, I had been their experiment. How many of my thoughts, my choices, had been my own? I curled in on myself, exhaustion dragging me under until I finally found sleep.

*

I awoke with my mouth ajar, and my head pressed down against Julian's journal. Coffee stained the edges where I had spilled it last night. I still had the Skorn deck in my hands. I gripped it in my hands, pushing myself back up.

Thoughts swirled around me—Sequoia, the cards, soul flight. In the last few days, several new clues had come to light. Not that I could say with any certainty that they were connected to Julian's case, but they were outstanding questions to answer, nonetheless.

The reading from the red woman at the Council flashed before my eyes. She had known why I was at Foresyth, but she breathed nothing about it. *Why?* It was another loose thread in the fabric of this case, one that was becoming increasingly distressing.

Then there was the matter of Sequoia and the other students using Skorn cards to access magick. Sequoia had mentioned something about a ceremony the night Julian died. Could it have gone dreadfully wrong, like what had almost happened to Sequoia last night?

Then there were the runic markings on the tree in the reading room. I looked down to where I had drawn the runic symbol and referenced it in my Runes dictionary. The symbol of two triangles stacked on top of one another was *berkano,* I discovered— representing birth, or a new beginning. Was this another message from Julian? Or was this just a random marking, and there were others on the tree that led to a full message?

And then there was Julian's journal. I tucked his journal in the middle of my own, in case anyone decided to come to my room. I had combed through it multiple times. Most of the pages were Julian's scribbled notes—from readings, transcripts from Circle, and his own streams of subconscious. The Hermetic magick sections were descriptions of ceremonial processions, many similar to the ones I used in my own Tarot readings.

The sections on Christian mysticism were the strangest of them all—they spoke about an evil God, imprisoning souls in human flesh. So much of the text was written in haste that it was impossible to decipher all of it. Another section was written in red ink with strange symbols resembling Latin letters and runes overlaid with one another. The only English text was on the header line and read, *"Blood of my blood."*

Flashes of Nina's dripping blood appeared in my mind's eye. The Tramping Grounds, another loose thread in the chasm of madness known as Foresyth.

Then a thought took hold of me. I raised the journal to my light source, examining the red ink more closely. The ink looked off. Too thick. The way it pooled in the paper's fibers, the way light refused to pass through it—it wasn't ink at all. I ran my finger along the edge, feeling the faint tackiness of dried fluid.

My stomach clenched. It wasn't ink. It was *blood.*

A flame of understanding ignited in me. *Blood magick*. That had to be the explanation. Inked blood to conceal a hidden message. A smile spread across my lips; I relished the finding.

I had to get this journal back to the Tramping Ground as soon as possible.

The Acolyte and the Alchemist: Part V

The archives, a subterranean labyrinth of knowledge incarnate, stretched endlessly before them. Shelves loomed six stories high, carved into the very foundation of the Conservatory, their ancient wood varnished to an obsidian gleam. The air was thick with the scent of aged parchment and candle wax, laced with something sharper—ink and the metallic tang of old magic lingering in the stones.

Quill and Hamra stepped forward, their footfalls muffled by age-worn rugs that stretched between the rows. Excitement rose in Quill's chest, heady and intoxicating, though he fought to steady himself.

They had been granted a single hour in the archives, no more.

A scribe had been stationed at their side, an older man in ink-stained robes, his expression neutral yet watchful.

"Remember, we have a list," Quill murmured, glancing at the small parchment folded in his palm.

"I know," Hamra whispered back, though her eyes were already darting between the artifacts displayed in glass cases along the walls. Her breath hitched. "Is that the original black mirror that the Knights Templar used to summon Beelzebub?"

Quill barely stopped himself from looking. He couldn't afford to be distracted—but it was hard not to be. Every inch of this place hummed. The air itself felt charged, as if the very walls had been inscribed with spells long since forgotten.

"We're here for research," he reminded her, though his voice lacked conviction. He, too, felt lightheaded from the sheer potential of what lay before them.

Hamra nodded, though her fingers twitched at her sides, resisting the urge to stray from their purpose. They split apart, weaving through the towering stacks, their movements swallowed by the hush of the archives.

By the time they reconvened at the librarian's desk, their cart was laden with books. It buckled under the weight of their discoveries, its brass wheels creaking against the marble floor.

The librarian, a gaunt woman with silver-streaked hair, peered down at them from behind the desk, her expression unreadable. "Did you find everything you were looking for?"

"Yes," Hamra said, a slow grin spreading across her lips. "And more." She traced her fingers over the spines of the tomes, reverent. "I can't wait to be an Advisor and have unlimited access to these archives."

The librarian's quill hovered over the catalog ledger for a fraction too long before she spoke. "Becoming an Advisor is a great honor," she said at last, dipping her pen into the inkwell and continuing her work.

Quill placed the final book, a leather-bound volume, its cover a gleaming obsidian mass, onto the growing pile.

"This one didn't have a code," he noted, adjusting the stack. Beneath his fingertips, the book thrummed, an almost imperceptible vibration against his skin.

The librarian stilled. "Strange," she murmured, reaching out but hesitating just before touching it. "That book has been missing for years."

Quill glanced at Hamra, a flicker of triumph in his gaze. "It wasn't on the list either, but I got it just for you. It's by your favorite author."

Hamra's fingers brushed over the cover, her eyes lighting.

Quill turned back to the librarian. "You can code it by the author. Last name Khorvyn, first name Aleric."

"Blood of my blood."

–*Julian Earhardt's journal,* dated March 15th, 1919

Chapter 19: Blood Magick

It rained in sheets for three days, turning the world into a blur of white. The downpour kept me confined to my room, save for the moments I ventured out to eat or attend Circle. I moved through the House like a ghost, slipping between doorways, avoiding conversation. Avoiding the Trees. I wasn't ready to face them—not after the other night.

The rain finally broke on the first of February, leaving behind a sky so crisp and empty it felt unnatural. It was a deceptive kind of stillness, but I'd take advantage of it anyway.

I crept down the stairwell, the journal pressed tightly against my ribs beneath the strap of my shoulder bag. The House was still, hushed in that fragile silence that never lasted long. By noon, the others would be descending for lunch. I needed to be gone before then—gone and unnoticed.

At the bottom of the stairs, I hesitated, looking back up to Sequoia's door. A hollow tug pulled at my chest. *Should I check on her?* The thought curdled the moment it formed.

Betrayal rose in my throat as sharp and bitter as nettle. She had meant to manipulate me—with the cards, with her charm. Had any of it been real? Had there ever been a moment between us untouched by her calculation? I searched the memory of our friendship for something honest, but all I found were the tainted shadows of our mutual deception.

My lips tingled with the phantom of hers. Lips that I had saved.

I tore my gaze from the door and pressed forward. No one in this House could be trusted.

I adjusted my bag and moved carefully down the main staircase, testing my weight against each step, avoiding the treacherous boards that groaned under pressure. A single misstep could summon a witness I didn't want.

I was making my way to the exit when I heard voices.

I froze outside the Meister's office, the low murmur threading through the thick wood. These weren't the other students. These were men—older, their tones edged with authority. I pressed my ear against the door, catching fragments of their conversation.

"We are . . . low on patience . . . Renate," said a clipped, deliberate voice.

"Your control over this House is slipping, Renate. The Council has been watching," said a more nasally tone, closer to the door.

"I am humbled by your support," the Meister said dryly, his voice laced with condescension. "But I have everything under control. The House is on its way to recovery, and so is our magick."

"Under your leadership, Renate, our magick has twisted into something else," the younger voice said. "Something unnatural—" The man's voice cut off. There was a wheezing sound like someone trying to cough.

"Our magick has become the most powerful the Council has ever seen, and you'd be wise to remember who secured your position, Beaufort," the Meister snarled.

Beaufort. The name struck a chord. It wasn't Leone, but a relative of his must be on the Council. What was the Meister doing to him?

"We do not question you, sir, but we do question that girl," the oldest voice said. "Wait—did you hear that? Is someone else here?"

Coughing erupted behind the door and I startled backward. The floorboard creaked under my foot and I cursed. A spike of adrenaline shot through me.

I stepped back, pulse hammering. I slipped into the nearest corridor just as the office door opened. Someone stepped into the hall.

I pressed myself against the cold stone wall, breath caged in my chest. A damp heat broke across my forehead as I willed myself steady.

The figure stood there only a moment before the door creaked shut again.

I waited, counting to ten.

Only then did I move, slipping back into the hall and sprinting for the exit. My fingers fumbled with the latch before I forced it open and slipped outside, swallowed by the waiting air.

I didn't stop moving.

*

The storms of the previous days had passed, and now the weather was warm and pleasant—the first inklings of spring. Sequoia had been right. I could hear the swallows calling in the distance, making their way back from winter. An assemblage of them dotted the sky, forming a "V." The brace of birds soared in rhythmic unity against the backdrop of a clear blue sky before disappearing behind the House's clock tower.

I traced their shape in the sky. They were too early, and winter would not let them rest easy here, not yet.

A chill ran through me as I recalled the conversation I had just overheard. *That girl*—had they been talking about *me*?

I was becoming increasingly convinced that the Meister had a hand in Julian's death. My suspicions were all but confirmed now. But it didn't make any sense—why would he summon me here if he killed Julian? How was the Meister corrupting magick? Julian's journal had hinted at forces beyond our understanding, rituals feeding something ancient. Could that be what they meant? Could he be drawing power from something the Council feared?

I walked down the cobblestone path to the gate, tracing the same path that Nina had taken me. Everything looked so different in the daylight. I remembered Nina and I following the edge of the forest that lined the area against the House's perimeter, and so I strode around the thick black bush. I followed the path about a mile down until reaching the fork. Faint mud prints guided me through the thicket until I lost them in the grass.

I looked around but every direction was the same, and I couldn't remember which way Nina went. *A white oak*. That was the tree that marked the way. I picked up a log and laid it down and stacked several others on top making cairns. The obvious human intervention would serve as my center point.

I reached into my bag and pulled out a spool of yarn. I tied it to a tree next to the cairns and started making spirals. I had to circumscribe several trees to keep the yarn from getting tangled, but this method was worth the time. Otherwise, I'd be making circles in the woods not knowing if I had traced the area or not.

On my third spiral I found it—a great oak tree with a smear of white across the trunk, like someone had painted it. The marker.

I tied my string to a neighboring tree, leading the path back homeward. I stepped closer to the oak, branches breaking under my feet. My swollen feet cried in my Oxfords, but I ignored them. I was getting close to the Tramping Ground; I could feel it. I found the narrow path uphill and began the ascension. My legs objected to the excursion, but I forced them up the way. I could see the ridge of the hill and increased the length of my stride, my shoes digging into the loose soil.

Stop, before you go too far, my father's voice resounded in my head. I pushed him away, just as I did the burning in my legs.

When I got to the top and saw the clearing, I stopped to catch my breath. Despite the fire in my lungs, my mind was clear and bright, free from the gloom of the House. I took in a hungry gulp of air, filling my chest and holding it there. I sighed, my pulse falling.

The Tramping Ground was right in front of me.

I stared at the cold, barren earth. The patch of dry soil was circumscribed with rocks, no doubt the work of Nina defining the grounds. The circle itself was perhaps only three yards in radius, but the dead bleakness of the ground was contrasted by the overgrown grass surrounding it.

Nina had called this *Sophia's* Circle. The same deity that Sequoia had seen the night when she nearly died.

A jolt of energy ran down my arms, and I wrapped my blazer tighter around my midsection. I took out Julian's journal and flipped to the pages stained in red, with what I now knew was blood.

He had left a message. One he didn't want just anyone to know—only those who had access to this Circle. And I was going to figure out what it was.

I came closer to the Circle and crouched down just a few inches away from its edge. I laid down the journal on the grassy side and stacked a few rocks on either side to keep it propped open. I reached inside my bag and took out my leather gloves. There was no way I'd touch the soil with my bare hands. I donned the pair and began to reach for the soil. It was hard and packed, as if someone had indeed been stamping around on it.

I dug my fingernails through the gloves, pinching the crust to break. It finally did, but at the cost of heat rising in my finger tips. It was *burning* my hands through the gloves. I worked quickly to coat the journal's pages with the foul soil until all the words were obscured.

It had only taken seconds for Nina's blood to disappear. The familiar buzzing surrounded me, and I tuned into the noise, no longer pushing it away. It was saying something, I realized, in a tight pitch.

Blood, it rang out.

I watched in awe as steam rose from the book, burning away the runic characters, leaving behind only the English written in red pen. I quickly dusted off the rest of the soil before it burned through the book.

I studied the marvel before me closely. It worked on organics. Blood, cellulose paper. Even the leather of my gloves was not impervious to its effects. I took out a small vial from my bag and scooped a pinch of the soil into the container to examine later.

I turned my attention to the journal in front of me. I raised it and shook out the dirt from the pages back into the Circle. To my delight, only the English writing remained. My heart lurched when I saw the entry was addressed to me.

Dearest Dahlia Blackburne,

If you're reading this, it means I'm dead. But don't worry, I caused enough trouble on my way out to make it worthwhile. Abyssus abyssum invocat—*hell calls for hell. My one regret is that we never met. I had hoped that, under different circumstances, we might have.*

The shadows over Foresyth run deeper than I feared, and I hate to think of you facing them. But Foresyth is in your blood, just as it is in mine. Blood of my blood. If you've found this Circle, then I know it's really you. I made sure only you would be able to uncover its location.

The Book *will call to you as it called to me. But if my theory is correct, you may have the power to resist it.* Resist it.

Be careful of the Meister. His power lies not just in magick—but in his deception. He bends truth to serve his needs, and that makes him more dangerous than anyone else. I've been studying the Gnostic texts, and I believe our rituals aren't just drawing power from the abyss—they're feeding it. The demiurge, the architect of the material prison, grows stronger with every invocation.

Find our father's journal. Only then will you understand the cycle of suffering in this House—and how to stop it. The coordinates are at the bottom of this page.

If there's one thing I regret, it's that we never met. I will look forward to it in another life.

Sub rosa,
Julian

The words on the page swam before my eyes, but one line stood out as though it had been etched into my bones: *Blood of my blood.*

My father . . . was Julian's father, too. The man I thought I knew, the man who raised me, had buried a past so deep I was only uncovering it now, in the dirt, in blood, like an animal. A scream was budding in my throat. My face paled, and I started to sway on my feet, reaching down to steady myself against the cold, barren earth.

I flipped back through Julian's journal frantically, searching for something—anything—that would explain it away. But it was right there, hidden in plain sight. His cryptic words, his obsession with Foresyth's secrets, and now, this. *Blood of my blood.*

Julian was my brother.

The world around me tilted. My knees buckled under the weight of the truth, and I reached out to steady myself on a nearby tree. My breath came in short, sharp bursts, each gasp pulling me deeper into the storm of realization crashing over me.

And how did Julian lead me here to this Circle? I hadn't found it, Nina did. But I had pulled the cards for her . . .

A sharp pain erupted at the base of my skull—a migraine threatening to split my head open. The Tramping Ground lay still before me, but the revelation roared in my ears, drowning out everything else. My father's ties to Foresyth, Julian's research, the dark call of power that lingered in every corner of this place.

They were all connected. My father had hidden so much from me, and now I was caught in the same web of secrets. Anger was replacing shock, rising like smoke in my chest.

I blinked rapidly, trying to clear my head, but the questions kept coming, each one more terrifying than the last. Who could I trust now? Definitely not the Meister, who was at the core of this betrayal. Aspen, who had always seemed one step ahead of me? Sequoia, who was tied so deeply into this magick that she'd nearly drowned in it?

Or could I trust none of them?

I had to find the truth. I had to finish what Julian started. The threats that loomed over Foresyth weren't just shadows of the past—they were real, living forces. And now, they were threatening to swallow me whole.

A branch snapped in the distance. I twisted my head behind me in the direction. Someone was here. Had someone been following me? My breath hitched.

I stood, dumping Julian's journal and the gloves back into my satchel and getting to my feet. I had to go quickly. If Julian's words were true, someone here didn't want me to find out the truth. I ran back down the thicket of woods, my eyes scanning for the white-marked oak.

Another branch snapped. Closer this time. I stumbled forward, heart hammering, searching for the white-marked oak—there. The string, my lifeline, should be here. I reached for it, fingers grasping at nothing but air.

The tree was bare. The string was gone.

My heart rate quickened. I burst into a run, tracing my steps as best as I could. I pushed away branches caught in my hair and jumped over fallen logs. But my bag caught in one of the branches and then the world tilted on its axis. I landed on my knees.

My senses reeled, my heart thundered against my ribs, and a metallic taste flooded my mouth. I tried to move, to scramble back to my feet, but something heavy pressed down on me, pinning me to the earth with an unyielding force.

Panic surged, each beat of my heart echoing in the silence of the forest. With a desperate gasp, I strained against the weight that held me captive, my muscles burning with exertion.

Then, as suddenly as it had descended, the darkness lifted.

A blinding light seared through the veil of shadows, and I squinted against its brilliance, disoriented and dazed. I glimpsed the silhouette of a figure looming over me, their presence ominous against the backdrop of screeching galls above. And then, a sharp blow struck my head, sending shards of pain ricocheting through my skull. Stars exploded behind my eyelids, and my consciousness slipped away like sand through my fingers.

Chapter 20: Trust Exercise

I blinked my eyes open, forcing them to focus on one point out in space. A mural floated in front of me, symbols shimmering in a sigil: the silhouette of a drooping rose, bound in a red circle. The smell of upturned soil filled my nostrils as I steadied my breath, trying to regain my senses. As my vision cleared, fear ripened deep in my gut.

My arms were bound behind my back, and I must have twisted my ankle in the woods because it ached in the unnatural position I was sitting in. I tried to adjust my legs from under me, letting out a hoarse cry from the pain shooting up my calf.

That's when I noticed the five cloaked figures seated around me in a circle. They raised their heads in unison and turned to me. It was too dark to make out their faces, but I knew who they were.

"Ms. Dahlia Blackburne," said the shrouded figure across from me. "Welcome to your Initiation."

My heart dropped. All I could think of were Julian's last words, penned in blood, warning me about the rites at Foresyth. Warning me about the *Meister*. Now I found myself shackled and at his feet.

Julian. I shot my eyes frantically around, searching for my bag. His journal, his confession. Where were they?

I caught a glimpse of the waxed leather of my satchel in the far corner of the room. As if the Meister noticed this, he stepped forward from the circle, catching my eyes and not releasing them.

"Foresyth is not just an academic institution, it is also a guild of magick practitioners. We embody our motto, integrity of the word, activation of the mind, transcendence of the soul. We enrich the academic community by safeguarding secrets long buried away and raise these powerful ideas up to consciousness. We devote ourselves, and our minds, to understanding the original sources—until the knowledge becomes core to our being." The Meister circled the rest of us as he spoke. "And now comes the time to welcome you to the final promise. True magick is born through transcendence."

Transcendence. The word echoed in my mind, tasting coarse and acrid. What exactly had been sacrificed to keep true to that promise?

"Over the past several weeks you have been welcomed to Foresyth Conservatory as a scholar," the Meister continued. "You might have realized you were being studied. Tested. Not every new scholar makes it up to this point unless they've demonstrated a certain magickal aptitude. The Council was part of that test, and you passed."

I swallowed hard, watching the Meister's footsteps trace in front of me. I hadn't doubted that I was being watched at Foresyth, or that I was being tested. But what had him thinking I had any sort of magickal aptitude?

What I had witnessed at Foresyth was inexplicable, but that didn't mean I believed it was magick. There had to be another explanation. I had held the sacredness of logic and reason close to my chest for as long as I could remember. Trained practically to it by my father. But there was a clear fission crackling in me that I couldn't deny.

Nina's blood.

Julian's journal.

My father.

"You came to Foresyth as a scholar, and now today, you join its guild as a practitioner."

The emblem in front of me glowed brighter, pulsing with every one of the Meister's words. The crack inside me widened with every word, every pulse.

"I have been waiting a very long time," he said, the Meister's tone changing. He wasn't speaking as the Head Meister of Foresyth in that steady cadence. No, his voice had a reverent fervor. A chill ran through me, expecting his next words. "For all the right elements to be here. And now they are."

One of the hoods turned to me, and I spotted Nina's eyes. She blinked slowly, as if to say, *It'll all be okay*. But the knot in my stomach wouldn't release. Had Julian gone through this? Had my father, when he was a student here? They undoubtedly had survived the Initiation, but both ended up dead sometime after it.

"I will now open the Circle to your peers, who will conduct the initiating rites," the Meister said, falling back behind the Circle. Another figure stepped out. I could recognize the saunter a mile away, even shrouded. That lazy, bohemian saunter.

Aspen walked forward to the center of the Circle where an altar was arranged—a chalice, an athame, candle, and mound of earth. One thing caught my eye in particular. Undeniably, a deck of cards sat on the altar. Aspen picked up the athame and stepped toward me.

I steadied my breath.

His first reaction betrayed him. His eyes opened slightly in warning. But it was gone just as quickly as it appeared. He tipped his hood back, an amused smile cresting his lips. He kneeled beside me with the athame still in his hand. All my muscles tensed, screaming for me to move, to run away. I leaned away from his reach, but he caught my arm with a stone grip.

"Get your hands off of me," I tried to say with a snarl, but only a hoarse whisper escaped.

He leaned his mouth closer to my ear. "I won't hurt you," he said it so softly I thought I must have imagined it. Then he circled behind me, picking me up to my feet so quickly I pitched forward. Before I could steady myself, I felt the cold blade of the athame between my shoulder blades. It dug into my skin.

The Meister moved forward again, breaching the Circle to cover the distance, his cloak billowing behind him. He floated toward us.

"Trust is an essential part of the equation, Dahlia. Accepting you into this sacred Circle means that you accept a blade behind your back. And trust that it won't pierce you."

Aspen steadied his grip on my shoulder, angling the blade to its point. The tip was dull, but with enough force, it could break skin. He applied the faintest pressure, trailing the blade down my spine. The sensation sent a shiver through me, my breath becoming unsteady.

This man must be insane to think I would trust him.

I swiveled my wrist, pushing up with all the strength I had. The blade clattered to the floor, and I moved back to pick it up, but Aspen was quicker. He had it across my neck the next second. A sharp pang shot across my wrist where Aspen was pinning me. An empty chuckle echoed against my back.

"You don't have to listen to me, but you should listen to *reason.* The Meister needs you; if he wanted you dead, you wouldn't be here." His grip softened on my wrists, and he traced apologetic circles with his thumb on the outside of my hand. But the hand holding the blade to my neck didn't soften, didn't give. I was pinned against his broad chest.

"Dahlia," the Meister said, his tone endearing as if talking to a child, "you must accept the blade. It is the only way to be Initiated."

I almost laughed. But I didn't because it might have sliced my throat. How had it only been a month and change since the Meister had walked into my store? And now I found myself on my knees, with a blade to my neck.

I had been a fool to trust him, to let him hire me. His motivations were laced in something much more sinister. I simulated the options in front of me.

Any option that required force would wind up with me dead, that I was certain of. Denying the Initiation wasn't an option either; if I was no longer a student at Foresyth, the Meister wouldn't have any use for me. And now that I was getting closer to his uncovering his ploy, could I really believe that he would just let me walk out of here?

He was the most dangerous of them all.

No. The only way out was *through*. Aspen was right. He wouldn't kill me, not now. Julian had survived Initiation. I likely would too. But the most convincing piece of evidence, the one that almost made me relax, was the Al-Ahmar. She wanted answers, too. I saw it in her eyes. The Meister wouldn't betray her, not when she carried so much weight on the Council.

The Meister wouldn't kill me. Not yet.

I braced against the weight of Aspen and nodded. He released the blade from my throat and trailed it behind me again.

"Say the words," the Meister pressed, his eyes glowing green. The silence stretched on in the chamber so long I started to hear my pulse. At Aspen's tug of my hand behind me, I finally found my words.

"I accept." The words tasted like crumbling rust in my mouth. Or was that blood? I dipped my head down, bracing for the impact of the blade behind me.

Instead, they sliced through my restraints in one quick motion. I fell forward, catching myself on my aching wrists, wincing at the pain.

"There is liberation in surrender," the Meister said, stepping forward and offering me a hand. I looked up to him, sending him the vilest look I could muster. "You'll have to stand for the rest of the ceremony," he said, looking down at my swollen ankle. Hatred bubbled up in my throat like acid.

The bastard.

I stumbled upward, placing the brunt of my weight on the right leg. I tried to keep from wincing.

He smiled, offering a hand. "Come," he said. I eyed his hand for several seconds before taking it. Shame tangled in my throat, but I pushed it aside. Survival was paramount, ego came after. Ego came when I'd uncover his murderous secrets for all to see.

I staggered behind his wispy movements to the altar where the athame had been replaced, a quiet Aspen back in the formation of the Circle.

"And now, the offerings," he said. My breath caught with an objection on my lips but died there.

The first to step forward was Leone. He wheeled himself to the center of the Circle, where I stood. His eyes narrowed to study me, as if discerning my worthiness.

It was a long moment before he spoke, but when he did, my heart could have stopped.

"Blood of my blood, bound by the Shattered Mother, I accept Dahlia Blackburne into this sacred covenant," Leone said picking up the chalice—evidently full of liquid—and blew a breath into it. He sat it down just as soft as he raised it and looked directly at me. He closed his eyes slowly, solemnly. I returned the gesture, a tingle of pride threatening in my traitorous chest.

What *was* that?

I wasn't used to feeling accepted. Not that I cared so much about it, given that everyone around me in Greenwich was barely worth my time, even if they were paying for it. But Leone—he was as close to a real scholar as I had ever known. His intelligence shone from his eyes, if not from his lack of interest in anything outside of his books. As much as I wanted to deny it, being accepted by him felt *good*. It felt validating.

Leone retreated back to his place in the Circle and Aspen mirrored his motion, breaking out of the Circle.

"Missed me already?" he said with a smile that showed his teeth. I scowled. He laughed quietly, his gaze drifting to his index finger and thumb. I didn't see how he lit a flame between his fingertips, but it glowed and cast his features in orange and yellow hues. He lifted the flame to the chalice and slowly extinguished it in the cup.

"Blood of my blood, bound by the Shattered Mother, I accept Dahlia Blackburne into this sacred covenant," Aspen said, pausing at my name.

Sequoia followed after him. As she approached the altar, I noticed her eyes were glistening.

"*I'm sorry,*" she mouthed silently.

I furrowed my brows. What part about this exactly was she sorry about? Lying to me, or having me beaten and kidnapped into this underground chamber?

I guess it didn't matter.

A single tear streamed down the curve of her cheek, and she caught it with her fingertips. She held it out over the chalice and flipped her finger over it. The teardrop collected into a perfect shape before splashing into the chalice.

"Blood of my blood, bound by the Shattered Mother, I accept Dahlia Blackburne into this sacred covenant," Sequoia said, barely an audible whisper. Her throat bobbed and I thought she would burst into tears at any second. But she took a deep breath and lifted her chin and nodded to me. And then she stepped down.

The last was Nina. She walked solemnly to the altar, any remnant of her usual sardonic disposition and biting humor replaced by a quiet reverence. She picked up the edges of the too-long cloak catching in her steps as she approached me. Her hood almost swallowed her face whole, but her black eyes shone bright like the moon.

She took out a single pebble from her cloak and let it drop into the chalice, giving me a wink. "Blood of my blood, bound by the Shattered Mother, I accept Dahlia Blackburne into this sacred covenant."

The words reverberated through my bones. *Accept.* Had I ever been accepted before? The feeling was strange, paradoxical almost, to be accepted by one's enemies. It felt too real, too raw, despite all the secrets. I cursed my gullible heart.

Perhaps I had read about a similar ceremony, or perhaps the fact lived in my subconscious, but I knew what to do next. I took the chalice in between my hands, tipping the rim to my lips and took a long, deep gulp. Warmth spread across my neck and chest as the concoction took effect. Everyone began to chant, and I somehow found the words and we were all chanting in unison. A deck of Skorn was placed in my hands and we all held it up to our foreheads, chanting in the sacred tongue. It wasn't any language I recognized, at least on a conscious level, but it felt natural—as if I had been speaking it for years.

I tried to fight it at first, but then a rush of warmth washed over me. The elixir was kicking in. All of the worry, the pain, the fear, slipped right off. I was everything and nothing at once.

The imprint of where the cards were on my forehead burned, but I didn't release my grip on them. They pulsed in my hands, pinning them there. The heat was rising, my neck slick with my perspiration. But I didn't let them go. An undeniable surge of power coursed my veins, and my entire body felt like it was pulsing.

I was accepted; I was one of them. It sickened and delighted me at the same time.

It was then I heard her name, her voice. She whispered it into my ear.

"Dahlia Blackburne—you all pray to a false God." her voice gurgling as if she was under water.

Sophia.

I heard her, but I couldn't make sense of the words. My grip loosened, but I didn't let go of the cards. They must have slipped from my hands as my vision became dark. The last thing I heard were the cards falling to the floor like a thousand claps of wings—like birds somewhere in the distance preparing for flight.

Chapter 21: A Promise

The next few days were a haze. My head throbbed like it was about to burst, and my ankle was swollen almost as large as a grapefruit. I stayed in bed for the majority of the time, save for when Nina would bring around meals. Sequoia would try to come in as well, but I never let her in. Instead, I watched outside of my window as the migratory birds drifted back from winter, embracing the rising warmth of spring. I watched them for a long time, studying their patterns in the bright blue sky.

When no one was around, I'd reach for the bag that I kept tucked away under my bed. It had been returned to me after the Initiation. Luckily, the journal was still intact, Julian's words stained in bright red. There were coordinates at the bottom of the page that I hadn't noticed the day at the Tramping Grounds. I traced the numbers with my fingertips so many times, I had memorized them by heart.

The truth about Julian was out there. The truth about my father, too. But I didn't allow myself to dwell on them, not yet. Not when my mind was as tender as my broken body.

When Nina came in to deliver me food, she tried to talk to me. She'd say silly things like *you're looking better*, or *the weather is so nice*. But I would just nod and go back to staring out the window.

I thought about my previous clients a lot. I distantly wondered if Carousel Michelle had ever made that trip up north without her husband. I also thought about Lady Florance's fat cat and wondered if the timed feeder I had made helped him to lose weight. I thought about my mom, opening and closing the threadbare curtains every day. I thought about Gabriel, sitting in that grassy plot in front of Greenwich Library, eating his lunch alone. I asked Richard every day if any post had come for me, desperate to hear from them.

I thought about everything except Foresyth.

"You know, you did brilliantly," Nina said one day, bringing me a steaming bowl of soup. She didn't need to specify what she meant; we both knew she was referencing the Initiation. "I knew you were ready after you accurately helped me pinpoint the Tramping Grounds. I'm glad the Meister finally decided to Initiate you after your debut to the Council. You did so much better than I did."

I gave Nina a soft smile, but my lips cracked. I tasted blood.

"I vomited the elixir at my Initiation," she went on. "They almost had my membership revoked for that," she went on. Then she came to my bedside and took a seat, the bed barely indented with her lightness. "But you—you were a *show*. You really earned that theatre concentration. You knew when to put in a fight, and when to give in. Sophia must have been very entertained."

"I heard her," I said blankly. I don't know why I decided to share it, but it felt good doing so. I was tired of secrets, even my own.

"We all did. It was the elixir—it increases your magickal sensitivity," Nina said, surely excited to not be talking to the brick wall I had been the past few days.

"She said that we all prayed to a false God. Do you know what she was talking about?" I asked. Her words had haunted me all these languid days in bed, but I hadn't wanted to address them. At least, not until now.

Nina's features sharpened but then became unreadable. "You must have heard wrong; she is our one true God, the emanation from Source," she said. I almost didn't recognize her in that next moment, her chiding self all but gone.

Sophia's voice had felt so real against my ear; I swore I felt her breath against my neck. I felt her *power* over me. It must have been a hallucination—I had been drugged, after all. But despite my reasoning, the Initiation shook me to the core.

Everything I held dear—reason, science, evidence—no longer made any sense.

I was starting to entertain the idea that magick was *real.*

"What was in that elixir?" I asked, my senses finally kicking in. There had to be a logical explanation for everything I'd seen at Foresyth, I couldn't give up on that. It might not have been poison, but it could have been mind-altering.

"It's an herbal tonic—myrtle, mugwort, a pinch of four-leaf clover, and *salvia divinorum.*"

"The sage of diviners?" I sat up on my wrists and only a dull ache bit back.

"Someone has been studying their Latin," a smile crept on her features before dropping. "Yes, the same. But with a very low concentration, I made sure of that. Enough to open ourselves spiritually, but not enough to hallucinate."

"Someone's learned titration," I teased back. A wave of relief washed over me. There was an explanation for everything. There had to be.

"It's jarring—I know. I didn't come from a magickal background, so this kind of thing didn't come naturally to me. But once you accept it, as it has accepted you, you gain access to power you could only dream of."

"I don't want power," I said, and it was true. Nothing good came from chasing power. I had always thought knowledge was a much more noble pursuit. Despite the fact that it was proving to be just as deadly.

"Of course you do—we all do. Power is *life.* And for someone like me, it's the choice between life or death. Power or despair. Power or death."

I scrunched my features, trying to discern her words. Nina seemed to have an inherent power, one that radiated outwardly and impinged everything she touched. I couldn't imagine her any differently. Did she not recognize it herself?

She uttered a soundless laugh. "I know it's hard to believe, but I was a lot different before I came to Foresyth. I was hungrier—I had to do a lot of things to survive back then, things I'm not proud of. I had been starving for power so long, I didn't know what it was like to be full." She looked away from me and at the window. A single crow landed on the windowsill, no doubt searching for his next meal.

"The way my parents died in their accident . . . The roads were slick, and their car went over a bridge." Her voice softened. I could see the memory flash over her features, reduced back to her childlike self. "I was with them. But I was so small, I managed to pry the door open enough to swim through. My parents did not. It was the hardest thing I've ever done—leaving them."

I reached for her hand instinctively. Despite the walls I tried to keep up from everyone at Foresyth, my heart strained against her words. I hadn't wanted to share my vulnerability with her, but it was hard not to give in when she shared hers so willingly. Her pain was palpable, I could almost reach out and grab it.

I pressed down on her hand instead. "I know what it's like to lose a parent," I said. "It's like a piece of you dies—your innocence, your childhood. You're forced to grow up quickly."

She nodded and two tears slid down her cheeks. She inhaled hard, wiping them away. "I'm sorry, this isn't about me. It's about you. I know this place comes with its own challenges, but I just want to tell you, it's worth it—the knowledge, the power. It doesn't fill the hole in your heart, but it comes close."

I thought of my father and his musical laughter. He rarely laughed, but when he did, it brightened the whole room. I tried imagining him laughing here at Foresyth, but the picture in my mind felt too incongruous.

"Do you ever wish you could bring them back?" I asked, the face of my father still freshly imprinted in my mind.

"All the time," she said gravely and squeezed my hand.

We sat like that for a while, with her hand in mine, watching the crows collect on the windowsill.

*

It had been a full week since the Initiation, but I finally made it down to the breakfast table. My ankle had healed significantly, thanks to one of Nina's tonics (without hallucinogenic effects, I think), and even my wrists were back to normal. My legs felt weaker though, from not moving regularly. I took a mental note of needing to develop an exercise regimen.

Coming down late to the breakfast table, I knew I had evaded Aspen and Sequoia who were early risers. Only Leone remained at the table, greeting me more chipper than usual.

"Hello, Dahlia," Leone said without looking up from his book.

"I think that's the first time you've acknowledged my existence."

"Well, you're a part of us now. I heard you survived the Al-Ahmar. Anyone who does that deserves respect."

I hesitated, the memory of the red woman flickering in my mind. "I didn't think she was all that impressive," I lied, piling biscuits onto my plate. Her face had haunted my dreams every night since the Initiation.

Leone glanced over the edge of his book, measuring my words. "That wasn't the only reason I accepted you," he said, finally closing the book with deliberate care. "You certainly stand out among the others—you're the only one taking the scientific part of our studies seriously. We need more skeptical practitioners like you."

The compliment felt almost backhanded, but I took it in stride. Leone had a way of speaking like facts were the only currency that mattered, and emotions were irrelevant. Still, I couldn't ignore the flicker of validation his words stirred. It wasn't often that someone at Foresyth acknowledged the virtues of logic.

Leone took a slow sip of his coffee, the dark liquid reflecting the early morning light. I could feel the conversation slipping away from me, and my pulse quickened.

This was my chance.

"Leone?" I ventured, trying to keep my voice steady. His gaze flicked up to me, slightly impatient, but curious.

I swallowed. "Now that I'm . . . accepted"—I stumbled over the word—"when can I learn about *The Book of Skorn*? The unpublished version?"

My heart thudded in my chest. The desperation was creeping into my voice despite my best efforts to mask it. My ankle still throbbed, and I wasn't in any condition to chase down my father's journal, but I still needed answers—Answers that Foresyth held within its very own cursed walls.

Leone raised an eyebrow, tapping the cover of his book absent-mindedly. "Well, typically, that's covered during the Circle after your Initiation. But since you've been . . . indisposed," he said, the slightest pause giving weight to his word. "I imagine you'll be brought in at the next Circle. Tonight."

Tonight. The word dangled between us, syrupy and thick with promise.

"I'll get to see the Book?" I pressed, narrowing my eyes, trying to gauge how much truth he was willing to share. Could I trust anything they said? The secrets, the manipulation—how much of what they told me was true?

"The oath of silence only applies to non-Initiates," he said, his tone flat, as if explaining something as mundane as the weather. His indifference made it clear he was ready to move on from the conversation.

Answers. The thought of finally getting clarity felt unreal, heady. I knew they wouldn't give me everything—not the full truth—but at least I'd have their version.

"The elected position of Meister at Foresyth Conservatory is one of the highest honors an Advisor can confer. To be eligible, a candidate must secure both the approval of the Council and the endorsement of seven patrons who vouch for the candidate's scholarship and abilities. Once appointed, Meisters typically serve for life, barring rare instances of resignation or a Council vote for removal. The Meister holds considerable influence over the academic and magickal trajectories of students, shaping which doctrines or belief systems are emphasized. The Council grants the Meister full authority over the daily operations and practices of Foresyth scholars."

—*Foresyth Conservatory: A Complete History, Unabridged*, 1891

Chapter 22: Their Version

Everyone was in their usual spots. Sequoia and Aspen on the loveseat, Nina sprawled on the chaise, and Leone on his own little island, book-in-lap. The only real difference was me.

I had changed. I was the one that had been Initiated.

As I approached, Nina gathered her limbs and made space for me on the chaise. The leaves of the giant oak tree swayed in the pre-dusk breeze and I shivered. I tried to not fixate on the spot where I had pulled back the bark to reveal a rune. From the corner of my eye, I could see Aspen trying to catch mine. I avoided his gaze, the phantom of the athame still at my throat.

Even if it was just for show, I had felt some part of him enjoying it.

The Meister entered the room, and everything became very still. The branches of the great oak themselves became quiet. His gaze drifted across the room but held mine longer than anyone else's.

"Dahlia," he let out in a sigh, after a long while. "So good to see you back and in good health." A saccharine smile broke out on his lips, but his gaze remained piercing, revealing his true meaning. I interpreted it as, *try to betray me again and you'll find yourself in even worse health.* How could I have overlooked him for so long? He was the lion-serpent welcoming me into his den.

"Very good to be back. I hope you'll excuse my absence granted the circumstances of my immobility," I said looking down at my ankle.

"Ah, you don't have to ask for my excuse. At Foresyth, we teach everyone to be the drivers of their own erudition. Missing time away from that only hurts you alone," he said slowly. "But no matter, you are here now." The Meister tapped his cane and we all rose. I winced, placing weight awkwardly on my ankle. Nina saw this and offered me her hand, but I shook it off.

"I'm fine," I said.

"*Sub rosa*," we all spoke by the Meister's five taps of his cane.

"Today's session, as you all know, is reserved for the newest Initiate. We all have a part to play in educating our Circle members. Thus, I will present the canonical story of our Shattered Mother, and you will fill in the rest in our typical Socratic method," the Meister said. Something about the cadence of his voice made me feel like he had said the line many, many times before.

He pulled out a hardcover book from underneath his coat, one with gold gilded edges and coated in a black resin. The tome was so dark, it seemed as if the Meister was holding night itself.

"This, Dahlia, you may not recognize, but is a tome I am sure you are very familiar with—*The Book of Skorn*," the Meister said. His eyes twinkled an emerald sheen, reminding me of the first night he had appeared in front of my bookshop.

He turned the book to show me the titular page. The Book was etched in cursive lettering, with a distinctive name underneath it. *Aleric Khorvyn.* He had been a member of the Founding Five, if I recalled correctly.

"The unabridged version," I said, almost entranced by a tome so rare. If my bookshop had ever held it, it would have no doubt been the most valuable item there.

"Exactly. It has never been published in this form, but I was lucky enough to acquire it from a friend." The Meister looked at the tome lost in a reverie. I wondered what the story behind his acquisition entailed. It took him a moment to collect himself, but when he did, he handed me the Book. "Here," he said, sharing the valuable possession. "It is as much yours as it is ours now," he said.

My hands grabbed the Book, impressed but not surprised by its hefty weight. A warmth spread from the base of my palm and up to my fingers, creating an outline of fog on the black mirrored cover. I wanted to deny the pulsing of my fingertips, the way my body both recoiled *from* and ached *for* the Book, and the way my breath caught in my throat. I wanted to deny all of those sensations. But I couldn't.

The Book felt like pure power.

Logic over emotion. Fact over fiction.

I could almost hear my father's words rattling in my mind. He wouldn't have settled for half-truths or rationalizations. He died settling that score, I knew, but only because it was more important than life itself. Truth *was* life.

There must be a heating mechanism imbued in the Book to make the holder perceive the warming sensation, like a joule heater. I had found a few filaments in Nina's lab that could do the trick. I turned the Book over in my hands, discreetly searching, but for naught. It was solid.

"Well? What do you think?" A knowing smile spread on the Meister's lips.

I nodded, swallowing hard, and opened the Book. I gasped when I felt the silky smoothness of its beige pages. It was like a paper I had never touched before. It felt *warm.* I traced my fingertips along its title, feeling every ache and pulse of my fingertip. I've read this Book from cover-to-cover multiple times, but I had never felt its power this strongly. There was a sacredness to it I couldn't deny.

"Khorvyn had many friends, but also many enemies. He wanted to hide his most potent findings from them, so that they wouldn't be used against him. But what he unearthed those many years ago might be the most significant finding in the 19th century. And now it's ours to study, to harness." He paused before waving a hand. "If I may guide you to page three-forty-two."

Curiosity led my fingers to brush the edges of the pages, prodding them to reveal their secrets. I opened to the page the Meister had instructed. I looked down, scanning the words, reading them faster than

I could ever speak them. I had never seen this section of the Book, but I recognized the ones that came before. It was an Appendix, entitled *Origins of the Powers of Tarot.* I had never seen anything like it.

"If you may, read the words of our prophet Khorvyn and the Shattered Mother," the Meister pressed.

My chest was tight with anticipation, but I forced my eyes back to the beginning of the text. I read aloud:

"In my dream I was visited by the lowest emanation, an Ǣon between the realm of the living and the divine, called Sophia. She spoke softly and I saw the story as she recalled it in her mind's eye. 'I am Sophia,' the emanation said. There was a low and reverberating quality to her voice, weighted down by a trace of guilt. 'And this is how the material realm came to be.

"'"My father—the Monad—was a strict ruler of the cosmos. He viewed our responsibility as Ǣons to populate the cosmos with material objects—planets, stars, comets, all inanimate but divine creations. My brothers, Valentinus and Charis, were skillful Artisans and competed with each other to see which Ǣon could create the most perfect galaxy. My youngest brother, Horos, meticulously created the Milky Way, but the others teased him for it only had nine planets and one meager Sun. But I loved the galaxy that Horos had created, with one planet in particular that caught my eye. Its blues were the deepest I had ever seen, and it filled me with both an eternal sadness and an overwhelming sense of hope.

"'"The cosmos were a very lonely place. They were vast and deep, and my brothers and I spent many eons traveling and creating worlds. But I wanted to create one just for myself, a very different kind of world: one with sentient beings like me whom I could talk to, whom I could love and nourish. Though I knew my father would disapprove, I was mad with loneliness, and in a moment of despair, I created a Being like myself.

"'"I created the demiurge: a sentient worker who would help me build the material world. But because of my lowly form, and no protection from my father or brothers, the demiurge overpowered me. He betrayed me, trapped me in the process, and became an evil creator of his own volition.

"'The demiurge created the physical universe and humanity. He also spawned the Archons to preside over the material realm, and to stop humans from ascending back to the divine realm. I tried to stop the demiurge, but he was more powerful than me, and I remained trapped in the metaphysical plane.

"'That is when I sacrificed myself. I shattered my soul into seventy-eight pieces and cast them onto the blue planet so that the pieces would enter all of the sentient beings. These are the Universal Truths, known as the Tarot. I gave humans the ability to read and access the Tarot in the hope that learning the Truths would give them a chance to escape the material plane.'

"Thus concludes the dream from which I learned from where the powers of Tarot came to be. I learned through Sophia's guidance that the cards are pieces of Sophia's Universal Truths, and allow us to tap into the cosmic fabric that binds us all and seals us from ascending from the material realm. If one can harness the power of the cards, tap into the Universal Truths, then one may access the power of the mother Ǣon, Sophia, limitless as it is on Earth."

I stared blankly at the page for several moments before blinking, looking back up to the Circle. The gravity of the text hit me like a boulder. I tried to form words, but they all died on my lips.

This wasn't a prestigious magick school, this was a cult, based off of an occultist's dream. I tried to hide the horror from my face.

The Meister studied my features, his eyes slightly narrowed in confusion. "Well, Dahlia, now you know the origins of Tarot, from where you and all of us derive our powers. By embodying the Universal Truths, we can tap into the illusion of the material world. And change it, even," he said. "This should make your research topic a little easier, hm?"

I suppressed a scoff. The origins of Tarot were the subconscious mind. But I recognized the power of saying what people wanted to hear. And so, I contained my true thoughts and instead spun sugar into his ear.

"These are the most beautiful words I've ever read," I said, fixing my eyes on the Book in awe. "Thank you for allowing me to read them," I added, bile rising to my throat. No one ever said I enjoyed lying.

"We are happy to have you a part of us, Dahlia. Your natural gifts of divination will restore power to the House," he said.

My brows twitched, wanting to furrow, but I didn't let them budge. "I do have one question," I said carefully. I couldn't let on any of my skepticism, but I needed to understand how exactly they thought this so-called magick worked. The Meister nodded for me to go on.

"If we only need to tap into these Universal Truths to access the power, then why the elixirs? Why dull our senses to do so? Wouldn't the strongest magick be elicited from our full sensing minds and bodies?"

My gaze drifted to Nina, the residential potion mixer. She gave me a familiar smile, as if knowing I'd ask that very question.

But the Meister answered instead. "It's true our magick is stronger when we are, but that's where the paradox lies. Our physical bodies and senses are a cruel trick created by the demiurge. By dulling our mortal senses, we allow our spiritual ones to awaken. We suppress our humanity in order to access divinity. That is where we create true magick, true art.

"You might have guessed now the connection between peculiarities at Foresyth Conservatory and our belief system. We adorn ourselves in bright, rich colors to remind ourselves that the material world is but a beautiful illusion. Same goes for our food."

Holy hell. The beautiful, tasteless food. The ornate House, and its gorgeous inhabitants. They were all a constructed reminder that the world was a co-created illusion.

I nestled these new findings into the story I had built around Foresyth thus far. An arts Conservatory dedicated to the study—no *practice*, of the deadliest art of all: magick.

Wasn't that what the Meister said about art? That it allowed for the transcendence of the soul? And then there was *Sophia's Circle.* Of course. The Tramping Ground itself was a testament to transcendence. No material form, or at least organics, could exist there.

I thought of Sequoia in the bathtub, ghastly white. Even now, though her parlor had improved, she was looking shyly at her feet, the faint trace of near death still fresh on her. She had killed herself to transcend into this state of spiritual awakening as the text had suggested.

And then there was Aspen's dagger at my throat. I didn't need any further explanation of how that had challenged my *material form.*

Transcendence of the Soul, Foresyth's very motto. How could I have missed it, when it had been in plain sight all along? It all made sense now. The single thread that connected everything. Escaping the material plane and using the cards to access the metaphysical one.

And then there was Julian. Had he also been trying to transcend? To access Sophia's power? This question burned on my lips, but I knew it was too dangerous to speak. Julian had warned me that secrets lurked even deeper in Foresyth. There was a feeling in the back of my mind that this only scratched the surface.

"I'll need some time with this," I said, clutching the Book in my arms.

"Unfortunately, that won't be possible," the Meister said. "The Book is a holy relic, the Council loans it out on an hourly basis. Its only here now so you can feel its powers." The Meister paused, studying my reaction. "You can feel it, can't you?"

My gaze drifted back to the obsidian Book. Its cover was glossy, such that I could see my own reflection. What I could *feel* scared me. But the fact that I couldn't explain it terrified me even more.

"Yes, I can," I conceded. At least I was telling the truth.

Sequoia's gaze jerked up and caught my eye. "You should work on cultivating your connection to the Shattered Mother." She covered her mouth with her hands, almost embarrassed. "I'm sorry Meister, I know it's not in the Socratic form, but I just wanted to share a piece of advice with Dahlia. The way I accessed my connection with the Mother was through embodying her in the form of the cards." *The Empress.* The essence of female divinity. And with it, a dangerous allure.

"I'm well aware of that," I said curtly. The last time I saw her accessing the cards she almost died. I had no interest in doing that. I very well couldn't solve a murder case that way.

"There are safe ways to do it, of course. We could do it here, if you'd like," Sequoia said, her eyes twinkling. I kept mine level with hers but said nothing. *Was she insane?*

"That's enough. You know that we don't practice magick during Circle. We only exchange thoughts, ideas, and teachings here. There is a time and place for everything." The Meister turned to me. "And ritual is strictly forbidden unless authorized by me. That being said, Sequoia is right. If you still have any hesitations about our philosophy, it's best you speak to the Mother yourself. She's spoken to you, hasn't she?"

I thought back to the Initiation. To the feeling of her breath on my neck, and her hand reaching *inside* my chest.

"I think so, but it's hazy," I said. Hadn't she said we prayed to a false God, echoing Julian's words?

"You will now understand that your research prompt—deciphering the origins of Tarot—has been an ongoing group project. Skorn is the predecessor to Tarot and the one true magick. Everyone here has collected experiential case studies concerning their own lives of how they have seen the Shattered Mother's powers manifested in them. You are the last piece, Dahlia. Your experience is the last case study we are waiting for, before presenting the findings to the Council," the Meister said with a gravity that unsettled me.

The last piece. Was that why the Meister had brought me here to Foresyth? Not for investigating Julian's death, but helping with this research project? Embarrassment burned bright on my chest and neck. I had been so foolish, thinking his offer was genuine. But I had been so desperate and impressionable. Anger replaced shame and burned through me. He might have welcomed me to the lion's den, but that didn't mean I would leave here without raising hell.

I nodded in acceptance, trying my best for a sweet smile.

"I know you won't disappoint us."

*

When Circle broke, I felt so exhausted I could have slept for a week straight. Perhaps the Book had siphoned my energy. *No*, I broke the train of thought. I was tired because I had been through an exhausting ordeal of pretending to say all the right things and not revealing my true feelings. Lying was tiresome.

I stepped out of the sitting room and started down the hall. It pleasantly surprised me that dusk had not fallen yet, despite it being after Circle. I hesitated by the window in the dining room, watching the pinks and purples in the clouds intertwine behind the blossoming trees.

"Beautiful sunset," Aspen said, coming up behind me. His eyes were fixated on me, despite remarking at the view. I instinctively jerked back.

"So, I guess you're not keen on knives," he said, raising both his hands up. "I'm unarmed, I promise," he added, raising his hands in defense. "And besides, it wouldn't be hard to pin you to the wall, knife or no." His smile beamed, showing his teeth in a way that made my heart skip. A low laugh rumbled from his chest. "Relax, Dahlia. Only joking."

"Why are you always following me?" I asked, heat rising to my face.

"Not much else to do in this old, boring House. And you're pretty interesting." He shrugged his shoulders in a way that made me believe him. "I think Koi would agree."

I narrowed my eyes at the insinuation. "Your idea of alleviating your boredom is to threaten me?" I asked.

He paused, considering. He traced a finger across his bottom lip in thought and my eyes followed. The motion was aggravating. Was he using the cards on me right now? I wanted to blame them for the curling knot of heat in my stomach.

"Well, no. Not quite. I came here to apologize," he said, moving closer. I took a step back, and he lifted his hands again. "I'm just trying to keep my voice low," he said, his eyes glancing at the open door of the dining room. We were only a few feet away from the hall. He stepped closer and this time I didn't move.

"What part? Kidnapping me, or threatening to slice my throat?" I shot back, but the harshness of the intended words was lost in the quiver at my throat. Tears threatened at the corner of my eyes, but I didn't let them fall. *Shit*, I was losing it.

Aspen's features softened, and he stepped closer to the window. "For all of it. Koi was right. We should have let you in much earlier. Prepared you better."

"If it hadn't been for the vow of silence toward non-Initiatives," I mocked. "I never took you as a rule follower," I said.

"I'm not," he said. "and telling you too much, too soon—well, you're hard to convince of anything you can't rationalize."

"Everyone should be."

His brows furrowed. "Just because you can't rationalize something doesn't mean it isn't real."

"It *isn't* real to me." He was so close to me I could smell the musk from his skin, clover and pine, and something earthy like beeswax. For a moment I forgot what we were talking about.

"What isn't real?" He teased, sensing my confusion.

"I saw it on you," I said, my mind flashing to when he held me against his chest, knife in hand. That smile, oozing satisfaction. It was unmistakable. I might be good at reading books, but I was damn prodigious at reading people. "You looked so satisfied, holding that athame to my neck," I said, my voice light. I meant it to be accusatory, but it had come out as if I was remembering a dream.

A corner of his mouth lifted. "I can't deny that I like being close to you, no matter the circumstances." His mouth was so close to my neck, I could feel the breath on the same spot where he had held the dagger just a few days before. His hand jerked upward, as if to brush my hair, but then fell to his side.

Snap out of it, a distant voice screamed in my mind. *He's using the cards on you.* Even though the thought was ludicrous, it broke me out of whatever trance I had found myself in.

He sensed my shift and took a step back.

"You're using the cards." I said, my eyes narrowing like darts. "To get close to me. Funny for someone who's such a shameless flirt, you need to rely on magick to get close to people." I was satisfied by how harshly the words had come out. Hurt flashed across his features, and I knew my words had hit their mark.

"That's not true." His jaw tightened. "I have never used the cards on you."

I searched him for a tell but couldn't come up with one. Though that didn't mean much given he was a prodigious liar.

"Admit it. You're manipulating me." I pressed harder, wanting him to give in. I might not be reading his cards, but I could still read his features.

He laughed but the sound came out hollow. "That's rich. Coming from the master manipulator. I've heard how you *read* for people. How you read for Koi," he said. The words stung because they were true.

"That's—" The words stopped coming out. I couldn't even deny it. The lies exhausted me.

"I'm not even blaming you for it," he said, running his hands through his hair. "I just— damn, I just want something *true*. And you're the closest thing I've ever seen to the truth. And what's so funny is that you don't even know," he said. "You try to hide your feelings, you try to manipulate us, but the truth is written all over that precious face of yours. You're the truest thing I've ever seen."

Red burst across my cheeks. Knowing that he could see it made me blush even harder. I swallowed hard before finding my words. How was it that my enemy saw me for who I was, when so many others never could? Either he was perceptive, or I had been a complete failure at hiding myself. Regardless of which it was, there was still a part of me that saw this as an opportunity. I wanted to prove him wrong. I wasn't *truth*; I was a liar, just like him. I'd lie my way to find the truth about Julian, and I'd use whatever means were necessary.

In a moment of reckless bravery, I gripped the collar of his shirt and pulled him close into me so that my lips touched the outer edge of his ears. "Fine, you want the truth? Then why don't you start, tell me something *real*," I said, letting the wind of my breath fan his flames. I knew he couldn't deny a challenge. I'd get the truth about Julian out of him one way or another.

Aspen's features mixed with surprise and delight, pulling his head back up to look me squarely in the eyes. His pupils dilated with excitement, green and brown streaks being swallowed up by black. "I would love to," he said, almost too eagerly, like he'd been waiting for the invitation. He put his hand over mine where I still held a clump of his shirt. Why did it feel like I'd already lost, even as he stepped willingly into my trap?

I swallowed my pride, trying to ignore how naturally his fingers threaded with mine, like they had with Sequoia's. I tried to ignore how the heat of his coarse palms flush against mine soothed the cold inside of me. I tried to ignore how his eyes, like burning embers, found mine equally transfixed to his. I really tried.

But I still followed him, out of the dining room and down the hallway, as if I had no choice at all.

The Acolyte and the Alchemist: Part VI

The two scholars tore through the Archive books, their fingers smudged with ink, their candles burning low. Each discovery unraveled another layer of untold history.

One book was a personal journal from Patty Mearsheimer, a member of the Founding Five and Advisor to Nikola Tesla. She claimed to have guided him in harnessing ocean magick—the rhythmic pulse of the tides—to shape electricity into the alternating current he would later perfect.

Another account detailed an Advisor's role using glamor magick to help negotiate a treaty with the Lakota Sioux. George Crook, a U.S. Army general, had relied on occult counsel to manage delicate talks over gold mines in the northwestern Americas.

But neither of these compared to the black tome Quill had pulled from the archives.

It was an unabridged version of *The Book of Skorn*, penned by Aleric Khorvyn, another of the Founding Five. Quill and Hamra hunched over it, flipping between its pages and the versions they had found in the library. Entire sections had never been seen before. It didn't take long for him to regret finding the book in the first place.

Quill frowned, skimming a passage. *This shouldn't exist.*

"Maybe it's a misprint," he said.

Hamra shook her head. "No. These sections were meant to be here. They don't just describe the use of magick cards, they discuss the origin of their power." Her voice dropped lower, almost reverent. "They say that the cards' powers come from the Shattered Mother, who imbued the cards with seventy-eight pieces of her soul."

Quill shifted. A low, almost imperceptible hum rang in his ears, like the faint vibration of a tuning fork.

"Does it feel strange to hold it?" he asked.

Hamra's fingers traced the cover. "It's as if the Book itself is infused with—"

"Magick." They both said it in unison.

A silence stretched between them.

Quill exhaled, setting the Book down as if it had suddenly grown heavier. "I think we should give it back." The tome felt intoxicating, its presence curled around his thoughts, pulling him under. This couldn't be right.

Hamra didn't even look up. "I think we should test it."

Quill's gaze snapped to her. "That is firmly Advisor territory. We aren't supposed to practice magick outside of leadership-sanctioned ceremonies."

Hamra smirked. "And why should all the power be reserved for the Advisors? Why let them keep it locked away when it's right here, at our fingertips? Why should we spend our lives preparing rituals for clients when we could use this for ourselves?"

Quill hesitated. She saw it, too—the slight dip in his shoulders, the line in his brow, the moment of doubt. And in that instant, her voice softened into crushed velvet.

"This could become our magnum opus," she mused. "Didn't you come to Foresyth for this very reason—to understand where power comes from? Well, here it is. Right in front of us. A theory waiting to be tested."

She stretched her arms out across the Book and intertwined her hand with his, her final play. The warmth rushing to Quill's head wasn't just from the Book anymore. Her skin was warm against his hands, and blood was rushing behind his ears.

A source implied that the magick was real, not simply persuasive ritual. This was the closest proof he'd ever gotten. What was the harm with testing a theory?

The Book sat between them, waiting. And Quill—despite everything—was already reaching for it.

Chapter 23: The Kiln

We were standing in front of a dark green door several down from the entrance to the lab. Aspen took out a key from his back pocket.

"No magick locks?" I teased.

"No, you don't learn that until third year," he said under his breath, fiddling with the lock. I could tell he was joking when a sly smile broke out on his lips.

"Where are we going?" The question came out sharper than I intended. I was tired of being led through secret corridors and shown hidden spots around Foresyth. If Aspen had any intention of killing me, this would have been the perfect opportunity. My father instilled in me the belief that no one could be trusted; that everyone was dangerous. But something deep inside—something I couldn't rationalize, something instinctual—whispered that this time, he was being honest.

"If you want to see something real, then follow me," he said and took my hand again. The thought of Sequoia seeing me with Aspen was enough to make my stomach twist. And yet, I found my hand instinctively curling into his. "No one else knows this place," he said, leading me down the steps. "And no one else has a key."

When we reached the bottom of the staircase, swallowed up by the subterranean darkness, the glow of a flame appeared. Aspen turned to me, his face cast in an orange hue. He was holding a match, perpetually burning without the flame consuming the wood.

"That's a cool trick," I said.

He scoffed and turned back to the room. In the dim glow, the room seemed to be a storage closet. Old furniture and mildewing books were stacked across every direction.

"This is it?" I asked. "Rotting furniture is your version of real?"

"Ye of little faith," he said, pulling me to one end of the room. A bookshelf was stacked with rotting books from floor to ceiling. "Hold on tight to your dictionary," he said, pulling down one of the books. The shelf started to shake and began to approach us. It swiveled open on a top hinge like a circular doorway. It led to an even darker room.

"Damn."

"I get a snide remark at fire magick but a hidden doorway impresses you?" Aspen said. I pushed him away, tracing my own path through the doorway. It reminded me of the false shelves in my father's bookshop—the ones that promised shelves of hidden tomes, yet led, in my imagination, to Babylonian vaults and cursed Alexandrian cities. I used to pretend every book I touched had teeth. The bite, I hoped, would jar me awake into a life I actually wanted.

"It's a tunnel," I said, staring out into the seeming never-ending darkness.

"Yes," Aspen said from behind me, his flame burning brighter, the orb seemed to grow in size to the proportion of space. "The school is full of them, connecting hidden rooms and workshops." I distantly wondered if there was a tunnel connecting to the lab.

"You can get into any room in the House through them." He winked, taking a large step through the door to guide us further into the tunnel. We walked single file for a few long moments in silence. We had already passed several diverts away from the main tunnel. This had to be an incredibly intricate system. We passed one sharp right turn that had several collapsed metal and wooden barricades in front of it. My grip on his hand tightened reflexively, and I was surprised when he returned my pressure.

"What's that?"

"Very old magick. I wouldn't go down those pathways if you can help it. They used to be warded when the House's magick was stronger, but they haven't been for a while. Whatever is down there, you don't want to be near it." Aspen spoke in a steady voice as if recounting a reading.

"Here, we're almost here," he said, leading me further down a turn. We passed several of those barricaded tunnel paths and I ignored the shiver running along my arms every time we passed one.

Old magick. Something was definitely there, magick or not. But the heat of Aspen's palm was a welcoming signal to follow.

I spotted a splotch of light up ahead. A skylight. Golden rays of sunset filtered through a grate and poured onto my feet.

"This leads outside," I said, looking up. A stray mockingbird flew overhead.

"The kiln has to be so many feet away from the House, and it needs an exhaust," he said. He unlocked the door with another set of keys and pushed it open, his muscles taut with strain under the weight. If Aspen struggled to open the door, I couldn't even imagine how well my attempt could go. Note bene: don't get locked in.

"You took me down a basement, through a hidden doorway, then a tunnel system, and now you think I'm going to go through this tetanus-ridden iron door with you?"

He grinned from ear to ear. "Of course you will, Alice. Don't you want to see where the rabbit hole leads?" Curiosity was one of my worst traits. I sighed, stepping through the door, following the glow of light on the other side.

At first, I was blinded by a sharp white light. I covered my eyes, looking away. But they adjusted in a few seconds, and I realized I was looking at what looked like a giant oven.

A kiln.

Metal pipes spanned the width of the space, all leading to the central cylinder. The place smelled of scorched sand and steam, of charred cedar, and wet ash. It was the mineral tang of something half-alive and half-alchemical, like the breath of the earth itself held captive. And at its core there was an impossibly white light. My eyes adjusted to the brightness, but I still couldn't look at it.

"You'll need to wear glasses if you're going to stare directly," Aspen said.

I turned my gaze back to him. He had extinguished the flame in his finger and was now rounding a wooden table at the opposite side of the room. Various tools, long pipes, some strange bulbs, and torches littered the top of the table.

His workshop. He had taken me to his workshop.

My eyes snapped back up to the kiln. Relief washed over me—too small to fit a body. Unless, of course, he planned to dismember me first.

"Tell me what you're thinking," he said, stepping closer.

"I don't think you want to know."

"There's nothing more I *want* to know."

I paused for a moment but finally yielded. "I'm thinking about how you'd go about stuffing me into that kiln," I said. The truth felt good on my tongue, even if it was only a half-joke.

He let out a roar of laughter. "I'm not stuffing you anywhere. Besides, it would ruin the kiln. Why do you think I'm so protective of it? I've never shown this place to anyone else."

A knot was starting to form in my stomach. *Not even Sequoia?* I didn't like thinking about the Trees keeping secrets from each other. And even more so them telling me a secret but not one another. And though I was still angry at Sequoia for keeping the cards a secret, there was still a part of me that didn't want to betray her friendship. Even if it sprouted from a bed of lies.

"You're a glassblower," I said, tracing my fingertips over the torch equipment.

"Mhm," he said, his eyes not falling from me.

"Interesting. I pegged you as more of the metal-working, Hephaestus type," I said in the most mocking tone I could muster. He was so far from Hephaestus it was painful.

"Ouch," he said, coming around the table next to me. "I started with metal. But the temperatures were too low—my sculptures were melting before they had a chance to solidify. As my magick grew stronger, I needed a medium that could handle it. Turns out glass can handle all two-thousand degrees of it," he said.

I scrunched my nose at him. "An interesting way of saying you're too hot to handle."

He laughed again, and I wished I could bottle up that noise and keep it with me. It was deep and true. I hadn't heard anyone laugh like that since my father was alive.

"I'm sure you can handle me," he said, smirking.

I ignored his flirtation, remembering the true reason I was down here. I needed answers, and the time was now. I had come this far; I needed to use his vulnerability. *Weaponize* it.

"Aspen." His name caught in my throat. I turned hesitantly to look at him, and he met my eyes. "Earlier, when you said you wanted me here. Why?" His motives were confusing, and his actions contradictory. He suspected I was investigating Julian's death, and yet he wasn't stopping me. His actions might even be aligned with *helping* me.

"Despite what you might think, I want you to figure out what happened to Julian. I don't believe for a second that he killed himself."

I met his steely gaze, encouraging him to go on.

"Julian isn't—wasn't—the melancholy type. He was jovial, brought a fresh perspective into the House. Something else must have happened the night of the ceremony; he was known for speaking out against the Meister's philosophies."

"What do you remember about that night?" I said, edging him on.

Aspen hesitated, the weight of his next words pulling the air tight around us. The ash was collecting in my throat. He finally drew in a long, deliberate breath. "We all had taken the elixir," he said quietly, his voice almost a confession. "The one Sequoia and Nina prepared . . . for soul flight. We all drank it." His gaze flickered to mine, searching for something—understanding, maybe. Or absolution.

"Dahlia . . ." His voice softened as he reached out, his fingers barely brushing my arm. The touch was light, but it sent a jolt through me, setting every nerve on edge. "I know you have every reason to doubt me. But I need you to believe this." His stare was molten. "I want to know what happened to Julian as much as you do. He was my friend . . ." His voice cracked, the words trailing off like the admission cost him something.

"And I think you're the only one who can figure it out," he whispered, the gleam from his eyes hardening. I could feel my eyebrows twitch into a furrow and I countered the movement, willing them to relax. How could he believe in me so fervently when I scarcely believed in myself?

We stood there for a moment, watching each other in silence. I wrestled with his words, not wanting to accept them, yet finding myself sinking into their weight. Finally, he spoke again, his voice quieter. "There's something else I need to show you."

He moved past me toward a pedestal draped in a linen sheet and, with a single graceful motion, unveiled it. What lay beneath took my breath away. It was the most beautiful sculpture I'd ever seen, even though I couldn't fully understand what it was. Entirely made of glass, it resembled a vase, yet appeared more like a puzzle—endlessly shifting, without a fixed form, beginning, or edge. The glass spiraled in continuous loops of deep Prussian blue, a color that felt strangely familiar. Just when I thought I could grasp its pattern, it morphed again, slipping away from my mind's eye.

"It's devastatingly beautiful."

"Yes, you are," he said.

I rolled my eyes and turned back to the sculpture. Staring at it was both unsettling and mesmerizing. The sensation felt oddly familiar . . . Then, it hit me. It was the same feeling I had while holding *The Book of Skorn.*

"It's forged with Skorn magick. Out of curiosity, can you guess which cards?"

I considered the object in front of me. Perhaps this was as close as I could get to reading Aspen.

"The Wheel of Fortune, of course. Representing the circularity, infinity. The Two of Swords. Duality, choice. Explains how I'm repulsed and entranced at the same time. And perhaps the Queen of Cups. The flow of water, emotions, ever fluid."

He studied me for a moment before replying. "Pretty good. But two are missing. There's a heavy pinch of the Seven of Cups, and a tad bit of the Devil in there, too."

"Ah, Satan's tricks. How could I have missed it?" I teased, eyeing him.

"A satyr that gets too much vitriol, if you ask me."

We both caught ourselves chuckling. He stared at me, his mouth still spread into a brilliant smile. *A crack*. This was the time in a reading when I'd push harder.

"Can I ask you something else?" I edged closer, sensing I was getting warmer, but I hadn't reached the heart of it yet. I had seen the fractures between the students, but now I was nearing something even darker—the cracks between them and Foresyth itself. The students didn't follow the Meister's decrees, at least not always. Sequoia hadn't. Maybe Julian's death was just one symptom of a deeper, festering wound, poisoning them all.

"Do you ever question this place? What it offers you?"

His smile faded, and he paused for a long time before replying. "There's a lot about Foresyth I don't agree with—most of us don't," he said quietly, as though afraid someone might overhear, even though we were far from anyone else in the House. "I thought I could change it from the inside, given that I couldn't escape it."

"What do you mean?"

"For one reason or another, we're bound to it. We're powerless."

The idea that Aspen was powerless was absurd. He had so much influence in Circle it was almost sickening. "Powerless? How?" I whispered, half expecting him to brush off the question. But he met my stare, the lines around his eyes tightening as if the truth caused him physical pain.

"The Meister has a very particular way of choosing us. He picks us, not just for our merits or lineage, but our family's debts." Aspen paused, his voice quieter.

I scrunched my features together, waiting for him to continue.

"My father, Titus, he didn't just amass his fortune from his cunning or luck." His eyes fell downward, back toward the tool bench. "He has been using the Advisors for years. And the price for that type of service isn't just money—it's *us*." Aspen looked up then, and I almost staggered back by the severity of his expression. "Sequoia too, her mother didn't earn her fame in the theatre just from talent, the Advisors had a hand in that, too."

My breath caught. The focus on lineage at Foresyth—it wasn't just an elitist prejudice, it was practical. Their parents had traded success for their children's future.

"That's cruel. You and Sequoia aren't at fault for the decisions your parents made," I said.

"Though that might be true, we all still answer to our parent's misdoings, one way or another," he said. "But don't misunderstand me: regardless of the debt, I want to be here. So does Sequoia. We're all scholars at heart, by birth or otherwise." My heart sank at the mention of her name. Was the warm, spiraling sensation in my chest . . . jealousy?

He looked toward the kiln, the light from the flames reflected in his eyes, yet he didn't flinch from the brightness like I had. "My father has exceedingly high expectations, and I admit that I sometimes put those on others. But it doesn't mean I don't question my own abilities."

"Everyone does. Especially those with the best of them." I paused, recalling the first conversation I had with Aspen in the breakfast room. "When you said you were here for the art, I doubted you. But now I see you were telling the truth. Your sculptures really are magnificent." My cheeks flushed at the admittance.

"Thank you," Aspen replied with a smile that didn't quite reach his eyes.

I looked away, my eyes traced the curves of the glass in front of me. "So this is your research work—what you'll be presenting to the Council at the Symposium. This is your magick," I said, rounding the pedestal to get another view from the other side. I couldn't imagine how these slight curves and features could have ever been forged by hand. The piece seemed as if it was assembled by magick. Something this extraordinary belonged in a museum, not buried in a tunnel like this.

He stepped closer, stopping just in front of the sculpture, and I felt the hairs on my arms rise. "Do you trust me?" he asked, his voice low, his eyes emanating their own source of heat.

My thoughts spun. I had been conditioned to trust no one, to be an impartial seeker of the truth. Of course I didn't trust him—I wasn't supposed to trust anyone. But despite that, my body betrayed me, instinctively drawn toward his presence, defying the logic of my mind.

"I don't know yet," I said.

"Then maybe this will convince you," Aspen said. And before I could react, his hand had swiped the glass sculpture to the floor. It fell so fast that I heard the crash in my ears seconds after seeing the pieces at my feet.

"What the hell—" I choked, my voice catching in my throat as I stared at the shattered remains at my feet. My heart pounded in my chest, the horror of what he'd done sinking in.

"Why did you do that?" I whispered, unable to tear my eyes away from the wreckage.

But before the shock could fully register, something else stirred inside me—a sudden, unexplainable heat. It unfurled slowly, spreading through my core like molten fire, each wave stronger, more consuming. I gasped, my breath hitching as the warmth surged lower, flooding my body with an intensity that made me rock and tremble.

I wanted to recoil, to scream, but I couldn't. Every part of me felt pulled towards Aspen and his devilish grin. Were those specks of amber in his eyes? It felt like we were tethered by some force far beyond reason. What had he done to me?

"You wanted to see something real. You wanted to know that I hadn't been using the cards on you." A dark undercurrent grew in his voice as he spoke, stepping closer to me. I winced as his feet crunched on the glass below. "Well, Dahlia. There's only one way to convince you of anything, and that's to show you."

My hands instinctively went up to his chest, as if commanded by an external force. The feeling I had from looking at the sculpture was now how it felt to watch him, his eyes narrow and serpentine, rounding every curvature of my cheek and flesh. The green in his eyes flickered in the kiln light, and I was entranced by the whorls and stripes of his irises. Their tendrils seemed to reach out to me—pulling me closer like an asp. The wave of inexplicable desire crashed over me, and even the faintest voice in my head, trying to warn me, seemed gurgling underwater. I was overcome by an almost primal need.

I *needed* him closer to me. I needed to know what it felt like to be bit by Eden's serpent.

He stepped closer. The flames behind him cast his shadow long across the floor. I crashed into him, my body caught in the pull of something dark and unspeakably sweet. My hands fell across his neck, our faces only inches apart, and our breaths mingling at one another's lips. I was pulled—and pushed—into him.

My lips found his, and relief flooded me at the warmth of him. He groaned in response. I inhaled the smell of sulfur and stone, relishing as it scorched my lungs. Our lips danced on each other's like a ballet, him supporting my every lurch and spin. It was as if we had danced many times before.

In the next instance, the spell was broken, and I pushed him off of me.

"What the hell?" I spewed, wiping the taste of him from my lips.

He considered me for a moment, the corner of his lips upturned. "I'll give you a second to figure it out."

I heard the glass sculpture breaking all over again. He used the cards. He wanted to prove to me that he'd been honest, that he hadn't used them on me before, and the only way to do so was to show me how it would be when he *did.*

The counter factual.

"We can't just channel the cards whenever, wherever. The use of magick requires sacrifice. Something we make, something we cast our energy into." He shrugged, stepping around his spoiled work. "I channel mine into these sculptures. Breaking these represents the sacrifice that Sophia made, all those eons ago. I forge, I cast, I break. Only then can the power be unleashed. Everyone has their unique method, but the underlying principle is the same. Unless you've seen me breaking vases around you, you can be assured I haven't been using any magick on you. Whatever you feel around me is yours, and only yours. It's real."

The words settled over me, and I grimaced.

"I can't believe you made me kiss you," I said, still reeling in shock. I had never been so overcome with emotion. "How disgusting." The feeling of the press of his lips still fresh on mine, I felt their absence.

His smile grew. "I'll have to challenge you on that one. Free will still exists, some argue. I can only amplify emotions, not create false ones."

He must have drugged me. Or confounded my senses in some other way. I couldn't believe that shattering some glass could completely overpower me.

"You must have done something else. Poisoned me or something," I started. My head was spinning, trying to come up with a logical explanation for what happened.

He laughed, but it was humorless. Not like the laugh from before. "Gods, I've never seen anything like it. You don't take magick for granted, do you?" he asked before continuing, "Damn, you *interrogate* it."

"Then how?" I almost shouted. All the thoughts in my head rattled against my skull, their cage. They begged to be free.

He took a long breath in. "The cards, they don't make up new emotions—they just heighten the ones you already have. Tapping into them is what gives you power. I forged this," he said looking down at the shambles at his feet, "thinking of you. Of your eyes. And how they made me feel like I was a puzzle, being endlessly turned this way and that, studied. A hypothesis, always changing with the introduction of new facts, new perspectives."

The color. I recognized it now. Prussian blue. They were the same as my eyes.

"I know you still don't believe me, Dahlia, and perhaps for good reason. You should be suspicious of everything—everyone—at this school. But I want to earn your trust. I want you here at Foresyth." The way he looked at me made me want to break down in tears. It reminded me of the desperation I saw in my patrons, them so desperately searching for answers to their messy lives. They thought I held all the answers, but I didn't.

"If you wanted me here so badly, then why did you poison me the first day?" The accusation was hot in my throat. I wanted to believe him, but the weight of everything I'd seen, everything I still didn't understand, was suffocating.

The look of confusion washed over him as he scrunched his eyes and nose together. He didn't even know what I was talking about.

"The first day—I came into the breakfast room. You piled my plate up high, and gave me a tea no one else was drinking," I explained. "It had an herb in it—something along the lines of a truth serum. I read about it in the library."

"Dahlia, I have no idea what you're talking about. I might have suggested a tea, but I didn't poison it."

My shoulders slumped, a wave of disbelief crashing over me. He had to be lying. He *had* to be. Why else would he have pressed me with all those questions afterward? He was the one who poured the cup, watched me drink it. But the uncertainty in his voice, the confusion in his eyes . . . it gnawed at my anger, unraveling the edges of my certainty.

"You need to be careful. You might be trusting the wrong person." He reached out, placing a hand on my shoulder, but the gesture felt too familiar, too invasive. I shrugged him off, the anger flaring again, hot and wild inside me.

"You're right," I spat, stepping back from his touch. "I *am* trusting the wrong person." My voice cracked, the words tasting bitter on my tongue. "I should go."

The look in his eyes—the hurt, the confusion, and something else I couldn't name—was almost enough to make me hesitate. Almost. But I couldn't afford to be swayed, not now. Not when I didn't even know if I could trust my own instincts anymore.

Before he could say another word, I bolted for the door, slipping past him and running through the tunnels as fast as my legs would carry me. The darkness closed in around me, swallowing every shred of light. The damp chill clung to my skin, but it was the suffocating panic that made it hard to breathe. Tears blurred my vision, but I wiped them away furiously, trying to keep the dam from breaking.

The sound of shattering glass still rang in my ears. It pierced, sharp and relentless, reverberating through the tunnels. And that's when I realized, it wasn't just the glass that had shattered.

Something inside me had splintered too—my grasp on reality, my sense of control. It felt like the ground beneath me had cracked open, exposing something dark and terrifying just below the surface. How could I trust anything—anyone—when even my own mind felt like that perplexing, ever-changing sculpture?

I ran faster, my feet pounding the stone floor. And in the back of my mind, a voice whispered: *Who are you really running from?*

Chapter 24: An Unexpected Visitor

Sometimes I found myself glad that my father was dead. At least he didn't have to witness how pathetic I was, running through tunnels, tears streaking down my face like a child.

Emotions are just a physiological response to stimuli. Control them. Don't let them control you. His voice echoed in my mind, sharp and clinical. I swallowed the tightness burning in my throat and forced myself to breathe deeply, methodically.

Inhale, exhale.

Bit by bit, my pulse slowed, the panic retreating like a receding tide.

I wasn't falling apart. I was just overwhelmed. Sleep—that's what I needed. Then I'd be able to think clearly. But before I exited the tunnels, I forced myself to stop, pulling out my notepad. I scribbled down the details of the tunnel system, noting which entrances were blocked, and the path back to Aspen's workshop. I'd need that information again soon.

Stick to what you can prove. Fact, not feeling. My father's mantra whispered in my ear, as if he were standing right behind me. Cold. Unyielding.

I needed answers. Not emotions. And I needed them soon.

My ankle throbbed with every step, swollen from my reckless escape, and my head felt like it was moments from splitting open. Somehow, I managed to sneak back to my room undetected. I tore off my clothes and collapsed onto the bed, feeling a sense of relief as the House's shadowed corridors closed around me. I'd been cautious, careful, yet part of me felt grounded here, tethered to something I couldn't understand. As if Foresyth had started to sink its roots into me, anchoring me into its dark soil.

I rolled over, my skin still tingling with the ghost of Aspen's touch. My lips burned with the memory of our kiss. How had I been so foolish? How could I have trusted him, even for a second? But in the back of my mind, the memory of his lips lingered, defying all logic, dragging me back into the feeling of that moment.

I couldn't afford to be reckless anymore. I couldn't afford to trust *any* of them. I was so close to uncovering the truth that Julian had taken to his grave. I just had to keep pushing a little longer.

Sleep didn't come easily. I tossed and turned for what felt like hours, my mind chasing shadows in the dark. But when exhaustion finally claimed me, the sound of shattering glass rattled through my dreams.

*

I awoke drenched in cold sweat, my throat raw from a tangled scream, and the vivid image of my father morphing into a serpent still searing in my mind's eye. I blinked hard, trying to shake it off. Glancing at my watch, I saw it was just after six in the morning. Plenty of time to investigate before the others stirred. I threw the covers aside and swung my legs over the bed, testing my right ankle with a slow, circular motion. It ached, but the pain was tolerable.

As I crept down the stairs, I was careful to avoid the boards I knew would betray me with their creaks. The House, as if aware of my plan, seemed to cooperate, granting me a soundless descent. The Meister's office was my first target. He was complicit in Julian's murder, and I just needed to prove *how*.

I reached the door of his office, an imposing slab of mahogany with a gold-encrusted doorknob. But the door was locked. He was likely away on Advisor business.

I ran my fingers over the keyhole, assessing the lock. Retrieving a hairpin from my bag, I crouched down and got to work, twisting and turning, but after five frustrating minutes, the lock refused to give. It was as though something was wedged deep inside, blocking my progress.

I sighed in irritation, dropping my satchel to the floor to free up my hands. As I did so, the deck of Skorn cards spilled out, scattering across the floor.

Use the cards, whispered a voice, faint but unmistakable.

I froze. My heart hammered in my chest as I whipped my head around. The hallway was empty, but the voice—that voice—I knew it.

Sophia?

A shiver crawled up my spine.

First, dreams of my father turning into a serpent, now disembodied whispers. I scoffed at myself, stuffing the deck back into my satchel.

"I'm losing my damned mind," I muttered under my breath. But even as I tried to push the absurdity aside, my fingers hovered over the cards again, an inexplicable urge pulling at me. What harm could it do?

Reluctantly, I sifted through the deck and pulled out The High Priestess. She stood at the threshold of knowledge, the keeper of secrets. I smirked to myself.

"Guide me through the doorway," I whispered half-jokingly.

Sliding the edge of the card between the door and its latch, I felt a heat build between my fingers. A faint buzzing filled my ears, low and steady, like a pulse. I worked the card along the door's seam, frustration mounting as nothing happened. Sweat beaded on my forehead, and I wiped it away, gritting my teeth. *This was ridiculous.*

But just as I was about to toss the card aside and resume picking the lock, there was a loud, satisfying *click*. And then the door swung open.

I stared at it, breathless. Pride ran through me in a hot wave.

The cards heighten your emotions. Aspen's words rang in my ears.

No. It had to be a coincidence. I'd just managed to work the mechanism from both angles. Any piece of cardboard could have done the trick. But even as I tried to rationalize it, something deep inside me edged otherwise.

The card had worked because I willed it to.

I shook the thoughts away, refocusing on the task at hand. I pushed the door open and slipped inside, quietly closing it behind me.

*

I spent the next thirty minutes scouring the Meister's desk and bookshelf. The antique oak desk—where I had once sat while he piled on research topics—loomed in the center. I shifted uncomfortably at the memory. He'd given me so many assignments, I could barely spare any time to investigate Julian's death. It was almost as if the Meister wanted me distracted.

I rifled through the drawers, coming up empty-handed. I wanted to find *The Book of Skorn* but knew better than to think it would just be lying in one of his drawers, unguarded. On the second pass, I remembered a trick my father used to hide case files. He'd stick them beneath the drawer, in a hidden compartment on the other side. With that in mind, I pressed my fingers to the underside of each drawer, feeling for any concealed papers or false bottoms.

Still nothing.

A groan of frustration escaped me as I slumped into the worn leather chesterfield chair. If I were the Meister, I wouldn't hide anything in plain sight. But maybe he wasn't as careful as he thought. Maybe he'd overlooked something.

I opened the top drawer again, this time rattling it side to side, hoping to jostle something loose. A flash of white caught my eye as a thin slip of paper slid between the cracks.

My heart leapt, and a smile tugged at the corners of my lips. Finally.

I slid my fingers behind the drawer, feeling for the papers that had slipped through. The first two sheets were bloodwork panels. One of them had my name on it.

What the hell? Why was the Meister analyzing my blood?

The second blood panel was Julian's.

They were dated for February 1919, almost a month before Julian died.

I surveyed through the other papers. Several of them were dismissal notices of students, issued by the Council for "academic misalignment." I stuffed the two pieces of evidence into my bag and then turned my attention to the letter. It was heavier cardstock, the kind reserved for deeds or wills. The paper was folded neatly into thirds, like a letter. My pulse quickened as I noticed an indentation between the two folds—a stamp. A circle enclosing a rose.

The symbol of Foresyth.

I ran my fingers over the mark, tracing the familiar grooves before carefully unfolding the letter. A weight settled in my chest, thick and heavy.

> *Dear Meister Christopher Renate,*
>
> *Given the grave situation in which this letter finds you and the school, your presence is urgently requested at Council. We would like to discuss the matter of contracting a detective over the disappearance of Julian Earhardt. The exact location will be telegrammed to you an hour before the meeting on December 10th, 1919. We expect to bring this matter to a close as swiftly as possible.*

The Council was involved in my recruitment. When I met them, they all seemed to know who I was. At first, I thought it was because of my father. *But what if it wasn't him*—my thoughts were interrupted by a knock at the door.

My head swiveled up before I ducked under the desk. The doorknob rattled and I held my breath and started to count. *One, two, three . . .*

After a few seconds, the knob stopped moving. Whoever was at the door must've turned away after confronting the lock. I sighed a breath of relief. *I needed to get out of here.*

I waited a few more minutes before I got up from where I was crouched and slipped the letter back in between the drawers. I traced my steps carefully, making sure I hadn't left anything upturned. When I finished, I slipped back through the mahogany door and crept back upstairs to my room.

*

The following few days at Foresyth, I kept to myself. The Meister canceled our mentorship meetings again, citing urgent Advisor business. But I knew the real reason: he didn't want to confront me because he knew I'd grown suspicious of him. He had brought me here for a purpose other than finding Julian's killer, and I was hell-bent on discovering what that was.

I bided my time before I tried locating my father's journals. I attended the Circle but remained withdrawn, only speaking when the others pressed me. Both Aspen and Sequoia tried to catch me before and after sessions, but I avoided them by feigning ill or busy and slipping away. It wasn't just what had happened with Sequoia that made me keep my distance, but there was a gnawing guilt over the kiss with Aspen. Not that I'd had much say in the matter—he'd practically tricked me.

But hadn't there been something real between us? I couldn't deny the attraction, the way he confidently carried himself in the Circle, the way he stood up for his beliefs, and pushed his fellow students to think critically, even if he did come across harsh. And his artwork—it drew me in, stirred something deep in me. Had he truly been friends with Julian, and genuinely wanted me to solve his murder? Or was he just another one of the Meister's pawns?

Circle had ended almost an hour ago, and I found myself sitting on the edge of my bed, shuffling the Skorn deck to keep my hands busy as my mind raced. *Aspen, the Council, the Meister.* Was everything linked or was I descending into madness, just as my father had? I needed to find my father's journal, and for that, I'd have to return to the tunnels.

I surmised that from the coordinates which extended beyond the reaches of the House. At least my encounter with Aspen hadn't been for nothing.

A knock at the door pulled me from my thoughts. "Ms. Blackburne," a voice called, snapping me out of my trance. I stood quickly, a card slipping from my hands. The Hermit.

My eyebrows knitted together, and my intuition flared. "Gabriel," I breathed.

I opened the door to see the familiar face of Richard. "I'm sorry to disturb you, Ms. Blackburne, but you have a visitor," he said. I pushed past Richard and rushed downstairs. And there he was—my childhood best friend, standing in the foyer with his hands shoved into his pockets, glasses slightly askew.

"Gabriel!" I ran to him, my breath catching in my throat. His face brightened at the sight of me, and he lowered his satchel to return my embrace. I hugged him tightly, inhaling the familiar scent of parchment, leather, and rain—the smell of Greenwich, the smell of home. A longing sadness settled into my chest.

"What are you doing here?" I pulled back, panic rising in my chest. Gabriel didn't belong here. He'd be in danger. The Meister could walk through the doors at any moment and see him, breaking Foresyth's strict code of no visitors.

"Dahlia, it's so good to see you. I got your letters." He smiled, missing the urgency in my tone.

"How did you find this place? You can't be here. It's not safe," I whispered, searching his eyes for understanding, willing him to realize the danger he was in.

"Is there somewhere we can talk?" he asked, his voice gentle but firm.

I sighed, leading him into the breakfast room and closing the door behind us. The hour was late, and no one should be coming in. Being with Gabriel felt like being back in the world I knew—safe, familiar. But it also felt uncomfortable. He hadn't changed a bit, whereas I had. His presence couldn't change that fact.

"How've you been, Dahl?" he asked, his eyes scanning my face.

"Fine." I forced a smile.

He wasn't convinced. "Come on, I know you better than that. You look . . . different." His gaze lingered on my clothes—a bright sweater Sequoia had picked out for me, paired with a black skirt that hit my hips just right. "More feminine."

"There's a stupid dress code here," I said, sitting down at the breakfast table.

"So . . . you don't like it here?" He leaned closer, concern etched in his brow.

"I . . . I don't know. It's confusing. I came here, well, for Julian. But I'm getting tangled up in this place. Managing research assignments, papers, relationships." The last word tumbled out of me before I could reconsider it. What did I even mean by that, relationships? Of course they weren't real, they were lies.

"Sounds like going undercover for your first assignment isn't as easy as you thought," Gabriel teased, but there was a seriousness beneath his words.

"Fine," I admitted, my voice quiet. "I'm in over my head, okay? I keep following the rabbit hole, and it just gets darker and deeper every step." My voice faltered as I leaned closer. Gabriel brushed a strand of hair behind my ear, the gesture familiar, yet unsettling.

I'd grown out of the version of myself he'd known in Greenwich. I was different, even though I couldn't quite explain how. But Gabriel couldn't recognize that I had changed, at least not in the ways that mattered to me.

"Is Estelle doing all right?" I asked, breaking the silence between us.

"She's fine. I've been checking in on her. She misses you." He paused, then added, "I'm the one who's a wreck, Dahlia. I haven't slept a full night since you left."

I lowered my eyes to my forearms, avoiding his gaze. I had barely slept, either, but for entirely different reasons that had nothing to do with Gabriel.

"Come back home with me," Gabriel said softly. His hand jerked to touch my cheek, but paused mid-air, as if he sensed my hesitation. "There's something wrong with this place." His tone darkened.

I lifted my head to meet his eyes. "I can't, Gabriel." His jaw tensed, and I saw the hurt ripple across his face. No matter how much I missed home, I couldn't leave now. Everything at Foresyth was connected—my father, Julian, and now me. If I didn't figure out what was happening at Foresyth, others could get hurt. Not just the current students, but the others after them. I had to stay, no matter the cost.

"Is it because of someone else?" Gabriel asked, his tone sharper. The word *else* felt like a dagger, implying that he was the one I was saying no to.

I furrowed my brows. "It's not like that."

"Have they tricked you? Brainwashed you?" His voice cracked, betraying the fear behind his question.

"No," I said, my voice too high-pitched. "It's not like that. The students here . . . they're under the Meister's spell. I agree that there's something wrong with this place, Gabriel. But I'm so close to figuring it out. I just need more time."

He clenched his jaw, his lines of frustration deepening. I could see how crazy I sounded, how reckless I appeared, staying in a place that was essentially a trap. But I couldn't abandon the investigation. I couldn't abandon my peers.

"This place—it's even more sordid than I thought," he said, opening his satchel. "I found this in the archives. Dahl, it wasn't just Julian. There's been a student every year for two decades."

My eyebrows knitted together. "What do you mean?"

"A student has died under mysterious circumstances, gone missing, or unenrolled inexplicably, for the last *twenty years*. Julian was just the last one."

I took the case file from him and thumbed through the newspaper clippings. A few were from 1893, then started again in 1904. Elizabeth Svenski, Michael Locke, Eden Kohnman, Jamie Gillard,

Thomas Wood, Lily Fraser. The names went on. Every name was like a vial of horror injected into my veins. Wait, *Lily Fraser*?

She was one of the names on the dismissal notices I had just found in the Meister's office. Students were disappearing, and the Council was covering it up as academic dismissals.

The cycle of suffering. This is what Julian had meant. This is what he wanted me to end.

"I can't leave now," I said, resolution ripening in my chest. For better or for worse, I was a part of Foresyth's history now. There was no sense or reason to explain what I felt, but I just knew it. Julian had known it, too.

"Why can't you just admit it?" he snapped. "Admit that you wanted to come here—to be a student."

"What?"

"It's all you've ever wanted, isn't it? To attend an elite school, to get a prestigious degree. Greenwich was never good enough for you. *I* was never good enough for you." He stood, his voice dripping with bitterness. His features, which were usually soft and demure, were now sharper, cutting in unison with his words.

"Wait, Gabriel, that's not true," I started, but his words had stung deep, laced with a truth I didn't want to face. It wasn't just Julian that kept me here. Hadn't I spent years longing for something more, something that Greenwich could never offer? Hadn't I craved the validation Foresyth offered? The acceptance of the students, the academic rigor, the feeling of being among equals?

I stood, trying to steady myself. "You should go. If you came to convince me to leave, I'm afraid it's not going to work. I'm committed to seeing this through." The words felt like stones in my mouth. I knew hurting him would make him fight less for me, maybe even forget about me. It was the only way to keep him safe. "And there is someone else," I added. *Two someones*, if I was going to be honest about it.

Gabriel scoffed, shaking his head. He slung his satchel over his shoulder, eyes filled with pain. "I hope this place is everything you've dreamt it would be, Dahlia," he said, walking toward the door. He turned to me one last time before leaving, and his anger was momentarily replaced with a flash of sadness. Then, he was gone.

My eyes drifted to the case file on the table, the newspaper clippings of missing students strewn about. I thought about the letter from the Council, and the bloodwork analysis of mine and Julian's blood. *Our* blood. I was bound to this place, whether I liked it or not. Julian had tasked me with ending the cycle, and I couldn't—I wouldn't—run away.

Gabriel had been right about one thing: Foresyth was turning out to be the exact nightmare I deserved.

Chapter 25: The Hunt is On

Gabriel's visit had reaffirmed my purpose at Foresyth: solving Julian's murder and understanding my father's connection to the school. I tucked my other motives, along with thoughts of Aspen and Sequoia, neatly behind a wall of guilt and set out on my next task. Equipped with a compass, a flashlight, a bobby pin, and Julian's coordinates, I began my search for the journal at quarter past midnight.

Tracing my steps back down to the seventh door along the hallway, picking the lock, and descending the rickety flight of stairs was easy enough. But keeping my breath steady and my heart from racing—that was harder.

I reached the revolving bookshelf after only tripping twice. Panic jolted through me when I realized I didn't remember which book Aspen had pulled to trigger the passageway. I racked my brain. What had he said to me?

Hold on to your dictionary.

I had to jump to reach the Merriam-Webster, but my fingers finally caught it, and I pulled down the spine. A few seconds of silence passed before I spotted the other one. I rolled my eyes. Of course, that pretentious bastard had used the Oxford dictionary instead. This one took a few more hops, but when I finally reached it, a mechanical click sounded, and I smiled in satisfaction.

My flashlight was less impressive than Aspen's eternal flame, but it got the job done, and it sat snugly between my ear and my skull, bound by my curls, allowing me the freedom of both hands. I took out my notepad and reviewed the rough map I'd sketched earlier. That, along with my compass, put me within twenty degrees north of the coordinates. I was only a few turns from Aspen's workshop when my compass started spinning wildly, as if I'd entered a magnetic anomaly.

I was facing a barricaded doorway. I took a step back, and my compass returned to normal.

Very strange.

I examined the doorway more closely, noticing a faint layer of dust. *Iron filings.* This magnetic anomaly wasn't natural; it was fabricated. Someone knew what was down here and didn't want anyone else to find it. I cursed under my breath, ready to turn back. But then, as if the House was sanctioning my quest, the barricaded door creaked open.

Old magick.

Had the door sensed my touch somehow? A ridiculous hypothesis, but I'd seen stranger things at Foresyth. It was then that I recalled something Julian wrote in his journal, something about the House itself being alive. I had taken it as a metaphor, but what if it extended beyond that?

I entered the room, bracing myself for whatever lay beyond. A wave of energy crested over me as I stepped through. This place felt *familiar.* Nothing about a barricaded room in an underground tunnel should feel familiar, yet somehow it was both unsettling and oddly welcoming.

You've come.

I swiveled my head, looking back at the entrance. I could've sworn I heard a voice, but there was no one. Lodging a thick stone between the door and its frame, I ensured I wouldn't get trapped. Then, I turned my attention to the room.

It was a sparsely decorated study, with a large oak desk in the center and cabinets scattered around the walls. A lone, moth-eaten chaise sat in the far-left corner, its fabric thinned with age. I began a methodical search, starting on the left side and moving clockwise. For locked cabinets, I used the back of a pocket screwdriver to break the hinges. Whoever used this office hadn't been here in ages; they wouldn't miss the furniture.

I was sweating by the time I'd upturned every cabinet, shelf, and book in the Godforsaken office. I couldn't believe it wasn't here; the coordinates had led me directly to this room. I checked my compass again to see the needle now spinning erratically. I cursed and returned the useless compass to my bag. Whatever magnetic anomaly coated the door must've been to blame.

Heading back out to the tunnels, I spotted peeling wallpaper behind one of the cabinets I'd moved. I went back and tore away more paper until it ripped in tiger stripes across the wall, revealing the image of a tree and markings speckling its trunk. Tracing my fingers over the symbols, I recognized them—the runic alphabet. This was a replica of the tree in the sitting room, except the bark had been stripped to reveal the runes etched beneath.

The Universal Truths beneath material form. I eagerly pulled out my notepad to copy down the drawing when I heard a sound. At first, I thought it was my own heart, pounding in my chest, but then I heard it again.

Thump. Thump. Thump.

My heart froze. There was a strange, jagged sound coming from outside the room. I stayed as still as I could, but my heartbeat betrayed me, growing louder as the noise approached. Weighing my options, I calculated a sixty-seven percent chance I could outrun it, given the three-second intervals of its steps and the length of its stride. I didn't like the odds, but the calculation was flawed anyway.

I made a run for it.

I jostled the stone holding the door open and dashed in the opposite direction of the noise. I spared a glance back, regretting it immediately. I didn't pause to rationalize what I saw: a creature with the head of a bird and the body of a bear, its eyes green and wild with a rage against its own foul existence. I ran faster than my lungs could handle, ignoring the pulsing pain in my right ankle. Fear rose with the bile in my throat, and I stopped, sparing a few precious seconds to consult my map.

I looked down, cursing again. I was far from any mapped areas—in unknown territory. The creature let out a mangled screech, making the hairs on my arms stand up. I charged further down the tunnel, utterly blind to my direction. Without a map or compass, I was done for. In my haste, I tripped over something long and jagged—a tree root. I looked up and around, realizing the tunnel was tangled with viny roots.

The House . . . it *is* alive.

The sound grew louder. I jumped to my feet and sprinted, only to slam into a locked door at the end of the tunnel. With no escape and the creature's screech closing in, I unhooked the dagger strapped to my ankle. If there was no way out, I'd have to fight. I took a deep breath, cursing myself again for not having a better map.

"What are you doing here?" a voice squeaked behind me, half horror, half surprise.

I spun around, ready to face a new threat. But two shining eyes stared back, and relief flooded me.

"Nina!" I gasped. "There's something out there. We have to get out of here."

"I know," she replied, her voice tinged with frustration. "It's this way." She turned and started down the tunnel—toward the creature.

"We can't go that way," I protested, but she'd already disappeared into the darkness.

The only way out is through, my father's voice echoed in my mind.

I started after her. The thumping grew so loud it overtook all my senses, the creature's agonized wail sending tremors through my body. I could feel its pain, visceral and consuming.

Nina's hair bobbed ahead, a beacon in the darkness. The creature was only a few yards away now, its phosphorescent green eyes hollow and soulless. As we crept closer, I realized it was blind—it couldn't see us. We slipped by, and Nina made a sharp turn to the right. I followed, barely missing the creature's crackling beak as it struck the tunnel wall. After a few more strides, when the monster's footsteps faded, I turned to Nina.

"What the hell was that?" I demanded.

She rolled her eyes. "Griffract. Best to avoid them. If their beaks don't get you, their claws will."

"I gathered as much. I mean, where did it come from?"

"There's a lot of . . . reject magick down here," she said, giving me a hard look. "You shouldn't be wandering alone, especially at night."

"I could say the same for you," I said, watching her closely. "What were you doing down here?"

"I could ask you the same," she replied, raising an eyebrow. "I was looking for mugwort. It grows underground. Now your turn." Her eyes narrowed, expectant.

"I'm . . . looking for something too. Someone sent me down here," I admitted. I hated to concede it, but Aspen was right. It was foolish to trust anyone here, even friends.

"Were they trying to get you killed?"

"I don't think so, but a warning would've been nice."

"Well, here's your warning: this place is crawling with failed magick. Don't wander here alone," she said, her tone unusually harsh.

But what was Nina doing down here, alone? Suspicion rippled through me and a sour taste coated my tongue.

"Fine, I'll make a date out of it next time," I lied.

We continued down the tunnel, and a familiar green door soon appeared.

"You're lucky I was here," Nina said, her pixie-like smile resurfacing as she flipped the latch and slipped through the doorframe, holding it open for me with a lightness that seemed almost careless after what we'd just been through.

"Thanks," I replied, and I meant it. If it hadn't been for Nina, I don't know if I would be leaving unscathed. My gratitude lingered like an unspoken debt between us.

The lab's sharp, chemical scent—a pungent cloud of formaldehyde that somehow felt comforting—enveloped us as we re-entered. The relief was so visceral that my chest loosened; I hadn't realized how tense I'd been until I was here, back in the world of the familiar.

I drifted to my workstation, letting my fingers brush over the cold brass of my instruments, their silence a welcome response. I could almost fool myself into thinking that nothing had changed—that I could simply return to the rhythm of work, the whirr of machines, the bite of chemicals in the air. But as I turned to leave, reality came crashing back with the weight of a half-dozen questions.

What *was* that thing out there? Radiation poisoning? A genetic anomaly? I kept trying to offer myself some rational explanation, but the truth felt slippery, the familiar logic I'd clung to unraveling into bare threads.

It was magick. Unmistakable, powerful, mind-shattering, magick. It almost felt good to give into the admission. My mind could rest now that it had found an explanation for the inexplicable, and my body could just take action. I started up the steps.

"Where are you going?" Nina's voice caught me, the note of hurt unmistakable. Maybe she'd expected me to stay, to linger in this pocket of safety with her. Maybe she needed the company more than I realized. But I couldn't afford to stay here, not now. I had too many questions clawing for answers, too many mysteries snapping at my heels.

"To find the Mapmaker," I called over my shoulder, already halfway up the stairs.

The Acolyte and the Alchemist: Part VII

The scholars began with small sacrifices.

An unsuspecting spider, swathed in its own web. A lizard, its glassy eyes reflecting moonlight. A goldfinch, its song cut short beneath their whispered invocations. Little things, barely a ripple in the vast pulse of the world's thrumming life.

They practiced only when the halls of the Conservatory lay silent, when the oil lamps had guttered to embers, and when the other students' dreams lay undisturbed. The first time, Quill had flinched. The second, his hands had merely trembled. By the third, he had learned how to steady his grip.

And yet, the magick did not answer them.

His hands, once dry and ashen from the endless turning of pages, had softened—warmed by the slick stain of blood. The ink of his studies had been replaced by something more sickly sweet.

But it wasn't enough.

"It's not working. We should stop," Quill murmured, his voice barely rising above the weight of his own revulsion. The latest offering lay twitching before him, its broken body still clinging to the last embers of life. A stray cat. A thing with a name, perhaps. A thing that might have purred beneath someone's touch.

His stomach twisted.

"This feels . . . morbid."

Hamra, crouched beside him, did not look away from the carcass. Her eyes—swirls of onyx and fire—were dark, too dark, reflecting none of his hesitation. Cards encircled them in a bright gold ring, gleaming under the moonlight.

"No," she said, fingers trailing the pages of *The Book of Skorn*, her lips moving as if deciphering a prophecy mid-chant.

"We're just misreading the Book. We need five elements represented." She looked over to their makeshift altar. "But what if they aren't just symbolic? What if they're . . . *people*?"

Quill's breath hitched. The air between them thickened, taking on the weight of something irreversible.

"You want to bring more students into this?" His voice was sharp, laced with something unexpected, even to him.

It should have been horror.

It should have been disgust.

But he named it for what it was: jealousy coursing through him, hot and thick, curling around his ribs like a vice. This ritual, this madness, was theirs. No one else's.

Breaching their pact would require him to justify himself, explain this madness to someone other than Hamra. He didn't know if he could do that.

Hamra lifted her gaze, watching him in that way she always did—like she already knew what he would say, what he would do, what he would become.

"It says here," she continued, unfazed, "that the elements breathe life into the cards, imbuing them with the power of transcendental magick. We need someone touched by water and earth magick. We already represent the others."

Quill swallowed. Somewhere, the rational part of him was screaming, clawing at the edges of his mind like a caged thing. Hamra must have seen it in his eyes, the quiet scream of doubt, because her voice dipped into that crushed velvet sound, soothing the scared boy.

"I will never feel the same about anyone except you."

The words curled between them like smoke, slipping into the cracks of Quill's hesitation, filling the spaces. He felt a head rush and his eyes dipped to her lips. How could anyone be so devastatingly beautiful?

"That's why I want to do this with you," she whispered, reaching for his hand. Her grip was warm, still slick with blood.

She rose from her crouch, moving to where he knelt beside the carcass. Her movements were slow, deliberate, as if the world had narrowed to just the two of them, to just to this moment.

Quill could feel the heat of her skin radiating towards him. He whispered to her, "Before we include the others, I have another idea—" But before he could finish, she leaned in, her breath warm against his lips. The scent of blood and cinnamon filled his lungs. The world blurred at the edges, the ritual swallowing them whole.

When she kissed him, her fingers still red from the fresh kill, Quill did not pull away. He accepted her lips like an unholy communion, baptized by their spilled blood.

Chapter 26: The Mapmaker

Once upstairs, I paused to catch my breath. My hands trembled, though I couldn't tell if it was from the cold sweat clinging to my back like a second skin, or the lingering terror still twisting in my gut. The House was silent this late at night, its long hallways stretching out in eerie stillness, the gas lamps casting jagged shadows against the walls.

I drifted toward the foyer, intending only to steady myself, maybe regain some sense of control before I moved again. That's when I saw it.

A red envelope, tucked neatly into my mail slot.

My breath caught. It hadn't been there before.

I swallowed hard and reached for it with slow, measured movements, my fingers brushing the thick, waxy paper. I glanced around, suddenly hyperaware of the empty corridors. It must have been delivered only hours ago.

I quickly dropped my bag and tore the envelope open, my pulse hammering against my ribs. The note inside was brief, but the weight of its message pressed down on me like a vice.

How's your research project going? I'm eagerly awaiting the results.

No date. No signature. But I didn't need one.

The Al-Ahmar.

The name slithered into my mind like the cursed lion serpent in my dreams. I could almost hear her voice, the amusement laced with quiet menace. She was reminding me of our trade. The Skorn deck in exchange for an answer to Julian's death. She must be trying to undermine the Meister, working around him. Maybe he was failing to deliver results.

My fingers tightened around the paper, crumpling the edges. The problem was, I still had no answer for her. What would she do if I failed her? I forced a breath, trying to untangle the knot forming in my stomach. I had to move.

My time was running out.

I needed to find Leone. Now.

*

I was stuffing my face with blueberry biscuits as I walked into the library. I probably should've kept the crumbs away from the books, but I was starving, and I wasn't there for the books. Not at two a.m. on a Monday night.

Everyone at Foresyth had a preferred letter in the stacks where they frequented, making it easy to find them. Leone was in the "C" section, bent over a particularly weathered cartograph.

Is everyone staying up late tonight?

"You're not allowed to eat in the library," he stated without even glancing up.

"I brought extra if you're hungry," I teased, even though I knew Leone's only appetite was for books and maps.

"No, thank you." He sighed with apathy. I leaned over his shoulder, catching a glimpse of the map he was studying. It was of an archipelago I didn't recognize, but the intricate craftsmanship was impressive. Even with my untrained eye, I could see why Leone deemed it worthy of his attention.

"Quick question, do you make maps, or do you just study them?"

Leone paused mid-scribble. "If someone's up this late working, it's likely because they have a deadline, not because they enjoy it. And as much as I value your conversation, I'm a bit preoccupied." His tone was flat and dismissive.

"Fine, then. I won't waste your time. I need a map of the underground tunnels at Foresyth."

Leone finally looked up, his expression impassive but not without a flicker of curiosity.

"Tunnels?"

"Cut the mysterious act—I know about them. And I almost got eaten by one of the Marie Curie experiments down there," I said, taking the chair across from him and placing my pack and half-eaten biscuit on the table. His eyes raked distastefully over my belongings, clearly not appreciating the proximity of my crumbs to his work.

"I might know something about them. But I haven't been down there myself," he said, his tone almost peevish. "Making a map without navigating a place takes a kind of magick neither of us can afford."

"I'm not asking you to conjure a map from thin air," I replied, though the sharpness of my tone surprised even me. I quickly softened. "There has to be an original blueprint of the tunnels from when this place was built." I recalled the maps that Nina and I had poured over to find the barren circle, but those were only of the House and the external grounds.

"Not to my knowledge," he muttered, clearly hoping to end the conversation. But I wasn't giving up so easily. Without a map, I'd be at a serious disadvantage, possibly even risking my life if I wandered down there again alone.

"Let's say I *did* want the magickal kind," I ventured. "What would you need to make that happen?"

"That kind of divination would require calling on multiple cards," he replied. "And even then, it would demand a substantial sacrifice. It would take a full semester to gather the magick needed."

The weight of realization cut through me like a sword: Leone believed in magick. And if someone as rational as him could, then maybe I could, too. I had witnessed inexplicable things with my own eyes where the only possible explanation was otherworldly. I didn't know exactly what type of sacrifice Leone needed, but maybe I'd try. If it meant getting a map, then surely it would be worth it.

"I don't have that kind of time," I snapped, frustration coiling tight in my chest. "Symposium is in three weeks. I need it by then."

The image of Al-Ahmar's bloodshot eyes flashed through my mind, her urgency mirroring mine. The weight of the red envelope was still fresh in my hands; the unspoken threat curled between the lines.

Leone studied me, unmoving, his gaze steady in that way that always made me feel like he saw past my words, past my face, straight into the hollow space where my uncertainty lived.

"Then you're going to have to be the one to bring the magick," he said simply. "I can't afford it."

I froze.

"Magick?" I echoed, the word a shape in my mouth, something tangible and heavy and ridiculous all at once.

I didn't know where to begin with that request. It felt like stepping off solid ground into the abyss. Like all the things I had dismissed as illusions or side effects were suddenly clawing their way back into my reality, demanding acknowledgment.

I swallowed hard. "I don't know how to do that."

"Yes, you do," Leone said, his pitch rising in annoyance. "Something *imbued* will work."

My mind turned, gears grinding. If Aspen had his sculptures, and Sequoia had her song, then surely I could create something, too.

I let out a slow, measured breath. "Fine," I said, the word tasting like surrender. "I'll do it."

Leone smiled, a rare sight, and one that sent a chill through me. He wasn't like Aspen or Sequoia, who wore their power on their sleeves, who reveled in their own performances. No, he wore his intellect like armor, like a sellsword—calculating and careful. And he was going to ensure he got something out of his work.

"I'll help you make the map," he said. "But you'll need to bring the magick *and* my payment."

"I thought we were friends," I said.

"The best friendships are built on mutual understanding," he replied evenly. "And I understand that you need something. So do I."

His expression barely shifted, but something flickered behind his eyes. He looked momentarily unsettled, almost vulnerable. "I want my Herbin. It was stolen from me."

I frowned. "Is that . . . a book?"

"No." His jaw tightened slightly. "It's a glass pen. One of the Trees has it, and they need to give it back. It was a rare instance of me losing a sabre match with Aspen last year . . ."

I blinked. "You want a pen?"

"I want what's mine," he replied, his voice edged with something sharper than frustration. "That's my price. And don't forget, you're also bringing the magick."

I hesitated. Something about the way he said it—the weight in his voice—felt off. This wasn't just a pen to him.

I could argue—tell him I'd find another way. But I knew Leone. He wouldn't be offering this deal unless it was exactly what he needed. And deep down, I already knew the truth: I'd do whatever it took.

"Fine." I sighed, knowing I was agreeing to something I didn't fully understand. "I'll bring you your pen. And the magick."

*

Leaving the library, I felt both triumphant and frustrated. I now had a plan for getting a map of the tunnels—an essential tool for navigating to Julian's coordinates. But I also had new tasks to complete, tasks that involved people I'd been trying to avoid. Both Aspen and Sequoia had become part of this puzzle, whether I liked it or not.

Julian the puzzle-maker. If he were still alive, he'd no doubt be giddy about the lengths I was going to solve his masterpiece.

Leone's words sat heavy in my chest, pressing down like a weight I couldn't shake.

You're going to have to bring the magick.

I had wanted to scoff, to push back, to tell him he was being ridiculous. *Magick* wasn't real. It wasn't tangible, it wasn't measurable, it was just belief. Faith dressed up in ritual.

But wasn't that what I had told myself when I first arrived at Foresyth?

Before I saw Nina's blood *fizzle* into the earth at the Tramping Ground, swallowed whole by the soil as if it had never been there? It didn't clot, didn't dry, didn't even stain. It had simply vanished. And the air had hummed when it happened, thick and charged, like something unseen had consumed it.

Before *The Book of Skorn* burned in my hands, not from heat, not from any chemical residue, but from a warmth that implied the Book was pulsing and *alive*? I tried to explain it away but failed.

Before I heard *her* voice.

You pray to a false God.

Sophia had whispered in my ear, her breath sweeping against my skin. I had felt it—felt *her*—the weight of an ancient deity pressing against my ribs. I had told myself it was the elixir, a side effect, a hallucination. But it didn't feel like a hallucination.

And Aspen—

I hated that my thoughts kept circling back to him, hated that my body still remembered the heat of him, the way my breath had caught when his fingers laced with mine. He had shattered his sculpture, and in that moment, the air between us had shifted. The pull had been instant, magnetic, unbearable. It hadn't been fully my choice to kiss him. Something else had been at work, something that had reached inside me and turned me inside out.

And the creature in the tunnels...God, that thing. That *thing*.

I had seen its eyes, green and phosphorescent, filled with hatred and hunger. Not a trick of biology, not some undiscovered species. It was something else, something created, something stitched together by hands that should never have touched the canvas of life itself.

So, what the hell was I still trying to prove?

I could keep pretending that magick wasn't real. Keep trying to twist it into rationalizations, into tricks of the mind and body. But deep down, I already knew.

The things I had seen at Foresyth—the things I had *felt*—they weren't illusions.

They were reality.

And that terrified me.

Because if magick was real, then that meant Julian hadn't just been killed by a human. It meant he had been killed by something far worse than I was prepared to face.

Chapter 27: The Lovers

The sound of cawing at my window ripped me out of a dreamless sleep. The crow was perched at my window, pecking at the seeds I had left. It jerked its head up, its black gaze piercing mine. I shooed it away irritably and reached for the tall glass of water on my desk. I took a long chug and then crumpled to the floor on the side of my bed.

You're so close. My father's voice caressed my ear as I clutched the glass so tightly that my fingers turned white. It was a feeling, not a thought, I realized. I honestly had no way of knowing how close I was to uncoiling the secrets at Foresyth or understanding my father's dark origins with this place. But I had a *feeling* that I was close.

And that had to be enough. So much for fact, not feeling.

When I had gathered enough strength and eaten a few more stray muffins from my bag, I made my way down the rickety stairs. I considered giving Leone the broken compass or the paperweight that sat on my desk as the magickal artifact needed for the map. But something inside me prevented me from pursuing that type of indifference.

If there was one thing I'd learned about magick at Foresyth, it was that it needed intention.

There was no truth in giving him a useless paperweight. It simply wouldn't work. As magickally uninclined as I was, even I knew that.

There were only two people I could count on to help me figure out how to imbue something with magick. I weighed my options carefully before landing on the fairer Tree.

It didn't take long to find Sequoia. She was humming in the sitting room, her legs draped across the chaise, a small book in hand. She looked up as I entered and smiled. The entire room became a few lumens brighter.

"Dahlia, there you are. How are you feeling?"

"Much better, thanks." I offered her a cracked smile in return. I should be as cautious of her as I was of Aspen, but that smile of hers was so disarming that I let go of my suspicions almost entirely. Almost.

"I've been thinking about what you said during Circle the other night," I started, rounding the chaise so I could take a seat next to her. "About how I ought to tap into Sophia's powers."

"Yes?" She closed her book, her eyes widening. The look on her face confirmed that I had found the right avenue for this misadventure.

"Well, I think it's a good idea. And I was wondering if you'd help me." My stomach curled at my deception, Aspen's accusations of me being the manipulator echoing back in my head. I swallowed my guilt down as I approached her.

She reached out a delicate hand and placed it on mine. Her skin was as soft as lace and smelled faintly of lavender. I wondered if she picked it from the garden outside the House.

"I'd be honored to," she said. "After you helped me and Aspen, I can't think of a better way of returning the favor."

I blinked. "Wait, what do you mean I helped you and Aspen?"

"You know, saving me. It's given us perspective, and we've put all the Julian nonsense behind us. There's nothing more arousing to a man than almost dying." She chuckled at this. Something hot and bitter was rising in my throat at the mention of Aspen. "Besides, the whole deal with the Tower in your reading was right."

"It was?"

"Yes, of course—it predicted my soul flight. Dying was like falling out of a Tower. That's how I knew I was dying; it was the falling that convinced me of it. And you and Aspen were there to catch me."

Her hair was pulled back to reveal the delicate flesh of her collarbone, sprinkled with a constellation of freckles. I distantly wondered if Aspen connected them to read her birth chart.

I understood, then, what Aspen found so mesmerizing about her. There was something so magical about holding on to a thing that could so easily break, that could crumble in your hands. She was like a paper mâché doll set next to a scalding hot furnace.

The potential of her destruction was awe-inspiring.

"I'm glad that it helped," I said, trying to keep my tone casual.

"It did. We haven't quarreled, and he hasn't been able to keep his hands off me since," she cooed. Heat rose to my cheeks, my heart sinking. I thought of Aspen's lips on me the day before: enthusiastic, lingering. Had all that been another one of his tricks? I turned away, embarrassed by my swell of jealousy. I was foolish to suspect anything besides his trickery. Trusting him, even for a second, had been a mistake.

"I'm glad it's all worked out," I lied through my teeth. But my tone didn't have the uptick of the earnestness it needed to be convincing, and Sequoia's eyes furrowed. I reached for her hand, quickly changing the subject. "And I'm glad you're in a better place now to help me channel the magick of the cards."

The fine line of her lips turned upward, and I sighed internally in relief. "Of course. We should start as soon as possible—tonight." Her eyes flickered back to mine with a gravity that was not lost on me. "After Circle, so we don't have any interruptions."

"Tonight," I agreed, swallowing hard.

*

I don't know what possessed me, but I decided to wear something nice. I found my finest, non-threadbare pair of slacks and a bright white blouse that fit me properly. It may have even accentuated what little feminine curvature I had. I even tried to tie my hair back—my mother always said I had lovely cheekbones hidden behind my curly mat of hair—but it didn't look quite right, so I let it down again. I couldn't help but feel insignificant next to Sequoia in so many ways. Perhaps by dressing myself up, I could feel less like a sack of potatoes. I never thought such things would matter to me.

But then again, a lot had changed since I came to Foresyth.

Sequoia and I stole glances during Circle, but I didn't let my gaze linger too long. I nodded attentively to the Meister, who was guiding us in a discussion on free will, keeping up my cover as the ever-diligent student as I still threatened to unravel his school. I disagreed with the premise of the discussion but wasn't in the mood to engage in rhetoric tonight, finding it better to save my energy.

"And what about you, Mr. Barlowe?" Out of the corner of my eye, I saw Aspen's eyes dart toward me. Anger rose in my chest again, too familiar, too recent.

"Contrary to the beliefs presented here, I actually don't believe in free will," he said, relaxing his arms behind him. Of course, he was ever the contrarian.

"And are you going to share with the group your reasoning?"

"There was an Advisor-supported research study in Oxford. Pre-synaptic neural spikes are fired in our brains moments before we commit an action. Our brain chemistry commands us to do things before our conscious thought," I could feel his gaze burning into my skull, but I kept my expression neutral. Was his double-meaning intending to bait me?

He was dressed handsomely this evening in a crisp white shirt, ironed trousers, and suspenders with his evening jacket resting behind him on the chaise. It was only natural, polite even, to keep one's eyes on the speaker. His lips curled upright when he caught my eye.

"And what do you think, Ms. Blackburne? You're a fan of the scientific literature; do you care to opine on the topic?" The Meister turned to me.

Aspen sat up, folding his arms on his knees. His eyes shone as if saying, *Care to dance with me?*

I gritted my teeth. If I didn't offer up my thoughts, I wouldn't hear the end of it. Someone had to put him in his place.

"I've read the study Aspen is referencing, but I wasn't convinced. It's been shown that conscious thought can rewire our brains—there's a growing field of cognitive behavioral work to support this. Granted, if someone is in possession of their full faculties . . ." I paused. "Then they can rewrite themselves to make the decisions they choose."

"Yes, but the only reason you're able to decide is because your brain is written into a configuration that allows you to. You only have the perception that you can change things, but in fact, the path before you has already been predetermined."

What was he even trying to say? That I was predetermined to kiss him through some cosmic force? That tapping into Sophia's powers was inevitable, and we were all puppets to the Meister's plan?

"Then why use the cards at all? If everything in life is preset, embedded into our spiral helix, why even pretend to play magician? Pretend to have power?" I knew he was antagonizing me for the fun of it, but my frustration was building to a crescendo, pouring out against my better judgment.

"Even our illusions of control are fated. We must act our part in the play called life." He feathered his fingers into a steeple, letting me know he wasn't going to budge.

My mouth opened, but no words came out. I wanted to refute his argument, but there was a part of me—the part that worshiped the truth—that knew that that night in the kiln, I had *wanted* to kiss him. That it had been *my* choice, and my choice only. His countering of free will was edging me to my stance, my conclusion.

Maybe the magick had given me *permission* to do it, to go after what I really wanted, but it was all me in the end. That was the truth, the proof point of my free will, that I couldn't share with him.

I swallowed all my unsaid words, burrowing myself deeper into the chaise, and let someone else take the argument. If I couldn't say what I wanted to, then I shouldn't say anything at all.

*

I walked into Sequoia's room an hour later, greeted by the scent of rosehip and hibiscus and the flicker of candlelight, a dozen or so candles lit and sprinkled throughout her room.

"I made some tea," Sequoia said, splayed on her bed, her hair pooling around her nightgown like spun sugar. The floral scent of the tea caressed my nostrils like soft ribbons before tying a knot in my throat.

"I'm fine," I said, recalling my first night at Foresyth, nursing a headache from ingesting a graciously offered potion of herbs. Aspen had said he wasn't the one who poisoned me—could it have been Sequoia? Or was he just deflecting blame away from himself?

"Oh, come on, Dahlia, there's nothing in here." She turned, reaching for something next to her dresser. "Unless you want there to be." She smiled, twirling a dark vial between her fingers.

I raised my hand, rejecting the offer. "Really, no thanks."

Her features fell for a moment, but then she perked up, reaching her arm out again. I took her hand without another thought and followed her to the bed.

Magick is an intimate affair. I recalled my first day at Foresyth, offering a reading at the dinner table. My cheeks burned at the memory. And yet, I now found myself in Sequoia's bed for the second time, for more magick.

"You're going to have to guide me . . ." I said. I considered if I should ask for Leone's pen first before getting into the cards, but based on her excitement, I didn't want to risk her turning me away.

"You brought your deck?"

"Of course," I said, pulling out the Skorn deck from my satchel. I went through too much stress with the Council not to always have it on my person.

"Good, you should do your normal preparations." She poured herself a cup of tea, the bright red liquid swirling into her cup. She started humming a tune as she mixed milk with the tea, turning it into a pink pool.

I obliged her request and shimmied the cards under my seat, as if preparing to do a reading. Sequoia sipped on her tea and let out a sigh of enjoyment into her cup. "You really should try this tea."

"No, you really should," another voice rumbled behind us. I didn't have to turn to know who it was. Aspen entered from the doorway, creaking the door closed behind him. "It'll relieve the tension in your shoulders, make the magick more permeable."

I stood abruptly, shaking the bed such that Sequoia's teacup spilled a drop of the rose liquid onto her white sheets. "I'm sorry—"

"No, I am. I startled you," Aspen said, rounding the bed across from us. He eyed me up and down, his gaze pausing on the new blouse I had donned, and at the seam where it met my waist. I felt foolish suddenly, embarrassed by the clothes, by finding myself so vulnerable with Sequoia, and for wanting to kiss him last night.

I felt like he read it all on my face at that moment. I was so mortified I wanted to bolt out of the room, but his stare kept me nailed in place.

"I know you only asked for Sequoia's help, but I'm here to offer mine as well," he said.

"I don't want any more of your help." I was almost turning before I felt Sequoia's grasp on the sleeve of my shirt.

"Stay," she said, her brown eyes wide with something startlingly sincere. She *meant* it. I saw it then—the unguarded truth flickering behind her gaze.

She actually wanted to help me.

And that was the part I couldn't reconcile. Why were both of them—Sequoia and Aspen—so willing to help me, when I was unraveling the very threads that bound this place together? Threads that included *them.* If the truth about Julian lay buried, I was digging straight through their secrets to reach it. And still . . . they wanted me close.

"There are two paths for you here, Alice. One leads you across the threshold out of this room and back into your bed. The other one is taking a sip of that tea, letting yourself relax, and us teaching you how to access magick," Aspen purred, his voice soft as velvet.

I closed my eyes, centering myself. It was true that I could likely figure out how to deliver whatever magical artifact Leone desired another way, perhaps even recruit Nina's help. But I needed that pen. Even if I couldn't trust them, I needed them to trust *me*.

"Free will?" I teased, taking my seat back on top of my cards. I sighed, faintly wondering if I was going to regret this. I reached out to the other cup Sequoia had set out and poured myself a cup of tea.

A smile broke out on Aspen's lips, illuminating his other features and the dimple in his right cheek. He was so handsome it almost hurt. It was part of his allure, the way he disarmed, like Sequoia. Being cognizant of it didn't make me immune to it. But a wave of calm settled over me as soon as I took a sip of the comforting warm liquid, and I sank deeper into the mattress and into the cards.

"Now what?"

"Now, it's up to you," Sequoia said. "What would you like to offer to the Shattered Mother to access her magick?"

Offer? I had nothing. A paperweight and a broken compass. A mismatch of clues that I didn't know where they led. I started shuffling around in my bag to see what else I had.

"It has to be an *emotional* offering," Aspen continued, reaching his hand over mine, still rummaging through my bag. His touch sent a jolt of electricity through me. "It can't just be something material. It has to come from you. It has to . . . elicit a feeling. Breaking out of your material form."

"I don't know if I have anything like that."

Aspen and Sequoia exchanged a glance that made me feel like I was speaking a different language.

"What's your medium?" Sequoia asked.

I thought back to my conversations with the Meister—my cover story. "I . . . I'm studying Tarotology with an arts concentration in theater."

"Then that's it . . . you have to channel the magick through story. That's your medium," Sequoia said, her excitement bubbling over. She inched closer to me, while Aspen sat still, watching us intently.

"Story . . ." I echoed. Maybe it wasn't so far from the truth. I did tell people stories through the cards—mostly reflections of the ones they told me with their eyes, their lips, the way they brushed their hair back. But those stories weren't my own.

"I tell stories when I read for people," I said. "But they're theirs, not mine."

"Then tell yours. Do a reading for yourself. Tell us the story of your life," Aspen suggested softly. "Instead of constructing someone else's narrative, construct your own."

"Yes. Dahlia should read for herself. Oh, the Mother will love that," Sequoia said with a bounce.

Panic set in, though I tried to hide it. I wasn't exactly the sentimental type. "I wouldn't even know where to start."

"At the beginning, of course," Sequoia said, smiling as I instinctively rolled my eyes. Beginnings were arbitrary. With clients, I often liked to start in medias res—right where the action was.

"Depending on how much magick you're trying to channel, the emotional weight of the story should match it," Aspen added. "You can't cheat magick; it has a way of coming back to collect unpaid debt."

"Fine, an epic *drama*. Got it," I said, wondering if I really did. "How will I know it's working? Let me guess, you just *know*?"

Sequoia smiled and nodded, cupping her chin in her hands.

I took a deep breath, pulling the cards from under me and letting their warmth seep into my palm. I had never read for myself before. I'd never wanted to confront myself in that way. Maybe there was a truth embedded into the stories I told. The same truth I was afraid to see in myself right now.

"I guess I'll do a life spread," I said. "A full pull of twenty-five cards, each set of five representing five years." I'd done it plenty for clients—mostly those looking to understand past traumas and find solace in naming them.

Aspen and Sequoia nodded encouragingly, their presence strangely comforting. I never thought I could do something like this alone. Sitting with myself, without a gadget to fiddle with or book to chew on, was maddening. My hands fiddled with the cards, shuffling them, my fingers shaking. I placed the deck in front of me and focused on my breath, as I would tell my patrons. I counted to ten before opening my eyes, pressing my fingers to the top of the deck.

At the touch, a spark jolted me upright.

I brushed it off as static, but then something deeper took hold. I felt a steady pulse radiating from my fingers, down my arm, through my chest, my core, my legs. I pushed the sensation aside and concentrated on pulling out the top five cards.

"Years one through five. The Eight of Wands and the Emperor. I was born under a blood moon; my grandmother used to say it meant I'd lead to the downfall of a king," I said, almost rolling my eyes, recalling my Bunica's habit of casting my fortunes based on the stars. "I don't personally know any kings, do you?" I joked.

"What else?" Aspen prodded.

"Let's see." I pulled out three more cards and laid them down on top of the two. "Five of Wands, King of Wands, the High Priestess," I said, frowning slightly. I had to pretend I was reading for someone else instead of myself. I needed to embrace the same process. I cleared my mind, listening to what rose to the surface. The Jungian way of reading cards involved listening to one's subconscious. It was a quiet, delicate task.

"I had a lot of interests as a kid. I'd follow my dad, represented as the king here, around his lab. It mesmerized me how he could look into a microscope or interpret jagged lines from his light analyzer to find the composition of matter. One day, he brought in a sample from a crime scene—a woman who'd died in a fire, supposedly started by a cigarette. But he didn't find any traces of tobacco or phosphorus, a common chemical in cigarettes. What he found was benzene. That was the evidence they needed to implicate her former lover. The way he could see things through those tools . . . well, that was magick to me."

Sequoia set down her teacup and her eyes lingered on the one card I had ignored. "And what about her?"

"The High Priestess? I don't know. I've never felt connected to her."

"She represents the knowledge within, turned inward, relying on intuition," Aspen said, his gaze steady. I nodded, recognizing the definition.

"That's not me. If anything, I've spent my life pushing my intuition away."

"It must have been there, at some point?" Sequoia suggested.

"Maybe, from my mother and grandmother. They read cards using intuition. But I don't . . . I look for facts."

Sequoia nodded with a knowing smile. "That *is* your intuition. What about the next years of your childhood?"

I swallowed, pulling the next five. "The Chariot, Ace of Swords, Five of Swords, the Magician, the Devil." I stole a glance at Aspen, regretting it immediately. Was he staring at my lips, or was I imagining it? I watched him swallow, the movement distracting me for a second.

"I . . . uh . . . started school, obviously. I studied a lot, fell in love with books—all kinds. School ones, the ones in my mom's bookshop, and, most of all, the ones I wasn't allowed to read," I said, pointing to the Devil, a symbol of rebellion. Out of the corner of my eye, I noticed Aspen biting his lip. I ignored the shudder it elicited through me.

I pulled the next five. "The Five of Pentacles, Ace of Wands." I flicked my gaze up at them, hoping they didn't know as much about the cards as I did. But of course they did. "First blood, the coming of age." I cleared my throat and continued. "The Hermit, Seven of Cups, Ace of Pentacles. Opportunities began to appear. I was admitted into Sawyer Academy; I would have been the first woman to go in the school's history. But my parents struggled to afford it. I told my father I'd study at home and become the Hermit, but secretly, I really wanted to go. My only friend Gabriel went." As I admitted this, the cards hummed under my hand. "But I didn't. That didn't stop me from reading all the books on the summer reading list, though, pretending I'd be there in the fall." The memory felt ripe, dripping like rotting fruit. I could taste my desire, my unfulfilled potential.

Who would I have been if I'd done more, become more?

"You're getting close, but you're not there yet," Sequoia said. "What do the cards reveal that you're too scared to face? Use your intuition."

My throat bobbed, and I already regretted the next set I was about to pull. "I don't know if this is a good idea," I murmured, my hands lifting from the deck. Sequoia's hands drifted to mine and pressed them back down.

"Yes, it is. You're doing great." She smiled, and I swear the candle flames flickered higher. I let out a breath, surprised by how comforting her touch felt. People begged me to tell their stories, but no one had ever asked for mine.

Pain mingled with relief in my chest as memories rose to the surface like bubbles. Telling my own story was uncomfortable but felt necessary. I was beginning to realize that Julian's death wasn't just his story, his puzzle to solve. It was deeply my own.

My fingers found the deck again, and I pulled. A humorless chuckle escaped, hot air filling my cheeks. "Adolescence: the Tower, Nine of Wands, Judgment, the Moon, the World. Heavy Major Arcana," I said, surrendering to the memory of that time in my life. "This is when my mother got sick. We closed the bookshop for months, in and out of hospitals. My father even paused his practice, something he'd never done. But I could tell he hated being a caretaker. I took it on, and while I knew he felt ashamed of his young daughter carrying the weight, I could see he was relieved," I said, tracing the Tower card's edge.

"I didn't have much of a life, but I became a recluse during those years. I stopped helping my father in the lab. My mother was my only company, along with a warehouse of books. I learned to read her every scowl, every grimace, every unspoken need. I lost myself in those years.

My only solace was the bookshop—no one could forbid me from any section. I read everything and more. But I was so alone," I said, my voice faltering. "I convinced myself it was for the best, that people were more trouble than they were worth," I said, and the words stung.

For someone so obsessed with truth, I'd become skilled at hiding from my own.

"But are they? Worth the trouble?" Aspen leaned closer, watching me thumb the cards in the candlelight.

"I still haven't decided," I said, meeting his gaze. "That was also when I reopened my mother's bookshop." I broke my eyes from his, looking back down at the cards. "The books didn't sell well, but the fortunes did." A sad smile crept up to my lips. "It was what little help I could offer my parents."

"It wasn't *little*," Sequoia said, and my chest lifted. I had never asked my parents for thanks. It was my responsibility to look after them, but their praise was non-existent, even when I felt like I was giving them my all.

"You wanted more than the bookshop, didn't you?" she asked gently.

"Of course. I wanted the world. I wanted to travel, to experience my own adventures, not just the ones in books. The darkest adventures always fascinated me," I admitted, my shoulders feeling lighter. "It was something in my blood—because my father had the same drive as I did. Or I had his."

I thumbed through the next five cards, but it was Aspen's hand that caught mine this time, warm and steady beneath my clammy fingers. I found myself welcoming it.

"The truth," he said softly.

"The truth," I echoed, my voice barely a whisper.

The deck felt alive under my fingertips as I pulled the next five. "And now, the last five years of my life. Death, Three of Swords, the Wheel of Fortune, the Fool, Ten of Wands." I let the cards settle around me, pausing before I spoke. As I did, a faint, almost imperceptible hum buzzed in my ears. I would have dismissed it as my blood pressure rising, but I knew better by now.

It was magick.

I shook my head, focusing on the cards, pointing a shaky finger at Death. "My father's death, just over a year ago," I said, my voice flat. "They found him with a bullet through his head, gun in hand, the blast powder on his fingers," I said, swallowing the sob that threatened in my throat. "It felt like a puzzle he left behind, one I was meant to solve, but there were no clues to follow. So, it must have been me; I must have been his undoing."

The buzzing grew louder, but my words felt detached, like they were spilling from someone else's mouth. "And now, the Wheel, I'm here, searching for answers to the wrong questions, in a house full of monsters, when I've always felt like the biggest monster of them all," I said, but the hum grew so loud that I could barely hear myself anymore. "That I was somehow . . . the cause of his death. I wasn't good enough, worthy of being his daughter." I blinked, trying to hold back tears, but it was Sequoia's gentle hand that wiped them away.

She pulled me close, letting me fall against her chest. She whispered something, but the words blurred. "Shh . . . everything . . . okay," was all I could make out. But what I felt, instead of hearing, was a sob welling up from deep within me, vibrating up to the top of my head. The sound, I realized, was muffled by Sequoia's hair. I took a deep inhale, the scent of rosehip and lavender flooding my senses, washing over me like a storm. She smelled like fresh rain.

"You did so well," Sequoia hushed against my cheek.

Then, there was another presence—the scent of musk and clover, maybe even something faintly burning. I felt Aspen's hands winding around mine, his thumb tracing gentle circles into the soft space between my fingers.

"We're here for you," Aspen said softly.

And for the first time, I believed him.

I melted into Sequoia's embrace, feeling her body against mine, our limbs tangling together. I found my steady breath again and broke the embrace, our cheeks brushing as I pulled back. The feel of her skin on mine sent a rush through me—a new, yet somehow familiar sensation.

Her eyes, brown and swollen—had she been crying too?—locked onto mine, and I felt pierced, almost breathless under her gaze. Her eyes drew to my lips.

I had always been like a lone seedling, desperate to sprout, but now I found myself in a new kind of garden. One full of strange, wicked growth beneath the surface. And yet, there were beautiful things here too, even if equally devastating.

I could no longer deny my truth. I wanted *her*. And I wanted *him*, too.

I stole a glance at Aspen. He was watching us, his gaze fixed, lips slightly parted, and fingers digging into his thighs as though he were bracing himself. A spark ignited in my core at the sight. He gave me an almost imperceptible nod. It wasn't permission, it was encouragement.

I looked back to Sequoia, her eyes equally alight with hunger. It took a fraction of a second before my lips met hers. Sequoia sighed into me and I tasted something I could only describe as spun sugar and lost innocence. I wondered what she tasted on me.

I didn't care that Aspen was watching. There was even a part of me that was thrilled by the thought of him seeing this moment, of sharing what he had once claimed as his own. I pulled away briefly to meet his heated eyes.

"Your hair . . . it's beautiful," he murmured, brushing a stray strand behind my ear. The hunger in his eyes raised my own desire above its breaking point. I looked back at Sequoia, her lips still parted, her gaze still locked on mine. I leaned in again.

We became a tangle of limbs and fingers, her grip mirroring mine, firm and unrelenting. Somewhere in the background, a teacup clattered to the floor with a soft thud. The cards scattered around us like rose petals, as if granting their approval through their constant, low hum growing louder with each touch. My fingers traced the delicate line of her neck, and at some point, she let out a quiet laugh, the sound sweeter than sunset.

I didn't think; I only felt. Every sense was heightened yet softened, as though we were drifting in a dream.

I broke my kiss with her just to find another warm, welcoming mouth waiting for me. As I kissed Aspen, he smiled against my lips, before biting my lower lip. His earthy scent of musk and clover and wax mixed with hers, lavender and lilac and rosehip.

It was intoxicating, like feasting in Eden.

Mouths opened, but no words formed—only sounds of different pitches and rhythms. A low groan here, a gasp there, a gentle sigh somewhere else. Nothing mattered except this moment, this suspended fragment of existence, where I felt myself transforming.

In that sacred, entangled embrace, I became something I had always longed for. No longer a solitary seedling, I was a blossoming bud of pleasure.

I was a flower in the garden.

Growing, growing, growing.

Chapter 28: The Tree and the Runes

The next morning, I woke to the gentle pattering of rain against my window, a soft rhythm against the glass that felt almost conspiratorial. My body ached, but not from exhaustion. The scent of rosehip and clover still lingered on my skin, woven into the sheets, as if the night had left its mark on me in more ways than one.

I turned onto my side, reveling in the cool press of linen between my bare legs. My fingers drifted absently over my arms, my stomach, recalling the weight of hands that weren't mine, the press of lips that had left no space between wanting and taking. Heat coiled low in my belly, lazy, lingering—until it collided with the sharper edge of regret.

My lips parted on a breath that felt too shallow. Sequoia's sigh against my mouth, Aspen's hand at the nape of my neck—it all flickered through me like an afterimage burned into my skin. I had let them in.

Worse, I had wanted to.

I had given in to the very thing I had spent my life resisting.

The realization settled over me like a second skin, both thrilling and suffocating. I had told myself I was better than this—stronger than my impulses, smarter than my desires. I had spent years pretending I was untouchable, that no one could reach inside me and unearth something real.

But I had let them, willingly.

My eyes shot toward my desk, where the Skorn deck lay in a scattered, chaotic spread. Twenty-five cards pulled and left askew, separated from the rest. *Imbued.* My pulse ticked up.

I sat up, the room spinning slightly as I pressed my palms into the mattress. The moment my fingers reached for the Skorn deck, a sharp pulse of static snapped at my skin. I flinched, exhaling sharply.

The magick was there.

I clenched my jaw, swallowing against the rising tide in my chest. My gaze snagged on Julian's journal, discarded among the wreckage of my choices. The sight of it tethered me back to orbit.

I had a purpose here. I had a mission.

I exhaled, dragging a hand through my tangled hair.

No. Nothing has changed.

I swung my legs over the side of the bed, the cold floor biting at my bare feet.

I was simply using them. Sequoia and Aspen. That was all.

What had happened—what I had done—was just another step toward the truth. Another move in a game where I could not afford to lose.

And if they got caught in the crossfire? A sharp pang twisted in my chest. My fingers curled against my palms.

So be it.

I grabbed the nearest sweater, tugging it over my head with more force than necessary. My trousers followed, my movements brisk, efficient, mechanical.

This was nothing.

This was a distraction.

I stepped into the hall before I could think twice, before I could look back and see the truth staring at me from the mess of cards and tangled sheets.

Before I could admit that I was already too far gone.

*

Breakfast was awkward. Everyone was already seated at the table when I walked in, plates in front of them. My heartbeat skidded at the sight of the Trees, shame stinging my face and neck. *No way but through,* I reminded myself.

I took my seat next to Nina and forced a smile.

"You sure look well-rested," she said, and a blush crept up my cheeks. Across the table, silence stretched too thin.

"I guess I am," I said, focusing my attention on my plate.

A few moments passed before Nina stood, stretching her arms. "You all are a lively bunch," she muttered, though her eyes lingered on me a second too long. I rolled my eyes at her, hoping the act mimicked normalcy enough to prevent further suspicion.

"Hmpf," she huffed before striding away from the table.

I finally broke my willpower and let my gaze drift up to the Trees. They were both staring at me, their expressions soft but steady.

"How are you feeling, Dahlia?" Sequoia asked, her voice light.

"Fine. Good, actually. Thanks for the help last night," I said, figuring it would be more awkward *not* to address it.

"Of course," Sequoia replied, her cheeks tinged pink.

I glanced at Leone, but he was so absorbed in his book that I thought he hadn't noticed. *I hoped* he hadn't noticed. But then, his eyes flicked up to meet mine before drifting to the Trees. The gesture was slight, but I understood it for what it was.

He was reminding me of our deal.

Aspen looked as relaxed as ever, but there was a flicker—something unreadable—lurking just beneath his gaze. I weighed my options. Approaching them together for the pen could backfire. If one resisted, the other might follow. Or worse, it could sow discord between them—and I couldn't afford to spark a rift I couldn't control.

I finished my plate at the same time they did, lingering as they picked at crumbs. Sequoia pressed a kiss to Aspen's cheek, murmuring something about an essay before leaving the dining room. As she passed me, she reached out, giving my arm a gentle squeeze.

"Let's talk later, okay?"

Aspen followed her out, but I caught up to him in the hallway. He met my gaze mid-stride.

"A word," I said in a whisper once Sequoia was out of earshot.

His brows lifted in amusement. "Back for more so soon?"

I rolled my eyes. "What happened last night—it doesn't change anything. You know why I'm here." I let the words settle between us, admitting it at last. Aspen had suspected I was investigating Julian's death. And after last night, it didn't feel right to keep lying—not when I had been so honest with other parts of myself.

He nodded, but for a split second, I swore I saw something like hurt ripple through his expression.

"And I still want to help you," he said.

I narrowed my eyes. "Why?"

Aspen hesitated. It was brief, but enough to make my stomach tighten.

"You told me you regretted not being more open with me," I pressed.

"I did." His voice was quiet. "But there are things I'm forbidden to say."

I scoffed. "Great. More secrets. Like I said, nothing has changed."

He sighed, and for the first time, he looked tired. "I do want to help you, Dahlia."

I shook my head, exhaling sharply. "Then prove it."

He watched me for a long moment before finally nodding.

"There's something I need," I said, lowering my voice. "A pen. Leone said you have it."

Aspen's confusion lasted only a second before a chuckle slipped past his lips. "That old sport is still after it," he mused, then lowered his voice. "Wait—you slept with us for a pen?"

Heat climbed up my throat. "No—that was—"

Aspen grinned, cutting me off. "Relax, Dahlia. I'm teasing." His voice dipped lower, a warmth behind it that made my breath hitch. "I figured you'd realize by now—that's how I show affection." He paused. "If you want the pen, I'll give it to you," he said finally.

I arched a brow. "And?"

"And what?"

"You're not going to ask for something in return?"

His lips curled at the edges. "What, you want me to ask you to solve a riddle?"

I groaned. "Whatever. Just bring it tonight."

But before I could turn, his hand closed around my wrist, firm but careful.

"What I said last night," he murmured, his breath brushing against my skin. "I meant it. We're here for you, we're your friends."

I swallowed hard. "You are," I said, though I wasn't sure if I truly believed it.

They were more than that, but still less than friends. Friends trusted each other, but I couldn't trust anyone in this House. Sure, I could trust them with my pathetic childhood stories, but not with anything that mattered. Maybe if things had been different: if I hadn't been a fraudulent student, if I hadn't been hired to solve Julian's murder, if I didn't have a dead father haunting me. Then maybe we could have all been friends. He finally released my arm, and I went upstairs without another word.

*

I had packed my bag, ready to head back down to the tunnels once I had the map, armed with the rest of my necessities: a second functioning compass, my deck of cards, Julian's journal, and my sharpened dagger. I only hoped that whatever Julian had left for me in those tunnels was worth all the trouble I'd gone through to get this far.

"We are building off of our previous discussion on free will tonight and examining the historical origins of predetermination. Aspen, this should be a favorite topic of yours," the Meister began.

I was already regretting attending tonight's Circle.

"And, Ms. Blackburne, you should have some research findings to report on the topic as well. From the Nordic sources, yes?"

Damn. I had been so preoccupied with Julian's case that I had completely let the Meister's side project fall to the wayside. I was going to have to rely on my working understanding of the runes and Norse system to get through this discussion.

"Of course. I'm happy to contribute," I lied.

As if sensing this, Aspen tilted his head to the side, giving me a slow, sideways smile. I furrowed my brows in return. I hated the way he could so easily read me—the way I read others. It was infuriating.

"I'm also fascinated by the topic," Nina chimed in. *Thank God.* They could carry the conversation.

Aspen and Nina went back and forth for a while before eventually turning to me.

"The concept of the Fates spinning the tapestry of the future—that symbolism exists in Norse mythos too, right, Dahlia?" Nina asked, looking at me. She didn't seem to realize she was setting me up to expose my ignorance. Or was she?

"Yes," I answered slowly, trying to recall the readings I had done weeks ago. "There are three Fates that mirror the Greek ones—they're called the Norns."

I let out a breath, relieved that I could remember something useful.

"And how are they tied to predestination? Is it through the runes?" the Meister interjected.

I racked my brain, trying to recall anything substantial about the Norns and the runes, but my mind kept circling back to the image of the runes carved beneath the grand oak's bark, my fingernails blackened from peeling it. And to the drawing I had seen in the tunnels, in that all-too-familiar office.

"The tree," I said quietly, something clicking into place.

I had read a text about a tree, but I hadn't connected it until now.

"There's a tree in Norse mythology called Yggdrasil, the Tree of Life. At its base lies the Well of Urd, the well of Fate." I sat up straighter, the memory sharpening. "And as far as the runes go, they were the gateway into the Norns' tapestry of Fate."

The Meister eyed me curiously, his gaze urging me to continue. I swallowed hard, recalling the next part of what I had read. I didn't like where my train of thought was leading.

"There's a story of Odin and how he acquired his power. It is said he hung himself on Yggdrasil for nine days and nine nights in order to gain knowledge of the Otherworlds and to understand the runes—to know the future and to possibly influence it."

"So, the Norse mythos did believe in predetermination, but they also believed there was a way around it," Aspen added. "Otherwise, Odin would have never sacrificed himself for that power."

"Yes, it seems so," I replied, but my voice was flat. I was no longer in the Circle, discussing an academic topic of predestination.

My mind drifted to the image of Julian's limp body.

Like Odin, he had hung himself from the tree, pointing me toward a message. Toward that symbol of the demiurge—the lion with the serpent's body. But what if the act of hanging itself was another clue?

It was as if he were reaching across time and space to tell me: *I died because of a sacrifice—one that I didn't make. A sacrifice to a false God.*

But what if it wasn't just *his* sacrifice?

The elements—the Meister's words echoed back to me: *I've been waiting for all the right elements.*

Of course.

I had pinned it the second he walked into my shop.

His pentagonal cane. The crystal I brought out with five-fold symmetry.

The night of Julian's death—maybe it wasn't just his sacrifice.

Maybe it was meant to be *all five of them.*

My stomach twisted, nausea climbing up.

"I'm sorry, I'm feeling unwell. I'll have to excuse myself," I said, standing too quickly.

Nina looked up at me with a furrowed brow, her mouth open mid-sentence. I had lost track of the conversation.

"Do you need any help?" Sequoia offered.

"No, I'm fine. I think I just need to lie down. If you'll excuse me," I said.

Horror lodged itself in my throat—raw, acidic, choking out anything else. I couldn't move, couldn't think beyond the sharp, metallic taste of it. But if that hadn't come first—if terror hadn't sunk its claws into me—I think the anger would have swallowed me alive. It pulsed just beneath the surface, waiting for the moment fear loosened its grip. I jumped out of my seat, feeling the urge to wretch.

The Meister gave me a curious look, as though suspecting I had made some realization. But in the next moment, he nodded, releasing me from the Circle. "Of course," the Meister said. "We are about to conclude. Rest, Ms. Blackburne."

*

"Are you okay?" It was Aspen at my door no more than twenty minutes later. His brows were knit so tightly I could have balanced a Skorn card between them. It made me suspect he actually cared. In his hand, he nervously twirled a pen made of spun and twisted glass, the delicate craftwork fragile in his tense grip. No doubt, it was *the* pen. I opened the door further to let him in.

"I'm fine. Something at Circle just made me need to step away," I said, not wanting to share the full truth but finding it hard to evade now.

"You can tell me what you're thinking," Aspen said carefully, setting the pen on my desk. I crossed the room and pocketed it before he could change his mind. "Even if you're distrustful, I still trust you, Dahlia. I didn't even ask why you needed this."

I studied him for a long moment. He'd shown me his workshop. He'd given me the pen. He'd done other *things*, too—offered pieces of himself I hadn't asked for but had taken all the same. The truth was, I'd already lost the battle of holding back from him. And God, I needed a friend. Maybe—just this once—honesty wouldn't be a mistake.

"The tree in the sitting room. It was the one Julian hung himself from," I said. Aspen's gaze was steely, but he nodded. "The tree itself is covered in runes. That's what I was noticing the night you came into the sitting room and found me by it. A piece of the bark had peeled off, and I realized there were runes all over it."

"That's strange," Aspen said, but his expression didn't match.

I knew it was dangerous to tell him what I was thinking, but there was something in the back of my mind that wanted to let him in. I had felt so alone these past two months—or years, really—that part of me relished his company, despite how dangerous it was. My dagger was in my bag, just under my pillow. I knew what I was about to reveal was risky, so I made my way to my bed and sat down, feeling for the hilt.

"When I was recalling the story of Odin in Circle tonight, something clicked. Julian hung himself to leave a message. He had died as a sacrifice—one that wasn't his to make. Sequoia told me that the night he died, you all were performing some kind of ceremony, and that you took a potion. Do you think it was meant to kill one of you, or all of you?"

Aspen's lips became a flat line. He came around my bed and sat next to me, and I gripped the hilt of the knife even harder, feeling my knuckles turn white. He was quiet for a long moment, and I felt beads of perspiration forming on my neck.

"Not all of us," he said finally.

I let the words sink in.

"But one of you," I pressed.

"Yes, one of us was supposed to die," Aspen said. He ran his hand through his hair, his nervous tell. "But it wasn't supposed to be Julian."

I waited for him to say more, but when he didn't, my pulse quickened as I let out the only word I could muster. "Why?" It was a simple question, but it dropped to the bottom of my stomach like an anchor.

"Damn it, Dahlia. I could be *killed* for telling you this," he said, turning to me, his eyes as sharp as the dagger I was gripping. He was torn—he wanted to let me in, but there was a primal fear in his eyes that was holding him back.

But then he finally unraveled.

"The Meister, he's much more powerful than you can imagine. He has us perform an elemental ceremony into soul flight once a year. It requires a lot of magick—it's the riskiest thing we do, right after the Spring Symposium. There's a chapter on it in *The Book of Skorn.* Khorvyn had written that if the ceremony works—when all the elements, fire, water, air, and earth are united—the practitioners would be able to tap into the material form of the Shattered Mother and access her purest form of power. Khorvyn claimed to have achieved it himself." Aspen paused, looking away at something out the window. "The Meister has been doing the ceremony for years. But every time it ends with the same outcome: a student sacrifice. The weakest among us don't survive the ceremony."

"If he's been doing it for so long, it must not be working. Why does the Meister keep trying?"

Aspen looked back at me, scanning his eyes around my room. "Look at this place, Dahlia. It's crumbling. The class size has been shrinking every year. The House has been dwindling in magick for years. He says he wants to save it, restore it back to the way it was when the Founding Five were here. But I suspect he wants to supersede the Al-Ahmar on the Council. With that kind of magick, he'd be the most powerful Advisor in history."

I searched his eyes, but all I saw was desperation and pain—all of it.

"He's been sacrificing a student every year for it," I said. That explained the string of missing students that Gabriel found. Maybe my father came to Foresyth as a detective first to investigate and was convinced into staying as a student. Just like the Meister had intended for me. Or maybe he just came here for the education, like I wished I could have.

"They don't always die. Sometimes they go missing, or go insane," Aspen said. "But *that* night, something went wrong. Julian wasn't supposed to die. I suspected someone must have intervened, either Leone or Nina. Julian wasn't the weakest of us; he was the *strongest.*"

I let the words settle over me before I spoke. "And the person who was supposed to die . . . it was Sequoia, wasn't it?"

"Yes," he said with a hollowness that uneased me. "She's always struggled . . . channeling her magick. That's why I'm so harsh with her. Because here at Foresyth, academics are a life-or-death matter, and we're bound to this place because of our parents' debts. I've strived to be her mentor, her protector, but some women seem to have a death wish, no matter what I do." His eyes locked onto mine and I detected a glimmer of a smirk before his face returned to stone.

"I suspect that's why she attempted soul flight on her own that night we found her in the tub. She wants to prove herself—wants to make sure she'll live through the next ceremony," he continued.

"The next ceremony?" I asked.

But when Aspen didn't answer, I said: "That's why you and Sequoia were fighting about Julian. You suspected he sacrificed himself for her?"

God, what if he had sacrificed himself to save *all* of them.

"No, that's not why we've been fighting."

"Then why?"

"I don't agree with the ceremony, or the intent of it. I think there are other ways to restore the magick of the House without sacrificing its students. Even if it meant my father would disown me, cut me off from his fortune, I wanted Koi and I to leave that night. But she begged me to stay, to prove herself. Julian even *sided* with her despite the fact he'd been vocal about his disapproval of the Meister's methods. But now I understand why. He stacked the cards that night, metaphorically speaking, and forced the outcome. He knew Sequoia would be safe, that he was the one that was going to die." His words drifted.

He reached into his pocket and uncrumpled a piece of paper, the words written in burgundy ink.

My eyes widened. "What's this?"

"He left me this that night," Aspen began, his voice low. "It was written in a scrawl, like he knew he was dying as he wrote it. It said, *Tuta sit, sed ne illi obstes. Let her be safe, but do not hinder her.*"

"Her?" I asked, a coldness prickling along my skin.

Aspen's gaze softened. "He knew you'd come."

I tried to process everything Aspen was saying, to untangle the puzzle Julian had laid out. Julian had somehow known I'd come here. He'd addressed me specifically in his journal, weaving a trail for me to follow, one he must have known would draw me in like a moth to a flame.

"Why are you telling me this now?" I finally asked, my voice quiet.

Aspen's expression softened. "When you first arrived here, I just wanted to make sure you were the person Julian had written about. That's why I took such an interest in you, asked you so many questions. But when you started suspecting me, I decided to do what Julian said, to let you figure out what happened on your own. I was still suspicious of the others, I couldn't rule out that something had gone awry, and I tried to help you. But it only pushed you further away." He hesitated, then reached for my hand.

"But now . . . I know it's selfish, and I know others could get hurt, but I almost lost Sequoia last year, and I don't want to lose you, too. Say the word, and I'll take you and Sequoia away from here." He raised my hand to his lips, pressing a gentle kiss against my knuckles. My traitorous heart fluttered before I could argue with reason.

"But you and Sequoia—" I said, unable to hide the confusion in my voice. He was with her, and yet he was here, confessing his feelings to me. "I'd only be . . . interfering."

Aspen let out a soft breath, warm against the place he'd kissed. "Koi and I . . . we're like a tree wrapped in poison ivy—we consume each other. We've known each other since childhood; it's hard to untangle that kind of bond. In this world and the next, we are bound."

"She mentioned something similar," I said.

"But our hearts are open. Koi falls in love with anyone, to be honest. I'm a bit more selective," he added, and a flush crept up my cheeks. His words hung between us, blazing like embers, leaving me with only stone and ash—and the truth. Isn't that what I'd come here for?

"Julian still needs me. This place and the students need me." I drew a deep breath, words spilling from the depths I rarely touched. "Before Foresyth, I felt like I was living in other people's stories, reading too many books, reading too many people who didn't care to even know me, the true me. This is the first time I feel like I have my own story, a purpose." I sighed deeply.

Even if Julian had written the story before he died, I was determined to rewrite it, to make it my own.

Part of me wanted to run away with him and Sequoia, or in the least, have him stand by my side as I unraveled the mystery Julian had left behind. But I couldn't afford to put any other student in danger, not when Julian had entrusted this to me.

Most importantly, I needed to start trusting myself.

"You need to protect Sequoia. I can take care of myself, I promise. And if I can't do it alone, I'll come find you," I said.

He hesitated for a moment but then nodded, and the glint in his eyes nearly brought tears to my own. I softened, leaning closer to him, the dagger beneath my pillow forgotten. Aspen leaned forward as if to kiss me, but paused, his face just a breath from mine.

Finally, he pulled away, tucking a strand of my hair behind my ear. A proud smile broke on his lips. "Go then," he said quietly. "Go finish your story."

The Acolyte and the Alchemist: Part VIII

Elizabeth Svenski lay in the children's hospital ward, counting the metal stars mounted on the ceiling. They twinkled faintly in the candlelight. Someone had put them there, she thought, appreciating the small, human act of kindness. She appreciated everything nowadays, now that her time in this world was dwindling.

Pain had become a passive part of her existence, a dull presence woven into her every breath. It gnawed at her bones, but she had learned not to flinch. Instead, she found solace in stories. She read until the words blurred and her body dragged her into dreamless sleep, her hands still curled around the pages. She had devoured nearly every book in the ward's modest library.

"I've heard you're a prodigious reader."

Elizabeth lifted her head. A woman in a red cloak stood in the doorway, her silhouette backlit by the dim glow of the corridor.

This morning, Elizabeth was feeling lucid. She blinked the sleep from her eyes, carefully placing her latest book on the bedside table, and folded her hands in her lap.

"I read like I'm dying," she said. "Because I am."

The woman stepped inside, the heavy fabric of her cloak whispering against the tile.

Elizabeth tilted her head. "I used to worry I wouldn't finish all the books I wanted before the time came." A small, sardonic smile played on her lips. "Now I know I won't."

The woman did not reply right away. Instead, she moved toward the window, placing gloved fingers on the glass. Outside, the town of Enderly stretched beyond the hospital walls, veiled in the blue-grey light of early morning.

"And your family?" the woman asked at last.

"They're gone." Elizabeth's voice did not waver. "Burned in a fire. I used to think I should have died with them. Prayed for it, even." She exhaled slowly, tilting her head back toward the stars on the ceiling. "I suppose someone finally listened. Who are you anyway? A sister of the Holy Cross?"

Silence.

Then the woman turned, stepping closer to the bed.

"What would you say," she asked, "to helping me with one final story?"

Elizabeth stilled, her heart sputtering. A small part of her thought that this might be Death, coming to claim her. But she would not show fear now. Not after she had endured the screams of her parents and younger siblings; her own was lost somewhere in her throat.

The candlelight flickered, and for the first time in a long while, something stirred in Elizabeth's chest—something that wasn't resignation. Her foolish heart might have even called it hope.

She sat up a little straighter.

"I'd say that depends on the story."

The woman in red smiled.

Chapter 29: Intuition as the Guide

I delivered the pen along with the twenty-five cards imbued with magick to Leone. He removed his glasses, slid one tip into his mouth, and chewed on it for several minutes before saying anything. I had never seen him so visibly unsettled. Finally, he set his glasses on top of the closed book in front of him.

"You got the pen," he said.

"I got the pen," I replied.

"And the cards?" His eyes darted to the slim deck I had placed on the table. "What did you do to imbue them? Will it be enough?"

I gave him a sidelong glance, ignoring the flush in my cheeks. "Trust me, you don't want to know what I had to do to imbue those." I gave up my defenses, my vulnerability in the most raw, intimate reading of my life. I didn't just give up, I gave *in*. "It'll be enough."

"If there's enough magick, the map should be ready by tomorrow morning," he said. I tapped the cards again, hoping he'd sense my urgency. If another ceremony was going to happen before the Spring Symposium, I didn't have much time.

"What would I need to pay you for a rush job? An inkwell?" I joked, but he didn't react.

For a moment, I considered revealing that I knew about the ceremony and the missing students. But if Leone had made it to his third year, it meant he had watched students disappear year after year.

Whether he was complicit or simply a bystander, I couldn't be sure. I respected him enough to give him the benefit of the doubt. But Aspen had a reason to be suspicious of him, and so did I.

"Do you ever wish things were different at Foresyth?" I couldn't believe I was saying this, but I needed to find a crack in his resolve. Even a small one.

He just stared blankly. "I believe in *The Book of Skorn*," he said, reaching back to the tome on his desk. I grimaced, cursing myself. Of course he did. As someone so close to becoming an Advisor, admitting any flaw in the academic system would likely unravel his beliefs. I needed a different approach; I needed something he actually cared about.

"Yes, but . . ." I moved to the side and took a seat. "You care about the truth, don't you? What if I knew for a fact that someone was deceiving you, and the only way to learn the truth was if you helped me?" My eyes flickered to the items on the table, the pen and the cards. "You once said I'd earned your respect. Then trust me this one time. I need the map as soon as possible."

Leone adjusted his glasses, pushing them up the bridge of his nose, and I detected a spark of curiosity. He regarded me thoughtfully before speaking. "Come back in an hour," he said. "But know I'm only doing this so I can finally get some peace and quiet."

*

Leone wasn't just a scholar: he was an artist. The parchment I held in my hands was meticulously crafted, the surface bearing a subtle sheen of gold. Each tunnel was wrought in detail as if he had drawn the labyrinthine maze with a needle, not pen. Golden lines winded and weaved, showing a mesmerizing dance of paths and chambers. I hadn't realized the system of tunnels underground were so intricate. I traced my fingers over the ones I had navigated, and the exact area where my own map became useless. My scrawled drawing was only a small part of the grand map I now held in my hands.

"How did you make this?" It was my turn to be astounded.

"Magick. Yours did turn out to be enough," he said. "And this pen." He turned it up to me so I could see the tip still glistening with a swell of gold ink. "It's a Mapmaker's pen."

I blinked, staring at the orb of gold at the tip. He must have had the map pre-made, I decided. There was no way it was possible for anyone, even an experienced artist, to ink something so beautiful, so quickly.

"I don't even want to bring this down to the tunnels, I wouldn't want to dirty it. Maybe I should make a copy," I said.

"You'll want the original." His tone was so harsh and immovable, so I didn't dare argue.

I nodded, still stunned by the piece of art I held in my hands, but glad for it. I had everything I needed now. Just some courage and an ounce of recklessness, and I'd finally unearth what secrets Julian had laid for me in this hellscape of a school. Hopefully it would bring me closer to incriminating the Meister for the *ceremonies* he was running behind the polished veneer of Foresyth's prestige.

"Thanks," I said, wrapping the delicate paper and placing it in my bag. "I owe you one."

*

The tunnels were darker and damper than I remembered. My Oxfords were not going to thank me for this. My feet splashed through muddy water as I descended the first tunnel, then the second. Holding my breath, I navigated the labyrinthine walls with one hand gripping the map and the other prying open the compass. It took only five minutes to retrace my steps from the other night and arrive at the abandoned office I had explored earlier.

As I carefully stepped over a pile of fallen rocks, the map changed. I blinked, wondering if my vision was playing tricks on me. I wished I'd taken a replica, because in the stark beam of my flashlight, surrounded by utter darkness, I could have sworn I was losing my mind. But no, there had been three walls and three tunnels between me and the coordinate just moments ago, and now there was only one. It was as if the pattern had rearranged itself.

The air shifted too, filling with a pungent, sweet scent, like overripe fruit. I looked down, stepping over a gnarled root, and ran my hand along the wall for balance, my fingers brushing against something bristly. I shone my light on it: mugwort. I tore a few sprigs from the base, stuffing them into my bag. Nina could thank me later.

The tunnel walls were speckled with all kinds of plants and fungi. Nina had mentioned that mugwort thrived in these tunnels. Strange, how anything could grow down here.

I rounded a corner, making a sharp right. My flashlight flickered, the batteries waning. Perfect. In the last few moments of light, I pulled out the compass to cross-check it with the map. Leone's map hadn't failed me yet, but I wasn't relying on it alone. I couldn't explain why I trusted Leone, but I did. He reminded me of the Page of Swords—honor bound and truthful.

His map couldn't lie, even if it wanted to.

When the flashlight finally died, I muttered a curse under my breath, shaking it uselessly. I fumbled in my bag for matches and struck one against the stone wall. I wished I had learned Aspen's trick to keep a flame steady, but my match burned out after only twenty seconds. I counted twelve matches in the box—two hundred and forty seconds of light. It would have to be enough to reach the journal and make it back.

The map would only guide me so far, and with the limited light, my compass was of little use. The darkness pressed in, and a deep-seated fear began to rattle inside me.

Use your intuition, Sequoia's voice echoed in my mind. It had seemed simple advice for a Tarot reading, but now, in the depths of this pitch-black tunnel, surrounded by who-knows-what, it felt impossible.

Still, I closed my eyes and listened. I just needed to read the House like I would a living, breathing patron. After a moment, I felt it, a faint, magnetic pull, guiding me forward. The more I trusted it, the stronger it became.

When I opened my eyes, I was standing in front of a door. Painted ruby red, its edges were sprinkled with rust. I reached for the knob, careful to avoid the jagged edges, and twisted. A sharp prick on my index finger took me by surprise. I jerked my hand back, noticing a smudge of blood, which disappeared as if absorbed into the metal. The door unlocked and creaked open.

You're here, a voice resonated in my mind, darker and deeper than before. Julian? I couldn't quite place the feeling, but I knew he was here—or at least, his energy lingered. The room was empty, save for a few splintered barrels and a dark, twisting crack on the floor. Roots, maybe? The room resembled an old wine cellar. After a thorough search of the western wall, I stopped and simply listened.

Something had led me here, and I didn't want to miss it.

Then I felt it again, a subtle pull, almost imperceptible, at the base of my navel. A faint buzzing filled my ears—the same sound I'd heard during my last reading. I followed the pull to the center of the room and looked down. The ground was tangled with roots except for one small, smooth spot, coated in a layer of white dust. I crouched down, pressing my hand to the stone, and felt it—the slight rise and fall of my hand, like the House itself was breathing.

The House is alive.

The thought unsettled me, lingering as I scanned the room. The roots clung to every surface, as if the House itself were holding back secrets, drawing me in, yet resisting my presence. This place wasn't just a structure; it was a *being*, a keeper of hidden arcana. I wondered if the House was pulling me toward answers or warning me to stay away.

I wasn't going to let it decide.

I dusted the stone, revealing a familiar symbol—a lion with a serpent's tail, the demiurge. The buzzing intensified as my fingers traced over it. I unsheathed my dagger and wedged it into the stone's edge, prying it up. After a few attempts, the tile gave way, revealing an opening. I struck another match and held the flame over the gap. A box lay inside, plain and unremarkable. It looked like one of those slim, metallic cases my father used to store evidence in.

Actually, it was identical to the one he'd carried.

I reached into the hole just as the match burned low. I'd have to wait to examine it in full light, but for now, I grabbed the box and stuffed it into my bag as the buzzing in my ears reached a crescendo.

When I turned toward the red door, two green eyes glared at me. The Grifferact.

It lunged, its beak grazing my shoulder just as I managed to duck and roll aside. Pain shot through my shoulder, where its beak had sliced the skin. I scrambled behind a barrel as the creature screeched, furious and flailing. I glanced at the dagger in my hand, realizing I had managed to stab it. Not enough to kill, but enough to wound. Just as it had wounded me.

I need to get out of here.

I took a quick assessment of my opponent. The Grifferact dragged its hind leg, injured. Its movements were jerky and erratic. It wasn't truly alive; it was *animated.* I remembered the Grifferact was blind—it hadn't seen me; it had heard me. I grabbed a piece of rubble at my feet, angling my good arm for a solid throw. I needed it to land far enough to divert the creature but not so far it bounced back toward me.

I threw the stone. It clattered in the center of the room, and the Gifferact turned toward it. I seized the chance, slipping past it and bolting for the door. Just as I made it through, the creature turned, claws extended. I managed to slam the door shut, narrowly avoiding a strike of its beak.

Without pausing, I sprinted down the tunnel. I was down to five matches, lighting them sparingly as I retraced my path. I was on my last match when I reached the bookcase threshold. My blouse was soaked in blood, my Oxfords sodden with mud and grime, and my shoulder throbbed with pain. But I clutched my bag tightly, gripping the stainless-steel case as if it was the very air inside my lungs, and hurried up the stairs, into the light.

Chapter 30: Blackburnes' Letters

I was bleeding, but that wasn't my main concern. My mind buzzed with the possibilities of what I'd just found, and the relief of survival. In my bathroom, I tore off my bloodied blouse and leaned over the sink to clean the wound. I was so focused on my task that I didn't notice the door opening.

"Dahlia, I heard you running. My Gods, you're bleeding!" Sequoia exclaimed, rushing to my side. She gently pulled my hair back so I could better wash the injury. I didn't bother looking at my disheveled reflection, focusing instead on scrubbing the wound as clean as I could.

"How bad does it look?" I asked.

"Uh, it's hard to say. It's in the shape of a triangle. Looks like a bird bit you or something. How did this happen?"

"I'd rather not talk about it."

Sequoia frowned, clearly frustrated by my secrecy, but continued tending to the wound without further questioning. "Hold this on it while I go grab a first aid," she said, pressing a washcloth to my shoulder.

"I have a medical kit in my room," I said. "I'll be fine."

"Let me help you. That's going to be tough to patch on your own." She was right; it would be quicker to let her help, even if it meant facing a barrage of questions, delaying me from retrieving the case in my bag.

"Fine," I sighed. I needed to get it closed quickly to avoid infection. We made our way to my room. I kept pressure on the wound as the pain in my shoulder grew sharper.

"There." I nodded toward my dresser where I'd laid out medical supplies and a small bottle of pain suppressant. "The bottle, too, please."

"At least you're prepared," Sequoia noted, gathering the supplies. She sat beside me, and I tried to ignore the memory of the last time we'd shared a bed. I opened the bottle and took a few drops of the tincture.

She worked with a gentle touch, her fingers cool against my inflamed shoulder. "It's not a clean cut. You might need stitches, or it'll scar badly."

"It'll be fine. Just stop the bleeding, and I'll live."

Even without looking, I sensed her pursing her lips. Sequoia wasn't the type to bear visible scars. Perhaps sensing my distraction, she hesitated, then said, "About the other night . . ."

I met her gaze. "It's okay, we don't have to talk about it."

"I know, I just don't want you thinking we used any magick on you," she said quietly. I placed my hand over hers as she finished the bandage, a wave of guilt washing over me. Sequoia was worried I might feel used by them, when in truth, I had been the one using her.

"I don't think that. What happened was as much my decision as yours."

Her face softened, and she offered me a small smile. "I'm glad you feel that way." Her fingers lingered on the bandage, adjusting it with care. "Aspen and I really like you. Even if you have a habit of getting yourself hurt."

I scoffed, easing back onto the bed with my uninjured shoulder. "I think I need to rest," I murmured, feeling a genuine wave of exhaustion.

"You're really not going to tell me what happened?" she pressed, her brow arched, though there was a hint of hurt in her voice.

"A bird attacked me," I offered. It wasn't far from the truth. Would she even know of the Grifferact if I had told her? "Isn't there a saying about that being good luck?"

She laughed softly, though I could tell my answer didn't satisfy her. Still, if she had her secrets, then I deserved to keep mine.

"Maybe you'll tell me when you're feeling better. Rest up. See you at Circle." She tucked a stray strand of hair behind my ear before leaving. It was a simple gesture, but one that held a quiet intimacy I wasn't ready to acknowledge.

I closed my eyes, fighting off sleep, and waited for the sound of her footsteps to fade from the room.

*

I opened my eyes, still groggy from the medicine, though the pain in my shoulder had dulled to a manageable throb. I pulled my bag from beneath my pillow, reaching for the case. Trying to pry it open, I quickly realized it was locked by a mechanism I couldn't decipher. Sitting up for a better look, I held it in the dim light of my room, catching my faint reflection on its surface. It had been a while since I'd really looked at myself, and the person staring back was almost unfamiliar. Her eyes glinted with a fierce, untamed intensity I barely recognized.

Tracing a finger over the case's engraved markings, I saw more runes, and a name, faint but discernible. It started with a "B." I exhaled a warm breath over the metal and polished it with my bedsheet until the letters were clearer.

Blackburne.

It was my name.

I shook, rattled, and even banged the case against my desk in frustration, but it wouldn't open. Groaning, I racked my brain for a solution. Maybe I could hammer it open or apply enough weight. But then, a more logical thought cut through my frustration. The doors I'd encountered in the tunnels had reacted to me instinctively, opening at the presence of my blood, as if they were attuned to something unique about me. A biomarker.

Blood magick. The phrase echoed in my mind, and instinctively, I knew what to do. I reached up to my fresh cut and peeled back the bandages. I hissed as I pressed my fingers to the opening, coating them in a slick of blood. I smeared a few drops onto the box, watching as a soft wisp of smoke rose, as if the blood had triggered a reaction within the metal.

With a satisfying click, the case unlocked.

I opened it eagerly, and what I found made my heart lurch.

Inside were three small notebooks, each marked with the missing years I had long searched for, along with multiple pieces of parchment. The handwriting was unmistakably my father's.

These were his missing journals.

But as I skimmed the entries, I realized they weren't travel logs as I'd assumed. They weren't research notes about his time abroad as I had imagined. In the corner of one page, he'd written: *Circle, March 10th, 1893.*

My pulse quickened as I unfurled the white parchment. But as I read the letter addressed to Julian, I stifled a gasp, pressing my nails to my teeth and biting until I tasted blood.

Julian, my son,

I hope you never have to read this. But if you do, it means I am dead, and I owe you the truth. No flourishes, no excuses, just the facts:

1. *I was desperately in love with your mother.*
2. *I was consumed by blood magick.*
3. *These two facts are gravely linked.*

When I came to Foresyth, I was newly graduated, convinced of my brilliance, eager to uncover the truth of magick—if it was real, and if its power could be harnessed. I believed myself to be a man bred on facts, not fiction, and that is precisely why the matter fascinated me so. My obsession led me to The Book of Skorn, a version no one else seemed to possess. I think it was drawn to my blood.

In the Book, Aleric Khorvyn wrote of an emanation called Sophia, of rituals designed to "transcend the material form" and claim her true power. I believed I had discovered something extraordinary.

It was around that time that I was seeing your mother, Hamra.

She was unlike me in every way. She relied on instinct where I relied on theory. She, unlike me, was bound to no text or teacher, yet wielded knowledge as intrinsic as breathing. We were rivals first, then collaborators, then something more. I let her see every part of me, even the parts I should have kept hidden.

We studied the Book together. And that was our undoing.

It started with small sacrifices—rats, lizards, trivial things. But your mother wanted more. I was too enamored—by her, by the Book, by the promise of understanding—to resist. But eventually it was at the cost of my soul.

We chose Elizabeth Svenski.

A girl, terminally ill. A life already slipping away. I told myself it was mercy, but that was a lie. We wanted to prove the Book's theories, to see if freeing a human soul from its material prison would unlock what Khorvyn had claimed.

It did not.

The girl did not die in a ritualistic transcendence. There was no ascension, no enlightenment. Only a quiet dimming of her light, a candle snuffed. And yet, something stirred in me. I felt it. A hunger not entirely my own started to fester deep within me.

The demiurge. The false God, the prison warden of this material realm, turned against Sophia, and created an unquenchable blood lust within me. It took but never gave, devoured but never satisfied.

The House knew that we had called on the demiurge. It fought back, attempting to right our wrong. Life erupted from underground—roots, vines, and a giant oak tree in the sitting parlor. But it wasn't enough to stop the death ripening within us. We were too far gone.

Your mother was convinced we had only done the ritual wrong. She believed the five elements had to be offered, not just in presence, but in blood. Five sacrifices. The demiurge would choose one to die and grant the rest power to manipulate the material plane from our sheer will.

And then she told me she was pregnant.

I wanted to protect you. I wanted to end this. I stole the Book and left, believing—foolishly—that if I hid it in the depths of my soul, the cycle would break. I buried myself in work, hunting men guilty of crimes that could never outweigh my own.

And yet, Foresyth continued.

At some point Hamra gave up, burying her research, and our dark history. She quietly raised you in Enderly while she ascended to power as one of the most influential Advisors in history. All the while Foresyth continued to fall apart at the seams.

The deaths stopped for a while. But when Renate was appointed as Meister, he came across Hamra's work. He was determined to finish what we started, and to restore the House's magick.

One by one, students began disappearing again. And at the behest of Renate, the Council ensured that no one would discover his sordid methods.

But I knew the truth. I had set this in motion.

I tried to stop it. I tracked the deaths, studied the patterns, but I had no proof. I was barred from the House, from Foresyth, and from you. The best I could do was keep the Book hidden. I locked it away, sealed with blood magick even the most desperate practitioner couldn't break.

I tried to move on.

I met Estelle. A woman of light in all the ways I was dark. She loved books—the good kinds—and together, we built something beautiful. Something untouched by magick. We were blessed with a daughter, Dahlia. A flower erupting through the tainted soil of my life.

I swore to protect her. To keep her from the path that had destroyed me. When I learned you were being groomed for Foresyth, I tried to keep her away from you, from any institution that might indoctrinate her.

But even then, the Book haunted me.

It spoke to me. Whispered things I cannot bring myself to write. The bloodlust never truly left. I told Estelle the truth, and it nearly shattered her. We tried everything to fix me, but it was no use. I became a ghost in my own home, watching my wife dwindle away, watching my daughter grow up afraid of the father who could never love her properly.

And now, the Book is back at Foresyth.

Renate has it. And I must stop him with what power I have left.

If you are reading this, it means that I have failed. It means that I could not protect you, and that you are in grave danger. So, I beg you, Julian, leave. Forsake the Book and walk away while you still can. Do not let it consume you as it consumed me.

I wish I could have known you, and loved you, as much as I loved your mother, Hamra. I have even come to forgive her, for the corruption she had let into her soul. I can only hope it doesn't fully enter yours.

For my absence, for my sins, I am sorry.

Your father, Daniel Blackburne

I let the letter roll over me like a storm, its weight settling in my bones, before turning to the second—this one penned in Julian's familiar hand. A terrible question began to rise: had my father's death truly been a suicide, or had he been silenced for speaking out about what was happening at Foresyth?

Anger surged in my chest, and I clung to it like a lifeline. It was so much easier—cleaner—to feel fury than to surrender to the guilt, the shame, the grief clawing at the edges of my composure. Easier to be furious with my father for all his secrets, with the Meister for pulling my strings like a marionette, and with Julian's mother for dragging him, and by extension, my father, into this spiral of darkness.

Rage, at least, gave me direction. The rest only threatened to consume me.

Reading my father's letter left me with a hollow, twisting ache, as though he'd carved something vital out of me. My father had tried to stop the Meister. I had blamed myself for his death, for his coldness and distance from me. I had thought that somehow, I had failed him as a daughter—that he withdrew because I wasn't enough, wasn't worthy of his affection. But now I know the truth. He didn't send me to Sawyer Academy—not because I wasn't good enough—but because he feared institutions and their indoctrination.

I hadn't failed him.

He was the one who had failed me, captivated by a sea so cruel he was never able to emerge.

My whole life, I had spent hours in the bookshop with customers asking me to divine their paths, to tell them how their lives might unfold. And now, in the presence of my own truth, my own lineage, I felt utterly unmoored, adrift in a sea I couldn't navigate. The binding of blood magick ran through my veins, an invisible shackle tying me to a history I had never chosen. I wanted to deny it. I wanted to scream. But that wouldn't change what I had read. I swallowed it down as I turned my attention to the next letter, penned by my brother.

Dearest sister Dahlia (if I may call you that),

Are you ready for the double death letter? No? Oh, well, I shall proceed, nonetheless.

Congratulations! You've discovered the dreadful powers of blood magick, imprisoning Gods, and cursed cards. You've made it all this way and now get to enjoy all these letters of death and madness. What a treat!

Sorry, is this too trivializing? You'll have to forgive a dying man for making a joke or two.

But it's only necessary for you to know the facts of our circumstances if you stand a chance of survival (two out of three are not great odds for the Blackburnes, as it stands). These precautions were necessary to guard what I'm about to share with you.

Our father was quite the man.

I received his letter a day after he died and was mortified to learn that I had a part in it (though I must admit, I had no affection for the man, having never known him). When the Meister assigned me an additional research project, I thought he was only doing it to torment me for speaking out against him to the Council.

But no, it was part of his plan. You see, the vault in which your father left The Book of Skorn was guarded by his blood magick.

The Meister sent me to that shop of yours on Wicker Street, and I glamoured him in his office and stole the Book. I even got to see a glimpse of you, sitting behind the bookshop counter, nose so deep in a book, I could barely see it. I thought you were so beautiful, but now I must admit I find the thought a little uncomfortable.

Oh my Gods, sister. I had no idea what I was doing. What would happen because of my actions.

There was a passage in the Book, the real version, that states that five blood types ought to be offered—Water, fire, earth, and air. But there was another element that was elusive. That, if it wasn't present, would make the magick unstable, and hunger for more.

Our father, just as we do, had the Bonder element in his blood but didn't know it. Truth-bound, he mistakenly thought he was the air elemental—how arrogant! If only he had been there for that first ceremony with my mother all those years ago, it would have stabilized the magick, and there wouldn't have been so many deaths to follow.

A dark twist of irony.

I'm not sure how things transpired, but at some point the practice passed hands from my mother to the current Meister you are so lovingly familiar with—Renate. My mother gave up the practices, stricken with the guilt of the havoc she'd caused, and determined to raise me in the opposite of her image.

But Renate found her research at the same time he became the face of Foresyth. The school was crumbling, but he was responsible for its ascension, or its demise. He was furious at her, and they started a feud on the Council, breaking it into factions. But despite my mother's power, he had the longer lineage and was practicing Skorn magick.

In an attempt to restore the school, he continued the elemental ceremony but to no avail. He didn't know about the fifth element in our blood, but he suspected the answer was in the Book. And he knew I'd be the only one who could retrieve it. That day in your bookshop, when I held that Book in my hands, I knew that it was far more powerful than the Meister could even dream of.

I heard its calling—the demiurge's bloodlust. Its desire to rid the world of its material forms in opposition to Sophia.

Naturally, I became suspicious and started to investigate the Meister. I have an affliction for puzzles, as you know, but no patience for not knowing the answer to one.

I started to investigate. I hunted the Meister's study and found his personal research journals and bloodwork analysis. He had discovered, with the help of the Book and samples of my blood, that there was a trace mineral unique to my blood that formed the Bonder.

Our father finding the Book wasn't a pure coincidence. The Book calls to those with the Bonder's blood. It's the only way to stabilize its magick, to satisfy the demiurge, and theoretically, tap into Sophia's power. It's a precarious art.

The Book was also what led me to the Tramping Grounds—like calls to like. I believe the Book itself was forged with the same earth as what lies there. I used it to my advantage to conceal my messages to you, entrusting that you'd be the only one to find the Tramping Ground, as it would call to you, just as it did to me.

I realized the night of the ceremony that delivering the Book to the Meister had been delivering my own death sentence. What he pieced together from the original Book, meant that I, along with the others, were the five sacrifices he needed to access the Shattered Mother's powers. I was the Bonder to bring all the other elements together.

I knew we were going to die, though the other students didn't suspect. They hadn't known what I did—they still thought that the ceremony killed off the weakest, just as your father had assumed. But it didn't—it wasn't going to.

It was going to kill me, along with the others.

Could I just leave, and never enter these haunting walls of Foresyth again? Certainly. But that meant the other's lives would be at risk. And I was a bit love-sick, if I must admit. Say hello to Aspen and Sequoia for me, would you? They were my dearest friends, despite our disagreements. And I knew that the Meister wouldn't stop. He'd find me, or worse yet, get to you before I had a chance to act.

That's when I made the decision to end it before he did. I didn't want to give the Meister that kind of power, or even the other students, after finding out what it did to our father. And besides, this gave me the opportunity to create the puzzle of my lifetime, my magnum opus. My final act.

Magick is all ceremonial, you see. And intention matters.

It came down to a matter of timing. If I died before the actual ceremony, then it wouldn't work—the Meister wouldn't succeed. I wished I could have thought of another way, but I had mere hours to lay out my plan. The Meister was going to kill me one way or another. But if I was going to die, at least I'd have a say on how it would happen.

And I had a back-up plan: I had you.

The Meister knew of your existence (thanks to your prolific Tarot-reading practice which made the January issue of the Greenwich Observer). I used that knowledge to my advantage. I knew that you'd be invited to Foresyth shortly after my death. The Meister would draw you here with some plot of his. And of course, you'd be curious. You'd hear the call of magick that's in your blood, and you'd come looking for me.

I apologize, dear sister, for laying out this plot for you and making you suffer it. I wish there had been a better way—another story in which we could all live together. But you are the last element, the one who can end this cycle of death. I laid out everything in Foresyth so you would slowly come to know its true nature, and the depth of its darkness, without being consumed by it. I couldn't trust anyone, even the other students. If the Meister was using me, he surely could be using the others. I made sure that you would be the only one with the full story. Maybe that was a mistake, but it's too late now.

You are almost to the end. But you're not there yet.

Take these letters as proof to the Council and have them see how corrupt the Meister has become. Until this moment, there hasn't been enough evidence to convict him. But my grand exit and written words ensured that there would be enough to challenge his rule. If you find my mother, maybe she'll help you, if she feels remorse over my death.

If you've gotten this far, then I know we would have been friends. But maybe, despite being separated by space and time, we can still solve this together.

Cheers!

Your dearest brother, Julian

When I finished re-reading the letters, I closed my eyes, trying to steady my racing heart. If nothing else, I had answers. The truth pulsed through me, rushing to my head, filling every vein. Now I understood why the Meister had brought me to Foresyth, why I'd felt so compelled to unravel the mystery of Julian's death, and why the magick called to me.

It was in my blood.

And most sickening of all was how Julian had treated this all like a game—his magnum opus. He treated his very own life like a puzzle, like one of Aspen's sculptures meant to be shattered. Like . . . Sequoia, drowning herself in the name of a God who wasn't even the source of her power.

And yet, here I had been—obsessed over finding Julian's killer, when he had discarded his life all along, refusing to fight. He had claimed to be under the manipulation of the Meister, but surely his genius could have found another way than to use his death to set off a chain reaction.

I tasted sourness on my tongue.

Something told me that Julian hadn't minded dying—that if it served a purpose, it was worth it. His lack of sanctity for his own life felt like the greatest betrayal of all. I could have ignited with rage, but I pressed it down and channeled it into something useful: a plan.

I had to save the other students, even if they were too stupid to value their own lives. Julian had said the final piece of the puzzle would be showing this evidence to the Council—that they could be trusted to enact justice. But I was tired of playing his game, of retracing my father's footsteps. I was tired of feeling like there was something wrong with me for feeling too much.

That my intuition was any less powerful than my logic.

Ignoring his gut, hiding his feelings—that's what had gotten my father killed. And following someone else's plan, along with his own hubris, had gotten Julian killed.

I was done with all of it.

I was done listening to men who thought they knew better than me—especially now that they were both dead. I was done believing that following my instincts was a weakness, that secrecy was power, that solitude was strength.

No, I wasn't going to follow Julian's plan anymore. Or walk in my father's shadow.

I had something very, very different in mind.

Chapter 31: Return to Blackburne

I walked the winding stone path along Wicker Street, my shoes scuffing against the uneven cobblestones. The scent of rain lingered in the cracks, mixing with the faint traces of chimney smoke curling from distant rooftops. The street was quieter than I remembered, or maybe that's what Sundays were like in Greenwich now.

Ahead, the bookstore stood still and solemn, its windows dark, its door marked by a hastily written sign: *Temporarily Closed.*

A heaviness settled in my stomach. I reached for the doorknob, my fingers brushing against the brass, cold and unwelcoming after months of absence. It had been almost three months since I'd left, and so much had changed.

But I wasn't here for nostalgia.

I was here for Estelle.

"Mother?" My voice wavered as I stepped inside, the bell over the door letting out a feeble chime. "It's me, Dahlia."

The scent of parchment and old incense wrapped around me like an embrace, familiar and grounding. I inhaled deeply, greedily. Home. I had missed home. The floorboards creaked beneath my weight as I moved forward, each step stirring dust motes in the dim afternoon light filtering through the curtained windows. These steps were worn with love, softened by the passage of time. Not like the floorboards in Foresyth—those were warped by decay, splintered by counter-magick.

"Mother?" I called again, climbing the stairs.

A faint voice, like a breath against the walls, responded. "Dahlia?"

I pushed open the door to her room.

She sat by the window, her thin frame curled into the armchair, hands resting lightly on top of a book. A cup of tea rested on the windowsill, long cold and forgotten. For a moment, the light caught her just so, illuminating her bright blue eyes. She was all the light to my father's darkness. Despite the lines of fatigue, the hollowed contours of her face, she still had that unspoken radiance.

"Dahlia!" she said again, louder this time, her entire face blooming with relief. "I knew you'd come back to me."

I studied her, cataloging the small changes. The silver threaded through her chestnut hair, the deepening shadows beneath her eyes. A hot tear streaked down my cheek before I could stop it.

"I thought you said Angelise was overfeeding you," I tried to joke, my voice unsteady. "You look thinner than the last time I saw you."

"Oh, hush now, child. Why are you fretting?" She waved her hand toward me. "Come sit beside me. I'm glad to see you've been eating better than I have."

I pulled a stool close to her chair and sat, my hand finding hers. I let the soft warmth radiating from her palm ground me.

"Mother, I . . . I wasn't honest with you," I admitted, my throat tightening. My fingers fumbled with the flap of my satchel before pulling out the letters. "I didn't go to Foresyth to learn about bookbinding. I went to learn about my father." I hesitated, then added, "And Julian."

At the name my mother stiffened. Her eyes flickered, something unreadable shifting behind them.

"Julian," she echoed.

"You knew about him?" That warm, sinking feeling twisted in my gut. A betrayal, thick and undeniable.

She exhaled, her other hand tracing slow patterns against the chair's yellow fabric. "Yes," she admitted. "I know of Julian."

"Why didn't you tell me?"

"You'll have to forgive a mother for trying to protect her daughter." A weak smile, an attempt at levity. "I wanted to keep you away from all of this."

"It's my history. You can't."

Her hand fell into her lap, resigned. "Of course," she murmured. "I should have known better than to think I could protect you when you've always been so good at protecting yourself." There was no coat of malice in her words, only observation.

"Then tell me," I pressed. "Tell me what really happened."

And finally, she did.

She wove the past into the present, mirroring the same thread of events I had pieced together from my father's letters. How Daniel left Foresyth before Julian was born. How she met him in the months that followed. How they built a life together—fell in love and had me. How she had agreed to let the past stay in the past, burying it beneath bookshelves and quiet evenings.

But I couldn't bury it. I couldn't forget. I dropped my hand from hers.

"I don't understand how you forgave him," I said, my voice thick with something between frustration and grief. "He killed Elizabeth Svenski—an innocent girl."

She looked at me then, and I saw it, the weight of her years and what she had carried.

"We all have regrets," she said softly. "I cannot judge a man's future solely by his past. I saw the light in Daniel that he never wanted to acknowledge. He turned his life around, he helped people, Dahlia. He brought criminals to justice. He gave families solace. He was an excellent husband, and in his own way . . . a loving father."

I clenched my jaw, my hands curling into fists in my lap.

"But the bloodlust," she continued. "That never truly left him. He described it as acid in his veins. We tried everything—herbs, tonics—but nothing worked."

"So, what did you do?"

She hesitated. "We went to a healer—an acquaintance of your grandmother, Tatiana was her name. She specialized in reversals. Lifted curses and hexes." Her lips pressed together, weighing her next words carefully. "But there was a cost."

My stomach turned. "What cost?" I breathed out.

But I already knew. I had learned to read my mother's face long before I had learned to read books. And right now, she was holding back something devastating.

"It was you, wasn't it?" My voice was barely above a whisper. "Your health."

She broke my gaze and looked back at the window.

"The reversal helped him," she admitted. "It stabilized him. He could be a father to you."

"At *your* expense. At the cost of *you* being a mother to *me*." My breath came sharp and uneven.

"We didn't know the full effects," she said quickly. "It was a blood exchange. I gave him my clean, unencumbered blood, but I had to take his in return, to help him carry the burden. My deterioration came slowly."

A slow, burning heat coiled in my chest.

"He made you sick," I spat, my voice shaking.

"I chose to help him," she corrected, tucking herself back into the chair, her frame suddenly impossibly small. "As we all make our choices in the end."

A sharp, hot streak of anger tore through me.

I hated them.

Hamra. Renate. Daniel.

I hated them all.

The heat of it tightened in my stomach, searing up my spine, urging me to run, to tear myself from this room, from the weight of my father's sins. I stood abruptly. I had come here for answers, and now that I had them, I needed to act.

"Please." My mother's voice cracked. "Don't leave me, too."

Something inside me fractured. I looked at her, really looked at Estelle: her frail body barely indenting the cushion of the chair she sat on, the hollowness of her cheeks cast by worry, the bright eyes still shining with life. She was the least guilty of them. She didn't deserve to suffer. For the sake of my mother, I steadied my breath. For so long, I had believed I bore the weight of her illness, of this bookshop. But I hadn't carried my mother's burden, I had carried my *father's*.

Who else would continue to suffer under his legacy if I didn't stop it? There were people at Foresyth I cared about. Sequoia, Aspen, Leone, Nina.

I couldn't let them carry my father's burden, too.

I turned to my mother, my voice steadier. "I will not leave you. I will stay with you tonight, but in the morning, I will keep my promises."

"In the spirit of intellectual rigor and communal discourse, any student holds the right to request an ad hoc Circle. Such gatherings, however, require the Meister's presence to be deemed legitimate, for the Meister alone embodies the authority and guidance necessary to preside over formal discourse. Any assembly convened in the Meister's sanctioned absence is considered an act of insubordination—not a mere gathering, but a mutiny against the institution's principles."

– *Foresyth Student Handbook*, 1920 edition

Chapter 32: Circle, Minus One

I returned to Foresyth the following Monday before the Meister could note my absence. I called a Circle—minus one. Technically, any student could call a Circle anytime, but I doubted anyone except Leone and I had read the Foresyth Handbook.

"What the hell, Dahlia? I was in the middle of something," Nina muttered, entering the sitting room and wiping something green and foul from her hands. I didn't doubt she'd been busy, but this was the only hour the Meister was guaranteed to be out with a client, according to his schedule book—information I'd uncovered after figuring out the lock on his office door.

"If Dahlia called a Circle, it must mean it's important," Sequoia chimed.

Aspen narrowed his eyes, though his voice softened. "What's going on, Dahl?" I didn't like the familiarity of his tone or the use of my nickname, but it softened me despite myself.

"I called you here because you deserve the truth—a truth that's been kept from you. We're not doing sub-*fucking*-rosa anymore," I began. I'd thought speaking plainly would come easily, but the words stuck, my anger getting the best of me. My father had taught me that trusting others with secrets was a weakness, a risk I could ill afford. But I wouldn't let his fears guide me any longer.

I let anger fuel the truth I was about to reveal. Trust might be dangerous, but it was necessary. And my pursuit of truth—unlike his—was going to set us free from Foresyth's magick.

"The Conservatory is killing its students. You've been promised power that will never be yours. We're all sacrifices for a bloodthirsty magickian who's using you," I said, looking around. Sequoia's face went blank, Nina looked annoyed, Aspen's expression twisted with concern, and Leone remained unreadable. "You're each an elemental component—water, fire, earth, and air. You're the intended sacrifices."

"So, you know," Sequoia replied, her gaze flicking to Aspen before meeting mine. "But, Dahlia, it's not like that. We participate willingly. The power is ours to share. And we understand the risks," she said, her voice calm.

"No, you don't understand. The Meister has lied to you. The Book doesn't promise power to everyone involved—just to the one offering the sacrifices to the demiurge, not Sophia. She isn't the one you have all been praying to."

"You must have misread," Leone interrupted. "I've studied the passages carefully. The elemental ceremony is supposed to grant 'spiritual transcendence and the Universal Truths of the seventy-eight cards of Skorn to each element.'"

I expected their skepticism; it was what I wanted. I wanted them to question the Meister as much as they questioned me.

"And when did you last read the text? What year?" I asked.

"My first semester," Leone replied.

My pulse leapt. "That was over two years ago. But the real *Book of Skorn*—the unabridged version—hasn't been here more than a semester. You must have sensed a difference in how the book *feels*." I'd learned from the Meister himself there were multiple versions of the Book.

"What are you saying, Dahlia?" Aspen pressed.

There was no turning back now. I glanced around, considering each one of them.

Did I trust them?

Sequoia—water. She embodied fluidity and intuition, qualities I'd once resented in myself. But she'd shown me how to trust my instincts, revealing parts of myself I'd kept locked away.

Nina—earth. Grounded and resilient, she had been the first to befriend me at Foresyth. Despite her losses, she wore her individuality like armor.

Leone—air. Truth-bound and meticulous, he sliced through facades with a curiosity I deeply echoed. He craved new territory, new truths, just as I did.

And Aspen—fire. He ignited something in me, a warmth and passion I hadn't acknowledged. I'd pushed him away not out of fear of him, but of myself. He saw me, stripped of pretense, and kept fanning my inner flames.

Ignoring the truth would have been easier, but I couldn't ignore what was in front of me. These were my friends, the ones I had to protect—those whom Julian and my father had failed to save.

After a pause, I met their eyes. "I have proof," I said. I pulled the letters from my bag, their weight heavier than before. My fingers hesitated over the edges, smoothed by time, stained with the ugly truth. I handed them to Leone first. If anyone could recognize inconsistencies, it would be him. "Julian was my brother—half-brother, technically. He discovered the truth about the Book and the Meister's intentions just before he died. He didn't have much time, but he left me these letters and our father's belongings."

One by one, they passed the letters around, their eyes moving over Julian's words. A silence thickened in the room, not of disbelief—but of realization. Then fear.

"The Book you read years ago, Leone, must have been fabricated to justify the ceremony. The Meister must have rewritten parts of it to support his theories. The true ceremony requires *five elements*: the four, plus the Bonder—me," I continued. "But Julian sabotaged the ritual by taking poison before the ceremony began, so the Meister couldn't go through with it. He must have signaled this to the Meister, sabotaged the prepared potion, then hung himself, leaving clues for me to follow. Without Julian, all of you would've died that night."

A long silence settled over the room.

"You're the Bonder—the one who's brought us together," Aspen said at last, reaching into his pocket to pull out a folded paper. "Julian left me a note, too." He said this mostly to the others, echoing our previous conversation. "I didn't realize why it had to be you, but now I understand it was because of your blood."

Sequoia looked at Aspen, hurt evident in her eyes. "You never told me."

"He asked me not to," Aspen replied, as if that was enough of a response. But I knew deep down that he didn't tell her because he meant to protect her.

"If Dahlia had left me a note, you would've known," Sequoia murmured, arms crossed.

Nina, who had been reading the letters, looked up, her voice flat. "We all would've died that night."

"Yes," I said quietly.

"Julian saved us, but he didn't trust us enough to tell us the full truth. To make our own decision," Aspen remarked. "So why do you trust us now?"

I hesitated but decided to let go of all logic, all reason, relying instead on what I now acknowledged as *instinct.* It was what made me a great Tarot reader, and what I believed would make me a good detective now.

"It's just a feeling," I said. "You're my friends. I care about you." I thought back to my framework on the greatest motivators of the human spirit: knowledge, power, or sex. But there was one that I had missed: love. It was the love of my newfound friends that were guiding my decisions now, despite how reckless or foolish they seemed.

"If the Meister intended to sacrifice us, he'll try again," Leone said, his voice edged with anger. He didn't like being lied to.

And neither did I.

"That's why I have a plan. But I need all of you. If you want to leave before the Symposium, I'll understand. But if you want to stay to incriminate the Meister, we have the chance to end this cycle tonight."

"I'm in," Aspen said. "I won't let Julian's sacrifice be wasted."

Sequoia's brow furrowed. "If we stop the Meister, who'll lead the school?"

"The Council would likely appoint someone new through a vote," Leone answered. "The House won't vanish—it seems like it's been resisting the magick with growth and life, even as it decays from the blood rituals."

The Council had turned a blind eye for decades, allowing the Meister's unchecked power to fester like rot. He hadn't just inherited his position—he had cultivated it, embedding himself within Foresyth's foundations, protected by politics and tradition. Even Julian, despite his mother's position as an Advisor, hadn't realized how tainted Foresyth had become until the very end.

Destroying the ceremony wouldn't be enough. If we wanted to end this cycle for good, we had to strike at the source—*The Book of Skorn* itself.

"We have to destroy the Book," I said, "so no one on the Council can use it."

"And neither can we," Nina noted. "We'll remain powerless." Nina's words threatened to stifle the air in the room as I noticed the others' shoulders drop. Of course, they all cared about the power. That's what'd driven them to go along with the Meister, with the sacrifices, for this long.

"You don't need it," I said, my voice growing with conviction. "Nina, you can transform corpses into art, recall the histories of hundreds of mythical creatures. Sequoia, you can light up the whole room from your presence alone and bring people to tears with your voice. Leone is the most erudite person I've ever met, and Aspen's sculptures belong in a museum. Each of you has incredible power already. You don't need the Meister's false promises."

Leone's face hardened, his voice resolute. "I don't take kindly to liars, especially ones who deceive so arrogantly."

Nina hesitated but then nodded. "No one sacrifices me without my knowing."

Relief washed over me, and I couldn't help but smile. For the first time, I had allies.

"What's the plan?" Nina asked.

"We'll go through with the ceremony. But this time, no one dies."

Chapter 33: Spring Symposium

Admittedly, the Blackburne line didn't have the best track record for survival. Evolutionarily speaking, we were losing—and badly. But I still had my mother's blood, and I clung to the hope that it might be enough to tip the scales in my favor. I pieced together the cold facts, stitching them together with something far older and wilder than logic. The magick I no longer doubted—my own intuition.

Magick was ceremonial. And so too should be the destruction of the Book, in the eyes of the person who gave its power life. It was through this ceremonial burning that we could put to rest what my father started all those years ago. He would be free to move on, and so would I.

The plan was simple. We would arrange ourselves as the Meister has orchestrated many times before. Nina would be assigned potion maker—she'd make the vial concoction and include the poisonous nightshade such as the Meister would see it.

For this, I gave everyone a generous wad of cotton to place in their cheeks to soak up the liquid (this time not sourced from the dining room furniture). It wouldn't be enough to completely eliminate the side effects, but the dosage would be diluted such that we wouldn't die. And that was the goal.

When the Meister himself was disarmed, that would be the time to strike. Aspen would be the one to fend off the Meister as Leone and I would handle getting a hold of the Book, and Nina and Sequoia would kindle the fire so that we could burn it then and there.

Ashes to ashes, dust to dust.

But the plan was contingent on one crucial detail: everyone's trustworthiness. If even one person decided to sabotage the plan, it could risk everything. I wasn't just betting on myself anymore. I was betting on my *friends*. And whether or not I trusted them.

I was in my room, going over the plan and preparing to take my work down to the Symposium. The House was buzzing with activity in preparations for opening it to the Council and the Advisors. This was the time all the students had been waiting for to dazzle and impress everyone. The Council members would each come around to our stations and evaluate our work, deciding if it was worthy enough to grant us another year at Foresyth. I had unfortunately been too preoccupied the last few weeks to make an impressive presentation, but I had scraped together something passable. After tonight, I could walk away from Foresyth, content that my role had been fulfilled.

But would *I* be fulfilled?

The thought was interrupted by knocking at my door. Aspen walked in with a sheepish grin and a flower in his hands. I recognized it instantly. It was a gorgeous bright blue Dahlia, fresh-picked.

"These are harder to find than you know, despite the sea of florals downstairs," he said admiring the petals. "They require a lot of sunlight—not something this place is known for." He stepped closer to where I was standing. "I just came to wish you good luck tonight. With everything," he said with one hand threaded through his hair and the other extended across to me. He was nervous. But about which part? The ceremony, or *us*?

But there was no us. There was only *them*, the Trees. I was a flower at the base of their trunk, never to reach their heights. Hadn't he implied as much the first time I met them?

"Thank you," I said, taking the stem.

"Are you sure about this?" he asked, his eyes scanning the bed where I had laid out my supplies.

"I'm sure." But I wasn't.

He smiled, but there was sadness in his eyes. "Julian was a master puzzle maker. He blew us all out of the water at the last Symposium with his disappearing act. Little did we know it wasn't the only trick up his sleeve."

I returned his gaze but didn't say anything. I thought of him and Julian, whether they got along, or if they fought in front of everyone else like we had. Were they like friends, brothers, or something more?

"Julian . . . he was more than just a friend to you," I said. I studied his reaction carefully, because of course I did. It was my natural instinct. His brows twitched only for a second, but it was enough for me to know I was getting closer to something I probably shouldn't.

"That's why you and Sequoia were fighting at my first Circle. I initially thought it was because Sequoia was involved with him. But . . . you were too." He looked down and I could sense the uneasiness in him—shame, perhaps. "But it was unbalanced. Perhaps he had a fondness for you that outweighed his for Sequoia."

Aspen started laughing. "That trick you do of reading people is impressive. And almost correct. But you know you could just ask, us being friends and all that," he cooed with a wink.

"Julian and I were close. But we had very different views of the school—of magick. Our fights were academic in nature. He was always too easy on Sequoia—too friendly. He coddled her, but I didn't. I never stopped believing she was more capable than people believed her to be. If we could have put aside our academic differences . . ." He smoothed out his hair with his fingertips and continued. "Perhaps in another world we would have all been something more." And for a second, I forgot he was talking about Julian.

"Is that why you were drawn to me? Because I'm like him?" I don't know why I said it, but I wanted to know if all of this had just been because of who Julian was, not who I was. I studied Aspen's face, searching for the truth between the spaces of his words. If Julian had left such a mark on him, if he had been the gravitational center keeping them all together . . . then where did that leave me?

I was still angry at Julian for giving up on himself like he had. He made me think of the Eight of Swords, imprisoned by a cage of his own doing. His own hubris had driven him to leave a puzzle in the wake of his death instead of fighting the Meister with the truth.

"You . . ." He paused. "You are the opposite of him—the puzzle solver to his maker. Julian was very secretive. He never let anyone get close to him. He told tall tales and dazzled everyone with stories, similar to you, but different. *You* were different. I noticed it the first time you connected with Nina, the sincerity of your shared interests, your shared admiration. Julian was a wall, but you've been more of a drawbridge, tethering on the verge of opening."

"Very poetic." I scrunched up my nose to feign my amusement. "And now I've let you all in," I said.

"And now you've let us all in," he echoed. When my eyes met his I was struck by the fierceness of them, the little specks of gold creating a dance of whorls and spirals in the light. They seemed to harden, the edges becoming sharper in focus. I hadn't allowed myself to trust him, not fully, until now. This was where he proved himself or destroyed me.

"Let's hope it's not a mistake," I said.

*

I could feel the vibration of the House under the footsteps of so many guests, but it was barely audible over the chatter of conversation. The posters and displays were set up in the sitting room where all the other furniture had been cleared, and the dining room table was now covered with a generous banquet—fruits and cakes of all sorts, sprinkled across the table like berry patches. The theme of this year's Symposium was "Eternal Spring," and a sea of violently blooming flowers covered the floors and tables from the entrance to the back hallway. The smell was intoxicatingly sweet.

I wore the only dress I owned and tucked the dahlia into my hair. The flower's contrast with my pale skin made me think that I was almost beautiful, like Sequoia. The dress was a sleek black that cut across my shoulders and cinched at my waist. On top of it, I wore a leather harness that tied into my utility belt where all of my items could be accessed in short notice. I hitched my black socks up high and slid into my Oxfords. I did not look entirely like myself, but perhaps a more feminine version of the menswear-donning self I had been a few months ago.

But maybe that was a good thing.

I stood by my haphazardly strung together poster entitled "Parlor game turned prophecy: the theatre of Tarot." I had replicated the images of several of my favorite cards and drawn arrows between ones where I connected concepts and themes. On the left panel of my trifold, I wrote out my pre-reading rituals, including the various cleanses and groundings I'd perform.

On the right side, I wrote my philosophy of reading, and how it was a collaborative, give and take, rather than a recitation. I didn't mention Sophia or the demiurge. I held a deck of cards, my old Tarot deck from the shop, to demonstrate my methodology and give on the spot one-card readings.

My real theatrics were being saved for later that night.

"It seems like Foresyth hasn't changed your methodology much." The Meister smirked, scanning my presentation board at my station. Foresyth has changed a lot of my thinking but not about reading cards.

"Why fix something that isn't broken? Pick a card," I said, outstretching my hand.

"Indeed," he said with a slanted eye and inched his fingers to my fanned deck I held. "Although, I do wish some of your work on the runes had made it into here." His tone implied I was holding out on what I had learned, and it was true. Did he suspect I connected the runes to human sacrifice, and back to his own horrid practices?

"I'm not ready to present those ideas to the Council. But when I am, they'll be the first to know," I said.

He feathered the cards with one finger before landing on a card. He pulled it out and gave it to me, not flipping it over. "And, uh, what about our other little side project?"

I turned over the card and stared at the Five of Swords. *Deception.* My stomach clenched. Of all the cards, it had to be this one. A duel with no victors. A warning, or a taunt from the universe?

My hands grew cold. He had a lot of gall bringing up Julian and his ploy to keep me here. I smiled, despite feeling like my teeth were going to fall out from clenching so hard.

"Julian died by his own hand," I said truthfully, "I haven't found anything that would indicate anything other than a suicide," I said.

"Ah, well that's good news then. I must have been wrong about the other students here."

"I was too," I said and meant it.

"I do hope you intend to stay, Dahlia, without the case to keep you here. You've made such a fine addition here," he said, smiling wryly. I almost scoffed. Of course he didn't intend for me to stay—he intended for me to die as his Bonder.

"I feel the same," I said, mimicking the sickly sweetness of the flowers around us.

He gave me a polite nod and then exited my station. I caught Aspen's eye across the room, next to the fireplace. But what stole my breath were the sculptures surrounding him. He was like Poseidon, in a sea of his own beauty. Vases erupted around him, various sizes and heights, all in that deep Prussian blue, the same as I had seen in his workshop. He smiled, catching my stare.

"God, I could gag from that smell. Did they really have to bring in that many flowers?" Nina said next to me.

Her station was right next to mine. She was also dressed in black, but with the addition of a large fur shrug which seemed to almost swallow her up. Next to her she had produced a collection of taxidermy entitled "Earth-bound," showing all types of birds with their wings torn off and replaced with stones and twigs and moss. She made a model of the Tramping Ground and lined up her creations around the miniature mound.

I almost asked her what it all meant but then thought better of it. Some art was better experienced than explained.

Sequoia's display was hidden behind the central tree in the room, but I could hear her song drifting across the room, a beautiful Gaelic rhythm. Leone's installation was next to hers and I peeked my head around to catch the very edge of it. Exquisitely marked maps adorned his poster board, gilded edges in gold and bronze. It was a beautifully wrought depiction of Dante's nine circles of hell.

All these art pieces, endless hours of toil, all wrought in the name of a vain God, the demiurge, and the opportunity to access Sophia's power. I hoped the students could see how powerful they already were without her. I was about to reply to Nina when my thoughts were interrupted.

"May I?" the Al-Ahmar appeared next to my station, her deep-crimson cloak obscuring the small station I inhabited from the rest of the room.

I looked up to meet her gaze and my pulse started to thrum in my ears. Her eyes looked so familiar, I could almost place them. That deep, rich brown that looked like upturned soil. Her red hood billowed behind her, obscuring the top of her head, but when she turned to my display, I caught sight of her reddish-black curls. The truth rippled through me like a stone skidding across a pond.

"You're Julian's mother," I said. My hand instinctively went to my belt and reached for the hilt of my knife.

Her glance skittered back to mine, her eyes opening wide. "How did you . . ." she said, but it was too late. I was holding the knife to her abdomen. Her layers of cloaks concealed the fact well, so nothing looked out of place to the others around us. I inched closer to whisper in her ear.

"You destroyed my father . . . you killed all of those people." I knew it was rash, what I was doing. It could very well destroy the plans I had for tonight, for ending the elemental ceremony. But my anger was raging. She was the one who robbed me of my father. He might have been around me physically, unlike he had been for Julian, but he had been haunted because of *her.*

"You don't want to do that," she said in a low voice, exuding too much calm for someone in her position. I jabbed the knife closer to her, feeling the rip in her cloak widen.

"Why not?" I said through gritted teeth.

"I know you're hurting—both of you were, and it was because of me. For that, I will be eternally sorry." Her eyes softened, and for a moment I saw Julian staring back at me, not the Al-Ahmar. "I loved your father more than anything, but the magick consumed me, burned away at me. Your father was stronger than I was to resist it."

"Your power, your status on the Council, it's all because of that disgusting Book—and Khorvyn's lies. You've been feeding them to the students, getting them to make an ultimate sacrifice just so you could hold on to it."

Her face contorted at my words, and a look of confusion took over her features. "I have long said my goodbyes to blood magick. It's true I practiced it for a few years after your father left, but without the Book, the magick dwindled. The House was collapsing on itself with all the unstable magick, we were forced to abandon it or be buried with it."

Her words were like cold flecks of water against my raging fire, only momentarily reducing the height of my flames. "You killed Elizabeth, and all the others."

"We only targeted those who were close to dying—the sick or on death row. We *never* planned on students dying. I never went through with the elemental ceremony." She lowered her voice. "I have paid dearly for my crimes." Her eyes began to glisten. "I tried to hide our research. I buried it all those years ago when we banned the practice of blood magick at Foresyth."

My grip on the dagger almost slipped at her words. "Banned?" The Council forbade blood magick, and yet it had still been practiced for so many years?

She looked away, down to the knife I still held at her. "It was too dangerous. No matter what it promised on the other side, it would only lead to more death."

"You don't know what's going on at Foresyth, do you?" My mind was so warped with all the layers of secrets and lies, it was hard to discern what was true and what was false. But I tried regardless. "The Meister, he's been practicing the elemental ceremony every year. Dozens of students have died or disappeared because of it. He's had Council members cover it up, citing false grounds for 'dismissal' for students who are never heard from again."

Her eyes closed and her expression turned solemn. "I knew students were leaving Foresyth at a higher attrition rate . . . but I didn't think he would be so soulless. When Julian died, I forced the Council to require him to hire a detective, but I had no idea it would be you—Daniel's daughter." She grabbed the hand that was holding the knife and squeezed it. "Dahlia, I'm so sorry. For all of this."

"That's not it." I could have almost laughed at the tragedy of it all. "The Book, he has it at Foresyth. It was stolen from my father, by Julian. That's why both of them died. I thought my father had killed himself, but I think he died at the Meister's hand, somehow. And Julian . . . he sacrificed himself before the Meister could complete the ceremony with all five elements."

The Al-Ahmar had seemed to be a thing of majestic power that night in the Council room when I had come to request the Skorn deck. When she had read my cards, sealing my Fate at Foresyth as an Initiate. But now, standing in front of me, I saw her as the woman my father fell in love with—as Julian's mother. The hard lines in her face, her stoic and knowing eyes, the lips that curved into a bow. The lips my father had kissed. Did I owe this woman mercy by proxy of my father?

"My son," she said, sadness overtaking her. She raised a hand to her mouth to stifle her cry. But in the next moment, she flicked off the tears and her expression became stone-like. "He'll die for this."

"Why didn't he tell you?" I asked.

Her brows knitted, pain blinking across her face. "Julian and I were estranged for much of his adulthood. Undoubtedly, that's why he didn't tell me about the Book or what has been happening at the school."

I finally lowered the knife. I might not trust her, but the Meister had killed her son. I could trust her motives were not in opposition of mine. I could trust her grief.

"I have a plan. For tonight," I said, conceding my last secret. If secrets were currency like Aspen has said, then I was laying out all of mine on a bet. I'd either find myself cashing in tonight or losing it all.

But then again, truth had always been my currency of choice.

She smiled with her eyes, even though her lips remained a straight line. "As the daughter of Detective Blackburne, I would have expected nothing less. But with this many Council members in attendance, we have the capacity to arrest him and take him to tribunal court based on your statement."

My mind was racing. "We don't have proof. I have a few letters, but those could be denied in a setting like that. Especially if he holds favoritism on the Council. We need to catch him at his own game—tonight. I have a device here," I said, pulling out a switchbox I had been working on for the past few weeks. "It's like a music box but it transmits sound in real time, including speech. Take it to the Council tonight, and when they hear him confess to his crimes, you can initiate the arrest."

"You did have a plan," she said.

"I wasn't planning on you being the one I gave this to," I said, giving her the switchbox. "But it's not you I trust, it's Julian. I trust you'll do what's right for him."

She grabbed the box from me and tucked it into her cloak. She pulled something out with her other hand. "I ought to give you this." She handed me what looked like a black pebble. "Daniel gave me this—years after you were born. He said if I ever meet you, that I ought to give you this. I've carried it with me ever since. Your father loved you very much."

I examined the stone in my hand, looking at it from all angles. My father had left me a clue, all those years ago? What did this common pebble even mean?

She motioned to take her leave, but I held her arm. "Wait, I don't know what this means."

"I have to go. We've been seen together long enough. I'll be listening with the full Council tonight. Good luck."

And with a flash of her red cape, she was gone, and I was left with the common rock in my hand, which I turned every which way. I stared hard at it for minutes, trying to sift through my library of memories. It looked familiar, but then again, it was a common pebble—from my father. Like something I'd find in his laboratory.

And that's when the memory fluttered to life. This was the same pebble that had disappeared in his jar of soil when I was a kid. It was the magic trick I had never figured out. I looked at it closely again and realized that there was something carved into it. But it was so small, so miniscule, I had to pull out my magnifying glass to make it out.

It was an *H* and then a dash, as if the start to a chemical formula. The stone wasn't an ordinary pebble—it was packed carbonate. And then, in that singular moment, I figured out the trick.

"Nina," I called, "if anyone comes around to my station, tell them I've gone to the bathroom. Say that I've gotten sick."

"Wait, what? You're sick?"

"Just cover for me," I said, cutting her a glance. She nodded and I shot out of the room, through the crowd of magickal Advisors and Council members, and headed straight to the lab.

Chapter 34: Things Fall Apart

The Symposium had dwindled into dusk with murmurs of conversation quieting. The Council members would take a day to evaluate our work, then submit their assessments to the Meister. Though he had no intention of sharing them with us, I thought bitterly, as the elemental ceremony was expected to be our final assignment.

A general sense of nervousness hung over dinner, though each of us showed it differently. Aspen was on his second glass of wine, Nina meticulously arranged her food, and Leone, uncharacteristically, didn't have a book with him. Conversation had naturally tapered off after the day's presentations, but I suspected the real reason for the quiet was the looming ceremony. I couldn't help but imagine Julian sitting here a year ago, knowing it would be his last meal. The thought alone made my stomach churn.

Doubt clouded my mind with a litany of things that could go wrong. Maybe I should have heeded the Al-Ahmar's suggestion and let her arrest the Meister, but I knew there wasn't enough evidence to convict him. My father had worked on the case for years to no avail, with no concrete evidence to overpower the Meister's political sway on the Council. We also needed to destroy the book and ensure that the practice couldn't trade hands like it had before. It was the only way.

"Is everyone . . . ready?" I asked, clearing my throat after managing only a couple of bites of dinner. I didn't have much appetite and found myself mimicking Nina's habit of rearranging food on her plate. I looked around the table to see reluctant nods and furrowed brows. The weight of putting them all in danger settled heavily on me. I tried to project confidence, but I knew I was falling short.

"Trust your instincts, Dahlia, they've gotten us this far," Sequoia said brightly, and I felt a bit lighter.

Us.

I might have felt weak then, but at least I was no longer alone.

*

We huddled back into the sitting room where Richard had rearranged the furniture. The room seemed eerily quiet after the activity of just a few hours earlier. Aspen and Sequoia took their usual spot on the loveseat, Leone by the fire, while Nina and I shared the chaise as usual. It was as if it were any normal night of Circle. But when the Meister entered, the atmosphere shifted; the air felt charged, almost electric. Even the hairs on my arms stood up at his presence.

"What a successful day." He sighed happily, cradling a parcel in his chest. His pupils were dilated, the same look of ravenous hunger I'd seen the night he first shared the Book with me, and the night he came to my bookshop. But he maintained a professional reserve over it, presenting himself as our mentor, as if ready to guide us through an innocuous lecture.

"The Council was very impressed by your presentations. I look forward to reviewing your evaluations tomorrow," he said, a smile creeping across his face. "Shall we do a quick reflection on the day before we start tonight's main event?"

We exchanged glances around the room, none of us eager to begin. My gaze remained fixed on the fabric bundle across the Meister's chest, containing the source of his evil. I dropped my eyes and forced myself to focus on the conversation instead.

We each took turns around the Circle, sharing our discussions with the Council members and their feedback on our work. After everyone had spoken, the Meister turned to me.

"And you, Ms. Blackburne? Anything of note?" he asked.

I licked my dry lips before answering. The only conversation worth recalling was with the Al-Ahmar, but I needed a cover story for why we'd spoken so long.

"The Al-Ahmar found my analysis intriguing. She suggested incorporating other types of deck and drawing comparisons," I said, offering up my own idea as conversational fodder to distract him.

"It looked like you were having a very interesting conversation. I hope you take her suggestion," he remarked. I clenched my jaw to keep from responding, then reached into my pocket and coated my lips with a thick layer of petroleum jelly.

"I just want to take this moment of reflection to share how very proud I am of you all. You've dedicated yourselves to this craft, and it shows. You're bringing honor—and life itself—back to the House." He paused, scanning the room. "Tonight, we have the ultimate privilege of honoring our Shattered Mother through the elemental ceremony.

"It's dangerous, I won't deny that—there's no way to conduct soul flight without risking not coming back. But it's our sacred duty to offer our mortal flesh to the Mother. If she deems us worthy, we may be blessed by her power, and we can restore the true glory of the House. Ms. Blackburne," he said, turning to me, "this will be your first time participating in the ceremony as our newest Initiate."

And my last.

"I'm honored to be a part of it," I said, with a sweetness matching the flower-strung halls.

"You know that this ceremony has been largely symbolic in the past, without yielding results. But I believe tonight, we shall all feast on the fruit of our collective efforts."

The Meister set the parcel on the table in front of him, which had been arranged as an altar with objects representing the four elements.

The gleam of the athame caught my eye, and the memory of Aspen holding it to my throat surged back. I met his gaze, and he offered me a slight bow acknowledging the memory.

I hoped my calculations about everyone were right. Aspen had told me all the details of the ceremony, but performing it was an entirely different experience. What had once been parlor tricks in my bookstore would now be a matter of life and death.

"Everyone in the Circle has their role to play," the Meister began, unwrapping layers of fabric to reveal the artifact within. The black box gleamed in the pale firelight, casting shades of orange and red across the room. "Nina, gather the ingredients. Sequoia, start the brew."

"Yes, Meister," they said, both moving to the altar to gather herbs into a small cauldron. Nina stoked the fire, ensuring it was hot enough to boil the mixture.

"Leone, you'll handle the reading," the Meister instructed. Leone moved to the altar, his face etched with lines of betrayal even in the dim light.

Sequoia made a show of each ingredient she added to the brew, pausing when she reached the nightshade. She looked up at the Meister, displaying the poisonous berries in her hand.

"Five berries, one for each of you," he commanded. She nodded, dropping them into the cauldron one by one, murmuring a prayer over each. When she withdrew her hand after the fifth berry, a prick of blood marred her finger from a stray thorn.

Aspen knelt beside her, taking her hand and placing her bleeding finger in his mouth, absorbing the blood and a lick of the poison. My heart dropped as I watched them, the depth of their connection evident by the gesture. It wasn't enough to dull his senses, but it could have been enough for Sequoia to feel its effects.

Two Trees entwined and ready to share everything, even poison.

I realized then that I would never be part of their world. A strange calm settled over me at the realization—I cared for them, yes, but I was not bound to them. I was untethered. And that was its own form of power.

I tore my eyes away from them and back to the altar. Once the potion was prepared, the ceremony proceeded exactly as described in *The Book of Skorn.* Nina handed each of us a ceremonial glass. I held it in my hands, feeling its chill leech the warmth from my skin.

"I'll explain the procedure, as our newest Initiate has yet to participate in the ceremony," the Meister said. "As you know, the ceremony's purpose is to transcend our material form and align with our Shattered Mother. In this state, we can tap into the Universal Truths as told by the cards of Skorn. Those who comprehend these Truths gain enlightenment and powers akin to the Mother herself, enabling manipulation of the physical world, which is only an illusion. This is why we practice art at the Conservatory—to use the material world as a pathway to the metaphysical."

Everyone arranged their cards in circles, starting with the Major Arcana, then the minor suits. I did the same.

"How will we know we've achieved it?" I asked, glancing up from the cards. "Soul flight, I mean."

The Meister's closed-mouth smile was chilling. He didn't answer.

Nina glanced back at me, her eyes red and unreadable, as if on the verge of tears. Or had she already been crying? I gripped my cup harder, licking my lips.

The fire crackled in the background, Aspen tending the flames. I spared him another glance, but his gaze was lost in the fire.

The Meister turned to the box, whispering a few words as he unlocked it. The air grew heavy as he opened the case, and a low vibration hummed in my ears. I wondered if everyone else could hear it. He removed the Book and handed it to Leone, whose face transformed from stoic to a mixture of terror and awe. His throat bobbed as his fingers tightened around the Book, his fingers shaking.

This wasn't good. I had felt the Book's power when I held it, but it hadn't overtaken me the way it was seizing Leone. Like it had overtaken my father. The Book fed on our emotions, and Leone was overcome with them.

I watched, transfixed, as Leone opened the Book.

"Page four hundred and thirty-two," the Meister ordered.

But Leone wasn't listening. He flipped through the pages as though any other book in the library.

"Page four hundred and thirty-two, boy. I won't say it again," the Meister thundered.

Leone glared at him. *Oh, God. Don't give us away.*

I silently pleaded for him to obey. The Meister held his breath as they locked eyes, but mercifully, Leone relented and turned to the page. I stifled my sigh and glanced at Sequoia, who was moving to serve the ceremonial tea to each of us, except the Meister, who would remain grounded, his soul intact.

With careful hands, Sequoia poured the thick, velvety liquid into my ceramic mug. The steam curled toward me like a dark invitation, its scent floral yet earthy. I took a deep breath and allowed myself to sink into the cushions around the altar. I reached into my pocket to check the switchbox was still there, relieved to feel its weight.

Sequoia began the chant in a harsh, foreign tongue. I struggled to enunciate the strange words with the cotton stuffed in my mouth, but I repeated them as the others did, shifting the cotton against my gums to keep it dry.

"And drink," the Meister commanded, his green eyes gleaming with anticipation. A shiver ran down my arms, and I adjusted my position to hide it. Around the Circle, everyone raised their cups to their mouths, their waxy lips glistening. I followed suit, carefully holding the cotton wad on my tongue to absorb the liquid. Even in that brief contact, warmth flooded my body. I steadied myself, watching as everyone else pretended to gulp as I had instructed.

The buzzing in my ears grew louder, but my pulse thundered when Aspen took up the athame. He angled it toward his palm and spoke in a low voice. "Shattered Mother of my Blood, Primordial Womb, Creator of Souls, I offer my flesh, my blood, my fire." He pierced his palm, letting blood pool.

The others followed with their own elemental invocations. When the athame reached me, I looked to the Meister.

I was the Bonder, not an element. But I wouldn't reveal what I knew.

"Repeat all of them," he said.

I pressed the tip of the athame into the palm of my hand until it broke the skin. I winced, but did as instructed and recited, "Shattered Mother of my Blood, Primordial Womb, Creator of Souls, I offer my flesh, my blood, my fire, my water, my air, and my earth."

We joined hands in the Circle, mingling our blood. Nina's and Sequoia's palms pressed into mine, our blood seeping between our fingers. This was the part I'd planned for. We needed a shared signal, so I began counting to ten. When we reached it, we'd move to secure the Meister and the Book.

One . . . two . . . three . . .

My eyes grew heavier. The cotton in my mouth was full of liquid, spilling onto my tongue.

Four . . . five . . . six . . .

I held the liquid, fighting the urge to swallow. Despite my efforts, I felt some of its heat course down my throat. Just a few more seconds, and I'd spit it out, right into the Meister's face. The buzzing building into a deafening crescendo.

Seven . . . eight . . . nine . . .

I couldn't wait any longer. I tried to signal—squeezing Nina and Sequoia's hands—but my body felt sluggish, like it was trapped in molasses. I opened my mouth to shout, but no sound emerged.

Ten.

And that's when I fell.

It was as if the earth had split beneath me, a chasm swallowing me whole. My body pitched forward, gravity itself twisting into something malevolent, dragging me down into an abyss. The circle of cards scattered around me, spiraling in my descent like leaves torn from the great oak. I clawed at the sensation, trying to tether myself to reality, but my limbs were useless. My eyes rolled back, the world blurring into darkness.

This is it, I thought. This is how I die.

The certainty was strangely liberating. For a brief, fleeting moment, the fear loosened its grip, and I floated on a cloud of warmth. My pulse slowed. I felt myself unraveling, surrendering to the void.

"*No. Not yet.*" A voice cut through the blackness, sharp as a blade and impossibly soft at once. A woman's voice. I strained to turn toward it, but my body was unmoored, unresponsive. I was nothing but a thought, suspended in emptiness.

Then came the light. It began as a faint glimmer, like a distant star, but it grew, spreading and spinning until it became a cascade of brilliance, like shards of silver glass raining from above. The spiraling stars congealed into a shape—a form.

A woman.

She stepped out of the light as if emerging from a dream, her every movement fluid and deliberate, like time itself bent to her will.

Sophia? I wanted to say, but the thought dissipated, swallowed by her presence. I couldn't speak; my body refused to obey.

Her tendrils of hair shimmered like molten silver, cascading around her in waves. Her eyes—liquid moonlight—bore into me, unrelenting and ancient, carrying a sorrow I couldn't comprehend. She moved closer, and as she did, I saw the fine glint of her lashes, the faint shimmer of tears pooling at the edges of her eyes. Was she crying?

"You have to make amends," she said, her voice resonating everywhere and nowhere, a sound more felt than heard. The words wrapped around me, a lifeline in the void. I tried to respond, to ask her what she meant, but my lips wouldn't move. Yet she understood. I felt it—our thoughts entwined. Hers vast and deep as the night sky, mine a flickering ember.

"They have strayed," she continued, her expression darkening, and the warmth around her turned sharp. "They do not worship me. They worship a false God—the demiurge." Her features twisted into a grimace, and her rage erupted in silver streaks of light, radiating outward in jagged, chaotic waves. It was beautiful and terrifying.

"The worker I created to shape the material world," she spat, her voice trembling with fury, "he is the one who fed Khorvyn false lies and created *The Book of Skorn*. He is the one who demands blood. Not me."

The demiurge. The lion with the serpent's tail, the symbol on *The Book of Skorn*. The creature my father had become in my nightmares.

I nodded, though I barely understood, but somewhere deep inside, the answers had been buried within me all along, waiting to be unearthed.

Sophia wasn't the God they worshiped, it was the demiurge.

"The knowledge I offer," she said, her voice softening to something almost tender, "does not lie in books. It lies within *you*." She raised a hand, her fingers as delicate as threads of light, and pressed a single finger to my chest. The Universal Truths, represented by the cards, accessed through our subconscious.

A searing pulse radiated through me, igniting something dormant within. Heat bloomed in my core, spreading outward, filling every corner of my being. For the briefest moment, I felt whole—truly, unimaginably whole.

And then the light vanished.

I was falling again, the warmth replaced by the cold rush of reality slamming back into me. Darkness claimed me, but her words burned in my mind, bright as stars.

"Dahlia," my father's voice sang in my ear. "You haven't figured out the trick yet." He shook a jar of dirt in front of my face. "Think. Your mind is your greatest resource."

I was ten years old, back in my father's laboratory, sitting on his metal stool, heels digging into the spindle. "I don't know, Father," I said. It was me, but it wasn't—it was like I was both observing and living as the little girl. "I don't like this game."

"The primacy of fact should prevail over the caprices of feeling—*fact*, not feeling, Dahlia," he said. "What could make the stone disappear?" His face was angled toward me, close enough that I could almost reach out and touch him. My heart lurched with grief. I saw it in him then—the matte of his eyes, the depth of his sorrow—mirroring mine.

The trick of the disappearing rock. It hadn't been Sophia, after all. *No, it was . . .*

Suddenly, my body became lighter, and I started to float. I drifted out of the lab and reappeared in my bookshop. There I huddled over the front desk, working on the ledger. It had been a grim day with very few sales. My father stood across the store.

"We didn't make much today," I said, defeated.

He puffed his pipe in great clouds, pinching his beard with his forefingers. "They'll come. When word gets out, they'll come."

"What word?" I asked in frustration.

"That all the knowledge in the world is here," he said, pattering his fingers across the spines of endless books. Something stirred within me then, but I only recognized it now, as I hovered above, watching.

I had *disagreed* with him.

Some knowledge, I thought, couldn't be found in books.

I watched myself running out of ink on the ledger and opening the bottom drawer—the drawer no one had touched in years. Inside, I found the pen, and beneath it, a deck of Tarot cards waiting for me.

When I touched the deck, I transformed again, this time to a point above the room. It was my father's office. He entered, wearing a wet overcoat and hat, as if he'd just returned from a rainy day on a case. The falling cards surrounded him, but he brushed them off like raindrops. He approached a painting of *The Destruction of Pompei* and opened it on hidden hinges, revealing a lockbox. He entered the combination, and a loud click followed.

I knew what should have been behind that safe.

I watched his last moments through his eyes. He stood there, staring at the open, empty space. He realized Julian had taken it.

I screamed at him. I knew it was futile, but I tried anyway, anything to stop what he was about to do. When he reached into his desk for the revolver, my heart could have burst. The cards continued to fall around him, rising to his ankles.

He must have known.

He must have known Julian had stolen the Book.

Blood of my blood.

Which meant he thought he had corrupted his own son with *The Book of Skorn.*

"But what about me?" I wanted to shout. "I did everything to be just like you. Why didn't you leave me anything?" The anger caught in my throat, and I tried to swallow it. I was beside him now, my arms desperately reaching for him, only to pass through air.

I couldn't reach him.

My heart shattered when he looked at me—gun loaded and cocked against his temple.

"I pray, Dahlia, that you turn out to be nothing like me," he said, his fingers trembling.

At the sound of the gunshot, the world erupted into black. But not before I caught the glint of two green eyes, piercing through the shadows.

Chapter 35: Strength

I awoke to the sound of my own name.

"Dahlia!" someone was shouting, but the weight of sleep pinned me down, pressing on my bones and skin. Distantly, I thought how nice it would be to curl up on my side. But the tugging on my lips pulled me from my torpor.

"For Gods' sake, Dahlia, wake up!" It was a man's voice. The floor was shaking, or maybe it was just me. My lids lifted, and I saw Aspen's eyes, swirling gold within green, like a snake encircling moss. He was wiping my lips, looking upset. "Thank Gods. I almost thought your lipstick routine hadn't worked on you."

"She saved me," I muttered, but the words were tangled in my throat.

My mouth felt dry as I reached for it. The jelly of poison was gone, wiped clean. Where had the cotton gone? I turned to the side and realized I'd spat it out—or maybe someone had pulled it from my mouth. My senses returned like a fog clearing. Across the room, I saw the Meister restrained with Leone's tie, just as planned. Leone, however, was slumped in his chair, a swollen eye marking his struggle.

"He wouldn't hand over the Book," Aspen explained with a shrug, pointing to the open Book lying beside Leone's unconscious form. I almost smiled at the brute force of it.

"Sequoia's vomiting, and I can't find Nina anywhere." Aspen's eyes darted around. "You were right about her—she poisoned the cups."

"What do you all think you're doing?" the Meister snarled, his eyes glowing green, full of hatred. Recognition pierced me like an arrow. He had just been in my dream.

I rose, despite my shaking knees, frantically reaching for the Book. I needed to pull my words together, get him to confess for the switch-box recording.

"You were there," I spat but my words slurred. "You were there when my father . . ."

The Meister's eyes sparkled as he rose, the knot of the tie coming undone and falling by his hands. "You children—you thought you could possibly restrain me?" He raised his hand into the air, twisting his fingers into a claw.

Aspen crashed down to his knees beside me, pulling at the imaginary fingers around his neck.

"*The cards*—" he choked out, faltering. I dropped to catch him. His eyes were bulging, his bronzed skin turning a nauseating shade of red. Panic rose to a fever pitch as Aspen contorted in my arms.

My eyes cut to the Meister. One hand was still outstretched in the shape of a claw, and in the other he was holding a golden Skorn card. An image of a sword shimmered as realization dawned on me—the Meister was doing this. I needed to get the card out of his hand as quickly as possible.

"I can manipulate the very air around your throat. This kind of power is only a fraction of what the Shattered Mother will offer me once I've completed the elemental sacrifice," the Meister exclaimed, curling his fingers.

I didn't have time to think. I only had time to act. I charged across the room.

My legs stuck to the floor like sap, but I pushed through my grogginess, aiming with my shoulder. In the next breath, I felt my shoulder shattering as it made contact with the Meister. The card dropped out of his hand, and Aspen spurted into a coughing fit. It was relief enough that I could ignore the blast of pain radiating down my arm.

I used my good hand to swipe a dagger from my belt, bringing it up to the Meister's face. I shifted my weight to firmly pin him to the floor, but his laugh rumbled through his chest, pushing me off.

"You are such a fool, girl. Your friends are dying tonight, and there's nothing you can do," he said, grasping onto my weight and tumbling me over. My dagger clattered next to us, and we both reached for it. He was faster and had it on my neck in the next heartbeat.

"You can't kill me—" I said, panic biting my chest. "You need me," I spat.

"You're right that I need you alive," he said, his scar across his eye glinting in the firelight. "But that doesn't mean I can't *hurt* you."

The Meister drove the dagger toward me, but I used my hands to brace his arm. His face was contorted into a mask of revulsion, lips parted with saliva gathering in the crease of his lips. The floor started to vibrate. Or was it my hands shaking against his?

A resonant creak of wood sounded across the room. I spared only a fraction of a second to see Sequoia behind the great oak tree. She was . . . *pushing* it down?

"Dahlia, you have to move!" she yelled.

"I'm preoccupied," I tried to say, but it only came out as a guttural scream. I fought to gain distance from the Meister, pressing the dagger further up in the air. His face contorted from anger to frustration, foam crusting his lips. His eyes were shining a liquid lime green as he drove the dagger down, now only a breath away from my throat.

The bark splintered in bursts—sharp, cracking noises like brittle bones snapping one by one. The air was thick with the low, reverberating moan of strained fibers tearing apart.

Before I could register the tree falling, a glint of metal flew across the room, and my fingers burst into pain. Aspen. He had kicked the knife out of the Meister's hand, but the force had echoed down my hand.

"Move!" he bellowed.

I scrambled for purchase, throwing all of my weight into forcing the Meister onto his back. Aspen swept me off of him, and we fell backwards, our landing softened by the chaise behind us.

The House shuddered. The roots strained against the earth with a final, reluctant pop, followed by the long whoosh of displaced air as the canopy collapsed. I felt Aspen's fingers covering my head, protecting me from the stray branches as they fell. They broke around us with brittle snaps, tangling and twisting like desperate hands grasping at nothing.

The impact was a dull, thunderous thud that echoed through my chest. The floor rumbled, rattling through bones and chests, before the sweep of silence rushed in. It was as if the House itself had exhaled.

The Meister was lodged right under the tree's trunk, a branch spearing his elbow. He let out a howl of pain.

I untwined myself from Aspen, rising to my feet. He was breathing heavily and covered in leaves, but otherwise unharmed.

"Sequoia," I said, my eyes darting to the opposite of the room. She lay unconscious beside the uprooted tree, a gilded card in her hand, her face angelic and calm as if in slumber. I squinted my eyes to make out the image of a flower-crowned woman, next to a tall, roaring lion. The card of Strength.

My God, she had *pushed the tree herself.*

"I'll take care of her," Aspen said, and lifted his chin with a grimace toward where the Book lay.

The Meister moaned in pain, trying to free himself, but he was pinned under the jagged bark. My whole body was pulsing in pain, but I forced myself to walk over to him and stare into those vicious green eyes.

"Is this not how you conduct the ceremony?" I spat over him.

He groaned, his arm spurting blood. "You might want to get that taken care of," I said and turned to the hearth where the Book lay.

My job wasn't done yet.

I forced my fingers to curl and pick up the Book, its weight unnaturally heavy, as if it carried the burden of every soul it had corrupted.

Power shuddered through me, starting at my fingertips and spreading like a spider's web through my arms and chest, threading into my very core. For a moment, my pain subsided. The sensation was cold and invasive yet intoxicating. I could feel it pulling at me, drawing me into its orbit.

I closed my eyes, centering myself, willing the world to fall away. The room dimmed, the noises dulled. All that remained was the Book, its voice a whisper in my ear, low and intimate.

"Dahlia Blackburne, your Bonder blood calls to us. Why don't you open our pages?" it purred, the words coiling around me like smoke. *"We have so much to teach you."*

The sound wasn't just in my ears—it was in my skin, my bones, resonating with the same eerie pulse I'd felt since entering this House. My fingers slid to its edges, brushing the cold, obsidian surface. They itched to open it, to peel back the veil and dive into its secrets.

The temptation was almost unbearable.

But I didn't move. My grip tightened instead, the reality of what I held sinking in. This was no ordinary tome. Solid carbon, compacted over years into stone, it was a relic of power and ruin. How many haunted hands had held its spine, known its true horror, and been destroyed by it? How many lives had it claimed?

It would not take mine.

"No," I said, my voice hoarse but resolute. "I don't need to learn from you."

Without hesitation, I hurled the Book into the fireplace. It landed with a heavy thud, an unnatural sound that echoed in the silence. The flames engulfed it, licking hungrily at its edges, and for a fleeting moment, I thought it would burn.

Then came the click.

The obsidian shifted, expanding with a mechanical elegance that defied nature. A shield unfurled around its pages, protecting them, deflecting the fire.

A low laugh echoed behind me, cutting through the crackling of the fireplace. The sound was bone-chilling, a mockery of mirth. It didn't match the Meister's twisted, monstrous face, but I didn't need to turn to know it was him.

"Stupid child," he gurgled weakly, his voice curdled thick with blood and hatred. "You cannot burn the Book. It is protected from the elements. Its power is eternal."

"Perhaps not with fire," I said, my voice steady despite the storm inside me. I reached into my pocket and drew out the black pebble, cold and sharp against my palm. "But I can with acid."

The Meister's laughter ceased. His silence was all the confirmation I needed.

I emptied the contents of my father's metallic case onto the flames. The Meister screamed in defiance, but I ignored him. The soil fell in dark clumps, mingling with the embers and smothering the fire. The room darkened as the last of the light disappeared, and for a moment, there was only stillness.

Then the soil began to work.

A hiss filled the air as the black earth settled onto the obsidian, eating into it like a living thing. The Book resisted, trembling as if alive, but the corrosion was relentless, and the black mass cracked, groaned, and then split. I smiled, watching the pages darken and disintegrate, curling into ash. Smoke rose in curling wisps, carrying with it the acrid scent of the Book's destruction.

The Book—its power, its horrors—was undone.

For the first time since entering the House, I exhaled. The weight that had clung to me since I first set foot in Foresyth lifted. Relief coated me, soft and unfamiliar, yet wholly mine.

I wasn't like my father. I didn't need *The Book of Skorn* or any other ancient relic to tell me who I was. The knowledge I craved wasn't buried in libraries or hoarded by elite institutions. It wasn't written on pages or carved in stone.

It was in *me.*

I turned to the toppled Meister. "The soil on your grounds is laced with an alchemical acid. The Book was forged, in part, with it. In small amounts, it's hallucinogenic, like what you add to the concoctions here.

But in higher concentrations, it eats through anything organic—and anything similar to itself in composition. In other words, like *dissolves* like," I said, gesturing to the pile of ash behind me.

The look on the Meister's face was priceless. He struggled against the tree, blood seeping from his arm.

"You foul girl! Without the Book, the ceremony cannot be completed. The House will never return to the power of its former legacy," he wept.

A part of me softened, almost feeling his longing—not just for power, but for the order he believed the House once held, perhaps even for the version my father had known Foresyth to be.

"I should have killed you sooner," he growled. And then all my sympathy vanished.

"But you couldn't, could you?" I retorted. "I was the Bonder. The Book needed my blood to complete the elemental ceremony."

His expression twisted.

"Julian left me a little goodbye present," I said, holding up the letters from him and my father. "I know you planned to use us to complete the ceremony. Did you really think a daughter of Detective Blackburne wouldn't discover your ploy?"

"I thought you'd be just as useless as your father," he sneered, and my blood boiled over. "I'm glad I killed him when I had the chance. And no one suspected that he didn't end his pitiful life himself." The Meister tried to laugh, but only a wet gurgling sound came out.

The horror pierced me like a dagger. My father hadn't died by his own hand. He had died by the Meister's manipulation, by his coaxing of the air around his fingers to pull the trigger.

"You were all supposed to die, every single one of you," he spat at us.

"You idiot," Nina hissed, her voice trembling with rage as she appeared behind me. She dropped to her knees beside the fireplace, clawing at the pile of ash and scorched debris left behind. "You destroyed the Book," she choked, her words breaking as her hands sifted through the embers. When she turned to face me, the raw hatred etched on her face was feral, almost inhuman. It cut through me like ice. "This was my only chance."

"You were working with him," I spat, still catching my breath. "You told him about the fire—the plan to burn it. You poisoned the rim of our cups." That was why I had instructed everyone— everyone except Nina—to don the jelly on their lips. I hadn't wanted it to be true but had instructed them just in case. I'm glad I did.

"The coating of mugwort mixed with nightshade should have paralyzed you," she murmured, speaking to herself. Her eyes darted to the shattered cups scattered across the room. Her hands dove back into the ashes, heedless of the heat, and the stench of burning flesh wafted up as she clawed at the remnants. Her desperation was almost as horrifying as her malice. "But you didn't die . . . why didn't you die?" she whispered, her voice shaking.

"You were working with the Meister from the beginning." My voice steadied, each word sharper than the last. "That tea on my first day, you poisoned it, not Aspen. You blamed him. You had looked up the truth serum in the library, that's why the book had been plucked out that night in the library. And those creatures in the lab . . . you were trying to bring them back, weren't you? To bring back your parents?"

"Why did you have to ruin it, Dahlia?" she shrieked, threading her fingers through her hair like she was trying to rip it from her scalp. Her nails left streaks of ash and blood across her face. Her whole body trembled as she lunged for the altar, grabbing something from its surface. "I was so close to fixing everything."

"Nina—" I began, but she spun toward me, her hand clutching the athame, the blade glinting wickedly in the light of the fading embers.

"You took away the only chance I had!" she screamed, her voice cracking as she charged.

It all happened too fast.

The flash of steel, her feral cry, and the crushing realization that I couldn't move in time. I twisted to avoid her, but the blade found its mark, plunging into my side with a sickening force. Pain shot through me, hot and searing, as blood bloomed black at my side, hot and syrupy.

My breath hitched, my eyes locking on hers. Aspen lurched toward her to contain her anger, but it was too late.

"Oh God, Dahlia," Nina gasped, her rage fracturing into horror as she stumbled backwards away from me. "I—I didn't mean to—" she stammered, falling to her knees again. "I'm sorry . . . I'm so sorry."

My legs gave out beneath me. The room tilted, shadows closing in, but I didn't hit the ground. A pair of arms caught me—gentle, steady.

"Shhh," a voice murmured, low and soothing. Sequoia. She was beside me, pressing down on the wound with both hands. "Stay with me, Dahlia. Just stay with me."

Her voice faded as my vision blurred, the edges darkening. My body felt heavy, too heavy to hold together.

For the second time that night, the world shattered and swallowed me whole.

Chapter 36: The Awakening

I awoke to the sharp scent of sterilizing alcohol. A woman in a white suit was dabbing at my side, and the sting made me flinch. "We're just getting this cleaned up for you. Looks like you tore a few of your stitches last night," she hummed. "Good to see you awake."

"Where am I?" I croaked.

"Mercy Hospital," she replied, draping a heavy blanket over me. "I'll let the doctor know you're awake, and he'll stitch that back up for you. Here, take these for the pain." She handed me two white pills and a glass of water before leaving the room. I rested my head back on the pillow, staring up at the buzzing string of incandescent lights, a sound that felt strangely familiar, like an echo from a bad dream.

I'm alive.

That was the only fact that mattered.

"Dahl?" someone called from behind the curtain next to my bed. I recognized the voice immediately, if not the moniker. I tried lifting my arm to part the curtain, but a sharp pain shot through my side, making me drop back down. The curtain opened anyway, and Aspen appeared. His face was pale, fading scratches dotting his cheekbone, but his eyes shone bright amber. My gaze fell to his bandaged hand.

"Are you okay?" I asked.

"I should be the one asking you that. You were the one who got stabbed."

"I'm fine," I lied, though I could tell he saw right through it.

Sequoia appeared behind him, and a wave of relief washed over me. Her eyes were swollen and pink, but she had the widest smile on her face.

My friends were safe.

"Oh, Dahlia, I'm so happy you're alive!" she said, her voice feeling like a hug. She reached for me, her hand cupping my cheek.

"I am too," I replied, managing a small smile. "What about . . . the others?"

"Leone will be fine; he's just in shock. He's taking a few days away from school. He's been obsessed with Foresyth and those books for years—he's reevaluating all he's known to be true," Aspen said.

Damn, so was I.

"Understandable," I muttered, turning my head against the pillow. Talking was exhausting, but I had to tell them about Sophia, the vision I had had before the ceremony had descended into chaos. "I saw Sophia. She's been trying to tell me something, but I finally realized what it was last night during the ceremony."

Sequoia scrunched her eyes together and I continued. "In *The Book of Skorn* it wasn't Sophia who asked for the elemental ceremony. Those visions that came to Khorvyn—it was the demiurge—he impersonated Sophia and dictated the Book, using sacrifices to feed his domain over the material world. It was never her," I said, my chest weak with the realization.

Had I really seen her, or was she my subconscious speaking to me? I didn't quite understand why I felt the need to tell them. But it was the truth I had longed for, and it finally tasted sweet on my tongue.

"Shh, you can relax now, don't lose your strength." Sequoia caressed my forehead. "I knew—that's what she told me when I went into soul flight in the tub, all those nights ago. That's why I agreed to help you," she admitted. "Besides my dear regard toward you." She smiled, her finger trailing the side of my face.

A shard of reality cut through me, as sharp as the cut on my side.

"And Nina . . . is she okay?"

"She's been placed in the rehabilitation ward," Sequoia replied sharply. Her tone, usually so gentle, surprised me. "Aspen was right—she didn't belong at Foresyth."

A pang of disappointment settled in my stomach, sharper than the ache in my side. I'd wanted to trust Nina; she had been the first person at Foresyth to show me an inkling of friendship when I needed it most. She and I were like two sides of the same coin. She came from a working-class family, clawing her way up to Foresyth through her own sheer skill and work ethic. I'd thought we could have been genuine friends.

But maybe I'd only seen what I wanted to see.

The small, quiet moments I'd observed—her murmuring over her creations in the lab, our shared excitement over the light analyzer—now felt tainted. I thought she understood the weight of power, its limits, its cost. I believed she was channeling her grief into art, not control. Yes, we both wrestled with death's finality, but I thought she at least honored the dead and their peace. But I was wrong. I thought back to the moments I'd doubted Aspen on her account, the times I'd given her my sympathy.

"She doesn't deserve your kindness, Dahlia," Sequoia said, fierce and unflinching. I saw a glint in her eyes that was new, battle-won. "She would have destroyed anything to get what she wanted—even you."

Her words cut through my regret, clearing the fog of disappointment. Nina had turned something that I held sacred—knowledge—into something twisted and unholy. Just as the Meister had. I could understand her grief over her parents, but not at the cost of her humanity.

I knew I'd be sitting with the grief of our friendship long after the cut on my side healed.

"My instinct knew it," I said. "She was working with the Meister, hoping for a share of the power for her necromancy. Aspen wasn't the one who poisoned me that first day—it was her. She framed him to throw me off."

"And it worked." Aspen smirked.

"It did work. But when I met her down in the tunnels near that creature that bit me, I knew she was up to something. Those poor creatures . . . they weren't alive. They were *animated*, soulless. She should have known that she couldn't bring back her parents. At least, not in the same way as they were before."

"If she was doing unauthorized experiments, the Council will deal with her too, in time," Sequoia said. "She really believed killing you would give her power. Killing *all* of us. Who knows what lies the Meister fed her about giving her immunity," Sequoia said.

Aspen looked away as Sequoia spoke. I noted that there was an irony to her words. She and Aspen risked the very same almost a year ago, and it led to Julian's death. They were bound to the school through their parents' debt, yes, but that did not change the fact they were complicit in Julian's death.

"You should rest, Dahlia." Aspen turned back to me, placing a cool hand on my forehead.

"The Meister. What happened to him?" I managed.

Aspen and Sequoia exchanged a look, almost like they were sharing a joke. "He won't be at Foresyth any longer. Thanks to that switchbox you rigged, the Council convicted him on charges of false practice and endangering students. Julian's letters are going to be used to charge him with murder," Aspen said.

"So, he'll be going to prison?"

"Not exactly. The Council has its own authority for dealing with magickal crimes. Though, I suspect his magick has been significantly weakened since the Book was destroyed," Aspen explained. "And we have you to thank for that, Dahlia," he said. "I'm so proud of you." He made a point to catch my eye before turning to Sequoia. "Both of you." He tipped her chin up.

When she pulled away, Sequoia's eyes were glistening, a small smile on her lips.

"I'll never forget the sight of you toppling down that tree," I mused. "How did you do it?"

"It was nothing. I think the House gave me the idea; it was already bending its way toward the Meister. I used the last of my power granted by the Shattered Mother to coax its roots from the ground."

"You saved me," I said.

"We all saved each other," she said, taking my hand along with Aspen's.

Relief, like fresh snow, settled on me. I didn't ask any other questions. I let the warmth radiating from our intertwined hands ground me and I allowed myself to feel safe. With that forsaken Book gone, the Meister and his followers were no longer my concern. I'd completed my father's work and avenged my brother. My responsibility was over.

"Do you think . . . you'll come back to Foresyth once you're healed?" Sequoia asked. "I think the Al-Ahmar will be the interim Meister."

My stomach knotted at the mention of her name. I still didn't know how I felt about the Al-Ahmar. I didn't have time to unravel the knots that she held with my family's history. But one thing I was certain of was that my history with Foresyth was coming to an end.

I stared into Sequoia's deep brown eyes, seeing her for what she truly was—not delicate, not in need of saving, but a force that was ancient and rooted. She had always seemed otherworldly, a figure spun from mist and moonlight, but now I understood. She was not fragile, she was formidable. The kind of strength that didn't demand but endured.

My gaze shifted to Aspen, his sharp edges softened by her presence, his fire tempered by her quiet gravity. He had always been her protector, her mentor, her lover. But love wasn't about protection, not really. It was about adaptation. Growth. I wondered how they would shift for each other over time, how they would bend and rise together, just as the canopy of trees twist and tangle, molding themselves to make space for one another—not caged, but entwined.

Aspen and Sequoia would continue to shift and grow, their roots tangled, bound to this place. But I was something else entirely—something that had never been meant to stay. Maybe I was a seed caught in the wind, drifting toward something new.

For the first time, that didn't feel like being lost. It felt like being free.

"I don't have a purpose at Foresyth anymore. I learned what I came to learn," I said, seeing her eyes fall. "But we'll stay in touch. You'll write to me."

"Of course," she said, taking a deep breath before leaning down to hug me. Even her slight weight pressed too much on my side, and I winced. "Oh, I'm sorry," she said, pulling back, her eyes brimming with tears. "I'm just so glad you're alive."

The curtain drew back, and a man in a white coat, glasses perched on his nose, stepped in. The creases beside his lips suggested he was good-humored, despite his profession.

"Lucky thing she is," he said. "When these two brought you in they said you fell down a flight of stairs and landed on a metal railing. This journal"—he held up a blood-stained book—"is the only reason it didn't pierce your liver."

I'd been wearing it on my belt when Nina attacked me. Her dagger had pierced the book, saving me from a deeper wound.

"Let's fix those stitches before the police come in," he said, approaching my side. "Your friends can stay for now, but when the officer arrives, they'll have to leave."

Aspen leaned over and spoke quietly to the doctor, his tone soft and persuasive, like the first time I'd seen him in his workshop. "That won't be necessary. She's already spoken to the appropriate authorities. You'll call them off."

The doctor's expression flickered with surprise, but he nodded, adjusting his glasses. "So, she has. Very well, I'll call them off." He turned his attention to my side, preparing to restitch the wound.

"We'll visit again soon, Dahl," Aspen said softly. "I'd tell you to take care, but I know you will." He added a wink, his usual smirk tugging at the corner of his lips.

For a moment, the edges of him blurred, haloed by the soft glow of the room. Or maybe it was just the medication settling into my veins. He looked almost regal, like an emperor draped in twilight. The image of the Emperor card flickered through my mind, weightless as a dandelion seed on the wind, before drifting away.

I blew them both a kiss before turning my head, my eyelids growing heavy.

I had been running on purpose, on anger, on the desire for the truth. But now, in this sterile, softly-lit room, I had nothing left to give. A deep tiredness settled over me, a heaviness not just of body but of spirit. I let my head sink deeper into the pillow, allowing myself, just for a moment, to drift—to let go of the responsibility, the constant vigilance, the weight of being the one who had to see everything, question everything, fix everything.

Just before I drifted off, I noticed the journal on a cracked tray beside me, its pages withered and stained with my blood. How lucky it showed up by my side just when I needed it most.

I guess Julian had saved me after all.

Epilogue

Three months later

I'd been sneezing all afternoon, stirred by the dust blanketing the last shelves of my bookstore. I knew it was my fault for not cleaning more often, but I cursed the books for gathering it. At least it kept my eyes cloudy with dust rather than tears. Although I'd always dreamed of selling the shop, packing the books into boxes to be shipped off to the public library in Greenwich made it feel too real.

In the long afternoon light, with most of the shop empty except for one shelf, I stopped to admire my work. The sun streamed through the windows, illuminating tiny motes of dust suspended in the air. The bookstore was all packed.

The last shelf was my father's prized collection of archaic magickal texts, which he hadn't let me touch (though I'd secretly read through them before I turned thirteen). I trailed my fingers over the cracked leather spines, feeling a faint static build beneath my fingertips. This set was reserved for another library, one that would make better use of it than Greenwich. But the invisible tug at my core stopped me from placing them in the special black box I'd set aside.

These books were the last pieces of my father. Giving them away felt like giving away a part of myself.

I reached into my pocket, my fingers closing around the pebble my father had saved for me. I reminded myself that not everything of his was gone.

A knock sounded at the door. I crossed the nearly empty shop, expecting my guest. It wasn't a client, as I'd closed my Tarot reading practice after returning from Foresyth. Perhaps the woman at my door would have an interest in the accounts, but I doubted she'd assign Advisors to the public.

"Dahlia," greeted the Al-Ahmar when I opened the door. She wore no cape or ceremonial garb this time, only a polished peplum blouse and long black slacks, elegant yet simple. Her curly hair was pulled into a sleek bun, and her eyes, outlined in dark pencil, studied me with a familiar intensity. "You look well."

"I am," I replied, meaning it. "Come in. I have the collection ready inside."

"Thank you," she said.

I offered her tea, which she declined with a polite smile. "We're grateful for your donation to the library," she began, "but there was something else I wanted to discuss with you."

"Truthfully, I expected as much," I replied, walking to what used to be my Tarot-reading table and motioning for her to sit. She nodded, taking a seat across from me. My hand reflexively reached for the shawl I once wore with clients, but I stopped myself.

I no longer needed it; I no longer needed a disguise.

"It seems you've been busy here," she said, noting the empty shelves. "Moving out?"

"Foresyth taught me that I can't live in books forever. It's time to move on from the past rather than be haunted by it. My mother, Estelle, and I are set to visit Dublin next week," I said, crossing my legs.

With the Book finally destroyed, a new life had entered my mother, her health all but fully restored. She still had to take frequent breaks, her body not yet as strong as her spirit, but I didn't mind. I had all the time in the world now.

Estelle was upstairs now, slowly packing our rooms as I sat with the Al-Ahmar. A conversation like this with the Meister would've unnerved me a few months ago, but with her, I felt calm. She seemed as at peace with the past as I was learning to become.

"That's a significant undertaking. I wish everyone could move on as you have," she replied, her gaze steady, almost assessing. "It's unfortunate that the Meister couldn't do the same. He believed old blood magick could restore the House, but really, it was draining it. Each failed ceremony only corrupted the place further."

"I wish he'd been stopped sooner," I said, feeling a simmering anger rise I thought I'd buried long ago. I thought I had let go of my anger toward them both—toward Julian for making me chase his ghost, toward my father for suffering in silence for so long.

But sometimes, closure wasn't a neat conclusion. Sometimes it was a wound that needed time to scab, scar, and heal. But even then, it would always be there underneath the surface. I'd just have to learn to live with it.

"We lost several Council members who sided with him, but we've reformed the Council now," she continued. "Understandably, many were afraid of his powers, but now with the Book gone, I think that type of power has been laid to rest. Our new leadership is dedicated to keeping magickal study separate from practice. We're an academic institution, after all."

When the silence between us stretched, she continued. "There's still much good you could do, Dahlia. Sometimes we must rely on what we already know to guide us to the good, rather than searching for it outside ourselves."

"I couldn't agree more."

The Al-Ahmar studied me for a long moment before speaking again. "The Council was impressed by you. You have a unique immunity to magickal relics—a talent that was evident that night of the ceremony. In fact, you were the only one able to handle the Book without being consumed. Have you wondered why?"

"I've tried to put that night behind me," I replied. "But yes, I have wondered."

I had felt the Book's pull—like a low, humming presence, something that wanted to burrow inside me, whisper secrets only I could hear. But it hadn't consumed me the way it had others.

I held it, I resisted it, and I burned it to ash.

"Our research suggests it has something to do with your Roma heritage on your mother's side," she said. "Dealers in magickal relics often need some immunity to them, and we believe you inherited this. Your father's blood contained Elyrium, which made the Book call to you. But from your mother, you inherited a marker that counteracts it. You're like a bloodhound that doesn't devour what it finds."

Elyrium? A counter magick? Thoughts tumbled through my head, curiosity sparking in my chest. But I gulped them all down.

"An interesting metaphor," I said, "but I'm not sure how it's relevant now; the Book is gone."

"The Book might be gone, but magick is not. As you said, belief itself can still compel people to evil. Your father, though tormented, was driven by justice. I thought perhaps you were too."

I swallowed. "I'm not my father."

"I think we can both be glad of that," she said, a soft laugh threading through her words. "But there are parts of him in you—parts drawn to darkness, and parts searching for light within it. The truth."

As she fell silent, I regarded her carefully.

Her words settled over me like dust, fine and inescapable. She wasn't wrong. I had always been drawn to the places others turned away from—the secrets buried under floorboards and behind locked doors. I had spent my life digging, prying, searching. If it was a patron seated across from me or a deadly Conservatory, it didn't matter, I pressed on the same.

But was it justice? Or was it morbid curiosity?

As the silence stretched, I realized something else. This wasn't just a conversation. This was another job offer.

"What exactly are you proposing?"

"You're too young to be an Advisor, not to mention I suspect that's not your path now, given you closed your practice. But there is an organization I think you'd find interesting. They're called the Arcanum, a group independent from Foresyth that investigates magickal crimes across the world. I recommended you to them."

I squinted at her. "That's not the kind of travel I had in mind. Estelle and I have other plans."

"You don't need to decide now," she said gently. "But I hope you'll think about it. Like I said, Dahlia, there's a lot of good you could do. Promise me you'll consider it?"

Her voice held a strange weight, an almost maternal urgency that made my throat tighten. I looked at her, and for a moment, it was as if Julian himself were staring back at me. The resemblance was uncanny—not just in the tilt of her head or the softness in her smile, but in something deeper, more ineffable. It was as though a thread had been woven between them, and through Julian, it now connected to me.

"I promise, I'll think about it," I replied, my voice steadier than I felt. Her smile deepened, and I returned it cautiously, my chest caught between a swell of relief and an ache I couldn't quite place.

She stood, and I followed her across the room. My eyes fell to the box resting on the counter—the relic of my father's life, his obsessions, his failures. For so long, it had weighed on me, like an anchor tied to my foot, pulling me down. Now, as I prepared to part with it, I felt that weight shift, not vanishing entirely, but becoming lighter.

"Are you sure you want to part with these?" she asked, her fingers hovering over the box.

"Yes, I'm sure," I said. My hand rested on the lid for a moment, realizing I was sealing it for the last time. I could hear Estelle's quiet footsteps above me, and I smiled to myself. "There's nothing in here I don't already know." The words felt true, but they still tasted strange.

The knowledge was mine now, not bound to these objects or the people who had held them before me. Letting go of those books felt like shedding a layer of skin.

She took the box and tucked it under her arm, and I followed her to the door, watching as she stepped into the street. I stood at the doorway until the car turned the corner and disappeared, swallowed by the narrow street. I stepped outside, onto the cobblestones of Wicker Street. The wind pressed against my skin, cool and full of familiar scents—salt, smoke, something sweet carried from a bakery down the way. The street stretched before me, endless in its possibilities.

Arcanum, I thought. At least they had one less thing to worry about, now that I had banished Skorn magick. I had seen the Book crumble into ash, its powers rendered void. No one could use the cards to hold sway over others, anymore.

But then, like a weed sprouting in a cleared garden, a thought pushed its way through the soil of my mind.

Aspen.

The Emperor.

THE END

If you enjoyed this book, would you consider leaving a review? Thank you from the bottom of my haunted little heart!

Acknowledgements

As an indie author, my team is small but mighty. This book would not exist without the brilliance, insight, and encouragement of their hands and hearts.

To my incredible beta review team—Rachel Broughton, Lessa Goss, Madison Horgan, Ishita Kamboj, and Kaitlyn Weaver—thank you for believing in this early concept and offering your sharp eyes and kinder words. Your feedback shaped this story into its best self and encouraged me to see it through. It wouldn't exist without you.

To the Cultservatory—my fearless, fabulous street team—thank you for making this journey feel like a movement. You are my people, and this book is for you. To my ARC team, your early enthusiasm means the world to me.

To my alpha reader and meticulous proofreader, William Harris: your honesty and insight kept this book on course and well-grounded. To my copy editor, Caitlin Lengerich: thank you for lending your precision and care to every last comma and clause . . . those ellipses owe it to you.

To my aunt, whose artwork brought the world of Foresyth to life in ways I could never have imagined—thank you for lending your vision to mine. To my grandmother, who first guided my hands to the cards and taught me how to listen—this story owes its magick to you.

To my "momager," Julia Hsain—thank you for being my anchor, my voice of reason, and my fiercest champion. To our mutual biggest fan, Mira, thank you for the cuddles and for always meeting me by the door.

To the many friends who told me—again and again—that this dream was worth chasing: you were right. Thank you for believing in me when I doubted.

And finally, thank you to you, dear reader, for giving my book a chance and being a part of the Conservatory magick.

www.ingramcontent.com/pod-product-compliance
Lightning Source LLC
Chambersburg PA
CBHW060816310726
48980CB00002B/309

* 9 7 9 8 9 9 8 8 0 5 6 0 8 *